Praise for

THE MEASURE

"What an incredible book! It's truly original with an intriguing premise that's beautifully executed. I loved the fact that it was written from so many perspectives, each adding depth to the overall narrative, which made it a rich and satisfying read. I found it gripping, poignant, and intensely thought-provoking."

—Ruth Hogan, bestselling author of *The Keeper of Lost Things*

"A compelling, heartbreaking story of life and love with a perfect, elegant premise." —Bridget Collins, bestselling author of *The Binding*

"Nikki Erlick has created an irresistible hook about a question that everyone asks but no one ever wants to answer. With thoughtful and compelling detail, she crafts a strange—and strangely familiar—world full of new moral and political conundrums, one in which people get to choose their own kind of freedom. And while the novel is full of ideas, *The Measure* has a strong emotional heart—with an array of characters exploring their frightening, but sometimes beautiful new worlds. Ultimately, *The Measure* is about the power of human resilience."

—Luke Allnutt, author of *We Own the Sky*

"*The Measure* is an utterly original and hugely compelling story, which drew me in from the very first page with its beautiful writing. Weeks after reading it, I'm still thinking about this smart, uplifting novel and its wonderful characters."

—Freya Sampson, author of *The Last Chance Library*

"*The Measure* is utterly original and wonderfully mysterious. Through Erlick's deft prose and clever logic, I threw away all disbelief and fully plunged into the unsettling but life-affirming world she creates."

—Jessica Anya Blau, author of *Mary Jane*

THE MEASURE

THE
MEASURE

A Novel

NIKKI ERLICK

WILLIAM MORROW
An Imprint of HarperCollinsPublishers

THE MEASURE. Copyright © 2022 by Nikki Erlick. All rights reserved. Printed in the United States of America. No part of this book may be used or reproduced in any manner whatsoever without written permission except in the case of brief quotations embodied in critical articles and reviews. For information, address HarperCollins Publishers, 195 Broadway, New York, NY 10007.

HarperCollins books may be purchased for educational, business, or sales promotional use. For information, please email the Special Markets Department at SPsales@harpercollins.com.

A hardcover edition of this book was published in 2022 by William Morrow, an imprint of HarperCollins Publishers.

FIRST WILLIAM MORROW PAPERBACK EDITION PUBLISHED 2023.

Library of Congress Cataloging-in-Publication Data

Names: Erlick, Nikki, author.
Title: The measure : a novel / Nikki Erlick.
Description: First edition. | New York : William Morrow, [2022]
Identifiers: LCCN 2021038062 | ISBN 9780063204201 (hardcover) | ISBN 9780063204225 (ebook)
Subjects: LCGFT: Novels.
Classification: LCC PS3605.R59 M43 2022 | DDC 813/.6—dc23/eng/20210929
LC record available at https://lccn.loc.gov/2021038062

ISBN 978-0-06-320421-8 (pbk.)

24 25 26 27 28 LBC 5 4 3 2 1

For my grandparents,

with love and gratitude

Tell me, what is it you plan to do with your one wild and precious life?

—*Mary Oliver, "The Summer Day"*

THE MEASURE

It was difficult to imagine a time before them, a world in which they hadn't come.

But when they first appeared, in March, nobody had any idea what to do with them, these strange little boxes that came with the spring.

Every other box, at every stage in people's lives, had a clear meaning, a set course of action. The shoebox holding a shiny new pair to be worn on the first day of school. The holiday present crowned with a looped red ribbon, skillfully curled on a scissor's edge. The tiny box with the long-dreamt-of diamond inside, and the large cardboard packages, sealed with tape and labeled by hand, loaded into the back of the moving truck. Even that final box, resting under the earth, whose lid, once shut, would never be opened.

Every other box felt familiar, understandable, expected even. Every other box had a purpose and a place, fitting comfortably within the course of a typical life.

But *these* boxes were different.

They came at the start of the month, on an otherwise ordinary day, under an otherwise ordinary moon, too early to blame the March equinox.

And when the boxes came, they came for everyone, all at once.

Small wooden chests—at least, they *looked* wooden—that emerged overnight, millions and millions of them, in every town and every state and every country.

The boxes appeared on finely mowed lawns in the suburbs, nestled between hedges and the first blooms of the hyacinth. They sat atop well-trampled doormats in the cities, where decades of tenants had passed through the threshold. They sank into the warm sands outside tents in the desert and waited near lonely lakeside cabins, gathering dew in the breeze off the water. In San Francisco and São Paulo, in Johannesburg and Jaipur, in the Andes and the Amazon, there wasn't anywhere, or anyone, that the boxes couldn't find.

There was something both comforting and unsettling about the fact that every adult on earth suddenly seemed to be sharing the same surreal experience, the ubiquity of the boxes both a terror and a relief.

Because, in many ways, it *was* the same experience. In nearly every manner, these boxes were identical. All were dark brown in color, with reddish tints, cool and smooth to the touch. And inscribed on every box was a simple, yet cryptic message, written in the native tongue of its recipient: *The measure of your life lies within.*

Within each box was a single string, initially hidden by a silvery white piece of delicate fabric, so even those who lifted the lid would think twice before looking at what lay underneath. As if the box itself were warning you, trying to protect you from your own childish impulse to immediately tear away the wrapping. As if the box were asking you to pause, to truly contemplate your next move. Because that one could never be undone.

Indeed, the boxes varied on only two accounts.

Each small chest bore the name of its individual recipient, and each string inside measured a different length.

But when the boxes first arrived that March, amid the fear and the confusion, nobody quite understood what the measure truly meant.

At least, not yet.

SPRING

NINA

When the box inscribed with Nina's name appeared outside her door, Nina was still asleep in bed, her eyelids twitching slightly as her dormant mind wrestled with a difficult dream. (She was back in high school, the teacher demanding to see an essay that Nina had never been assigned.) It was a familiar nightmare for someone prone to stress, but it was nothing compared to the one awaiting her in the waking world.

Nina woke up first that morning, as she usually did, and slid off the mattress, leaving Maura undisturbed in her slumber. She slipped into the kitchen, still wearing her plaid pajama set, and switched on the burner under the plump orange teakettle that Maura had found at a flea market last summer.

The apartment was always deliciously quiet at that early hour, the silence only interrupted by the occasional hiss of a droplet escaping from the lid of the teapot and landing with a sizzle among the low flames of the stovetop. Later, Nina wondered why she hadn't heard any commotion that morning. There were no screams or sirens or televisions blaring, nothing to alert her to the chaos already unfolding outside her home. If Nina hadn't turned on her phone, then perhaps she could have stayed in the stillness for just a while longer, savoring the time before.

But instead she sat on the couch and looked at her phone, the way she started every morning, expecting to read a handful of emails and scroll through various newsletters until Maura's alarm went off and they debated eggs or oatmeal. It was part of Nina's job as an editor to keep herself informed, but the sheer number of apps and outlets had grown with every year in the role, and it sometimes overwhelmed Nina to think that she could spend an entire lifetime reading and never keep up.

That morning, she didn't even have a chance to start. As soon as she unlocked the home screen, Nina knew something was wrong. She had three missed calls from friends, and the texts had been piling up for hours, mostly from her fellow editors in their group message.

WTF IS HAPPENING?!
Did everyone get one???
They're EVERYWHERE. Like the whole world. Holy FUCK.
Is the inscription for real?
Do NOT open until we know more.
But inside is just a string, right???

Nina felt her chest constrict, her head tingling with dizziness, as she tried to piece together the full story. She clicked over to Twitter, then to Facebook, and it was all the same, filled with question marks and all-caps panic. But this time, there were photos. Hundreds of users posting pictures of small brown boxes outside their doors. And not just in New York, where she lived. Everywhere.

Nina could make out the inscription in a few of the photos. *The measure of your life lies within.* What the hell did that mean?

Her heart was beating alarmingly fast, keeping pace with the questions in her head. Most of the people online, faced with the same obscure message on the box, had quickly rallied around a single, terrifying conclusion: Whatever was waiting inside that box claimed to know just how long your life would last. The time you'd been allotted, by whatever powers may be.

Nina was about to scream and wake up Maura, when she realized that *they* must have received them, too.

She dropped her phone on the couch, fingers trembling, and stood up. She walked to the front door of the apartment, a little woozy on her feet, then took a deep breath and peered through the peephole, but she couldn't see down to the floor. So she slowly unhooked the double lock and timidly opened the door, as if a stranger were waiting on the other side, asking to be let in.

The boxes were there.

Sitting on the doormat with the Bob Dylan quote that Maura insisted upon bringing with her when she moved into Nina's place. "Be groovy or leave, man." Nina probably would have preferred something simpler, a neutral lattice mat, but that quote always made Maura smile, and after weeks of trudging home to it, Nina had grown to love it, too.

Covering most of the cursive blue lettering on the mat sat a pair of wooden-looking chests. One for each of them, apparently.

Nina looked down the hall and saw an identical box waiting for their neighbor in 3B, an elderly widower who only came out once a day to toss his trash. She wondered if she should alert him. But what would she possibly say?

Nina was still staring at the boxes at her feet, too nervous to touch them, yet too shocked to leave, when the whistle of the kettle roused her from her trance and reminded her that Maura still didn't know.

BEN

Ben, too, was asleep when the boxes arrived, only he wasn't at home.

He wriggled in his narrow economy seat, eyes squeezed shut against the glow of his neighbor's laptop, while millions of boxes swept across the country like a fog, thirty-six thousand feet beneath him.

Ben's three-day architectural conference in San Francisco had concluded in the early evening, and he had boarded the red-eye to New York before any sign of the boxes had reached the Bay. His plane departed just before midnight in the West and landed just after sunrise in the East, none of the passengers, nor the crew, aware of what had transpired during those dark hours in between.

But when the seat belt sign clicked off, and the cell phones of every traveler turned on all at once, they were instantly made aware.

Inside the airport, crowds formed around the base of the giant televisions, each network offering a different spin.

MYSTERY BOXES APPEAR ALL OVER GLOBE.

WHERE DID THEY COME FROM?

BOXES PURPORT TO PREDICT THE FUTURE.

WHAT DOES YOUR STRING REALLY MEAN?

All upcoming flights were delayed.

A father standing near Ben was trying to calm his three children while arguing on the phone. "We just got here!" he said. "What should we do? Come back?"

A businesswoman staring at her iPad had taken to informing fellow passengers of the latest news online. "Apparently they only came for adults," she announced aloud, to nobody in particular. "No kids have gotten them so far."

But most people were screaming the same question into their phones: "Did *I* get one, too?"

Ben was still squinting at the neon screens above, his eyes dry and sore from an uneasy sleep. Flying, to Ben, always felt like sidestepping time, the hours on an airplane existing outside the normal continuum of life below. But never before had he so clearly exited one world and returned to another.

As he started walking quickly toward the AirTrain to reach the subway, Ben dialed his girlfriend, Claire, but she didn't pick up. Then he called his parents at home.

"We're okay, we're fine," his mother assured him. "Don't worry about us, just get back safely."

"But . . . you did *get* them?" Ben asked.

"Yes," his mother whispered, as if someone might be listening. "Your father put them in the hall closet for now." She paused. "We haven't opened them yet."

The subway into the city was distinctly empty, especially for the morning rush hour. Ben was one of only five in the car, his carry-on luggage tucked between his legs. Wasn't anyone going in to work that day?

It must be a safety precaution, he realized. Whenever something cataclysmic might be striking the city, nervous New Yorkers avoided the underground. Few places seemed worse to potentially be trapped in than a small, airless train car below the earth.

The other commuters were quiet, on edge, sitting far apart from each other and consumed by their phones.

"They're just little boxes," said a man slumped in a corner. He looked, to Ben, like he was high on something. "People don't need to be freaking out!"

The person nearest to the man shifted away.

Then the man started singing deliriously, conducting an invisible orchestra with his hands.

"Little boxes, little boxes, little boxes made of ticky tacky . . ."

It was only then, listening to the man's raspy voice, the eerie tune, that Ben truly started to worry.

Suddenly distressed, he rushed off at the next stop, Grand Central Station, and raced up the steps, grateful to be back on street level among the comfort of the crowds. The terminal was much more populated than the subway, with dozens of people boarding trains to the suburbs. Where were they all going? Ben wondered. Did they really believe that the answer to these mysterious boxes resided outside the city?

Perhaps they were simply running toward family.

Ben paused by an entrance to a vacant track, trying to orient his thoughts. About a quarter of the people around him were carrying brown boxes under their arms, and he realized that even more might be hiding in backpacks and purses. Ben felt surprisingly relieved that he hadn't been home when it arrived, snoring obliviously in bed, separated from the invading box by only a shamefully thin wall. It felt like a lesser violation, somehow, when he was gone.

On a typical day at the station there would be plenty of tourists milling about, listening to audio guides, staring upward at the famous celestial ceiling. But today nobody stopped, and no one looked up.

Ben's mother had pointed them out to him once when he was a child, the faded gold constellations above, explaining each zodiac in turn. Was she also the one who had told him that the stars were painted backward on purpose? That it was meant to be seen from the perspective of the divine, rather than humanity? Ben always figured it was just an excuse concocted afterward, a pretty story covering someone's mistake.

"The measure of your life lies within," a man was enunciating into his headset, visibly frustrated. "Nobody knows what it means! How the hell should I?"

The measure of your life lies within. Ben had picked up enough information by now, from the strangers at the airport and his phone on the subway, to recognize that was the inscription on the boxes. The mystery was only a few hours old, but some people were already interpreting the message to mean that the string inside your box foretold the ultimate length of your life.

But how could that *possibly* be true? Ben thought. That would mean the world had flipped around, like the ceiling above him, the humans now seeing from God's perspective.

Ben leaned against the cool wall behind him, faintly light-headed. That's when he remembered the bout of turbulence in the middle of his flight that had jostled him awake, the plane shuddering up and down, nearly spilling his seatmate's drink. Like something had briefly rocked the atmosphere.

Ben would realize, later, that the boxes hadn't appeared all at once, that they came during the night, whenever night happened to fall in a particular place. But there, standing in Grand Central, when the details of the prior evening still remained hazy, Ben couldn't help but wonder if that shift in the air marked the moment the boxes had arrived down below.

NINA

Nina did not want to open the box.

She read the news every day, as she always had. She pored through Twitter for updates. She told herself it was work as usual. But she wasn't just looking for stories.

She was looking for answers.

Online, competing theories seeking to explain the strings' inexplicable origins ranged from a messenger of God to a clandestine government agency to an alien invasion. Some of the most avowed skeptics found themselves turning to the spiritual or the supernatural to justify the sudden arrival of these tiny boxes, just six inches wide and three inches deep, on every doorstep around the world. Even those currently houseless, erecting their dwellings in the streets, even the nomads and the hitchhikers, all had awoken, that morning, to chests of their own, waiting wherever they had laid their heads the night before.

But very few people, at first, would admit to believing that the strings could *actually* represent the length of one's life. It was too frightening to imagine any external entity with such unnatural omniscience, and even those who professed faith in an all-knowing God had difficulty understanding why His behavior, after thousands of years, would suddenly alter so radically.

But the boxes kept coming.

After the first wave covered every living adult twenty-two years and older, each new sunrise brought a box and a string for anyone who turned twenty-two that day, marking a new entrance into adulthood.

And then, near the end of March, stories started to spread. News circulated whenever the prediction of a string came true, particularly when people with shorter strings died unexpectedly. Talk shows featured the grieving families of perfectly healthy twenty-somethings with short strings who had passed away in freak accidents, and radio programs ran interviews with hospital patients who had abandoned all hope, before receiving their long strings and suddenly finding themselves candidates for new trials and treatments.

And yet no one could find concrete evidence to trust that these strings were anything more than strands of ordinary thread.

Despite the nagging rumors, the mounting testimonials, Nina still refused to look at her string. She thought that she and Maura should keep their boxes closed until they knew more about them. She didn't even want them in the apartment.

But Maura was more adventurous and impetuous than Nina.

"Come on," Maura groaned. "Are you worried they're gonna catch fire? Or blow up?"

"I know you're making fun of me, but nobody really knows *what* the hell could happen," Nina said. "What if this is like those anthrax mailings on a massive scale?"

"I haven't heard of anyone getting sick from opening them," Maura said.

"Maybe we could just leave them out on the fire escape for now?"

"Then somebody might steal them!" Maura warned. "At the very least, they'll be covered in pigeon crap."

So they settled on storing them under the bed and waiting for more information.

But it was the waiting part that riled Maura.

"What if it's real?" Maura asked Nina. "The whole 'measure of your life' thing?"

"It just *can't* be," Nina insisted. "There's no scientific way for some piece of string to know the future."

Maura looked at Nina solemnly. "Aren't there just some things in this world that can't be explained by facts or science?"

Nina didn't know what to say to that.

"And what if this box can really tell you how long you'll live? My god, Nina, isn't the curiosity *killing* you?"

"Of course it is," Nina conceded, "but being curious about something doesn't mean we should rush into it blindly. Either it's *not* real, and it's not worth freaking ourselves out over nothing, or it *is* real, and we need to be absolutely certain what we want to do. There could be a lot of pain waiting inside that box, too."

When Nina convened with her fellow editors and a few reporters at the conference room table to discuss the upcoming magazine issue, the chief political correspondent said what everyone was thinking. "I guess we have to scrap everything and start over now."

The issue had initially been planned as a series of interviews with the new presidential candidates, after most had announced their campaigns that winter. But the events of March had far eclipsed any interest in a presidential race that suddenly seemed eons away.

"I mean, it's gotta be these strings, right?" the correspondent asked. "That's all anyone's talking about, so it has to be our lead story. The election's still a year and a half away. Who knows what the world will even look like by then?"

"I agree, but if we don't have any actual facts, then we risk just adding to the noise," said Nina.

"Or fearmongering," said another.

"Everyone's *already* afraid," one of the writers interjected. "Some people have tried checking their security cameras on the night the boxes appeared, but nobody's been able to get a good look at what happened. It seems kinda shadowy, and then once the footage clears, the box is just there. It's fucking crazy."

"And the boxes still haven't appeared for anyone under twenty-two, right? That's the youngest age I've heard."

"Yeah, me too. Seems a little unfair that the kids aren't exempt from dying, just from knowing about it in advance."

"Well, we still don't know *for sure* that they predict when you'll die."

"At least we're just as in the dark as everybody else." The correspondent raised his hands in defeat. "The easiest article would probably be to ask a bunch of people what they're doing about it, whether they're building bunkers for the apocalypse or just ignoring everything."

"I saw a story about couples who've split up based on different beliefs about the strings."

"We're a newsmagazine, not a gossip rag. And I think most people have enough of their own drama right now, they don't need to read about everyone else's," said Nina. "They want answers."

"Well, we can't come up with answers if there aren't any." Deborah Caine, the editor-in-chief, spoke in the same calm tone as always. "But the people deserve to know what their *leaders* are doing about this, and that's something we can actually tell them."

Predictably, government offices at every level and in every nation had been dealing with an onslaught of frantic phone calls since the very first boxes arrived.

A cadre of financial leaders from the Federal Reserve and the IMF, as well as the world's most powerful banks and multinational corporations, had immediately assembled, just days after the arrival, to shore up the global economy, hoping that a familiar combination of methods—lowered interest rates, tax rebates, discount loans to banks—might fend off any instability stemming from a very unfamiliar threat.

At the same time, the politicians, faced with a growing number of questions, turned to the scientists for answers. And, since the boxes had appeared all over the world, the scientists turned to each other.

At hospitals and universities on every continent, samples of the strings were chemically analyzed, while the material of the boxes themselves, so like mahogany in appearance, was simultaneously tested. But neither substance proved a match for any known matter in the laboratories' databases. And though the strings resembled common fibers, they were bafflingly resilient, unable to be cut by even the sharpest of tools.

Frustrated by the lack of conclusions, the labs called for volunteer subjects with strings of varying lengths to be brought in for comparative medical testing, and *that* was when the scientists began to worry. In some cases, they could find no discernible difference between the health of the "short-stringers" and the "long-stringers," as they soon came to be called. But, in others, the tests on many of those with short strings revealed dire results: undiscovered tumors, unforeseen heart conditions, untreated illnesses. While similar medical issues also turned up in the subjects with long strings, the distinction was alarmingly clear: Those with long strings had curable ailments, while those with short strings did not.

One at a time, like dominoes, each lab in each country confirmed it.

The long-stringers would live longer, and the short-stringers would die soon.

While the politicians were urging constituents to remain calm and maintain normalcy, the international research community was the first to confront the new reality. And no matter how many NDAs were signed, something this monumental could not be contained. After a month, the truth began to leak through the cracks in the laboratory walls, creating small puddles of knowledge that eventually grew into pools.

After a month, people started to believe.

BEN

"So, you seriously believe that these strings are some sort of lifeline? That they tell us how long we're going to live?" the woman asked, her eyebrows arched. "You don't think that sounds certifiably insane?"

Ben was sitting in a corner of a coffee shop, studying the blueprints of his firm's latest venture, a flashy new science center at a university upstate. Back in February, Ben couldn't stop thinking about this project, imagining all the future students who would someday study and work in the classrooms and labs that he helped design. Perhaps they would even make some world-changing discovery in the very building that he had first sketched out on a page at the back of his Moleskine.

But then, in March, the world did change. And now it was hard for Ben to even keep his focus on the plans in front of him. When he overheard the woman's questions at the next table over, he couldn't help but listen.

The woman was clearly an adamant denier, as at first many were.

But their ranks were dwindling week after week.

"I don't know," her companion said, less sure of himself. "I mean, the fact that they could just appear, out of nowhere, all over the world, has gotta be some sort of . . . magic." He shook his head, perhaps not quite believing that this conversation was even occurring.

"There just has to be another explanation. Something *realistic*," the woman said.

"Well, I guess some people are still talking about groups of vigilante hackers who've pulled some pretty big stunts before," the man offered weakly. "But I don't see how a group of nerds could ever be large enough to pull this off."

Indeed, one of the most popular of the early rumors posited that an international network of hell-raising geniuses had come together to execute a prank of mind-blowing proportions. Of course, Ben saw the appeal: If it were all just a hoax, no one would be forced to accept the existence of God, or ghosts, or wizardry, or any of the other, more challenging theories currently swirling about. And, most importantly, nobody would have to confront the fate supposedly dictated by a piece of string in a peculiar box.

But this was too far-reaching for a man-made prank, Ben thought. And there was no one who seemed to profit from the boxes' arrival, no clear intention other than catapulting the world's inhabitants into a state of fear and confusion.

"So you're comfortable concluding that it's *magic*?" the woman asked.

It was strange for Ben to hear the strings referred to as "magic." To him, magic was the handful of card and coin tricks that his grandfather taught him during family vacations at the beach in Cape May. Magic was sleight of hand, it was, "Pick a card, any card." It may have *looked* amazing, but there was always an explanation behind it.

These strings weren't magic.

"Then maybe it's God." The man shrugged. "Or multiple gods. The ancient Greeks believed in the Fates, right?"

"They also executed nonbelievers," the woman said.

"That doesn't mean they were wrong! Weren't they the ones who figured out algebra? And democracy?"

The woman rolled her eyes.

"Okay, well, then how else do you explain all those stories about the short-stringers who died?" the man asked. "That fire in Brooklyn? All three of those guys had short strings."

"When your sample size is the entire world, you're bound to find anecdotes that support *any* theory," the woman said.

Ben wondered if this was a first date. If it was, it didn't seem to be going very well.

Like a reflex, Ben recalled the last first date he had gone on—with

Claire, nearly two years earlier, at a café not unlike this one. How nervous he had been. But those first-date jitters, in the time before, suddenly seemed so trivial, worrying that you might knock over a coffee cup, or get spinach stuck in your teeth. Now you wondered how quickly the subject of the strings would come up, if your theories would align, when you might broach the sensitive question you were all too curious not to ask.

"Did you look at yours?"

The man lowered his voice when he asked it.

"Well, yeah, but that doesn't mean I believe it." The woman leaned back in her chair and crossed her arms defensively.

The man hesitated. "Can I ask what it was?"

Too forward for a first date, Ben thought. Perhaps a fourth or fifth, then.

"It was pretty long, I think. But again, it means nothing."

"I haven't looked at mine yet. My brother's still deciding if he wants to, and I'd rather we look together," the man said. "He's the only family I've got, so I don't know what I'd do if our strings were different lengths."

His vulnerability seemed to shift something in the woman, and her expression softened. She reached out and touched his arm tenderly. "They aren't real," she said. "Give it a little more time, and you'll see."

Ben tried to concentrate on the floor plans in front of him, but instead he thought only of his own opened box, and the short string inside that had been lying in wait.

Maybe this woman was right, Ben thought, and his short string didn't mean a short life. He prayed that she was right.

But his gut said she was wrong.

NINA

In April, Deborah Caine was the first in Nina's office to receive official confirmation. She called a small group of editors into a conference room and told them what her source at the Department of Health and Human Services had just divulged to her.

"They're real," she said slowly. "We don't know how, and we don't know why, but it would appear that the length of your string does, in fact, correlate with the expected length of your life."

Everyone in the room sat silently paralyzed, until one of the men stood and began to pace across the floor. "That's fucking impossible," he said, turning away from Deborah so he couldn't see her response.

Nina's mind and body both went numb, but she could somehow hear herself speaking, and her voice sounded surprisingly relaxed. "And they're *sure* about this?" she asked.

"Several international task forces have all come to the same conclusion," Deborah said. "I know this is . . . calling it a 'bombshell' sounds almost too normal. I know this information may be life-changing, for many of us. The president is expected to make an announcement tomorrow, and I believe the UN Security Council is also planning something, but I wanted to let you all know as soon as I heard."

Gradually, Nina's emotions seemed to return. She began to scratch at her left thumbnail, chipping off the pale pink polish, and she could feel that she was about to cry. She hoped that she could run to the bathroom before it started.

The man behind Nina stopped pacing and looked directly at their boss. "What do we do now?"

"About this month's issue?" Deborah asked.

"About everything."

After Deborah dismissed the group from the room, Nina locked herself in a bathroom stall and began to sob, leaning against the tiled wall to keep herself steady. There were simply too many feelings to process at once.

She could still see it vividly. The moment, just one week earlier, when she and Maura had finally opened their boxes together.

Despite Nina's insistence on keeping them closed, in the end Maura couldn't help herself. She had come to Nina one evening with remarkable sangfroid. "I want to open my box," she said calmly.

Nina knew that Maura was determined. They could *both* be stubborn like that. But this wasn't something simple, like picking out a couch, and there was no such thing as a compromise. They either looked or they didn't. There was nothing in between.

Nina was afraid to open her box, but she was also aware of something even *more* frightening, and that was the prospect of opening one's box all alone. Nina was the eldest child, the big sister with a tendency toward overprotection. And now that same feeling, the urge to shelter and care for everyone around her, encompassed Maura, too. Nina couldn't let Maura look by herself.

"We'll do it together," Nina said.

"No, that's not what I'm asking." Maura shook her head. "You don't need to do that for me."

"I know," Nina said. "But I can't fight the fact that the world seems to be hurtling toward the point where everybody looks. And I'd much rather look with you by my side."

So the two women sat cross-legged on the rug in their living room and gingerly opened the lids of their boxes, peeling back the paper-thin piece of shimmering cloth inside.

At the time, they weren't able to interpret the exact meaning of the lengths of their strings, but they placed them between their fingertips and held them out next to each other. One thing was instantly, sickeningly clear: Maura's string was barely half the length of Nina's.

They had only just celebrated two years together, only recently begun to share a home. Though they hadn't explicitly spoken about marriage, Nina had seen Maura steal a peek in her dresser drawers right before their anniversary dinner. They both knew well enough that Nina hated surprises and thrived on planning, so perhaps they each assumed, subconsciously, that Nina would be the one to propose.

As with most people in love, Nina felt like she had known Maura for much longer than two years, but their life together was really just beginning.

And now Nina knew for certain. The life of the woman she loved would be a life cut short.

Standing in a cramped office bathroom stall, Nina couldn't even savor the joy and relief of her own long string, of knowing that a full life stretched before her. She couldn't celebrate the truth of her string without mourning the truth of Maura's.

Nina's chest started to heave, her lungs hyperventilating. Maura's string had *looked* short, but what did that really mean? How much time did they actually have left? The initial question plaguing the world had at last been answered: The strings were real. But so many questions remained.

When Nina heard another woman enter the stall next to her, she tried to cover her mouth and quiet her sobbing. She knew that no one would blame her for succumbing to her emotions, but she felt embarrassed by her public display, as if the world were still normal and not radically altered.

Nina would have to tell Maura that night, so the truth came from someone who loved her, and not some talking head on the news.

She would have to take back everything she had said to Maura on the night that they had looked. All the claims that she had made—that she had genuinely *believed*—about the strings being fake.

"It can't possibly mean anything," Nina had said, trying to hold her voice steady. "It's just a piece of string."

"That's not what everyone else thinks," Maura whispered.

"And what does everyone else know? We don't live in some crazy world where magical boxes predict the future," Nina said. "We live in the *real* world. And these strings *aren't* real."

But nothing Nina had said could dispel the invisible tension that loomed between them ever since that moment, exerting pressure on them both, each night when they went to bed and each morning when they woke. They hadn't had sex since the middle of March, and nearly all of their daily interactions were tinged with a quiet anxiety.

As if they had both known, all along, that something terrible was coming.

Once the other woman exited the bathroom, Nina stepped out from the stall and ran a paper towel under the tap. She wiped her face and the back of her neck with the damp compress, trying to regain the strength in her limbs and hopefully stop breathing so heavily, or else she might pass out.

After she told Maura the truth, Nina would have to tell her family, too.

She would have to call her parents, still living in the Boston suburbs where Nina and her sister had been born, close enough to spend any holidays together, far enough to indulge their daughters' preference for independence. And she would surely need to tell Amie.

Nina's younger sister had resolutely decided *not* to open her box, and every time they spoke of it, she remained adamant about the choice. But now that the strings were conclusively real, would Amie change her mind?

Nina threw away the paper towel and looked at herself in the mirror, the glass streaked with water stains. Nina rarely wore makeup, but her face appeared even more naked than usual. It looked pink and raw and vulnerable, stripped down to its core.

Whenever she stared in a mirror, Nina couldn't help but notice the slight pinching of the skin near her eyes and the two subtle creases in her forehead. ("Maybe if you weren't so serious all the time, you'd be wrinkle-free like me," Maura had teased, playfully stroking her hand against the smooth, dark skin of her cheekbones.) Nina was only thirty, just one year older than Maura, but she was clearly starting to age. And she knew, now, that her long string meant she would one day look in the mirror and see a very old woman gazing back. Until today, Nina had simply assumed that Maura would still be standing next to her.

But the strings had destroyed that illusion in one horrifying instant, and Nina's future suddenly felt just like her reflection in the mirror now. Sad, defenseless, and alone.

BEN

Ben found himself crossing the Times Square subway station for the first time since the strings had arrived.

Transferring from the 1 train to the Q, he passed through a dank passageway where the ceiling leaked even when it wasn't raining and the walkway was perpetually lined with mustard-colored trash bins collecting the droplets. When he emerged, he was standing in the large underground intersection where the passengers from nearly ten different train lines emptied out simultaneously.

The busiest of all New York's subway stops, the Times Square station had always been chaotic, the perpetual foot traffic fostering the ultimate soapbox for evangelicals, doomsayers, and anyone else with an opinion to shout. But now the usual chaos felt even more frenzied.

Two women in ankle-length skirts implored passersby: "Trust in God! He will save you!" Megaphones amplified their high-pitched voices to a booming volume that their petite frames could never accomplish. "He has a plan for you! Do not fear your string!"

The women of faith were competing with at least four other preachers that evening, but thanks to the bullhorns, they were winning. As Ben politely dodged their pamphlets and approached the entrance to his track, he could distinguish the words of one of their competitors: a middle-aged man in a stained button-down shirt with a less hopeful message to deliver. "The apocalypse is nigh! The strings are just the beginning! The end is coming!"

Ben tried to maintain eye contact with the floor until he had walked far enough away from the man, but he looked up at the overhead screen to see when the next train would arrive, and unluckily met the speaker's gaze as he posed a question to the crowd.

"Are you prepared to face the end?"

He meant, of course, the end of the world, the end of days. But his words struck Ben with an uncomfortable force. Ben was here in this station, after all, because he was heading to the first session of his new support group on the very topic of preparing to face the end.

"Living with Your Short String" was what the group's flyer had said. A title that appeared more ironic than promising, Ben thought wryly, since the very fact of possessing a short string meant that there wasn't much living left to do.

A variety of support groups for short-stringers and their families were swiftly formed in the wake of the boxes' arrival, and Ben found one that met every Sunday night from eight to nine P.M. in a classroom at the Connelly Academy, a private school on the Upper East Side.

He arrived early on his first night, while the hallways were still eerily quiet.

Raised by two high school teachers, Ben felt a strong nostalgia toward schools, and it only took a quick glance at a colorful bulletin board—this one happened to be space-themed, with each of the students' photos glued inside a yellow star—to bring him back to the days when he was little, accompanying his parents to the school where they both taught, gawking at the teenage students who towered above him like giants.

It was always odd for Ben to watch his parents command a classroom, to see that there were all these other children who *also* had to listen to them, to learn from them, and he sometimes felt jealous or defensive, not wanting to share his mom and dad with these strangers. But the highlight of his visits came when he would sit in the back of a classroom, scribbling messy drawings of tiny, oddly proportioned houses on the sketch pad he carried with him everywhere, and a few of the older girls would fawn over him.

"Who lives inside that little house?" the girls cooed at him. "An elf, or a fairy?"

Ben was tempted, in his juvenile bravado, to explain that he was far too old to still believe in elves or fairies, but he enjoyed their attention too much to risk losing it.

The memories from his *own* classrooms were less comforting. Walking past the walls of lockers on his way to the support group that night, Ben wondered if any had been left open with a sliver of tape covering the lock, the preferred method of students who didn't care to memorize their combinations. Ben had taped his locker door only once, in ninth grade, after he saw a group of football players doing it and asked them for a piece of their tape in what he now understood was his pathetic attempt at infiltrating their fraternity of the broad-shouldered. It took less than an hour for Ben's cell phone and jacket to be pilfered from his unlocked locker.

He reached the threshold of Room 204, where the plastic chairs had been pulled out from their desks and rearranged in a circle, but only one man was inside.

Embarrassed by his early arrival, Ben stepped back into the hallway.

"Too late! I've already seen you."

Ben reemerged and forced a grin that could rival the cheeriness of the voice he just heard.

"Hey, there, I'm Sean, the group facilitator," the man said. "You must be one of the newbies tonight."

Shaking Sean's hand, Ben tried to appraise the man who would ostensibly be guiding him on his path toward peace and acceptance. He was somewhere in his late thirties, with a thick beard, and wearing loose-fitting jeans. He was seated in a wheelchair but still projected an impressive height.

"Nice to meet you, I'm Ben. And yeah, it's my first time," he said. "Does that mean there are other new people coming, too?"

"Yup, you and a young woman both signed up this week."

"Sounds great," Ben said, his damp hands seeking shelter in his pockets. He could feel his natural shyness threatening to take over, and he hoped that he hadn't made a mistake by joining this group.

Damon, a friend from college and one of the few people whom Ben had told about his short string, had convinced him to try the support group. (Though Damon was a lucky long-stringer himself, his father was a recovered addict who relied upon AA meetings, and Damon was a true believer in the virtues of group therapy.)

Ben wished he could have brought Damon along with him, at least for the first session. Ben had never been good at opening up to new people, and after the recent disaster with his now-ex-girlfriend, Claire, Ben feared his sense of trust had been permanently severed.

"So, if you don't mind me asking, do you also have . . ." Ben couldn't quite finish the question.

"Well, no," Sean said. "My string is a bit longer than the folks in this group, but I'm licensed as a clinical social worker, and helping people through difficult circumstances is what I've always wanted to do."

Ben nodded quietly, as an approaching brunette rescued him from any ensuing small talk.

"Hi, Sean," she said, placing her tote on the nearest chair.

"Ben, meet Lea. Lea, meet Ben." Sean swiveled between the two.

"Welcome to the party." Lea smiled sweetly.

The remainder of the group filed in quickly. The oldest was a physician in his early forties. (At least Ben assumed he was a doctor, since a few of the others greeted him as "Doc," though he introduced himself simply as Hank.) The rest appeared closer to Ben's own age, scattered throughout their twenties and thirties.

Chelsea, a strawberry blonde who looked like she had just left the tanning salon, entered the room while reading something on her phone, trailed by a series of men: the burly, bearded Carl, his face slightly obscured by a Mets cap; the lanky Nihal, in a Princeton sweatshirt; and the dapper Terrell, whose gleaming black oxfords made Ben glance shamefully at his weathered canvas sneakers.

The final arrival was Ben's fellow newcomer, a woman named Maura, who sat down next to Ben and offered a half smile and a half nod that Ben received as a silent summation of the entire group's unspoken sentiments: *It sucks to be us.*

But at least there is an us.

MAURA

Maura hadn't wanted to join the support group. Joining felt like admitting defeat, and Maura was no defeatist. She only agreed in order to placate her girlfriend.

Nina hadn't even wanted to look at their strings when they first arrived, which wasn't very surprising. Nina was always the cautious one.

But when they finally opened their boxes at Maura's urging, she instantly wished they hadn't.

Nina had tried her best to allay Maura's fears, to convince her that the strings weren't real. But Maura had been fighting a queasiness, a lack of appetite, and a general sense of dread ever since the day they'd looked.

And then, about a week later, Nina returned home from her office and told Maura to sit down, that she had something she needed to tell her.

"Deborah got a call today," Nina said slowly. "From someone at the Health Department." Her eyes had already turned glassy, and she was struggling to find the next words.

But Maura understood.

"Just say it, Nina. Just fucking say it!"

Nina swallowed. "They're real."

Maura jumped off the couch and sprinted to the bathroom, crumpling onto the cold tiles. When she vomited into the toilet, Maura could feel Nina holding back her dark curls, and she knew Nina was holding back tears.

"It's going to be okay," Nina kept saying, gently rubbing her hand up and down Maura's back. "We'll get through this."

But for the first time in their two years together, Maura couldn't find comfort in Nina's words.

They sat in front of the television the following night, their hands clutched together, as the president made a speech urging citizens to stay calm, and the secretary of the Department of Health and Human Services made a speech outlining the researchers' findings, and the director of the World Health Organization and the UN secretary general both made speeches calling for global solidarity and compassion during this moment of uncharted crisis.

The Pope even emerged on his balcony in Vatican City to address the millions of frightened souls who were no doubt waiting for his guidance.

"I would like to remind everyone of the words we repeat at each Mass: 'The mystery of faith.' We know that faith, *true* faith, calls upon us to accept that some mysteries will always lie beyond our comprehension while here on earth," the Pope declared, his words translated for all. "Our knowledge of our Creator will always be imperfect. As we read in Romans 11:33, 'Oh the depth of the riches of the wisdom and of the knowledge of God! How incomprehensible are his judgments, and how unsearchable his ways!' Today, we are faced with the incomprehensible, the inscrutable. We are asked to believe that these boxes contain knowledge that has, until now, been reserved for God alone. But this is not the first time that we have been called upon to believe in what was once unbelievable. Even the Apostles did not believe, at first, that Jesus Christ had risen from the grave, but we know it to be true. And just as I have no doubt in the resurrection, I have no doubt that these boxes are a gift from God to His children, for there is no one else more powerful, more knowing, and more giving than the Lord our God."

But Maura did not see her box as a gift.

Every day, as hundreds of thousands of people celebrated their twenty-second birthdays by awakening to a new wave of boxes, the situation grew increasingly urgent. They couldn't just keep guessing at what their strings foretold.

A team of analysts collaborating between the U.S. and Japan was the first to offer a solution: a government-sponsored website that would enable at-home users to interpret the length of their strings.

The researchers had amassed the measurements of thousands of different strings, down to mere fragments of millimeters. They had concluded, based on the earliest data, that the length of one's string did not, in fact, equate with the time *left* to live, as some had initially posited. The measure of the string held instead the full measure of one's life. From the beginning until the end.

Presuming the longest possible string accounted for the rare life span of approximately 110 years, the researchers had gradually worked their way backward to establish an estimated guide to string length and its corresponding life span. They couldn't offer an exact date; the science wasn't quite that precise. But users could visit the website, enter the length of their string, and—after clicking past three more screens designed to make absolutely certain that they wished to proceed, and agreed not to sue over any bad news—they would finally see the result, printed all too clearly in black Times New Roman. The time in which their life would end, narrowed to a window of barely two years.

What was, at first, a vague awareness that Maura's string was not nearly as long as Nina's soon crystallized into something crushingly concrete.

Maura's string ended in her late thirties.

She had fewer than ten years remaining.

Through the early days of April, Nina wanted to talk with Maura about what was happening, and she often did talk with Maura, but she worried that she couldn't offer the same type of support that a fellow short-stringer could.

"You know that I will *always* be here for you," Nina said, "but maybe there are others who can be there for you in a different way? My sister said that her school has even started to host some string support groups."

"I appreciate that you're trying to help," Maura replied, "but I'm not sure I want to be surrounded by a bunch of people weeping about their unfinished business."

"Well, apparently they have different types of sessions based on how, um, how much time is remaining on your string. So there are groups for people who have less than a year left, and groups for people with maybe twenty years left, and then a group for those in between, like . . ." Nina looked unsure if she should continue.

"Like me," Maura finished for her.

"Obviously you should only do what you feel comfortable doing, and I'll support you no matter what."

Maura looked at Nina, whose slight frame appeared even more fragile in the dim light of their third-floor walk-up, and she agreed to try the support group, if only to wipe away the watery mixture of guilt and grief that had pooled in Nina's eyes as she spoke.

Less than a week later, Maura found herself walking toward the school that would house her group therapy session.

The streets had become a familiar scene; at least one business per block was boarded up by now. Often the owners placed signs on the locked doors and metal gates of their shuttered stores and restaurants with scribbled sentiments like "Gone to live my life," "Spending more time with family," or "Off to make some memories." Maura passed by a piece of paper taped onto a former jewelry store: "Closed. Looking for closure."

More disturbing than the signs, though, was another encounter—rarer, but not entirely uncommon—of stumbling upon a stranger's discarded box peering devilishly above the rim of a garbage bin or from within a curbside pile of broken furniture.

In the days and weeks following the revelations of the strings, those reeling from the truth had found different methods of handling the unwelcome chests that had intruded upon their lives. Some, choosing willful ignorance in the hope of attaining its promised bliss, threw away their boxes to avoid temptation. The melodramatic hurled them into rivers and lakes or locked them away in a remote crevice of their house. The more cavalier just tossed them in the trash.

Still others attempted to obliterate the boxes in fits of rage, but these powerful chests, like the black box of an airplane, simply could not be destroyed, no matter how many times they were burned or smashed or violently trampled upon.

Pedestrians who came across an opened box that had been left on the side of the road, or perhaps flung out of a nearby window, tended to avert their eyes and quicken their steps, as if passing by a panhandler whose gaze they wished to avoid.

Luckily, Maura didn't see any abandoned boxes that evening as she approached the entrance to the school. The quiet, brownstone-lined streets of the Upper East Side were either too genteel or too uptight for such a public display of emotion, she thought.

Fitting for its locale, the building looked old and fancy, the architectural equivalent of an elderly philanthropist dressed up for a benefit. It had one of those elaborate prewar exteriors that realtors love to point out, adorned with tiny gargoyles shaped like gryphons.

As she walked up the wide interior staircase, past marble plaques quoting Plato and Einstein, Maura's fingers crept up to her face, touching the small turquoise nose ring she had worn since college that would surely violate the dress code of a place like this. Nina's younger sister, Amie, had taught at this school for several years now, but Maura had never stepped foot inside before tonight.

She heard murmurs when she reached the second-floor landing and followed them to Room 204. Thankfully, she was the last to arrive.

AMIE

Apparently she had never finished *Atonement*.

Amie's arm was stretched painfully under her bed, fingers splayed, feeling for a pen that had seemingly rolled into oblivion, when her thumb brushed unexpectedly against the spine of a book. She pulled out the paperback, covered in a light layer of dust, and saw that her bookmark—gold-plated and monogrammed, a gift from an ex-boyfriend that had long stopped reminding her of their brief intertwinement—still rested in the furrow between pages, two-thirds of the way through.

Amie had been reading the novel back in March, and she couldn't believe she had forgotten about it, she had been so engrossed in the story. But she had nodded off that night, the night the boxes arrived, with the book sleeping next to her in bed, and in the commotion of the following morning the novel must have slipped off the duvet and into the past, a sudden relic of the days before.

Before.

Amie held the book in her hands, remembering that morning. She had slept in late, as usual—a habit that her sister, Nina, never understood—unwilling to extricate herself from that night's reverie, no doubt inspired by her reading. In the dream, she was a student at Cambridge in the 1930s, courted by a young man who spoke like Hugh Grant, and Amie remembered feeling faintly disappointed to have woken up alone in bed.

By the time Amie rolled off her mattress that morning, Nina had already left two panicked voice mails. (She was only a year older than Amie but had long deemed herself the voice of authority.)

"Call me as soon as you get this!" Nina shouted into the phone. "Don't go outside yet, don't do anything. Just call me first! Please!"

Nina hadn't believed in the boxes' inscription and wanted to wait until she had met with her news team at work. But the truth was Amie wouldn't have looked anyway. These boxes had shown up *everywhere*, clearly powerful beyond belief. The world had somehow tripped and tumbled through the looking glass, and Amie had read enough novels to recognize that this was the part of the story where nobody knew what the hell was going on, where the characters made rash decisions whose consequences would only be revealed chapters later.

Fortunately, the strings had arrived in the middle of spring break, so nobody at the Connelly Academy had to make the last-minute decision to cancel classes. (Very few schools had actually canceled that day, though Amie heard that most classrooms were only half-full, with both students and teachers failing to turn up.)

"Your students will, of course, have questions," the principal had addressed the staff the following Monday. "And I'm sure that you all have formed your own opinions by now. But we cannot go telling our students anything we don't know for certain."

The teacher next to Amie had leaned in and whispered, "So . . . basically that means we can't say anything at all?"

More than a month had passed since then, the gravity settled over the world. But the situation at school felt largely unchanged, the administration still trying to shelter its students as much as possible. Access to YouTube had even been blocked on school property, after a teacher realized that half of the pupils in the cafeteria were watching videos of a teenage boy attempting various means of destroying his parents' strings. The teachers later watched some of the clips in their lounge, and Amie looked on anxiously as the boy tried cutting the strings with pruning shears, dipping them in a fizzy homemade acid concoction, pulling strenuously on one end while his bulldog chomped down on the other.

"Look, I certainly don't want the kids getting inspired by these stunts, or watching them in my class," Amie recalled her colleague saying. "But we can't just act like it's not happening. I can't keep teaching them *history* and pretending like we're not living through it right now."

In a way, Amie thought, wasn't that incredible?

She was well aware of the pain the strings had wrought—Nina's girlfriend, Maura, had a short string. But Amie still hadn't opened her own box, so she could see the world through unsullied eyes, and though she would never admit this in front of anyone, there was something almost . . . thrilling . . . about the strings' arrival. Frightening and confusing, of course, but also, perhaps, wondrous? As a child, she imagined herself swept up by adventure, stepping inside the magical wardrobe, touring the chocolate factory, tessering through time. (Once, when she skinned her knee while playing outside, she even pressed her finger in the tiny wound and smeared a few droplets of blood on her cheek, envisioning herself as a warrior princess in a faraway land, to Nina's germophobic dismay.) And now, the fantastic, the unbelievable, had suddenly entered her world. And *she* was there to witness.

Amie stood up slowly from her bedroom floor, *Atonement* in her hand. She had a few more papers to grade, then she was eager to finish reading. But she realized, as she placed the novel atop her dresser, that this was the first time the world outside of her books had ever rivaled the stories with its very own plot twist.

NINA

Nina and her colleagues were shocked, their eyes fastened to a computer screen in the middle of the office bullpen. The footage showed a group of police officers assembled near a bridge in what looked like a medieval village, cordoning off photographers and curious onlookers.

An incident in Verona had just made its way into the news cycle in New York. A young Italian couple, recently married, had jumped off a bridge together, hand in hand, after opening their boxes on their wedding night and discovering that the bride possessed a devastatingly short string. The groom survived the joint suicide attempt, while his wife of three days did not.

Nina winced when she realized that the tragic act, set in fair Verona, would undoubtedly spark an onslaught of tasteless Shakespearean puns in the tabloids.

"It's so horrible," said one of the reporters.

"But you know what's really crazy?" asked a fact-checker. "The guy knew he wouldn't *succeed* in killing himself. They looked at their strings, so they knew that hers was short and his was long. Even if he did something completely dangerous, he knew he wasn't going to die."

"Well, maybe he knew he wouldn't *die*, but obviously he was pretty messed up about it. He still risked paralyzing himself by jumping off a fucking bridge."

"Oh, yeah, of course. But it's weird to think about."

"I don't know, to me it's just more proof that nobody should look," said the reporter. "Clearly, seeing their strings drove them both insane."

They weren't *insane*, Nina thought. They were heartbroken.

But she didn't expect her coworkers to understand. They couldn't look past the dramatic spectacle to see the ordinary, everyday anguish that lay just underneath it.

Their staff was small, dwindling every year in tandem with the magazine's budget, and as far as she knew, Nina was the only member of the office with such an intimate connection to a known short-stringer.

Her colleagues had been timid at first, understandably wary of breaching any work-life boundaries, but the team had always been close enough to speak freely about breakups and weddings, pregnancies and deaths, and eventually they opened up about the strings.

A third of the staff hadn't looked in their boxes; the rest seemed fairly content with their findings. After learning about Maura, several coworkers even offered to cover Nina's desk, should she ever need some time off.

But for Nina there was no such thing.

Surrounded by the news all day, Nina could never escape the strings. She found herself begging Deborah to assign her to some other story, *any* other story, but it seemed as if there weren't any. The field of presidential candidates was taking shape and global temperatures were rising, but nothing captivated readers the way the strings could. There was hardly an hour in the day when Nina wasn't thinking about them, wondering if she would ever know the truth.

Maura often described Nina as a lovable control freak, always needing to store the Tupperware containers with their proper lids, never buying a new skirt unless she already owned a matching top. Part of what Nina loved about being an editor were the *rules*, the clear and comprehensible laws of grammar and linguistics, and she loved wielding the power of the red pen to enact them. Before her promotion, when she was still trying to prove herself as a reporter, she reveled in seeking out the *facts*, burying herself in piles of research, charged with the hunt for the truth. But everything about the strings unearthed an even deeper desire for knowledge, for control. The lack of answers—where did the strings come from? why now? do they actually control the future, or simply possess the knowledge of it?—kept Nina from sleeping through the night. Everything was too murky, too gray. She needed things in black-and-white.

And Nina was forced to helplessly watch Maura suffer, because nothing could be done. Any semblance of control had been ripped from them both.

Nina felt powerless, like she was reliving one of the worst days of her life, back in senior year of high school. She had spent an hour, that morning, with the school's guidance counselor, seeking advice on coming out to her friends, unaware that a catty classmate had been eavesdropping through the door, and by the time that Nina had left the office, she didn't need to worry about finding the right moment to share. The truth was already out.

Even now, as an adult, Nina could still see the gym's locker room: the curious glances, the subtle nods, the embarrassed whispers. For someone who refused to let even one sentence be printed in the school newspaper without her explicit editorial sign-off, she had entered a new circle of hell. Nina's meticulous planning, her weeks of internal debate, everything was scrapped in an instant. All her power, her control, had been stolen away. She had only intended to tell a handful of friends, but word quickly slipped across multiple grades.

Of course, two days later, her news had been eclipsed when half the soccer team was suspended for smoking pot behind the field, and hardly anyone could remember the gossip from before. Except for Nina.

She would *always* remember.

More than a decade later, living in the apartment she rented with Maura, Nina could still feel the anger and humiliation, could still recall vowing to protect herself from any other agony, from ever losing control again.

Amie and Maura often asked her to be less controlling. To loosen up. To let it go.

But Nina couldn't let go. Not when she lived in a world of betrayal and heartache, of mysterious boxes and painfully short strings.

If Nina let go, then whatever it was that she was trying to protect—her younger self, her future with Maura—would be left unarmed and vulnerable. Out of her control.

The boxes were now a part of her life, Nina couldn't change that. But she was determined to regain a sense of power and clarity. And so, in the wee hours when she couldn't sleep, or when Maura was away from their apartment, Nina found herself scouring the Internet for answers.

What had started as a simple Google search—Where did the boxes come from?—quickly unspooled, after Nina clicked over to Reddit and landed in the middle of a popular new subreddit, r/Strings. She instantly realized there were *hundreds* of ongoing discussions, all attempting to decipher the mystery of the boxes.

Normally Nina was too private a person, too self-disciplined, to enjoy the public abandon of most social media, but she surprised herself with how easily she could slip into the conversations and suddenly lose two hours online.

Nina landed on one photo posted by gordoncoop531957 of a box illuminated under UV light, fingerprints glowing on the outer casing. "Proof," the photo was captioned.

```
Posted by u/Matty 1 hour ago
  Proof of wut? That ur an idiot?

Posted by u/TheWatcher 1 hour ago
  Definitely extraterrestrial. It's why the prints
  are invisible to the naked eye.

Posted by u/NJbro44 2 hours ago
  Dude those are probably ur own fingers.
```

Another user, offdagrid774, posted a picture of his box being kept inside a microwave, urging everyone to do the same: "Don't let the NSA listen to you!"

```
Posted by u/ANH 1 day ago
  Ur right, the boxes are def bugged. The gov spying
  not just on Americans but the whole world!! How
  else would they have ur name and address? Keep it
  out of ur house!!
```

```
Posted by u/Fran_M 1 day ago
  Offdagrid774, do you think there's a camera
  inside, too?
```

The religious contingent occupied a smaller corner online, though equally vocal. A Bible verse, shared by RedVelvet_Mama, had recently gone viral as an alleged testament to the boxes' divine provenance.

"Do not judge, so that you may not be judged. For with the judgment you make you will be judged, and the measure you give will be the measure you get." –Matthew 7

Nina didn't believe anything she read, it was all just conjecture. But it was comforting to know that there were thousands of people, millions even, who were just as unnerved as she was, and just as interested in finding the truth, if such a thing even existed.

On Sunday evening, when Maura was at her support group, Nina thought about the man in Verona, and what her coworker had said. It was an unsettling thought that someone was essentially immune to dying until they reached the end of their string—especially strange for those, like Nina, with long ones.

Sitting in bed, Nina pulled out her laptop and searched "long string + death" to see if anything might come up.

The query led her to a new site, Don't Try This at Home, with its own ongoing discussion. When she reached the forum, it was filled with the accounts of seemingly reckless long-stringers pushing the limits of their strings.

I have a long string and a few days ago I OD'd on painkillers but my roommate found me and here I am!! Thanks string!!

My girlfriend and I had been wanting to play with asphyxiation for a while and we both have long strings so figured now is the time. 10/10 would recommend ;)

Happy 22 to me! Got a long one! ☺ Looking for some Special K to celebrate

Nina had to stop reading. How could so many people be willing to experiment with their lives?

But hearing their stories only made the mystery of the boxes that much more disturbing, the power of the strings even more potent. It was like the strings *knew* your response all along, as if they were somehow able to account for any daredevil tendencies when determining your final measurement. They could somehow *see* which drugs and games and jumps would be fatal, and which would merely end up as morbid one-liners posted online for whoever happened to be browsing.

Nina felt sick. She closed her laptop and curled up her legs under the sheets, hoping Maura would come home soon.

MAURA

Despite her early reluctance to join the group, Maura left that first session already looking forward to the next Sunday night. She knew that Nina purposefully swallowed any discussion of the strings in her presence, trying to maintain some chimera of normalcy in their lives—and for that Maura was usually grateful—but it was actually quite freeing to enter a space where no subject was verboten, where the kid gloves came off.

"I'm so depressed," Chelsea opened a session, one night in late April.

"About your string?" Maura asked.

"No." Chelsea sighed. "Well, yes. But tonight I'm *also* depressed because *Grey's Anatomy* just got canceled."

"Hasn't that been on forever?" Terrell asked.

"That's why it's so crazy! It ended out of nowhere. TMZ thinks somebody high up at the show must have gotten a short string and quit."

"Well, you're welcome to shadow me at the hospital." Hank smiled. "Though I can't promise any torrid affairs."

"Did you hear the Spice Girls might get back together?" Lea asked. "Rumor is that one of them's a short-stringer now and wanted to reunite before . . . you know."

As curious as she was, Maura couldn't help but feel sorry for the people they were discussing. Sure, they had chosen a public life, but wasn't this somehow different, off-limits? Speculation and gossip were running rampant by then, and not just about actors and singers. In the checkout lines at stores, during previews at the movies, at the next table over in any

restaurant, it was common to hear people guessing at the length of someone's string. Quitting a job, getting engaged, being unusually cagey at a
party, anything could be construed to support either side, long or short.
"They claim they haven't looked, but I *know* that isn't true," was a wildly
popular refrain. It made Maura wonder what people said about her, the
ones who didn't know.

What's worse, Maura realized, it was all their fault. They had brought
this upon themselves. Even before the boxes appeared, the traditional
barriers of privacy had long been collapsing, hers already a society of
over-sharers. Maura, like so many others, had posted photo after photo
online—of decadent meals, of the view from her office, of weekends at
the beach with Nina—each one encouraging people to pry deeper and
deeper into others' lives, to expect a certain degree of transparency. Until, finally, even the act of looking at your string—what should have been
the most intimate, the most personal of moments—became just another
insight into your life that no longer belonged to you alone.

Had the strings arrived in any other century, Maura reasoned, nobody
would have dared ask what was inside your box, leaving each household to quietly mourn or celebrate on their own, behind closed doors and
drawn curtains. But not now, not in this modern era when feuds and flir-
tations played out online, when family milestones, professional achieve-
ments, and personal tragedies were all on display. Celebrities dodged
interview questions about their strings. Athletes were probed about their
"career prospects." Song lyrics were ruthlessly examined for hints of a
string-related message. Happy hour proved unexpectedly dangerous,
with friends and coworkers fishing for drunken confessions. Members of
the royal family, child stars, the sons and daughters of politicians, anyone
with the misfortune of turning twenty-two in the spotlight, awoke that
fateful morning under the nosy gaze of paparazzi lenses, aiming to cap-
ture the million-dollar reaction. The public demanded to know.

"I have an idea for something different tonight," said Sean, snapping
Maura's attention back to the present. "And I want everyone to keep an
open mind as I explain it."

Maura glanced at Ben seated next to her. "Gird your loins," she whispered.

"Already girded." He smiled.

"Some of my colleagues from other groups have talked about the fact that not everyone feels comfortable sharing things out loud, which is perfectly natural," said Sean. "And while I hope that this is a safe space where nobody feels intimidated to speak up, I think it could be helpful to try a different method of processing our thoughts."

Sean pulled two yellow legal pads out of his satchel, followed by a dozen blue pens. "I want everyone to take a pen and a few pieces of paper and write a letter."

"Is there someone specific we're writing to?" asked Nihal, ever the good student.

"Nope." Sean shook his head. "You can address the letter to your current self, your younger self, your future self. Or to someone else whom you'd like to say something to. Or you can just put pen to paper for ten minutes and see what comes out."

"Sounds like a waste of time," Carl mumbled.

The notepads made their way around the circle, and Maura stared at the blank page in her lap. Nina would love this exercise, Maura thought. She was so much better with words.

Dear Nina, she wrote.

The next line was proving more difficult. In a world of rumors and meddlesome strangers, Nina was the only person who actually deserved to know everything about Maura's life, and there were few things that Maura hadn't shared with her during the past two years.

And through each late-night confession, they had stayed together.

Nina wasn't bothered by Maura's restless nature, the fact that in seven years she had held five different jobs, from a downtown gallery to a mayoral campaign to a brief stint at a start-up that abruptly imploded. And she had gone through just as many girlfriends as careers.

While Maura had jumped from career to career, from fling to fling, Nina was never burdened by that sense of restiveness. She had worked her way up at the same magazine since college, and she had had two rather undramatic relationships before Maura, with zero one-night stands in the middle—all of which Nina would speak about almost shamefully, as if it made her seem boring, unadventurous. But Maura actually admired it. Nina was loyal in a way that seemed rare nowadays.

After they'd opened their boxes, Maura had given Nina the chance to leave. But she refused.

"I know that you love me," Maura said, "but I don't even have ten years left, and you deserve someone you can spend the rest of your life with."

Nina was shocked. "I *do* love you, and that's why I would never leave."

Maura suggested that Nina take some time to think. "You wouldn't have to feel guilty about it." She held Nina's hand tenderly. "I wouldn't blame you."

But Nina had insisted. "I don't need time to know how I feel."

Still searching for inspiration for her letter, Maura looked around Room 204. It was clearly an English classroom, decorated with black-and-white portraits of famous authors. They reminded Maura of the posters in her old studio apartment, where the bed took up nearly half of the space, and her collection of vintage celebrity mug shots graced the low white walls.

On their fourth date, the first time that Nina came over, Maura had watched as she studied the photos intently: A stoic David Bowie in a Rochester precinct. Frank Sinatra in the thirties, his tousled hair falling over his forehead with a boyish sexiness. Jane Fonda raising a clenched fist in Cleveland. Bill Gates, looking like a blond Beatle, actually grinning in his portrait from the seventies. And Jimi Hendrix, unfazed, in 1969, with his shirt unbuttoned to reveal a pendant necklace.

"Most of those were just drug-related, pretty minor offenses," Maura explained. "Bill Gates was arrested for driving without a license."

"I think they're fascinating," Nina said. "I almost want to put them in a four-page spread in our next issue."

"So, you're on a date with me, and yet you're thinking about work?" Maura sat down on the bed and crossed her legs flirtatiously. "How's that supposed to make me feel?"

"I'm so sorry." Nina smiled, leaning down to kiss Maura lightly. "I'm actually embarrassed to admit I didn't know a lot of those people ever got arrested."

"That's sort of why I hung them up," Maura said, looking across the display. "They're a reminder that sometimes we screw up, and sometimes the system screws with us, but if you live your life with enough passion and boldness, then *that's* what you'll be remembered for. Not the crap that happened along the way."

Ten minutes had nearly passed, but Maura's letter was still blank.

She looked around the room and saw that most of the other group members hadn't stopped writing since receiving their pens. Ben had already finished his letter and was doodling a sketch of the New York skyline. At least Hank seemed to be struggling, too.

Dear Nina,

What could she write that Nina didn't already know?

There was only one answer, but Maura couldn't tell her now, not after all of their discussions and decisions. Not when Nina thought that the matter was settled.

And it *was* settled, Maura had convinced herself of that. What good would it do Nina to learn that Maura was having doubts?

HANK

On the first day of May, nobody at New York Memorial Hospital could have predicted the large-scale tragedy that would occur there in just two weeks' time. At the beginning of the month, the doctors and nurses and patients were still preoccupied, as always, with the tragedies unfolding on smaller scales all around them.

That morning alone, Hank had seen three people come into the hospital with tears in their eyes, faces pale with fear, desperately begging to speak with a doctor about their short strings.

In the early weeks, back in March and April, Hank and his colleagues would invite these short-stringers into the hospital and run a series of tests: blood panels, MRIs, ultrasounds, EKGs. Sometimes they would find something of concern and the patient could return home, if not with hope, then at least with an answer. It was far more difficult to send someone away with no explanation at all.

But the short-stringers appeared with greater frequency as the weeks passed and more people became convinced that the strings were real. And so, by the first of May, after the government had confirmed what everyone had feared, the hospital board decided that short-stringers exhibiting no present symptoms could no longer be "indulged." The sick and injured would never be turned away, of course, but the otherwise healthy couldn't be admitted solely because of their string, which could equally imply an imminent accident as it could a medical ailment. The emergency room was too crowded already, and the legal team worried that doctors who released short-stringers with a clean bill of health might be flirting with a lawsuit.

Hank had just stepped into the ER lobby to discuss a patient's results with his family, when he saw a man arrive, box in hand, and approach the triage nurse screening patients at the entrance.

"My name is Jonathan Clarke," the man said frantically. "I need help."

"Can you tell me what's wrong?" the nurse asked, warily eyeing his box.

"No, but . . . it's so short," Jonathan pleaded. "It's so soon. You've gotta stop it."

"Are you currently experiencing *any* symptoms, sir?"

"I don't know. No. I don't think so," Jonathan stammered. "But you don't understand, it's almost done. Somebody's gotta help me!"

"Sir, if you aren't experiencing any symptoms, unfortunately I need to ask you to leave." The nurse gestured toward the exit. "We have patients here who need immediate attention."

"*I* need immediate attention!" Jonathan shouted. "I don't have any time!"

"Sir, I sympathize with your situation, but unfortunately there's nothing we can do. We recommend making an appointment with your primary care doctor instead."

"How can you say that? This is a fucking hospital! You're supposed to help people!"

A few of the patients and families waiting in the ER had turned to watch the scene, riveted like rubberneckers on a roadside, but most locked their eyes on the floor, both embarrassed and saddened for the man.

"Sir, I need you to calm down," the nurse said firmly.

"Stop calling me that!" Jonathan shook his box in the air. "I'm gonna die!"

One of the nearby security guards, a former wrestler, was coming over now as backup.

"How can you do this to me?" Jonathan was screaming. "How can you just let me die?"

"Sir, we know this is a difficult situation," said the guard, "and we don't want to call the police, but if you don't leave, we're going to have to." His hand hovered near the baton at his waist.

Jonathan fell quiet, and his eyes scanned the lobby, eventually settling upon Hank, the only white-coated figure in the room.

"Fine," Jonathan said. "I'm leaving."

He looked back at the nurse and the towering guard. "I don't want to spend my last days in a fucking jail cell," he said. "Maybe another hospital will have a goddamn heart."

From his post in the ER, Hank felt like he had been watching the world move through the stages of grief, inching closer and closer to some form of acceptance, a new notion of normality. But it seemed to him that, at every stage, more and more people had been left behind, trapped within each phase, unable to transition out.

Some were stuck in the early throes of denial: A few blocks from Hank's apartment, a dozen demonstrators often gathered to shout their assertions that the strings were a hoax, a government ruse, and that any accurate string predictions were merely self-fulfilling prophecies, testaments to the weak human spirit so easily swayed.

The bargainers pleaded with God to lengthen their strings, promised to turn their lives around. And perhaps those still refusing to open their boxes were engaged in a kind of bargaining as well, Hank thought. Every day that they didn't look at their strings, they bought themselves more time in an unaltered life.

But the people imprisoned in the more emotional stages, mired in anger or depression, were the easiest to spot and painful to watch. Jonathan Clarke belonged to the angry.

Hank waited as the sullen man exited the ER, and the feeling that had been growing inside of him since all of this began—a virulent sense of his own impotence—seemed to boil over in that moment.

At the close of his shift, Hank told his supervisor that he would be resigning from the hospital at the end of the month.

AMIE

May was unusually warm that year, the early morning sunshine hinting at the sticky summer heat to come, and Amie decided to walk across Central Park to her school on the east side instead of waiting for the crosstown bus.

The park was one of the few places that felt rather unchanged. Sprinters and bikers still rushed by, while joggers pushing strollers swerved past Amie on the walkway. Children climbed atop playground equipment and slid down plastic yellow slides, their parents and nannies watching from nearby benches.

Unfortunately, the beautiful weather did not go unnoticed by Amie's students.

"Can we have class outside today?"

As soon as Amie walked into her classroom, the predictable question came from a predictable culprit, a precocious boy with a smattering of freckles. His constant requests—Can we eat lunch during class today? Can we watch a movie in class today?—always roused the others, though Amie secretly admired his tenacity.

She looked at the entreating eyes of her fifth-graders. "I don't think that would be a good idea, since the pollen outside can make some of your classmates sneeze and cough, and we wouldn't want that," she said.

Her explanation sufficed for most, though a few sneered or rolled their eyes.

Truthfully, she wouldn't have minded leading class outdoors. She sometimes dreamt of herself as a college English professor, inspiring devotion in her students like Julia Roberts in *Mona Lisa Smile*. She pictured herself surrounded by a ring of eager scholars, seated on the quad with open novels in hand, notebooks and coffee cups strewn through the grass.

But bringing a rowdy group of ten-year-olds outside just wouldn't do.

"All right, now, who wants to talk about the ending of *The Giver*?" Amie asked.

She called on Meg, who was seated near the window as usual, though the desk next to her, once occupied by her best friend Willa, was now empty. Amie had been informed by the principal that Willa's mother, upon learning she had only a few years left to share with her daughter, took Willa out of school for an indefinite sabbatical abroad.

"I guess I felt . . . hopeful," Meg said. "Jonas's world is scary and unfair and confusing, but he gets to escape it in the end. And even if we don't really know what's waiting at the bottom of the hill, those lights down below make me feel like it's someplace nice. So, maybe, I don't know, whenever things feel scary and unfair and confusing for us, there's another, nicer place that we could find, too."

Amie wasn't quite sure what to say. Her students were young, they didn't use fancy words or figures of speech, they didn't quote philosophers or historians, but sometimes they simply left her speechless.

"That's beautiful, Meg, thank you. How does everyone else feel?"

On her walk home from school, Amie called her sister. Even when Nina was busy, she always answered for Amie.

"What are you working on?" Amie asked.

"Um, a piece about the airline industry's response to the strings," Nina said vaguely.

"Is now a bad time?" Amie could sense her sister's distraction, her eyes skimming the pages on her desk. Amie wondered, what exactly *was* the industry's response to the strings? Perhaps the airlines would suffer, too many short-stringers fearful of a fiery crash. Or maybe the strings would spur more people to travel, to explore the world while they still could.

"Sorry, no, now's fine," Nina said.

But Amie was still thinking about planes. "Do you remember when I wanted to date a pilot?"

"Of course." Nina laughed. "You went on, what, two dates with the guy from Delta?"

"Because I hoped the third date might've been in Paris," Amie said wistfully.

"I'm guessing that's not what you called to talk about."

"I'm trying to think of a book for the kids to read over summer break," Amie explained. "Preferably something historical, but relatable."

"Hmm, well, what did *we* read in fifth grade? Something about the Salem witch trials? Honestly, now might be a good time to talk about how people react to something they can't understand."

"I guess I'm just a little wary of bombarding them too much with the string stuff," said Amie. "I know they're aware of so much more than we give them credit for, but . . . they're still just kids."

"I get it," Nina said, then both sisters fell quiet.

"You, um, you would tell me if you changed your mind, right?" Nina asked timidly.

"Of course, you'd be the first to know. But I probably don't even have to look," Amie said cheerfully. "Yours was super-long, and you and I must share the majority of our DNA, so I'm sure mine's pretty similar."

"Oh yeah, definitely," Nina said. "And there's still no stopping Mom and Dad."

Amie smiled at the thought of her parents, thankfully still healthy in their early sixties, who had chosen, like Amie, not to look at their strings. To focus instead on the blessings in their latter half of life, filling their weekends with gardening and book clubs and tennis, those simple pleasures made all the more pleasurable for feeling so ordinary in an extraordinary time.

"Well, I'll let you get back to work," Amie said. "I'm going to stop by the bookstore and see if any inspiration strikes. Say hi to Maura for me."

Amie stepped into the bookshop near her apartment, the bell chiming as she entered. The small television mounted overhead was playing an interview with one of the newest presidential candidates, Anthony Rollins, a smooth-talking, good-looking congressman from Virginia who was no doubt pontificating about why *he* should be the man to shepherd the country through such alien times. Amie was still upset that the shop owner had installed the television last year. She came to the bookstore for relief from the endless news cycle, the stresses of the world outside.

She tried to ignore the man on the bright screen above her and slipped past the table of popular titles up front, where *The Iliad* and *The Odyssey* had both taken up residence in recent weeks, thanks to renewed interest in Greek mythology and the Fates, alongside a cluster of self-help books and meditations on mortality by doctors, philosophers, and theologians. *The Five People You Meet in Heaven* was a bestseller again.

Once she was in the main room, surrounded by the tall wooden shelves and the familiar scent of thousands of pages, Amie felt herself relax. There were few places where she felt more contented than a bookstore. She had a sometimes overwhelming tendency to disappear into her daydreams, so Amie took comfort in being surrounded by the equally prolific dreams of others, preserved forever in print.

When she and Nina were younger, their mother would often take them to the local bookshop after school, where the owner didn't mind if they spent an hour reading on the carpet before even making a purchase. By then Amie was already pulled toward fantasy and romance, while Nina preferred factual biographies of women like Marie Curie or Amelia Earhart (though her unsolved disappearance troubled Nina for weeks). As they read together, Nina developed a habit of pridefully pointing out any typos she found in a published book, which never failed to annoy Amie. She always wished that her sister could just let go and lose herself in the story.

As they grew up, Amie and Nina even founded a tradition of passing along the books they were reading, as soon as they were finished. It was originally Amie's suggestion, a balm for her fears that as the two of them aged, and their lives started to diverge—Nina came out as gay, then they both headed off to separate colleges—their newfound differences might threaten their closeness. For the five years they spent living apart, both sisters sent each other dozens of paperbacks through the mail, complete with sticky notes on favorite passages and inside jokes scribbled in the margins. Nina made fun of Amie's blubbering when she received her copy of *Never Let Me Go*, the last pages wrinkled with tears, and Amie griped at Nina for sending *Outliers* with a distracting amount of highlighted sections.

In the bookstore, Amie paused at the section for dystopian fiction, where she had come across *The Giver* back in January and, flooded by fond memories of her own fifth-grade book club, decided to assign it in class—before everything changed that spring. One spot over, *The Handmaid's Tale* sat snugly beside *The Hunger Games*, two books she remembered reading rapturously as a teenager. On more than one occasion, she had lain in her bed past midnight, unable to sleep, envisioning herself as a tribute in the Games, fending her way through a dark, dense forest grown inside her mind.

At least the future they had been doled seemed more promising than those on the shelves in front of Amie, in which women's bodies were stripped solely to their reproductive capacities and children murdered each other on television at the government's behest. Each novel seemed to imagine a world bleaker than the last. If those were the alternatives, Amie thought, perhaps they should feel lucky that the strings were all they got.

But Amie wondered, as she did almost every day, if she was making the wrong decision by refusing to open her box and rejecting the knowledge that had given so many of her friends and colleagues—nearly all of whom had long strings—an unprecedented peace of mind, the greatest gift they could ask for. Even Nina, whose thoughts were so often consumed with worry about Maura, had admitted to

Amie that she couldn't help but feel relieved when she saw her own long string.

But Amie's mind was constantly in motion, depicting herself in different scenarios. She had vividly imagined every possible outcome—a long string, a short string, a length in the middle, she once even conjured an *empty* box—and she reasoned that the safest choice was simply shoving the chest to the back of her closet, behind a salt-stained pair of winter boots that she only wore during snowstorms.

On Monday morning, Amie arrived at school, armed with two dozen copies of *Tuck Everlasting*.

"Excuse me, Miss Wilson?"

Amie turned around to see one of the school's custodians pulling a folded piece of yellow loose-leaf from his pocket. "I found this on the floor of your classroom as I was cleaning up last night, and I didn't know if I should throw it away or put it somewhere. I'm guessing one of your students wrote it?"

"Oh, thank you." Amie took the sheet of paper, a miniature rendering of the Manhattan skyline drawn on the back. She glanced at the names mentioned in the note inside. None were her students.

"Where did you say you found this?"

"Just lying under one of the chairs, near the bookshelf."

"I guess it might belong to someone," she said. "Thank you for saving it."

He nodded. "Anytime."

Amie smiled and stepped into Room 204, taking her seat behind a cluttered desk crowned with two notebooks, one tiny cactus (a gift from Nina that was "more practical than flowers"), two empty coffee mugs, a near-empty stapler, and a tabletop calendar with the theme of "banned books" that the history department had given her. May was *The Catcher in the Rye*, although Amie's calendar had been open to May ever since April 3, when she decided that too many of her students were asking what *Lolita* was about.

She placed the sheet of paper atop a small stack of essays, unsure if she should read it.

Amie turned her attention to the day's grammar lesson on commas and semicolons, but her eyes continued to drift toward the paper until she finally slid it off of the pile and onto the desk in front of her.

Sean told us that we needed to write a letter, so here goes.

A few faint marks after the period betrayed an impatient tapping of the author's pen.

Carl still thinks this is a stupid exercise and looks like he's poking holes in his paper with the tip of his pen, to Sean's dismay. And Chelsea might be drawing something, it's hard to tell.

Amie didn't recognize anyone.

Ten minutes is longer than I thought. Plus, it's been a while since I've written a letter like this, with a pen on paper. I feel like one of the soldiers in an epic war drama, hunched over a notepad writing a message to his girl back home.

It actually reminds me of visiting the WWII museum during a road trip down south. They had a bunch of those soldiers' letters framed on the walls. Of course I spent a good 20 minutes looking at them all, and now I can only remember one. The guy was writing to his mom and asked her to do him a favor and tell Gertrude: "No matter what happens, I still feel the same."

Not sure why that one stuck with me. Maybe it was the oddness of seeing such a private sentiment displayed so publicly. I almost felt embarrassed to read it. Or maybe it was just the name Gertrude.

Amie was struck with a sudden sense of guilt, reading the thoughts of this stranger. But the letter had been found in *her* classroom. It had to be written by one of her students, right? Only, she couldn't think of any of her ten-year-olds writing with this level of self-awareness—or with penmanship that was this neat. And yet it sounded like the author was writing some kind of school assignment? But there were no teachers named Sean that she knew of.

That's when Amie remembered what a colleague had said last month, that the school would be hosting short-stringer support groups in the evenings and on weekends.

Her stomach tightened as she realized what she had just read, and she felt a surge of pity for the writer, whose words must have been coaxed out of him as some form of therapy.

As she continued to grip the edges of the paper, uncertain what to do with it, Amie turned her thoughts to Gertrude. It was easier to think of a name in a distant museum than the short-stringer who had sat in her classroom mere hours ago and left this letter behind. So, instead, she imagined Gertrude and her sweetheart at war, like *Atonement*'s Cecilia and Robbie, the poor woman anxiously checking her mail for the tear-stained missives from a boy on a ship somewhere. No matter what happens, he still feels the same.

BEN

A week later, on Sunday evening, just before the session started, Maura pointed it out to Ben: the sheet of yellow loose-leaf, folded neatly in a square and placed on the floor beside the bookshelf in Room 204. There was an etching of the New York skyline on the page facing up.

"Isn't that yours?" Maura asked.

"Oh wow, yeah," Ben said. "I was wondering if I dropped it somewhere. What are the odds that it's been here this whole time, and nobody threw it out?"

Maura seemed just as surprised. "Maybe they saw the drawing and thought someone might come back for it. You're actually quite talented."

"*Actually?*" Ben laughed, and Maura smiled as she pulled out her chair.

Ben slid the paper into the pocket of his jeans, and it wasn't until he arrived home, after the session, that he finally opened it up to reread it.

Underneath his original letter, something else had been written.

A response.

Did you ever learn what happened to Gertrude and the soldier? I only ask because I've been thinking about them a lot, and I've grown curious about the actual meaning of his words.

At first, I interpreted his letter as the ultimate romantic promise—that no matter what happened to him in the war, his love for Gertrude would never fade. But what if that's not right? Since I haven't read the letter in full, I can't say for certain, but if he truly just wrote, "No matter what happens, I still feel the same," then maybe his words meant the exact opposite? Maybe he had already rejected the poor Gertrude, and no matter what physical and emotional horrors he would face, his feelings would not change. He still wouldn't love her the way she loved him. And he needed to call upon his mother as a conduit because he didn't have the courage to tell Gertrude himself.

Of course, this is just my wild conjecture (and perhaps I should be concerned that I am searching for sadness in what is most likely a beautiful expression of love?), but I would be curious to hear if you know anything else about Gertrude and her soldier.

—A

HANK

Hank didn't see the man come in, but he heard the gunshots from behind the pale green curtain while examining an elderly patient admitted to the emergency room at New York Memorial Hospital with severe chest pain.

Hank had been a doctor for more than fifteen years. He had seen the most intense expressions of anxiety in his patients while describing their symptoms or awaiting their results. But never before had he seen unmistakable fear dash so quickly across a person's face as at that very moment, on the morning of May 15, when they both heard the shots. One of the worst parts, Hank would realize later, was that neither of them experienced even a second of confusion. They had both seen enough news footage and read enough articles about this particular terror. They both knew exactly what was happening.

For a moment Hank's entire body clenched, and he didn't know if he was still breathing.

And then he thought, *A.B.C.*

An NYPD officer had visited the hospital a few months earlier and told them what to do in the event of an active shooter. *A.B.C. Avoid. Barricade. Confront.* In order of preference. Avoidance is best, barricades should be built if necessary, and confrontation, preferably by a large group, was only to be used as a last resort.

By the time the third and fourth shots were fired in rapid succession, Hank had reasoned that they sounded far enough away, near the street entrance to the ER, for him to evacuate the patients in the back rooms.

Dozens of frightened people in blue paper gowns raced toward the emergency exits, while doctors and nurses frantically pushed wheelchairs and gurneys behind them. A fifth and sixth bang reverberated through the room, and arms instinctively flew up to protect heads and faces, despite the fact that the noise was still coming from behind a set of closed double doors.

Hank was moving as quickly as he could while rolling the IV pole of a woman who didn't have time to disconnect the tubes flowing from the dangling bag of medicine into the veins in her wrist.

Seven, then eight.

He secured the woman behind the exit doors, along with a young boy dressed in all black, eyes blinking and twitching from both the current terror and the high concentration of methamphetamine in his system that had brought him here in the first place. Hank sealed them both behind the doors, then turned around and ran toward the noise.

But he had missed the worst of it, arriving only in time to witness the fallout.

The bodies on the ground, trembling and bleeding, were being lifted to the nearest beds. The people helping the victims were shouting. A security guard was collecting the attacker's weapon off the floor, where it must have fallen when the guards finally got a clean shot, killing the assailant. It was a small handgun, and Hank realized he had been expecting an assault rifle.

When he crouched down to press his hands onto the wound of a victim to stanch the blood flow, he couldn't help but steal a two-second glance at the face of the man responsible for such horror.

A face that Hank instantly recognized.

NINA

Two days had passed since Deborah Caine rushed out of her office to alert her staff to the shooting at New York Memorial Hospital.

Nina and a few reporters had spent that morning discussing the latest news out of North Korea, where all boxes were now required to be turned over to the government. Anyone who hadn't yet opened their box was no longer allowed to look inside, and every new box received by those turning twenty-two was to be handed over to officials unopened.

It was the first of such mandates to be enacted.

Back in March and April, the governments of the world had been too concerned with confirming the veracity of the strings, with keeping the global economy from spiraling, to realize that they weren't entirely powerless. They couldn't control the boxes' arrival. But perhaps they *could* control how people used them.

That spring, several nations within the European Union had quietly sent some additional troops to their most contentious borders, anticipating that frightened short-stringer migrants might seek out those countries with greater access to health care, to some final fragment of hope. The U.S. Border Patrol was said to be equally on guard. But this North Korean ruling was something *new*, beyond politics as usual. The directive was rumored to be the result of bubbling unrest and a fear among the supreme leader's circle that a few impassioned short-stringers with nothing left to lose might foment an insurrection.

"Obviously it's an extreme tactic, but maybe they're on to something," said one of the writers. "If everybody stops looking inside their boxes, then life can go back to normal."

"Except for the ones who already looked," said Nina. "It's too late for them."

"Well, I guess all we can do is hope the short-stringers *here* don't become a threat."

Nina was surprised by the ominous comment. "Why would they become a threat?"

Before the writer could answer, Deborah appeared in front of their desks, a strained look on her face. "There's a report of shots fired at New York Memorial," she said. "Multiple casualties."

Forty-eight hours later, the final number of fatalities, excluding the shooter himself, had settled at five, the victims ranging in age from twenty-three to fifty-one. Five short-stringers who may not have even known they were short-stringers, or who had come to the hospital looking for help, unaware that the very fate they were hoping to avoid was waiting for them just behind the ER doors. A fate that arrived in the form of a gun-bearing fellow short-stringer identified as Jonathan Clarke of Queens, New York.

The crime beat reporter opened the morning roundtable: "What are we thinking for the in-depth hospital piece? 'Inside the Tragedy at Memorial'?"

"Possibly. How do we feel about the word *tragedy*?"

"We've had this debate before. Didn't we decide it should be based on the number of deaths? I thought someone said that it had to be ten or more deaths to be called a 'tragedy.' This was fewer than ten."

"I think we called that home invasion two weeks ago a 'tragedy,' and only one person died."

"Yeah, we probably shouldn't have done that. Personal tragedies aren't the same as news tragedies."

"Well, this was a mass shooting, and those are always tragedies."

"Did this one definitely qualify as a *mass* shooting?"

"If we're using the criteria of at least four victims, then yes."

"Of course it's a tragedy. Shootings like this can usually be prevented. The sick bastards are almost always bragging online about their fucked-up beliefs beforehand. Something's a tragedy if we could have stopped it."

"We're getting lost in the semantics here. This isn't some neo-Nazi shooter with an online manifesto. The real story here is the strings."

"It sounded like the hospital refused to admit the shooter, even though he claimed he was about to die."

"I heard they just couldn't afford to keep giving CT scans to every short-stringer showing up looking perfectly healthy."

"I wonder if the hospital could've predicted that something bad was about to go down if they had known that the waiting room was full of people at the end of their strings."

The table was silent for a beat.

"Look, the only winners here are the gun lobbyists and the politicians in their pockets," someone said. "It's the first shooting in this country that they can easily wash their hands of: Don't blame the guns, or the laws, or the health care system. A short-stringer did it. Blame the strings."

"That's our angle," Deborah finally interjected, after quietly observing her editors argue about the nature of tragedy and the number of human lives lost to satisfy a legal definition. Deborah had once confided in Nina, after her third drink at the holiday party, that whenever the team discussed a shooting or a natural disaster, she was struck by how lightly their words were tossed about. In her three decades as a journalist, as the headlines seemed to grow ever more grim, Deborah had seen the words shed their weight a little more with each occurrence, until they barely resembled the dense nouns and heavy adjectives that once pressed upon entire rooms. But that was the only way to continue working, Nina thought, to shield your soul from breaking.

"This is the first mass shooting in the new world order," Deborah said to the table. "How does that make it different? How does that change our response to it?"

She stood to leave the room, then turned back briefly.

"And five people died," she said, sounding exhausted. "You can call it a tragedy, for fuck's sake."

At home that night, Nina stared at the open page on her laptop, the article she was supposed to be editing. But she was thinking, instead, about Jonathan Clarke.

What would happen if *Maura* went to the hospital now? The two of them often rented bikes and cycled along the river. What if Maura collided with a taxi and was rushed to the ER? Would the doctors be allowed to ask about her string?

Nina knew that her girlfriend, as a Black woman, was already at a heightened risk in a medical setting, that women's pain and Black people's pain had a long history of being misdiagnosed or ignored. And now *this*? The injustice never failed to astound her.

Of course, Maura wouldn't *have* to tell them about her string. She could lie and say she had never looked. But would they actually treat her differently, if they knew the truth?

It might not be a conscious decision, Nina realized. Surely, if a doctor had to choose between saving a patient who was eight or seventy-eight, they would save the child first, right? Maybe this was the same? Help the long-stringer first?

Nina was terrified by the thought that Maura might be abandoned as a hopeless cause simply because of her string. But the part that really created chaos in Nina's orderly brain was the question that emerged from it all: Did a patient receive less care because her string was short, or was a patient's string short *because* she received less care?

It felt like the world's most fucked-up version of the chicken-or-the-egg conundrum.

Nina closed the article and clicked on the Outlook tab, where a handful of new emails had been stacking up in her inbox. She deleted the message from Anthony Rollins's presidential campaign soliciting donations. She wasn't even sure how she had gotten on his list. A few of her colleagues had just been discussing Rollins, lamenting the fact that his slick charisma and family wealth apparently qualified him to lead the country. Nina found him too cocky, and she had seen an interview, back in February, with an old college classmate of Anthony's who claimed he had been the sexist president of a sketchy fraternity.

But, of course, that was before the strings. Nina had other things on her mind now.

She replied to a few emails from work, and then she couldn't help herself. She typed "short-stringer + hospital" into the search bar. But what was she even looking for? Some confirmation that Maura wouldn't be turned away at the door?

Most of the top results were about the recent shooting, but on the second page, Nina happened upon a new website called String Theory. It appeared to be a public message board, but the comments seemed different here. There weren't any posts about aliens or God or the NSA. The problems felt more urgent, more real.

Any other short-stringers seeing impacts on their health insurance? I had informed my insurance about my string and was just denied coverage for tests that I thought would be covered! Also heard rumors of some short-stringers' premiums increasing suddenly.

Please help my brother: He's an amazing chef, it's his DREAM to open his own restaurant in New York, and he only has 3 years left to do it. But the bank denied his loan application because of his short string! Check out our GoFundMe to help him raise the money.

I confided in a coworker about my short string, and now I just got laid off from my job as part of "long-term fiscal planning." AKA my life isn't "long-term" enough for this company to keep me employed?? If there are any lawyers reading this, do I have the grounds for a wrongful termination suit?

Nina kept scrolling down the list.

What is the government doing to help short-stringers?? It's like they did all the research, proved the strings were real, and then left us to fend for ourselves. We need legal protection!

Has anyone collected data on string length vs. demographics? Wondering if there might be higher prevalence of short strings among POC or low-income groups? This could be actual proof that generations of systemic abuse + lack of opportunities are KILLING the people in these communities!

One of the responses to the last post was currently gaining traction.

Do NOT go digging for that data. It will only get twisted around and come back to bite you. Pro-gun groups are already blaming the hospital shooting on the strings. What's next? "It's not OUR fault that you're poor and sick and jobless–it's the strings! It's out of our hands!"

Maybe Maura was right, Nina thought. Maybe it didn't matter anymore *where* the strings had come from. Even if they were sent from heaven, or beamed down from outer space, or traveled back in time from the distant future, it was *people* who decided what to do with them now.

Once the truth of the strings had been acknowledged by all but the final few holdouts, the new world came into focus: a garden in which many inhabitants had eaten the apple, while the rest remained too scared to bite.

The weight of this revelation, this once-unthinkable knowledge, continued to solidify in people's hearts and minds. It grew heavier and heavier, applying more and more pressure, until finally, inevitably, some cracked underneath it.

Homes and possessions were sold; jobs were abandoned—all in the pursuit of making the most of one's time. Some wanted to travel, to live on the beach, to spend time with their children, to paint and to sing and to write and to dance. Others dove into an abyss of anger, envy, and violence.

In Texas, a week after the incident at Memorial Hospital, another short-stringer gunman opened fire in a shopping mall.

Two back-to-back shootings perpetrated by short-stringers set off a media frenzy. SHOULD WE FEAR MORE ATTACKS BY SHORT-STRINGERS? the chyrons asked.

In London, three computer scientists nearing the end of their strings hacked into the accounts of a major bank and made away with ten million pounds, presumably in the hope of living out their final years on a secluded island without extradition.

Stories circulated on social media of couples calling off their weddings just days in advance, upon learning each other's fates, while others eloped in Las Vegas, their rushed nuptials like a raised middle finger to the boxes at their doors.

A small number of short-stringers decided to use their remaining time to take revenge on those who had wronged them. When the target of one's rage had a long string, any murderous efforts would inevitably prove futile, so other ways were found to exact pain. Ordinary folk behaved like mafiosos. Windows were smashed, homes were burned, legs were broken, money was stolen. Both embittered and emboldened by the knowledge that they wouldn't live to suffer a lengthy imprisonment, some short-stringers felt almost invincible. There was no need to fear death row if you were already sitting there.

And the risk-taking of those with the shortest strings was matched by those with the longest. Buoyed by the assurance that they would live through old age, they went skydiving and drag racing and experimented with hard drugs. They forgot that having a long string only promised them survival. It didn't preclude them from injury or illness. It didn't mean they would go unpunished. News anchors, doctors, talk show hosts, and politicians urged long-stringers to remember they were not invulnerable. You've been given the ultimate gift of a long life, they said, you don't want to spend it in a coma or in prison.

But despite the dramatic acts of those with long strings, it was still the short-stringers who caused the greatest alarm. Surely those who turned to violence accounted for only a minuscule fraction of the full population of short-stringers, but there was a sharp enough rise in criminal acts to stoke public anxiety. And, while most of the world's long-stringers could sympathize with the short-stringers' anger and grief, they couldn't help but grow fearful.

People began whispering about those with "dangerously short strings"—a particularly ill-fated community with members in every city and every country who found themselves staring into a future whose brevity ensured little to no consequences for their actions and whose rapidly approaching end served as a blunt and brutal reminder that there would be no cosmic rewards for ethical behavior, no late-in-life blessings, no tangible motive to do good.

This caricature of the extremist short-stringer with regard for neither public law nor moral order seeped into classrooms and boardrooms, into hospitals and households. And it eventually trickled into the offices of high-ranking politicians in countries across the globe.

In America, where the populace had proven time and again to be particularly susceptible to paranoia, suspicions took root deeply and quickly. It was estimated that the number of short-stringers—those whose strings ended before age fifty—hovered between five and fifteen percent of the country's total population. A small number, yes. But not small enough to be ignored.

A few short-term measures had been enacted, a bandage on a gaping wound. Several states formed dedicated hotlines, under the slogan "Don't Look Alone," encouraging residents to speak with a trained professional while opening up their boxes. Congress debated special aid to short-stringers—eviction bans? onetime payments?—but ultimately fell to gridlock, as the particulars proved unmanageable. (Just *how short* must a string be to qualify? And was there a risk in offering a financial incentive to look, pressuring those who had chosen otherwise?)

But nothing could stop the swelling rumors, fed by every act of violence, until the mayors, governors, and senators began to quietly discuss a *different* matter, distinct from earlier efforts to help. Though it wouldn't be until the events of June 10 that the president would decide the "short-stringer issue" had reached a boiling point and significant action needed to be taken.

ANTHONY

When the strings appeared in March, most Americans briefly forgot about the next year's presidential election, the campaigns for which were just getting underway. Many of the major magazines and newspapers even canceled their planned features on the candidates.

But Anthony Rollins did not forget.

A blue-blooded congressman from Virginia, with uninspiring polling figures, Anthony Rollins saw the strings as a blessing from God.

At the end of February, before the arrival of the strings and just after Anthony announced his candidacy, a former college classmate appeared on CNN to claim she had once overheard a drunken Anthony make crass, sexist comments about female partygoers at his fraternity. She also recounted that freshman girls were warned not to drink the punch at Anthony's frat house, after several incidents in which women experienced memory loss after a party, and a male student even died from alcohol poisoning.

Anthony's team quickly crafted a response noting that Anthony, as the son and grandson of several remarkable women, had always treated the opposite gender with the utmost respect. The statement confirmed that Anthony had attended various events hosted by his college fraternity, during which occasions alcohol had been consumed by all, but that he had no recollection of any particular "punch."

Before any other classmates could appear on any other national news outlets, the boxes mysteriously appeared, and any interest in Anthony's college antics dissipated overnight.

That morning, almost three months ago, Anthony and his wife, Katherine, brought their two small boxes into the living room and debated what to do. Anthony called his campaign manager, who advised him not to open his. Anthony was a public figure, after all, and if the message on the box were indeed true, then any sensitive information about Anthony's life was at risk of being stolen and leaked to the press.

Katherine called her friends from church, who also advised her not to open the box, warning that the end times were surely near.

"Do you think that's really what's happening?" Katherine asked her husband, clutching her King James Bible. "It says right here in Revelation, *Behold, the tabernacle of God is with men, and he will dwell with them, and they shall be his people, and God himself shall be with them, and be their God*. Maybe these boxes are some sort of tabernacles? God dwelling among us?"

Anthony was skeptical. "Doesn't it also talk about waves of destruction, and water turning to blood? An entirely new world emerging?"

"Well, how else can you explain it, then?"

Anthony took the Bible from his wife's hands and placed it on the table, next to their unopened boxes.

"A few days ago, our campaign was under attack," Anthony said. "Now people couldn't care less about what that woman *thinks* she remembers from college. I believe these boxes are a sign from God that He's looking out for this campaign, protecting us from harm."

Katherine wasn't fully convinced, but she took a breath and let her shoulders loosen. "I hope you're right."

Anthony smiled and kissed his wife. "Besides, even *if* the world were ending," he said, "you and I are shoo-ins to be saved."

It didn't take long for Anthony and Katherine, along with the rest of the world, to understand the truth of their strings. When they ultimately opened their boxes to reveal strings of substantial length, promising at least eighty years for them both, they knew they had been blessed with a wondrous gift, rewarded for their faith.

At church the following Sunday, they gave thanks for their good fortune and asked for guidance on the long campaign ahead. Katherine even

wore her lucky suit—a crimson skirt and matching blazer that comple-
mented the color of Anthony's favorite tie and made her look like a young
Nancy Reagan. It was the same outfit she had worn on the cold morning
in January when Anthony had been sworn into Congress, and the same
one she sultrily peeled off whenever the two of them role-played as Mr.
and Mrs. President in bed.

As the man at the pulpit assured his congregation that God would
lead them through this tumultuous time, and Katherine dutifully nodded
along, Anthony sent up a prayer of his own—that their two long strings
were just the beginning, a harbinger of even greater things to come.

Throughout March and April and May, Anthony's small campaign staff
continued to canvass and tweet and poll voters, while most of the world
was busy deciding how to react to the irrevocable changes around them.
And, despite the underwhelming turnouts, Anthony insisted on continuing his rallies and engagements. (After all, it was his *wife's* family signing
most of the checks.)

Anthony had married his college sweetheart, Katherine Hunter, on
her family's three-hundred-acre estate in Virginia nearly twenty-five
years earlier, when he was just a young prosecutor in the District Attorney's Office and she was a new board member of the Daughters of the
American Revolution, both equally hungry for something bigger.

And now they were on the cusp of it.

Anthony and Katherine didn't have any children, but ever since the
campaign's kickoff back in February, members of the Hunter family had
attended nearly all of Anthony's events. (It was especially helpful whenever Katherine could convince her camera-shy nephew, Jack Hunter, to
appear with them onstage, sporting the crisp-cut uniform of a twenty-
two-year-old army cadet and reminding voters just how strongly Anthony supported the troops.)

But even with the Hunters' help, Anthony knew his campaign was still
struggling to be heard over the commotion of the strings and the voices
of the better-known candidates, and as the spring pressed on, Anthony
waited for something, *anything*. The catalyst his campaign desperately
needed.

At the end of May, he got it.

One of the campaign volunteers, an older woman named Sharon, told her supervisor that she needed to speak with Anthony and Katherine directly.

When they gathered in an office, Sharon explained that her daughter attended college with Wes Johnson, Jr., the nineteen-year-old son of Ohio senator Wes Johnson, Sr., who happened to be the candidate currently polling just ahead of Anthony.

"Small world," said Katherine, intrigued.

"Well, my daughter is friends with Wes Junior's girlfriend, and that's how she heard Wes's father is close to the end of his string," Sharon said. "Wes is devastated. The son, not the father. Although I imagine the father must be devastated, too."

Anthony's eyes narrowed, already running through the options in his head. "Obviously that's terrible news," he said soberly.

"Tragic," said Katherine.

"But we appreciate you sharing it with us." Anthony shook Sharon's hand.

Once Sharon and her supervisor left, Katherine turned to her husband. "I don't know about you, but I think we have a duty to inform our fellow citizens that if they elect Wes Johnson as president, he may very well die in office."

"We'll have to tread carefully here," Anthony cautioned. "But once this gets out, Wes will surely have to withdraw."

Katherine wrapped her arms gleefully around her husband's waist. "You were right, honey," she said. "God's on our side."

BEN

Ben was finally able to concentrate on work again.

Perhaps his friend Damon was right, and the support group had given him the outlet he needed, a way to compartmentalize his life. On Sunday nights, Ben was a short-stringer, but from Monday to Friday, safe inside the glass walls of his office, he was still the rising architect he had always been before the boxes arrived.

On Monday morning, Ben walked past the scale model of the university science center, soon to break ground, and he sat down in his private office with all the trappings of success: the ergonomic chair, the adjustable-height desk, the view from the twenty-seventh floor. Ben had a team of eager young architects working underneath him, hoping to *become* him in five years' time. And everything he had done to get to this place—drilling the multiplication tables in the kitchen with his dad, leaving the bar before ten P.M. to finish grad school applications, even the many hours he spent alone with his childhood sketchbook—had all been worth it. If Ben had been asked in an interview where he wanted to be by age thirty, this would have been his answer.

But it was strange for this one piece of Ben's life to feel so *together*, triumphant even, while the rest of his life had crumbled. The top of his desk still felt bare, now that the framed photo of him with Claire wasn't sitting there anymore. Sometimes Ben thought he saw the phantom picture at the edge of his vision: the two of them smiling, naively, on the pier at Coney Island.

Ben leaned under his desk and pulled out a sheet of paper from the inner sleeve of his briefcase, pressing it between his thumbs. It was the letter that he and Maura had discovered at the back of the classroom the night before, with the mysterious reply from "A."

There was a part of Ben that wondered if he was being punked. Something about returning to a middle school made him particularly suspicious that the letter might just be a cruel prank by one of his fellow group members, like the time a few lacrosse players had removed all of the batteries from Ben and his teammates' calculators right before the Math League contest. But Ben wasn't that geeky boy anymore. A cursory glance around his office could remind him of that. And he simply couldn't believe any members of the support group would ever toy with him like that. Their bond was too special.

So the only explanation, Ben concluded, was that someone else inside the school had found his letter during the week and decided to write a response.

When he phrased it like that, it almost sounded normal.

Which made Ben feel better about *his* decision to write back.

Dear A,

I'm sorry to disappoint, but I know as little as you do. I'd like to think that your first reading was correct, and that nothing, not even the war, could interfere with the soldier's love for Gertrude. But after the past few months that I've endured (including a bad breakup, a long story), I'm not sure that I'm the best person to ask about love.

I'd honestly rather think about the war. Do you ever wonder what might have happened if the strings had appeared before WWII? Or any major war? If millions of people across the world—entire generations in some countries—had seen their short strings, would they have known that a war was coming? And would that have been enough to stop it?

Maybe they would have just assumed that a plague was about to break out, and the war would have happened anyway.

But it does make me wonder. Why didn't the strings come then? Why now?

Of course, having the answer to either of those wouldn't help with the
question that I most want answered.
Why me?

—B

It was surprisingly easy for Ben to share his thoughts on paper, much
easier than speaking up in front of the group. But, as he reread his letter, he realized what he had written—essentially confessing to being a
short-stringer—and wondered if he should start over, remove that final
part. The stranger on the other end certainly didn't need to know about
Ben's string. Yet there was something about the physical, intimate act of
writing a letter that made him want to be honest. If knowing about Ben's
string scared off this anonymous correspondent, so be it.

Besides, Ben needed some practice telling the truth if he was going to
tell his family that weekend.

Equally as difficult as Ben's struggle with his string was his decision to
share the news with his parents. For weeks he had kept it a secret, not
wanting to saddle them with the horrible truth that would only corrode
their golden years.

It was Lea, from support group, who convinced him otherwise.

"I know exactly what you're going through," she said. "You're worried that telling them will ruin the rest of your time together. But *not*
telling them, and living with this secret festering inside of you, combined
with the guilt of keeping something this important from your family,
that's what would ruin your time together."

"How did your parents react?" Ben asked.

Lea paused. "They cried a lot."

Ben nodded sympathetically.

"When I was a little kid," she said, "it felt like the worst thing in the
world to see my parents cry. It only happened a few times, like at a funeral or some rare national crisis, but there's something so deeply upsetting about seeing your parents sob. And apparently you never grow
out of that."

Lea pulled her sweater down over her fist and wiped the corner of her eye.

"But I still think you should tell your family," she said. "It's too big of a burden to carry alone."

I'll take your part when darkness comes, and pain is all around.

The haunting rhythm boomed throughout the station, in a voice like Ray Charles's, silencing all those who heard it, and Ben stood anxiously on the subway platform, breathing in the deep bass of the busker.

Like a bridge over troubled water, I will lay me down.

An elderly woman next to him closed her eyes and swayed.

Like a bridge over troubled water, I will lay me down.

The man's singing was eventually swallowed by the screeches of the approaching train, and the elderly woman dropped a few coins into the baseball cap resting at the singer's feet before following Ben onto the subway car and settling into an empty seat.

Ben's gaze drifted from passenger to passenger as the train sped through the tunnels, finally returning to the older woman across the way, now mumbling to herself.

Ben looked aside, not wanting to appear rude, but he could still hear her quiet, garbled utterances, which seemed to be gaining in speed and conviction. He noticed a few other passengers staring, as well.

"There's even more crazies now than before," a man next to Ben said with a sigh.

But Ben felt sorry for the woman, whose muddled conversation with herself continued on until his stop.

As he was exiting the train, he quickly glanced down at the woman's lap, where her hands had been resting behind her purse, hidden from everyone's sight.

Her fingers were shifting from one bead to the next. She was praying the rosary.

Ben's parents lived in a one-bedroom apartment in Inwood, at the northernmost tip of Manhattan, where the rent was cheaper and the pace was slower, just what they wanted in their retirement. His father had spent more than four decades teaching twelfth-grade calculus, and his mother, the same years in ninth-grade history. They liked to joke that their son became an architect as a means of satisfying them both: Buildings were physical records of a city's history—and the correct math was needed to make them stand.

As Ben sat down at the table with his parents, he realized, painfully, that the last time he had eaten dinner in this apartment was with Claire, about a month before their breakup, before the strings arrived, before everything fell apart in one catastrophic cascade. But he shoved that memory aside, focusing on the meal in front of him.

Ben's parents had both chosen not to look at their strings, and it wasn't until the lasagna had been finished and the final scoop of coffee ice cream was melting into a puddle in his bowl that Ben rallied sufficient strength to tell them about his.

He laid down his spoon and looked up, but his mother interrupted first.

"Oh, Ben, we forgot to tell you the most wonderful news!" she said. "You remember the Andersons, down the hall?"

Ben's mother grew up in a small town in the Midwest, and she refused to become the type of urbanite who didn't know her neighbors.

"The couple whose son had that rare blood disorder," she reminded Ben.

"Oh yes, of course." Ben nodded. He remembered his mother baking a crumb cake to bring to them last month. "How is he?"

"Well, that's just it. He turned twenty-two last week, and the poor boy was terrified to open his box, but he decided to do it, and . . . his string is long!" Ben's mother clasped her hands excitedly.

"That's . . . wow," Ben said, trying to mask his surprise and, truthfully, his envy.

"The doctor had told them not to give up, that the treatment might still work, and now they know it will!"

Ben's father leaned back contentedly in his chair, the wooden frame creaking under his weight. "The family's planning a big celebration this weekend and invited us to join," he said.

"It's proof," Ben's mother added. "Miracles happen."

She smiled as she stood to clear the empty plates, and Ben found himself thinking about the woman with the rosary beads. He knew that his parents believed in God, but his upbringing had never been particularly religious, no prayers were said at dinner. Any pious fervor that once existed on either side of his family had apparently dimmed with each generation. But maybe his parents had more faith than he realized.

"Do you really believe in those?" Ben asked. "Miracles?"

His mother slid the last plate into the dishwasher and straightened her back. "I do," she said. "I mean, maybe not the walking-on-water type, but . . . inexplicably wonderful things *do* happen, every day. Remember when you flipped off your bike and didn't break a bone?"

Ben smiled and nodded at his mother. But he was suddenly rethinking his decision to tell them, to crush his parents with the devastating truth that they would likely outlive their child.

It was better, Ben thought, to believe in miracles.

MAURA

For the longest time, Maura rarely thought about children. She had difficulty even imagining herself as a mother.

At age twenty-nine, she still saw herself as only slightly more mature than the teenage girl who snuck out of her parents' house to attend underground concerts and once let a friend pierce her ears. (The infection lasted for weeks.) That stubborn, irresponsible young girl couldn't possibly be a parent. She didn't want to swap her late nights lingering at the bar for early mornings breastfeeding. She certainly didn't want to deal with nine months of pregnancy and god knows how many hours of brutal labor, nor had she ever wished that upon any of her girlfriends over the years. She wanted the freedom to stay home all day in her sweatpants and do nothing at all, or to quit her job and travel the world, to someday own a second apartment in London or Madrid.

What's more, the rare pangs of anything even resembling maternal desire occurred so infrequently—only when she saw a particularly adorable infant or learned of a friend's new pregnancy—that Maura could easily dismiss them as a minor biological nuisance. If she *truly* wanted kids, she would have known by now. She was almost thirty, after all.

When Maura first met Nina, she worried that her non-maternal instincts might cause a rift in their relationship, but Nina, focused solely on becoming editor-in-chief, fortunately felt the same. She hadn't grown up playing house like her sister, and she rarely dreamt of her future family, especially after she realized that the domestic bliss she saw on television—the sitcom husband and wife—didn't reflect her own desires. All she really wanted was a partner in life, Nina said, someone to share in the journey. And Maura was satisfied, their futures aligned.

Until she opened her box.

The pangs became more frequent, more intense. Maura would have assumed that a woman's yearning for a child was purely emotional, but for her it became somehow physical, a palpable sensation inside her body.

When she thought about having a child, she could feel her stomach tightening, scrunching up around a hollowness. Her hands and arms felt a subtle tingling, a restlessness stretching down into her fingers, wanting to touch something that wasn't there and hold something that didn't exist.

On her way home one evening that spring, Maura turned a corner just as a young mother was exiting a brownstone with her son. The little boy, maybe four or five years old, wearing an impossibly small blue backpack on his shoulders, quickly grabbed hold of his mother's hand as he bounced down the steps and onto the sidewalk, just ahead of Maura.

He tilted his head up toward his mother. "That was a fun playdate, right?"

His mother agreed.

The boy paused for a moment, before venturing to ask, "Do you think maybe we could have him over to our house sometime?"

Perhaps it was the surprisingly high pitch of the little boy's voice, or the way he sounded so shy and unsure, like he didn't know if everyone else had enjoyed themselves as much as he had, or if his mother would ever allow him to have another playdate again. Maura didn't know what it was. But her feet suddenly stopped moving, and she felt herself starting to cry, right there in the middle of the sidewalk.

The little boy and his mother didn't notice and kept on walking, while Maura just stood there crying, for no apparent reason other than the innocence of what she had witnessed.

Later that night, while Maura tried to sleep, the pangs were so strong that she turned on her side and nearly tapped Nina's shoulder to ask if she might change her mind about having kids. With two moms, of two different skin tones, the decision would surely be layered: Would they adopt or use a donor? Would they choose the sex? Choose the race?

But all of those looming questions suddenly felt so small when compared to Maura's string, to the realization that struck her with a nauseating blow.

Her child would be seven or eight years old, and Maura would already be gone.

She spent a sleepless night wondering *why* she might want this now. Was it a selfless act, so as not to abandon Nina, leaving her all alone? Did she hope that Nina would remember her whenever she looked at their child? Was it vanity? A legacy? Some piece of herself to live on? Had she fallen victim to the sexist myth that she was *supposed* to want a baby? Or are we simply doomed to want whatever we can't have?

The mere presence of all these questions, swimming around in her head, ultimately proved to be the answer. Maura knew that she couldn't bring a child into this world, under *these* conditions, without feeling certain. And she wasn't certain.

But she also knew that the pangs would never fully disappear, and when she stared at the slope of Nina's back, rising and sinking as she slept, Maura wondered if it was dishonest to hide these thoughts from Nina, whom she swore to share everything with.

But Maura simply couldn't tell her about the pangs or the boy with the impossibly small backpack.

Try as she would, Nina could never understand.

The next morning, Maura's emotional somersaults and lack of sleep conspired to form a hellish hangover. Nina was already brushing her teeth when Maura rolled over in bed and squinted against the bright bathroom light.

"Are you okay?" Nina asked.

"I'm just not feeling great this morning," Maura said.

"Do you need me to get you something? Should I call the doctor?"

"No, no, I'm fine," Maura assured her. Ever since they had learned about Maura's short string, any semblance of illness, however minor, could send Nina into a tizzy.

"Are you sure?" Nina asked, her brow furrowed in concern.

"Yeah. I'll just take a sick day and sleep it off," Maura said. She glanced around for her phone but couldn't find it, then eyed Nina's laptop at the foot of the bed. "Can I use your computer to email work?" she asked.

"Of course," Nina said, turning back around to rinse in the sink.

Maura pulled the laptop across the duvet and propped herself up on the pillows. After sending a message to her boss, she opened Facebook for a mindless perusal. But she was quickly bombarded with a strange series of ads that she had never seen before.

A travel agency was hawking its "Short-Stringer Bucket List Trips," whisking you around the world in just a few months, while a pair of sleazy-looking lawyers touted their short-stringer discounts on civil suits. "Were You Wronged in the Past? Make It Right, While You Still Can!"

Why was Nina receiving these dubious ads clearly targeting short-stringers? Had she actually been searching for some cliché short-stringer vacations? For a lawyer?

Normally, Maura tried to espouse a laissez-faire attitude when it came to her partners' online activities. She didn't mind if they watched porn when she was away, or occasionally emailed their exes, as long as they were honest when asked. But there was something off about these ads.

Nina was dressing by the closet now, and Maura's cursor hovered over the "History" tab on her computer. She was hesitant, acutely aware of the intrusion, but too curious not to click. Like opening her box, all over again.

Nina's most recent links covered a common array of news sites, but farther down the list, the content changed. There were dozens of Reddit pages, with varying degrees of apparent outlandishness, plus a number of visits to a site called String Theory, which appeared to be some sort of forum for disgruntled short-stringers. None of it looked like your typical day of browsing, especially for Nina.

When she finished getting ready, Nina came back over to the bed. "Are you sure you're okay? I'm happy to stay home with you."

"What's String Theory?" Maura asked her.

"You mean, like, in physics?"

"I mean this website," Maura said, turning the computer around so Nina could see the screen. "And all the other pages you've been visiting."

"It's nothing." Nina shrugged.

"It doesn't look like nothing."

"I know it looks weird," Nina said, her face starting to flush. "But I was just doing some Googling, and I guess it got a little out of hand."

Perhaps hoping to avoid interrogation, Nina turned her back toward Maura and started to pack up her purse, double-checking that she had all her usual items: a few spare pens, tissues, a notebook.

Maura stood up and faced her girlfriend. "There are *hours'* worth of searches on there, Nina. Like you fell completely down the fucking rabbit hole."

Nina looked up from her purse, brushing her hair away from her face with an irritated swipe. "I think you're overreacting," she said.

"You know, for someone with a really long string," said Maura, "you're awfully interested in the plight of the short-stringer."

Nina was startled. "What's *that* supposed to mean?"

"Nothing," Maura said, suddenly mindful that she was sidling toward a dangerous edge. "I guess I'm just surprised you never mentioned this . . . obsession."

"It's not an *obsession*," Nina insisted. "I was just . . . I don't know . . . looking for answers."

"And did you find any?"

Nina rolled her eyes in response.

"I didn't think so," Maura said harshly, turning away from Nina and walking down the hallway.

"Where are you going?" Nina yelled after her.

When Maura didn't respond, Nina ran down the hall and reached for Maura's arm, spinning her around and trapping them both in the narrow space between the walls.

"Why are you so pissed off about this?" Nina asked.

Maura stared into Nina's panicked gaze. She knew that she was hurting Nina, and she didn't want to. But she was exhausted and fractious and still thinking about last night. While Maura was facing one of the greatest challenges of her life, Nina was off with her nose in some tinfoil-hat conspiracies.

"I just don't understand why you're so fixated on these strings, when *you're* not the one whose life's been completely fucked!" Maura shouted.

Nina's breath stuttered, and the flush of her earlier embarrassment drained in an instant. Her hand dropped limply from Maura's arm.

"I may not have a short string," she said quietly, "but you and I *share* our lives now, so whatever you're going through affects me, too."

"I can't believe you're making this about you," Maura said bitterly.

"I'm not trying to!" Nina's hands flew up in frustration. She was fighting hard not to get angry. Maura felt like she could practically see Nina's mind searching for a way to defuse the situation, before it was too late.

"Look, I know that I can get a little compulsive sometimes, and yes, it's killing me not to know the truth about these strings," Nina said. "And maybe that's how this whole thing started, but I swear it's only because I was thinking about *you* and your safety. I was worrying about you. I'm *always* worrying about you."

"Well, it doesn't really matter what you find on these websites, because it won't change anything," Maura said firmly. "What's going to happen is . . . still going to happen. You're only wasting your time."

Maura watched as Nina struggled against her tears.

"And I don't need you worrying about me all the time." Maura sighed, finally ready to relent. "It'll only drive us *both* nuts. What I need is for you to keep your shit together. For me. Do you think you can do that?"

Nina nodded.

"Good," Maura said. "Because there's only enough room in this apartment for *one* of us to go crazy and, given the circumstances, I'm hoping *I* can reserve that right."

Dear B,

I wish I had an answer for you. A coworker of mine (full disclosure: a long-stringer) spent our entire lunch hour trying to convince the table that the strings are actually a gift to humanity. He said that we've always been inundated with songs and poems and needlepoint pillows urging us to remember that life is short, and we should live each day as if it were our last, and yet nobody ever did that.

So maybe he's right, and the strings really do offer a chance to live with fewer regrets, because we know exactly how much time we have to do it. But isn't that still too much to ask of people? I can hardly count the number of lives I've led in my mind—equestrian, novelist, actress, world traveler—yet I know I'm rather incapable of pursuing most of them.

I suppose I should tell you now that I haven't opened my box, and I don't plan to.

Since the strings arrived, so many of our conversations are about such big, heavy ideas, literally life and death. And I miss talking about the little things, especially in a city filled with so many wonderful little things.

Last night, for instance, I was waiting for a cab outside my apartment, and across the street, I saw an old man leaning out of his window, waving goodbye to an elderly woman on the sidewalk below, as she was exiting the building. He kept waving to her as she walked away, and she kept turning around and waving back. On and on, they both continued waving like children, until the woman was nearly at the end of the block.

And even when the woman stopped turning back and continued forward, the man still kept his head out the window, watching the corner where she disappeared.

Gertrude and her soldier, perhaps. Reunited and happily retired in Manhattan.

—A

Dear A,

Here's a little thing: About a year ago, I was walking home around midnight, when an old song started playing out of nowhere. "Que Será, Será." The original Doris Day version. My grandma used to hum it sometimes. The song got louder and louder, until I turned around to see a bicyclist riding down the middle of the empty street, wearing this outrageous purple jacket, with a stereo strapped to the back of his bike. And he just pedaled slowly past me, playing his music, as if he were any other cyclist.

I had forgotten about him until, just a few months ago, I heard the same music on the street, again in the middle of the night. "Que será, será. Whatever will be, will be . . ." And there he was again: the same man, the same song, even the same jacket.

Some might think New York is a greedy, selfish, aggressive place, and they're not entirely wrong, but it's also a place filled with generous people who share their spirit with the world. Maybe this man is on some sort of rotation, spending the quiet hours of every evening bringing music to a different corner of the city. And every few months, he ends up in mine.

It's possible that he's changed his choice of song since then, after the strings arrived, and the future now is ours to see, at least partially. But I like to think that he still does it. That maybe he believes in music, in its power to uplift and unite. Maybe he knows that we've always needed that—and we need it now more than ever.

—B

JACK

Jack's mother loved music. It was one of the few things he remembered about her, the fact that she would whistle to herself in the kitchen and sing to him at night, both of them equally mesmerized by the sound of her soft, soothing voice.

After she left, Jack's father said that he was too old for lullabies and refused to indulge his requests. His aunt Katherine at least attempted to sing to him, on the evenings she put him to sleep, but she only knew the same half dozen hymns from church, and eventually Jack stopped asking.

But it was still those memories of his aunt, perched politely on the side of his bed and crooning, shrilly, about God's love and Jesus's sacrifice, that made Jack feel like he *had* to say yes, when she asked him to attend the rallies.

"Uncle Anthony and I would *so* appreciate if you could join us onstage," she had said. "You'll look so handsome up there in your cadet's uniform."

And Jack had agreed, despite the knot in his stomach. In the Hunter family, "Yes" was the only acceptable answer.

Several cousins or in-laws usually joined him onstage, but Jack was the sole member of the Hunter clan who seemed embarrassed to be up there, squirming in his combat boots. He typically tried to position himself directly behind his aunt or uncle, blocked from the prying lenses of the cameras, wishing himself as invisible as possible.

Unlike the rest of his family, Jack had no interest in sweating under the beams of the national spotlight. He was simply trying to survive his final year at the military academy without drawing any *more* attention to himself. And Anthony Rollins wasn't helping.

Jack's roommate Javier was the only person he could confide in.

"I just don't know how to get out of it," Jack complained, as the two of them entered the gym to practice the obstacle course.

"Why can't you tell them you're uncomfortable?" Javier asked, pulling the pair of dangling ropes toward them. "Can't you say you have stage fright or something?"

Both boys hoisted their bodies up on the ropes and began to climb.

"Fear is no excuse with them." Jack panted as the prickly fibers of the rope dug into his palms.

"But they are your *family,*" Javier said.

Jack sighed, looking up at the soles of Javier's sneakers inching along the rope above him, already two feet higher than Jack. "Yeah, that's how I *know* they won't understand."

Javier pulled himself off of the rope, onto the wooden platform above, and nodded at Jack, just as two members of the rugby team entered the gym below.

"Hey, Hunter! Don't look down!" one of the boys jeered.

"Yeah, it's too bad your uncle isn't president yet," said the other. "Maybe he could've gotten you out of the ropes course."

Jack's anger flared, his fists tightening around the rope, but Javier shot him a discouraging look from the landing above: *It's not worth it.*

It wasn't the first time that Jack's family had caused him trouble, and it sure wouldn't be the last. The Hunter reputation was well known both on and off campus. They had the rare distinction of claiming an actual Revolutionary War soldier as an ancestor—the original Captain Hunter— and every generation since the 1770s had sent at least one family member into the military. Only a shattered kneecap during a high school soccer game had kept Jack's father from enlisting, too.

Indeed, the only blemish in the Hunter family history was Jack's own mother, who left when he was young. From the scraps of information gleaned from his family—and his own scattered memories—Jack had reasoned that his mother was always too independent, too free-spirited, for the Hunters. She may have loved Jack's father once, perhaps even softened his edge, but *his* wasn't the life she wanted. An accidental pregnancy and a hasty marriage had simply forced her into it. When she finally told him she was leaving, Jack's father refused to give up his heir, and her lawyer was no match for the Hunters' longtime attorney. Jack's dad was granted full custody, Jack's mother was granted her freedom. The last Jack heard, she was somewhere in Spain, living with a fellow expat, trying to make it as a musician. And Jack's father made it clear that his son's enrollment at the academy was never even a question.

The Hunters had always been respected within Virginia society and military circles—those who didn't enlist in the army became state senators and board chairs—but Anthony and Katherine's foray into national politics had raised the family's profile to unforeseen heights. And though Anthony had surprised everyone by declaring his presidential candidacy before acquiring much name recognition outside his home state, the Hunters collectively vowed to help get him elected.

"I know I promised Aunt Katherine that I would go, but is it really necessary for me to be at *all* these rallies?" Jack asked his father on the phone that night. "I'm worried I'll fall behind on studying," he explained, "and I swore I would get to the gym more this semester, and—"

"This is your family, Jack. And families support each other," his father said. "*Especially* ones like ours."

Jack loved his aunt Katherine, he wanted to support her, but he never understood what she saw in Anthony, other than breeding and a strong jawline. It was Anthony who had inadvertently revealed to him that his conception was unintentional, when a young Jack had listened, from the top of the stairs, as his aunt and uncle conferred with his father, soon after his mother left. It was one of Jack's only childhood memories that remained sharp to this day, hardening over time the more he returned to it.

"Let's just keep this within the family for now, as quiet as possible," Jack's dad had insisted, unaware of his eavesdropping son. "I don't want people talking."

"Honestly, you're better off without her," said Katherine. "She was never quite . . . *aligned* with the rest of the family. And at least you have sweet little Jack."

"Just make sure he's not *too* sweet." Anthony laughed, and Katherine scolded her husband with a click of her tongue.

"You're right, I'm sure Jack will be fine," he added. "And who would've thought that getting knocked up was the only good thing that woman would ever do? We were so worried about the liability, but . . . now you've got your legacy."

Jack was too little to comprehend in the moment, but he later asked his cousin to explain what Anthony had meant. In the coming years, whenever Jack felt like a stranger in his own family, he could trace that sensation right back to the stairs, when Anthony had casually mocked him, framed his very existence as an accident.

Jack had hated his uncle ever since.

And, truthfully, a part of Jack was always envious that Anthony had earned the acceptance—indeed, the approval—of the notoriously critical Hunter brood without even considering service in the army, while Jack was grinding his way through a military school he never wanted to attend.

As his uncle gained political prominence, Jack found him increasingly abrasive and insincere, his ego growing at an unconstrained clip. Every time he came calling for a campaign favor—or, more likely, asked Katherine to call on his behalf—Jack thought about his comments, his laughter, that night downstairs with Jack's dad.

By the springtime, Jack clung to two slivers of hope: his imminent graduation from the academy, and the recent arrival of the strings.

Though the timing of their appearance may have diverted attention from Anthony's slew of bad press, Jack felt convinced that the strings would ultimately spell the end of his uncle's campaign—and the end of Jack's own proximity to the limelight. Something so cataclysmic, so frightfully unknown, would inevitably require a familiar face in the White House, a tried-and-true candidate whom everybody recognized, with the training to handle this unusual moment and calm the nation's nerves. Surely this would call for a seasoned secretary of state, perhaps a former vice president, someone with decades of experience weathering such times of perilous change as the world faced now.

Anthony Rollins was a congressional novice, riding on the coattails of the Hunter family. He had never gone to war; he had never led through crises. He couldn't possibly win now.

And Jack was relieved.

JAVIER

Jack Hunter and Javier García had been roommates since their first year at the academy, perfectly paired, as both were more introverted than their fellow cadets—not to mention a few inches shorter and more than a few pounds lighter.

At first Javier had depended on Jack for guidance. Javier was the first in his family to even attend college, whereas military medals hung like ornaments from every branch of Jack's family tree. Jack's second cousin had recently graduated from the academy herself, and Jack knew the history and traditions, the ins and outs of campus, the way only a legacy could.

It wasn't until their third or fourth week that Javier started to see the *real* Jack, to realize that all those decorations in fact weighed heavily on the branches, nearly causing them to splinter.

When a handful of new cadets announced their plans to get "Death Before Dishonor" tattooed on their forearms, Jack thought they were nuts.

"Not a fan of tattoos?" Javier had asked him.

"Not a fan of the sentiment," Jack answered.

In daily training, it was painfully clear that Jack wasn't as fast, as strong, or as innately disciplined as most of the other cadets, and many of them were all too eager to prove themselves superior to a member of the eminent Hunter tribe.

One night, early in the fall, one of the brawnier guys recognized Jack's last name from a school plaque honoring his great-grandfather and challenged him to a fistfight.

"Come on, Hunter!" he taunted. "You don't want your great-grandaddy looking down on you and thinking you're a pussy!"

The brawl lasted all of two minutes, with Jack crumpling after three hard punches, but the smirks and the snickers were even worse than the blows.

Afterward, Javier walked a deflated Jack back to their dorm, then snuck into the kitchen to find an ice pack for his roommate's swollen nose.

"Thank you, Javi," Jack moaned, cramming the cold bag against his rapidly bruising face.

"It's nothing." Javier shrugged.

"I don't just mean the ice," said Jack. "I mean all of it. Treating me the same as any other guy."

"You mean because I *didn't* challenge you to some public pissing contest?"

"Because you don't treat me any differently than the other guys on campus, and you never probe about my family," Jack said. "Which is new to me. And it's nice."

"Well, I'm sorry to dent your ego, man, but you *are* just any other guy," Javi said. "Sure, you've got an extra-helpful sense of how things work around here, but I didn't grow up in this world. Your name means nothing to me." He smiled kindly.

And he meant it. Javier didn't understand why he should place Jack on a pedestal built from the accomplishments of his forebears. But he wasn't oblivious to Jack's unique position, either. Javi had pieced together enough of the family history based on a handful of reluctant snippets from Jack and the gossip from fellow cadets: the *nine* generations of Hunters who had fought for their homeland since its founding, all the honors they had received and donations they had given, year after year after year.

And Javi understood the burden facing his roommate—the added scrutiny, the demand for success—having known his own particular strain of that pressure. Only ten percent of the cadets on campus were Latino. They couldn't afford to be seen as failures.

"*Why* are people so concerned with your roommate?" Javi's father asked on the phone.

"Well, his family is pretty well known in certain circles," Javi tried to explain. "I guess they see themselves like the Kennedys."

"And now *my* son is in the same school as theirs," his father said. Javi could hear the awe in his voice.

Javier's parents were incredibly proud of all that their son had achieved, of the man he was fast becoming, and though applying to the academy had been Javi's decision, it was certainly influenced by eighteen years of listening to his parents expound the virtues of American freedom while sorting food donations at church. They worked long days and weekends at his father's store, saving up so their child could enjoy the education neither of them had received. But they always carved out time for Mass on Sundays and volunteered at the soup kitchen whenever they could, modeling a life of service and diligence and family, a life that only seemed possible in a place like America, where, despite its flaws, a boy like Javier was free to learn, to play, to rise, to *choose*.

Javi wanted to choose a path that his parents would admire, something to honor the lessons they had taught him and the way they had lived their lives.

When Javi told them about his acceptance—and the fully funded scholarship—they celebrated with their first family vacation in years.

So Jack and Javi endured four of the toughest years of their lives, but they survived together, and by May they were just weeks away from officially becoming the newest members of the U.S. Army, marking the end of a very strange semester. Jack's uncle had announced his campaign back in February, to both Jack's and Javi's displeasure. (Javier had met him only once, at a Hunter family dinner, but could instantly sense that Anthony was a glutton for power.) And then, in March, two small brown boxes had arrived outside Jack and Javier's dorm room.

Neither cadet had dared to open the lids after reading the inscription on the box and assuming it was some sort of test from the academy, to see if temptation and curiosity would get the better of them in the final months before graduation. But even after they had learned that it wasn't a test, that the entire world had in fact received the same chests, the boys still chose not to look. Theirs was a dangerous profession, and the risk ahead was much easier to accept when that was all it was: a risk, not a guarantee.

And in the blissful days of May, the last before graduation, while they tossed Frisbees on the lawn and toasted the end of final exams, neither Jack nor Javier had any idea that the events of June would change everything.

HANK

The rest of May had blurred past for Hank, and his final day at the hospital, a day that he had once thought he wouldn't see until his hair had turned silver and his fingers were too arthritic to suture a wound, had actually arrived. Anika, one of his fellow doctors, invited him to lunch to mark the occasion.

"It's not really something to celebrate," said Hank, as the pair sat down in the cafeteria.

"Well, we're not celebrating you *leaving*. We're celebrating all of your accomplishments from your time here." Anika smiled and raised her coffee cup.

Hank was glad that he and Anika could part as friends. Given their history, it wouldn't have been odd for them to strictly avoid each other. But now that he was leaving the hospital, Hank wondered if he would ever see her again, Dr. Anika Singh, the most gifted surgeon he had ever known and the second great love of his life (after Lucy, his girlfriend during three years of medical school, who accepted a residency in San Diego when Hank moved to New York). In Hank's mind, he and Anika were the perfect match. They understood the demands of each other's livelihoods, they were equally driven, and they pushed each other to become better doctors. Perhaps Hank had pushed a little too hard, since Anika ultimately felt that she couldn't commit to him the way she was committed to her craft.

At least her decision seemed to be working out for her. Anika was on track to become chief of surgery someday. Plus, she hadn't given up on Hank *completely*.

At least once a month since their breakup two years prior, either Hank or Anika took advantage of their continued friendship when they were in need of a particular release. It was just so easy between them. All the embarrassment and modesty and awkwardness had long since disappeared, and neither was offended if the other received an urgent call from the hospital in flagrante.

But, sitting at the table with Anika now, Hank couldn't even think about those evening liaisons without remembering the night in April. The night Anika had learned the truth.

The sex had been especially good that night, the kind of desperate, greedy intensity that you only really tap into when the stakes feel heightened, when the world outside is going to shit. And that spring, the world sure went to shit.

When the boxes first arrived, Hank hadn't opened his right away.

He was wary of the inscription and wanted to wait until there was more information. But once the strings were officially confirmed, Hank still couldn't decide what to do. A part of him saw the boxes like a routine medical test: If something's happening to your body, then you should want to know the truth. Even if you can't alter the final result, there might be *something* you can do to improve your life. But the other part of him, the part that dealt with the anger and grief of patients and families on a daily basis, wondered if perhaps it was better to postpone any pain as long as possible.

In the end, though, the scientist within Hank won out. He simply couldn't run away from the knowledge on offer.

So he opened his box and measured his string with the at-home calculator and learned that he was fully, irrevocably fucked. He had already entered his final window, the thin span of time in which his life would end.

He should have just kept the damn box closed.

Hank briefly contemplated quitting his job to spend his final months traveling, but he was lucky enough to have already seen a great deal of the world, spending two summers abroad in Europe and the year before med school backpacking through Asia. And besides, his job was all he had. The sterile white walls of the hospital were the boundaries of his life, his coworkers his only friends. But Hank had never really minded the fact that he spent most of his hours in the ER. He liked his job. He liked the adrenaline and the challenge and the fact that he was saving lives, something many people aspire to, but few actually *do*.

He knew that he was sometimes selfish, perhaps deriving a little too much pleasure from the gratitude of patients he helped, but he reasoned that if heaven or its equivalent did exist, he had probably earned a spot up there. And it couldn't hurt to keep saving lives in the meantime.

Hank hadn't really dated in the two years since Anika, his father had already passed away, and he didn't want to send his seventy-six-year-old mother into shock, so he decided not to tell anyone about his string. He didn't want to burden someone else with the news, and he didn't want pity or charity. He only wanted to stay strong, and he wouldn't be able to do that if everybody started treating him like a victim.

Hank had seen enough tragedy and lost enough patients—enough short-stringers, before they were *called* short-stringers—that he didn't bother asking, *Why me?* Hank was no different from the patients who had been wheeled into his ER every day for the past two decades. Why *them*, before? And why *him*, now? These were pointless questions that only fueled the hurt.

About a week after he opened his box, Hank was changing in the hospital locker room at the end of an all-day shift, about to head home for three days off, his first real break in months, when he suddenly realized that he didn't want to go home. A full seventy-two hours without any patients, any work, any distractions, sounded like a nightmare. He couldn't spend that much time alone with his thoughts.

Hank felt his whole body clench with dread, thinking of the anxious days awaiting him. He slammed his locker shut and smacked it harshly with his hand.

"That bad of a day, huh?"

Hank turned to see Anika, still in her scrubs, staring at him with concern. And something inside him caved.

"Do you want to get a drink?" he asked.

One drink turned into more drinks and, soon enough, Anika was back at Hank's apartment, and the two of them enjoyed their particularly good sex, and for the briefest of moments Hank actually forgot about the box in his kitchen with the short string inside.

After they were finished, Anika left Hank relaxing sleepily against the pillows and slipped into one of his T-shirts from the dresser beside the bed, maneuvering around his apartment as if it were her own.

"I'm going to get a glass of water," she said, and Hank didn't think to stop her.

But when she walked down the hall to the kitchen, she saw it.

Sitting on the table, exposed.

Hank's box, the lid open. And the string, just beside it.

Throughout March, Anika had remained a vocal denier. Despite all the anecdotal evidence, Anika was a woman of science, and without any *scientific* explanation for the strings' predictive powers, she couldn't accept them. She had managed to hold out until the Department of Health outlined the results of its study, and then she finally broke down and looked at her string, which ended somewhere in her late eighties. As good as she could have hoped for.

But when Anika saw Hank's string out on the table, she froze. Why was it sitting there? Had he been measuring it just that morning?

She knew, of course, that she should turn around, forget the glass of water, return to bed. But she couldn't. Only three, maybe four steps lay between Anika and the string.

She and Hank had never actually talked about their *own* boxes before, their conversations filled instead with patients and procedures, both more comfortable discussing others than examining themselves. But Hank had left his string out in the open, she reasoned. Practically inviting her to look. Besides, Anika and Hank had spent nearly three years together, sharing every secret with each other, and they were *still* close now, albeit with a different arrangement. There were times when Anika even wondered if she had made a mistake ending their relationship.

All of her muddled feelings toward Hank seemed to collude with her terrible nosiness in that singular moment, when she decided to take those final four steps. And when she did, her hands flew up to her face, her nimble surgeon's fingers silencing her gasp.

Anika had only recently measured her own string, so she quickly recognized that Hank's was about half the length of hers. Which meant that he would die in his early forties.

And he was *already* in his early forties.

In her shock, Anika realized why Hank must have invited her that night, and why the sex felt more intensified than ever, fraught with something bigger than just their two selves. Hank knew that the end was coming—and coming quite soon.

When Anika walked back into the bedroom, Hank was sitting upright, and in the dim light he could just barely make out the strange expression on her face. She sat next to him on the bed and rested her warm hands on his forearm.

"I am so sorry, Hank."

"For what?" he asked.

"You don't have to be stoic anymore. It's *me*."

Hank shifted uncomfortably against the pillows. "Seriously, Anika, what are you talking about?"

"I know I shouldn't have looked, but . . . I did," Anika whispered. "And I don't know what to say, except that . . . I'm sorry. And I'm here for you, whatever you need."

It took Hank a second to piece it together, to connect her sudden sympathy with the string he had so carelessly left on the table. She had *looked*, and now she was sorry, staring at him with unmistakable pity.

"Shit!" Hank jerked his arm away from her touch. "Why the hell did you look?"

Anika stared back at him helplessly. "It was just *there*, when I went into the kitchen. It's not like I went searching for it!"

"Well, I didn't exactly plan on bringing you back here!" he yelled. "You could have just walked away! You didn't have to look. Does my privacy mean nothing to you?"

Hank could feel his heartbeat gaining speed, the blood throbbing in his veins. His body was kicking into fight-or-flight, a familiar feeling for an ER veteran. But he couldn't run away from this; Anika already knew.

"This was a mistake," Hank said angrily. "Tonight was a huge mistake."

Anika's face puckered in a remorseful wince, her eyes starting to well with tears. "Maybe I shouldn't have said anything, but I *know* you, Hank. I know that you would choose to go through this alone, thinking that you're sparing everyone else," she said. "So I wanted you to know that you *aren't* alone. Not if you don't want to be."

Hank could still feel the stress hormones coursing through his body, readying him for battle. He could still feel the anger inside him. But hearing Anika's words and watching her cower shamefully at the edge of the mattress, Hank's own T-shirt draped loosely across her trembling frame, Hank realized that he wasn't really angry at her.

He was angry at his string.

A part of Hank still loved Anika. There was even a time, a few years back, when he thought he would marry her one day, accepting her flaws for better or worse. Tonight, when she looked at his string instead of just turning around, was certainly worse. But she didn't leave, after looking. She came back to bed. She told him that he wasn't alone.

Hank didn't want to fight. He didn't want to make enemies of the people he loved, not when he had such little time left with them. He let out a long, tired sigh, then reached out his hand and placed it on hers.

And Anika looked up at him gratefully, biting her lower lip to stop it from shaking. "I know I shouldn't have looked, Hank. But were you *really* not going to tell me?"

"I wasn't going to tell anyone."

Anika's eyes were red and anguished. "But it must be horrible to do this by yourself."

"Not as horrible as that look you're giving me right now," Hank said.

"Maybe it's not true!" Anika tried to sound hopeful. "I know *I've* told patients they only had a few months left, and then watched them live years longer."

"You know this is different," he said.

Anika sighed deeply. "Well, I promise I won't tell anyone, if that's really what you want."

Hank still believed in keeping his secret, though he knew that his resignation from the hospital had already incited some rumors. (He insisted that he simply needed a break, that the deluge of short-stringers looking for answers had quickly worn him down.) But speaking with Anika, saying the words aloud, he actually felt a small sense of relief that *one* person knew about his string. It was grueling to conceal it from everyone, to keep worrying that something he might say or do would reveal the truth inadvertently. Now, at least, he could loosen his guard around Anika. He didn't have to pretend that all was perfectly fine.

"You know, I've been so focused on not letting anyone at the hospital find out, and not telling my family," Hank said. "And in the meantime, I haven't really cried or screamed or done whatever else you're supposed to do."

"Why not?"

Hank knew why he hadn't cried at his father's funeral, when he'd tried to stay strong for his mother, and why he hadn't cried as Anika broke up with him, when he'd wanted to save face before the woman he admired. But this time, he didn't know what was holding him back.

Anika picked up one of the pillows and offered it to Hank.

"Do you want me to punch it or something?" he asked.

"You can do whatever you want with it," she said. "You wouldn't know it when I'm in the OR, but I've always been a fan of a good pillow cry myself."

Hank reluctantly took the pillow from Anika and stared at it silently.

"Do you want me to leave you alone?" she asked.

Hank looked up at her through blurry eyes. The black hair falling across her shoulder, even darker against the white of his shirt. The wet remnants of mascara smudged beneath her brown eyes. The sharp, pointed chin that she would rest atop her hands whenever she was working through a problem.

Suddenly Hank crammed the pillow against his face and began screaming violently into the soft fabric. Anika watched the veins in his forehead bursting underneath his skin, like they were howling as loudly as he was.

When he had fully exhausted himself, Hank dropped the pillow into his lap. "Do you think you could stay?" he asked.

Anika wrapped her arms around his broad shoulders, and Hank

finally allowed himself to be carried away by the waves of deep, full sobs that would appear, overwhelming him, squeezing all the air out of him, and then disappear, leaving him calm and quiet, a moment to recapture his breath, before the next wave inevitably swept him back beneath its undertow.

And through it all, Anika never let go, until Hank, at last, pulled away.

When Hank ran into her at the hospital the following week, Anika asked how he was doing.

"Well, I usually tell my patients in this position to try some sort of therapy or support group," he said, "so I'm thinking I should put my money where my mouth is."

Anika gave him the address of the Connelly Academy, a school near her apartment where several groups were being held, and Hank showed up that Sunday, a half hour late after a busy shift in the ER.

He peered through the door to Room 201, where those nearing the very end of their strings had gathered. Everyone was crying, rubbing each other's backs, passing around a box of tissues. It looked depressing as hell. Hank wanted this group to make him feel better, not sadder than before.

He was about to leave when he heard faint laughter coming from three doors down, in Room 204, home to the short-stringers who still had more time left, who still measured the remainder of their strings in years instead of months. And Hank decided to check it out. Nobody needed to know that he didn't actually belong there.

MAURA

"Tonight, I want to talk about secrets," Sean said, opening the evening's discussion.

"Oh good, we haven't had a theme in a while," Maura whispered to Ben.

"And it sounds like a juicy one," he added.

Ben and Maura's proximity on their first night had led to a regular habit of sitting together. Maura appreciated Ben's receptiveness to her sideline commentary, and Ben seemed grateful that Maura never took the sessions too seriously. Each of her lighthearted remarks poked a hole in the shell of doom and gloom that might otherwise have proven suffocating.

"I'm sure many of us spend a lot of emotional energy keeping things bottled up," said Sean. "But when you're already dealing with something so . . . significant, like your string, maybe it would help to lighten the rest of your load. If you're comfortable, of course."

"This ain't fucking confession," Carl grunted.

Maura's thoughts briefly turned to her fight with Nina, the online obsession she'd been harboring for weeks. But hadn't Maura been hiding something, too? She never did tell Nina about the pangs in the night, the little boy with the backpack and his mom.

"Well, *I* have something I'd like to get off my chest," said Terrell.

Clearly pleased, Sean motioned for him to continue.

"It's the whole Ted affair," said Terrell.

"Who's Ted?" asked Nihal.

"My ex-boyfriend," Terrell said. "I stole an eight-hundred-dollar watch from him."

Everyone waited for an explanation.

"Well, let me first say that I consider myself a very respectable person," Terrell said, "and this is my only shameful deviation, like spending your whole life eating salads and then one day inhaling an entire chocolate cake. But, to make a long story short, Ted and I had been dating for almost a year when he decided to cheat on me in the most uninspired manner."

"With your best friend?" Chelsea guessed.

"With a coworker during a late night at work. Like an idiot, he came home from the office with the wrong belt on, because apparently it was dark and every man in finance wears similar ugly black belts. So obviously I found out, and we broke up, and I decided to exact my revenge by taking something he cared about."

"The watch was really important to him?" Ben asked.

"It wasn't a family heirloom or anything like that. It was just a really fucking expensive watch. And the bastard owed it to me. I had to get back at him for wasting the past ten months of my life. He stole all of that *time* from me, so I couldn't think of anything more apropos than stealing his watch."

Terrell rolled up his sleeve and wriggled his wrist with a sheepish grin, the gold wristwatch gleaming in the fluorescent light of the classroom. Even Sean couldn't help but smile.

"Oh man, I wish I had thought of that," said Chelsea. "When my ex had the nerve to dump me by text, I just took a baseball bat to his rearview mirror."

"Why did you break up?" Nihal asked.

"Well . . . he found out," Chelsea said, and each member of the group could fill in the gaps.

He'd found out about her string.

"But it's not all bad news," Terrell said, deftly rescuing the group from further despair. "Technically, this is *also* a secret, but I happen to know that a new Broadway show is currently in development with an entire cast and crew of short-stringers. Writing, directing, lighting, choreography . . . the whole shebang! All short-stringers. People are flying in from all over the country to work on it. And, best of all, *yours truly* will be on the producing team."

"That's incredible," said Ben.

Maura wasn't surprised. "You can always count on the artists to step up," she said, "especially during a crisis."

"*And* to do it in song." Terrell smiled.

"That reminds me, some of my old college buddies are launching this home exchange program exclusively for short-stringers," added Nihal. "You can match with someone in another state, or even another country, and swap homes with them for a period of time. It's supposed to make it easier for short-stringers to travel and see the world."

"You *have* to let us all be beta testers!" Chelsea squealed.

"I actually have a pretty big secret, too," said Lea, buoyed by the change in mood. "But you all have to promise not to tell anyone . . . yet."

A few of the group members actually leaned forward in their chairs.

"I'm pregnant," she said.

"Oh my god!" "Holy shit!" "Congratulations!" The group showered Lea with shock and excitement.

Maura was the only member of the group who stayed quiet, though nobody seemed to notice. Of course she was thrilled for Lea, but she couldn't help but feel stunned. Lea was a short-stringer, too. Did she not suffer the same fears, the same burdens? Maura wondered if Lea had made all the same calculations, yet arrived at a different answer.

"Thank you, guys," Lea said. "I figured I'd have to tell you all soon. It's *twins,* so I'll be showing in no time."

Twins, Maura thought, at least that was good. At least they would have each other.

"Who's the father?" Chelsea asked, and a few others shot her an alarmed look. "What? Is that like a taboo thing to ask?"

"Don't worry," Lea said. "I'm actually a surrogate for my brother and his husband, so my brother-in-law is technically the father. But the eggs were mine, so we're hoping the twins might bear a slight resemblance to my brother, too."

A collective "Ohhh" rippled through the group, but the revelation had a strange effect on Maura. A part of her felt relieved, there was no need for envy. Another part felt a little sad.

"Your brother and his husband must be so grateful to you," Hank told Lea.

"Well, they did say that if it's a boy and girl, they're naming them Lea and Leo." She laughed. "I sincerely hope they're joking."

Terrell touched Lea's hand softly. "You're giving them the greatest gift," he said.

And Lea smiled. "That's exactly what they said to me." She rested her hands on her stomach. "It's strange, because my brother and his husband both have fairly long strings, so it seemed to me like they already *had* the greatest gift," she said. "But maybe they didn't see it like that. And now, it turns out, *I* was the one who could give it to them."

Maura remembered when the Pope had appeared on his balcony, declaring the boxes a gift from God. Perhaps for some people—like Lea's brother, or Sean, or Nina—they were. But for everyone else, for the people in Room 204, at least there were other gifts, as Lea said. The trouble was simply recognizing them.

The musical that Terrell had mentioned—the dreams of a hundred short-stringers gracing the Broadway stage—sure sounded like a gift.

The moment, each morning, when Maura woke next to the woman she loved, a woman with every reason to leave.

The fact that she and Nina could even love each other, freely and openly, at all.

She decided, right then, to tell Nina the truth.

An hour later, Maura sat on the edge of the bed, looking at her girlfriend.

"I should tell you something," she said. "I know that we never planned on having kids. And my string has only made it *more* clear that we shouldn't. But, honestly, sometimes . . . I struggle with that."

Nina looked poised to interject, to offer something kind and encouraging, perhaps even reopen the subject. But Maura shook her head.

"We don't need to get any deeper into it," she said. "It is what it is. But I didn't want to keep any secrets from you. I just wanted you to know how I feel. That apparently it's possible to regret something, or at least *wonder* about something, while still knowing it was the right choice."

"I didn't even know it was bothering you," Nina said.

"Well, I can put on a pretty tough face," Maura confessed. "I know I'm lucky, I've never been lacking in confidence." She smiled thinly. "But sometimes that can make it difficult to be . . . vulnerable."

Nina sat down next to Maura. "I'm glad you told me," she said. "You can always be vulnerable with *me*."

"Do you ever find yourself . . . rethinking it?" Maura asked.

"Honestly, I don't know," Nina said quietly. "It's not like I ever made the choice to *not* have children. I just never made the decision *to* have children, you know? And then, once you and I found each other, I just felt . . . complete."

Maura nodded and took a breath. "I know how you feel," she said. "But the crazy thing is that it wasn't even something I wanted, until I realized that I probably couldn't have it. It's like the door slammed in front of me before I could really take a look at what was inside. And maybe it isn't even *really* about children. Maybe it's the fact that now I can't stop thinking about all the *other* doors that might be closing, too. Like, what if I never find a job I really love? What if I don't get to see that much more of the world? What if I never do something that . . . leaves an impact?"

Nina looped her arm around Maura. "You leave an impact on everyone you meet," she said. "You're just that kind of person. You're almost *annoyingly* impactful." Nina smiled.

And Maura laughed at that, softly and somewhat restrained, but a laugh that made her realize that she was okay. They were okay.

"Well, maybe Amie will hurry up and have some kids, so we can be the cool aunts." Maura grinned. "Or at least *I* can be the cool aunt, and you can be the one who reads them the newspaper at bedtime."

And they both laughed again, a heartier burst this time, until Nina kissed Maura deeply, and the two women fell back onto the bed.

Dear B,

During a vocab lesson today, one of my students defined "foolhardy" as "funny," and I had to tell her that she was wrong. She looked so confused, and then she said, "I'm sorry. I thought it meant what I wanted it to mean." I've never heard a student phrase it like that before, and I've been thinking about it all day.

Maybe the boxes are like that, too. Nobody can offer any foolproof explanation for them, so they just end up meaning whatever we want them to mean—whether that's God or fate or magic. And no matter how long your string is, that, too, can mean whatever you want it to—a license to behave however you want, to stop dieting, to seek revenge, to quit your job, to take a risk, to travel the world. I don't have any desire to leave my students, but sometimes I do imagine myself spending a year abroad, on a pilgrimage to my favorite literary sites, wandering the dramatic moors of Emily Brontë, bathing on the beach of Fitzgerald's Riviera, bundled up against the winter of Tolstoy's Russia (though I'd probably wimp out and go in the summer).

Every morning, I wonder if today will be the day that I just break down and open it.

If it's not too personal, can I ask—do you regret looking?

—A

BEN

Ben didn't know why he was surprised. He should have expected the question eventually.

But it took him a while to craft a response. He tried procrastinating with a sketch of a new building, until he had erased and redrawn the design so many times that he ended up back at the original, and that's when he knew that he had to start writing. But it was so much more complicated than the author's simple query—*Do you regret looking?*—made it seem. And it threatened to dredge up every emotion from that night, the night he learned of his short string. All the shock and sadness and fear. The look on Claire's face as she wept.

He believed that the stranger on the other end of his letters had always been honest with him, and he wanted to be open with them in return. But he found that he couldn't quite bring himself to share the story in its entirety. He preferred not to relive that night. At least, not yet.

Dear A,

I feel like there was a time before my box was opened and a time after, and they're just so completely separate. There's no way to ever go back to the time before. I know that sounds cliché, but it's true. Once you know something, you forget what it was like to not know it.

And yes, most days, I do regret knowing. But I try to tell myself that this initial regret will pass, and that one day, I may even be grateful to know.

Of course, if it turns out that I die suddenly in some accident, then maybe I would have been better off not knowing beforehand and just being hurled into oblivion instantaneously with no time to think about mistakes or what-ifs. But if it turns out to be a slow ending, with no shortage of time for self-reflection, then I have to take comfort in the fact that it will not come as a horrible surprise, and I will hopefully have spent the previous 14 years living the way I wanted, so I can look back and feel as content as one can hope to be.

Ben felt drained after writing the letter, like he could fall asleep right then. But there was something else he wanted to say.

I have to assume from your most recent letter that you're a teacher, and now that it's June, perhaps you'll be heading off on summer vacation somewhere, away from the city.

Ben didn't know how to conclude. Should he reveal his name? Leave his address? Suggest they meet in person?

He was honestly surprised that the letters had even lasted this long. His only similar experience was after sleep-away camp, when his bunkmates had sworn to stay pen pals throughout the school year, even sealing their pledge with a spit shake. By winter, though, once the boys' lives were consumed yet again with classes and sports and music lessons, nearly all of the exchanges had died off. It was Ben who had written the final letter, never to receive a response.

The last letter made it clear that "A" was a teacher, but Ben didn't know if his current pen pal was a man or a woman, young or old. Perhaps he should investigate, now that he had more information, maybe finagle a visit to the school on a weekday and ask which teachers used Room 204. But wouldn't he look suspicious? A thirty-year-old man snooping around?

Besides, Ben wasn't sure that he wanted to know. He wasn't ready to lose the mystery that made these letters so special. He knew that it might just be a trivial diversion for "A." Maybe they simply pitied him. But he didn't want them to disappear.

The handful of friends whom Ben had trusted with the news of his string—all long-stringers themselves—had kept in touch with him frequently, at the beginning, always calling or texting to check in. But lately the outreach had been slowly fading. Even Damon, who had encouraged Ben to join the group back in April, used to inquire every Monday morning about the previous night's session, but he had missed the past two weeks in a row.

Perhaps they all felt powerless to help Ben, or uncomfortable in their grief, or guilty about their own long strings. Maybe they just didn't know what to say.

But I'll still be coming to this classroom every Sunday night, in case you find yourself here this summer.

And, if not, then I wish you the best of luck, and I hope you find peace in your decision, whether you look at your string or not.

—B

Ben waited until the group had dispersed and he was left alone in the empty classroom. He pulled the sheet of paper out of his satchel, folded in half, with the letter *A* written on the front. Then he bent down to set it like a miniature tent pitched at the foot of the bookshelf.

When Ben turned around, Hank was standing behind him, puzzled.

"I think I forgot my headphones," Hank explained.

"Oh, um, I can help you look for them," offered Ben.

The two men filled the awkward silence by shuffling around the room, necks tilted down.

"Do you mind if I ask what you were doing with that piece of paper?" Hank finally ventured.

Ben thought for a moment. "Would this be covered under doctor-patient confidentiality?"

"Sure, why not?" Hank laughed.

So Ben told Hank about the letter he had left behind during an earlier session, and the mysterious reply he received.

"And now I'm sort of writing back and forth with a total stranger,"

Ben explained. "Which I realize sounds ridiculous when I say it out loud."

Hank squinted curiously at Ben. "You really have no idea who's writing to you?"

Ben shook his head. "My best guess is that it's one of the staff at the school," he said. "But I think they might also host some AA meetings and a few other groups here on different nights, so I suppose it could be one of those members, too."

Hank shrugged and smiled reassuringly. "Well, I guess the only way you'll ever find out is if you keep writing back."

"Thanks," said Ben.

"For what?"

"For not making me feel crazy."

"We're all in uncharted waters here. It's hard to call any reaction crazy." Hank peered under the table where Sean had set up snacks.

"You work at Memorial Hospital, right? I'm sorry about what happened there."

"I actually quit at the end of May. But I had already given notice before the shooting," Hank said. "I just realized I can't recall what you do?"

"I'm an architect," said Ben.

"Oh wow. Have you designed any buildings I'd recognize?"

"Not yet," Ben said wistfully. "One in progress, but upstate."

Hank sat back down in one of the plastic chairs. "What made you want to be an architect?"

Slightly surprised, Ben sat next to him. "I'm not really sure," he said. "But I didn't have any siblings growing up, and both my parents worked, so I spent a fair amount of time doodling little houses and towns and imagining the people who lived there."

Hank frowned at him with pity.

"Oh no, don't get me wrong," Ben stammered. "My parents are great, and it wasn't like I was lonely all the time. I just really enjoyed drawing those tiny worlds."

"And now you want to make bigger worlds?"

Ben laughed. "Let's just say that school wasn't always easy for me, and back then I thought that if I could create something as big as a New York skyscraper, it would be impossible to ever feel small."

"And what about now?"

Ben looked out the window, where the stately apartments of the Upper East Side blended together against the darkening sky.

"Now I want to make something permanent. Something that will keep on standing even after . . ."

Hank let out a knowing sigh, and the two were quiet for a minute, unsure if the conversation would continue. But Ben was curious. "So, if it wasn't about the shooting, why did you quit?"

"I think I was tired," Hank said. "Tired of seeing people come into the hospital crying, scared, completely desperate, and begging me for answers that I couldn't give them."

"That sounds awful."

Hank screwed his mouth to the side, thinking.

"You know, that actually wasn't the only reason. That's what I told my boss and my colleagues, but the truth is that I just didn't want to be a doctor anymore. There I was, thinking that I had brought hundreds of people back from the edge of death. That I had confronted death and won. And then I found out that maybe I hadn't. Maybe I had only saved the ones who weren't going to die anyway, the ones who still had more time on their strings. And, as for the other ones who I tried to save and failed, maybe they couldn't have been saved. No doctor could have helped them."

"That sounds like it might almost be comforting?" Ben asked.

"Except it's hard to keep fighting against something once you realize it's not a fair fight," Hank said. "And I guess everyone else could shift their focus better than I could. Even if we can't affect someone's longevity, at least we can still impact their quality of life. And I know they're right, but I can't get past it. I worked in an ER. I've spent my whole career fending off death. But it's the one thing we can't defeat."

"Well, wasn't that true even before the strings?" Ben asked.

"Yes," Hank said. "But before the strings, I could still delude myself into thinking that I actually stood a chance."

Ben nodded somberly. "I'm sorry about that."

"I'm sorry I won't get to see your skyscraper."

Ben pretended to be insulted. "Hey! I've still got some time left to build it."

Hank looked down at his feet. "I'm not like the rest of you," he said.

"What do you mean?"

"I'm much closer to the end of mine," Hank said. "But I didn't really want to attend the group for short-stringers with just a year left. Too damn depressing. So I came here instead."

"I'm so sorry." Ben's voice was barely a whisper.

"Well, some days can get pretty dark," Hank said, "but other days, I just try to remember that I've lived a good life. I did my best to help people. I fell in love a few times. I tried to be a good son." Hank leaned back slowly in his chair. "You know, I watched a lot of people come to the end, and everyone around them kept begging them to fight. It takes real strength to keep on fighting, and yes, usually that's the right answer. Keep fighting, keep holding on, no matter what. But sometimes I think we forget that it also takes strength to be able to let go."

Dear B,

Don't worry, I'll still be around. I'm teaching summer school and tutoring.

But even if I weren't, I've found that I look forward to your letters enough that I might even risk my job and break into the school after hours—I should hate to miss even one week.

As long as you'd like to keep writing, I promise I'm not going anywhere.

—A

HANK

On June 9, Maura asked if their support group could meet an hour earlier, so the session would end in enough time to watch the first primary debate of the season.

Hank didn't particularly care for politics. He cared, of course, in a broad sense about matters that immediately impacted him and his work—health insurance, crime rates, taxes—though he didn't have the time to spend hours debating the minutiae of policies or reading long political think pieces. But Hank had heard the rumors that the candidate from Virginia, Anthony Rollins, was planning to make a big announcement during the debate. To Hank, he was just another suave millionaire, detached from the realities of most Americans' lives, the realities that Hank had borne witness to every day in the emergency room. But he was still curious enough to tune in.

He was sipping a beer on his brown leather couch when the moderator asked the question that Hank hadn't realized he was waiting to hear.

"I'd like to begin tonight with the subject that's on every voter's mind: the strings. As I'm sure we've all heard, China has just released a new nationwide mandate, taking the opposite approach to the recent North Korean ruling and instead requiring all citizens to *open* their boxes upon receipt and file a report with the government indicating the length of their string. While most congressional efforts to address the strings here in the U.S. have largely stalled, certainly we've all been following the tragic events of late, including last month's shootings at a New York hospital and a Texas shopping mall, that appear to be connected to the strings' arrival. So, candidates, has the appearance of the strings caused you to rethink any of *your* positions or proposals?"

Anthony Rollins was primed. He ignored the bulk of the question and dove straight into the speech he had clearly rehearsed.

"The presidency is the highest office in our land, and whoever is elected is expected to serve his or her country for four full years, and perhaps even *eight* full years. Running for president is a promise to the people of this great nation that you are willing and able to commit yourself for your full term, and perhaps even *two* terms, in the Oval Office. That is why I humbly submit to you the people—alongside my tax returns and my Twitter history—something even more important. My string."

With this, Anthony took out a small box from behind his podium, opened its lid, and held up a string that everyone, by now, could quickly recognize as one of considerable length.

"Should I have the honor of becoming your candidate, I assure you that I will serve for as long as you'll have me. And I ask that my fellow candidates, in the spirit of transparency, present their own strings, so the voters can head to the polls armed with as much information as possible about the person who may lead our country for years to come."

The audience didn't quite know how to react. While most clapped and nodded in agreement, several boos and heckles rose above the applause.

"All right, all right." The moderator calmed the crowd. "Let's hear what the other candidates have to say."

"I made the decision, along with my spouse, that neither of us would look at our strings," said Dr. Amelia Parkins, a Harvard professor of political science running as the Washington outsider. "I believe it is an entirely personal choice whether or not to look, and asking candidates to share something so private seems unjust and unethical, not to mention un-American. Congressman Rollins's request feels more in line with the authoritarian regimes mentioned earlier."

"Thank you, Dr. Parkins," said the moderator. "Governor Russ, any thoughts?"

"I believe that what Miss Parkins fails to comprehend is that to be an effective and trustworthy public servant, you need to accept that most of your private life will *become* public," the governor said. "Certainly that's true of the presidency. Even if candidates refuse to show their strings, you can bet the tabloids will go digging anyway. And I can already see the headline: 'Country Elects President Who Will Die in Office.'"

In keeping with her reputation as the "family values" candidate, Kentucky congresswoman Alice Harper added, "I would like to think that any candidate who had the misfortune of having a short string would withdraw from the race to spend their remaining time with loved ones, and not on the road campaigning for a job that they wouldn't be able to keep for long anyway."

While the other candidates spoke, Senator Wes Johnson, Sr., was thinking.

He was the only African American onstage, and he must have known that his words would be doubly scrutinized, Hank thought. Johnson waited until the others had each said their piece, and the moderator asked if he had anything to add.

"Yes, I do," Johnson said. "The American people should elect the person whose values they agree with, whose positions they support, and whose proposals they believe will improve our nation. Having a short string does not erase those qualities, and choosing *not* to elect a qualified candidate simply because of their short string is akin to punishing them for something entirely out of their control. We've made it illegal to discriminate on the basis of race, gender, disability, and age, but forcing candidates to show their strings would be condoning an entirely new category of discrimination."

Some scattered applause led the moderator to lean toward his microphone, but Johnson wasn't finished.

"Some of our greatest leaders died while still in office," he continued, "and some of our least effective politicians have been blessed with longevity. If John F. Kennedy had revealed his string, and the voters had punished him for it, the Cuban Missile Crisis might have erupted into nuclear war with the Soviets. If Franklin Roosevelt had revealed his string, and the voters had punished him for it, the Nazis may never have seen defeat. And if Abraham Lincoln had shown his string, then the men and women who look like me and my children might still be enslaved, and our country might have been torn apart for good. I shudder at the thought of what our world would look like today if those men had been denied the chance to govern simply because of the unfortunate hand they had been dealt, and I hope that my fellow Americans can see the danger in Congressman Rollins's proposal."

Hank breathed a sigh of relief as the audience cheered in response, and Rollins looked on blankly. It was in the final shot of Wes Johnson's face, just before the camera moved on, that Hank could have sworn he saw the senator's eyes shimmer with tears that he couldn't afford to release on television.

And that's when Hank realized that he and Wes Johnson must share the same fate.

Hank quickly lost interest in the rest of the broadcast, picking up his phone and turning instead to people's reactions online. While many were supportive of Johnson's stance, Rollins had ignited . . . *something*. Tweets and blog posts were emerging from all corners of the country calling for candidates to reveal their strings, arguing that a short-stringer couldn't be trusted with the nation's most important job. Short-stringers are too distracted, they said. Too anxious, too depressed, too volatile.

It didn't take long for the conversation to move past the presidency. Maybe all political offices should require a string disclosure? they asked. And what about the CEOs of major companies? Any thoughts on medical residents? Why would a hospital want to spend time training someone who couldn't return its investment?

Hank threw his phone across the couch.

The next morning, June 10, around 9 A.M., approximately three months after the boxes first appeared, a short-stringer detonated a homemade bomb just outside the Capitol, killing multiple bystanders. And Hank knew that somewhere, in some bland hotel room in some midwestern state, Anthony Rollins must be pleased.

SUMMER

ANTHONY

The suspect in the June 10 bombing was killed in the blast—taking several other short-stringers along with him—but he left a message for the authorities to find upon searching his apartment later: *The people suffer and die while our leaders do nothing*.

An elite emergency task force, convened by the president to deal with the fallout, agreed rather quickly that there was nothing the government could do to stop short-stringers from suffering and dying. What the committee *did* decide was that something needed to be done to keep rogue short-stringers from causing any additional damage.

A week after the bombing, Anthony Rollins flew home to D.C., leaving his wife to sip cups of Earl Grey and eat cranberry-walnut scones at an afternoon tea with prominent donors in Charleston.

The next day, the president's emergency task force prepared to welcome its newest member.

The team already comprised three senior senators, two top officials from both the FBI and the DHS, and the chairman of the Joint Chiefs of Staff.

"We know it's a bit unprecedented to bring in a representative on something this high-profile, and especially a primary candidate," Anthony was informed by the chairman. "But these are unprecedented times. And the president won't hold office for much longer. He needs to think about the long game, who's going to hold the nation's hand through the next four years of this nightmare. Apparently your performance at the debate really lit a fire in some segments of the party."

"And I'm sure you've seen that my numbers are spiking fast," Anthony added. He knew that some pundits had already dubbed him a fad, predicting his imminent burnout, but this assignment could cement his rise. "It seems that the whole *country* is listening to me."

By the afternoon, the task force was listening, too.

The following morning, the nine members of the committee gathered in the Oval Office to offer their thoughts on the so-called "short-stringer situation" to the president himself.

String disclosures should be required for high-ranking government posts, they argued. It should be treated the same as a background check or a physical fitness exam. If you're going to hold a position of power, you need to prove that you're committed, that you're physically and mentally capable. Frankly, a short-stringer is a liability, they claimed. You never know if they're going to snap, like the bomber and the shooters before him.

Agent Breslin of the FBI was the only woman in the room, and for most of the meeting, she stayed quiet, letting the men continue to think aloud while she processed her thoughts internally.

"There's something else that we haven't thought of yet," she finally interjected. "If we can check the strings of every applicant for field agent positions or active military duty, and *only* send those with longer strings into the field or into combat, then we can effectively eliminate all risk of death. They're guaranteed to survive."

The agent looked around the room of men, who were nodding in bewildered agreement, and she smiled.

"Except survival is just that," said an older senator. "It doesn't mean we won't be sending our boys home in a coma, or missing their arms and legs."

"That's better than a body bag," she countered.

"Are we limiting this to military and federal positions?" asked another. "I imagine police departments and other high-risk jobs will want to follow suit."

The president had been listening intently in silence, but his task force seemed to be hurtling toward a powerful consensus. He needed to weigh in.

"All right," he said, raising a cautious hand. "I agree with what you're saying, but there need to be limitations. We're the United States, not China or North Korea. We'd never get away with requiring everyone to open their boxes and tell us what's inside. Plus, if we allow this to spill over into every industry, I'm afraid there'll be no jobs left for short-stringers."

"What do you propose, sir?"

"A compromise," said the president. "We require string disclosures for active-duty military personnel, FBI field agents, and government officials with the highest security clearances. But everything else stays the same. At least for now."

A few days later, Katherine rejoined her husband in suburban McLean, where they had purchased a relatively modest four-bedroom house after Anthony's election to Congress.

"I still can't believe the president himself called you in," Katherine said breathlessly. "He must think you're going to win."

"Let's not get too far ahead of ourselves," said Anthony. "We've still got a long way to go. The president simply recognized the truth, that I was the only one brave enough to say publicly what a lot of others have been thinking already."

Safely inside their living room walls, Anthony divulged what he could to his curious wife, without sharing too many specifics.

"There are going to be some changes," Anthony said. "But the people like us will be just fine."

"We'll be better than fine." Katherine grinned.

And Anthony couldn't help but agree with her.

MAURA

The changes were announced in a televised White House press conference on a Friday night at the end of June.

Maura and Nina had been waiting for the twice-delayed conference to begin, distracting themselves by watching one of those crime procedurals known for picking plot lines out of the news. The show itself had just made headlines by becoming the first television series to introduce the strings into its fictive universe, and Maura was stunned to watch the episode unfold, the team of police officers hunting down two vicious short-stringers on a crime spree, leading to the climactic shootout where they both lost their lives. A portrayal that wouldn't do any good for short-stringers in the real world, she thought.

Nina seemed just as upset by the story, fidgeting on the couch before switching channels, where the president of the United States finally appeared on-screen amid the muffled coughs of reporters and a few camera flashes. Flanked at the podium by senior members of the military and the FBI, he announced his most sweeping executive order to date: the Security and Transparency in Appointing and Recruiting Initiative, or the "STAR" Initiative for short. A similar bill would likely be introduced in Congress soon, but the attack on the Capitol had made it clear, the president argued, that immediate action was warranted.

"They must know that people will be angry," Nina said after the conference had ended. "That's why they announced it on a Friday night. They're hoping there'll be less media coverage on a weekend, and maybe people won't pay as much attention. As if that could ever happen."

Maura stayed quiet, taking it in, while Nina rambled on anxiously. "I mean, I did hear that the primary debate had shifted the conversation in Congress," she said, "but I can't believe that it's gotten this far, this fast."

Nina looked at Maura. "Are you okay?" she asked softly.

"Am I *okay*?" Maura asked. "First I have to watch that smear campaign against short-stringers masquerading as a TV show, and now *this*? The president just created two classes of citizens, based on strings."

It was clear Nina didn't know how to respond. "I know that the cop show was . . . not good, but I don't think this STAR Initiative could be that bad," she said reassuringly.

Maura pushed herself up off the couch. "It's all part of the same problem!" she yelled.

"Well, maybe the announcement *seems* more extreme than it actually is," Nina offered.

"They just told me that, solely because of my string, I can't be a soldier or an FBI agent or do some NSA-level shit. How the fuck can they do that?" She started pacing the room. "It's like we're moving back in time. What's next? 'Don't Ask, Don't Tell' about your string?"

"I honestly can't believe it, either," Nina said. "But technically it's not that you *can't* serve in the military or the FBI, it's just that you're limited in terms of what you can *do* in those roles."

"Seriously, Nina? Are you trying to defend them?"

"No, of course not," she said quickly. "It's horrible."

"Everyone's been saying that what's happening in those other countries could never happen *here*," Maura said. "And now look!"

"It's probably a stupid, knee-jerk reaction to the bombing," Nina said. "And they'll call it off once they realize it was a mistake."

But Maura sighed and shook her head. "That's not the way I see it."

Maura loved Nina, but she was always trying to comfort her, to point out the path to the bright side. Being with Nina may have been Maura's umbrella, but it didn't stop the rain from bearing down, and sometimes she just needed space to get mad.

All her life, Maura had been aware of the loathsome stereotype, never letting herself appear too angry, too loud. She knew that the world liked to praise the saintly, those who accepted their hardships with peace, rather than rage or complaint. But when something felt this random, this unfair, how could anyone be faulted for feeling pain and expressing it?

In the confines of Room 204, at least, Maura could bathe in that anger, surrounded by those who shared it.

The Sunday after the press conference, she walked into the classroom, where several others were already discussing the news, and dropped her bag on the floor. "Is everyone else pissed?"

Murmurs of "Fuck, yeah," and "Of course" echoed throughout the group.

"I'm sure that emotions are running high, and I'm happy to discuss everyone's feelings in turn," said Sean, wary of his session devolving into disorganized rants.

"Maybe we're all overreacting," Nihal said.

"I think there's only *one* way to react," said Maura.

"What do you think it means for us?" Lea asked, her eyes searching among the group for an answer.

Hank met Lea's gaze. "Unfortunately, it means that things might get worse."

"I don't see how it can get much fucking worse than it already is," said Carl. "It's not like they can make our short strings shorter."

"But we don't even have time anymore to feel badly about our strings, or angry about our own lives," said Maura. "Not when there's so much other crap going down in the world that we need to get angry about."

"And it's not just the government," said Chelsea. "It's *everyone*. I heard about a new dating app that's only for short-stringers, called Share Your Time. You can even filter by string length. They're selling it as a way to find people who are similar to you, but clearly it's a ploy to get us off the regular apps, so god forbid long-stringers don't accidentally fall in love with one of us."

"Like some sort of deranged Darwinian attempt at exclusion." Terrell shuddered. "It actually reminds me of a pretty disturbing story from some friends of mine trying to adopt. Neither of them opened their boxes, but the agency was apparently pressuring them to look. It sounds like they're up against couples who are touting their long strings as part of their qualifications for being good parents."

"That's *beyond* fucked-up," said Chelsea.

"My guess is that short-stringers looking to adopt are like the new gay couples," said Terrell. "It's not impossible, but it sure won't be easy."

"Well, I'd like to believe that people will see how wrong all of this is and demand a change," Lea said, anxiously rubbing her growing midsection.

"But this is what humans have always done," Maura said, her anger swelling inside. "We segment ourselves based on race or class or religion or whatever fucking distinctions we decide to make up, and then we insist on treating each other differently. We never should have allowed them to start labeling people as 'long-stringers' and 'short-stringers.' We made it too easy for them."

Hank nodded solemnly. "Nobody seems to care that we all look the same when we're open on a table."

The room was quiet for a moment.

"But do you really think it's fair to compare different strings to different races?" Terrell asked.

"Why not?" Maura said. "We all heard the news. We've just been banned from holding the most powerful positions in the country. No short-stringers need apply! It's like we're living in a fucking time loop where no one's learned anything from history! Once people start believing that a certain group is out to get them—that immigrants are stealing their jobs, and gay couples are undermining marriage, and feminists are falsely accusing them of rape—it doesn't take much to get us to turn on each other."

"Well, at least plenty of people feel nothing but pity for us," said Ben. "That should hopefully make them more compassionate."

"Except it's not just pity, or compassion," Hank cut in. "This is different. Ever since that first incident at the hospital. Now anytime there's violence involving a short-stringer, that sympathy gets more and more diluted with fear. And fear is a far more powerful emotion."

"But why should *they* be afraid of *us?*" Nihal asked. "They have everything, and we have nothing."

"Nothing to lose," Hank answered.

He recalled the night of the primary debate, when audience members had applauded Anthony's callous call to action, and he spent hours scrolling through online discussions asking if discrimination against short-stringers was justified.

"They're saying that short-stringers can't be trusted," he explained. "That we're too much of a liability, too unpredictable. And of course it's all bullshit, but Maura's right. It's how things have always worked. All we need is one more shooting or bombing or god knows what else, and I don't even want to think what might happen."

Nihal's face was stricken, and Lea looked like she was going to cry.

Carl turned toward Hank. "You know, for a doctor, you're not very good at delivering bad news."

"But it's the truth," Maura said. "And unless we keep talking about it—and keep getting *mad* about it—then nothing will ever change."

"So that means there's still hope, right?" Lea asked.

"Look, I may not know what it's like to have a short string," said Sean. "But I *have* lived my whole life in this chair, so I do know a thing or two about how it feels when people see you as somehow . . . *other*. I know that life can sometimes feel like a battle to be recognized for who you are, and not your circumstances. It's why I signed up to lead this group in the first place. And I'm living proof that *one* long-stringer in this world can empathize with all of you. So I think that's at least *one* reason not to give up hope."

JAVIER

When the president debuted the STAR Initiative on national television, Jack Hunter and Javier García—along with every other member of the military—knew instantly that their careers, their lives, had forever changed.

The two friends had graduated from the academy on a sweltering Thursday at the end of May, formally commissioned as second lieutenants in the U.S. Army, and the pair moved into the D.C. apartment that Jack's father had purchased for his occasional trips in from Virginia. The arrival of the strings had been particularly jolting for those in the military. The leaders needed time to regroup. So Jack and Javi and their fellow grads had been granted the summer as a short reprieve before embarking on officer training.

Hoping to enjoy their final season of freedom, they came home each night to cold beers and cold pizza and *Madden NFL*. They dragged a discarded foosball table from the curb into their living room. And they took turns serving as wingmen at the Georgetown bars on Saturdays.

But then, on a Friday evening in June, the ground shifted underneath them.

"What exactly does this STAR thing mean?" Javi asked.

"I think it means that we have to look," Jack said. "That we don't have a choice anymore."

Before the strings arrived, branch assignments for new lieutenants had been determined based on the graduates' interests, coupled with the needs of the army. But the world had changed in the past three months. There was new information to consider.

After the president's announcement that all military positions would require a string disclosure—to be completed in person, by presenting your box to the commanding officer overseeing your geographic region—word quickly spread among Jack and Javi's former classmates that certain roles, such as those involving active combat in high-risk areas, would no longer be open to short-stringer soldiers. Though it was believed that many of those already deployed would have the chance to be grandfathered in, finishing their service regardless, the newest recruits would be placed according to string length.

"They're forcing us to look at our strings, even if we didn't want to," Jack ranted. "And for what? They think they can change fate? As if not sending a short-stringer into combat would somehow save their life? I bet they're just trying to save themselves."

"I don't know," said Javi, more ambivalent than his friend. "Maybe they feel guilty marching a band of short-stringers into a battle zone without even *trying* to do something about it."

But neither had time to do much complaining, or to properly sort out their feelings, as they were promptly assigned times to report to the nearest army recruiting office, their respective boxes in tow. It was recommended that those who hadn't yet looked at their strings do so in advance of their appointment, to avoid any shock in the room.

They had two weeks until they were called.

Jack and Javier sat on the couch with the two small boxes on the cushion between them and the string calculator queued up on Jack's iPad.

Their bodies and minds had overcome plenty of challenges in recent years: arduous obstacle courses, new cadet hazing, boxing matches, navigating hilly, swampy, wooded terrain with only a compass in hand. But the task before them now was by far the hardest yet.

"Do you think you'd try to quit?" Jack asked. "If it's short?"

"Well, I worked really hard to get this far," said Javi. "And I made a commitment—to the army *and* to myself. So I think I've got to keep going. No matter what's inside."

Javier's parents were both devout Catholics, so he sent up a silent prayer in their honor, and then gave Jack a nod. He was ready.

Because he *had* to be.

When Jack measured his string, he sighed a full exhale of relief that broke into a smile.

But Javier fell quiet.

Javi chose not to tell his parents. They were too thrilled to see him in uniform, a graduate of one of the finest colleges in the country and someone who commanded respect from every person he met. It was everything they wanted for their son.

Jack spent the next week caring for his grieving roommate, bringing food to his bedroom, constantly asking if there was anything he needed.

A few days later, the only thing that Javier needed was to get out of the apartment and run.

The two boys followed their usual route along a handful of blocks where many of the shops and restaurants had been boarded up since April, giving the streets an eerie bareness, though the emptier roads did make for easier running, without as many cars or shoppers to dodge. And the boys could use a particularly angry burst of graffiti on one of the barren storefronts—"Fuck the strings!!"—as their three-mile marker.

For a lot of the run Jack was quiet, only the heavy patter of their sneakers on the pavement making noise. It wasn't until they reached the midway point that Jack spoke up.

"Javi?"

Javi kept his eyes focused ahead. "Yeah?"

"What if . . . what if we switched?"

Javi still didn't crack his concentration. "Switched what?" he asked.

"Switched our strings," Jack said.

That's when Javi stopped abruptly. "What did you say?"

A biker behind them started frantically ringing his bell, but Javi stood frozen in the road.

"Watch out!" the cyclist yelled, and Jack quickly pulled Javi out of the way, just before the rider whirred past, flipping them off.

"Are you okay?" Jack asked. "You almost got hit!"

But Javi couldn't focus on anything else. "Did you actually say *switch* our strings?"

Jack nodded. "Am I fucking nuts to even be saying that?"

Yes, you are, Javier thought. "But . . . it wouldn't really change anything," he said.

"It might not change the ending," said Jack, "but it sure as hell would change everything else."

Javier still didn't get it. "Why would *you* want to pretend to have a short string?"

Jack paused for a moment, clearly uncomfortable. "Look, I feel like an asshole saying this, because obviously I'm happy about my string, but . . . I'm also kinda freaking out. I mean, I know that I owe them a couple of years in *some* capacity, but what if the army wants to send me into combat for life?"

Every terror that the academy had tried to expel from Jack had apparently come rushing back. He had no illusions about his physical prowess, he could barely hold his own in a stupid scuffle with a classmate. How could he possibly fight in a real war?

"And maybe if the army thought I had a short string," Jack said, "they would just stick me behind some desk here in D.C. for a bit. I could basically disappear."

Javier just nodded. It seemed unlikely that Jack's worst fear would be realized—the army couldn't *force* him into unending service, no matter what his string foretold—but after four years as friends, Javi wasn't exactly surprised by Jack's reluctance to be sent into battle, his instinct for self-preservation. It was the audacity of Jack's proposal that was most shocking now. Switching strings? Was that even possible?

"I was thinking about how you said that you owed it to yourself to keep going," Jack added. "And we both know that you ranked higher than me in class *and* in the field, so if only one of us could get the chance to really prove himself, it should be you."

Javi was still processing, but he couldn't just keep standing. His legs felt as antsy as his mind. He turned and started to run again, leaving Jack to catch up.

And as Javier ran, focusing on the rhythm of his breathing, he began to evaluate his options.

Jack was asking him to intentionally *lie* to the United States Armed Forces, to the very people who had educated and trained him. Not only did it *feel* wrong, it was definitely illegal. The STAR Initiative stated that any service member who refused to comply—to show their string—could face dishonorable discharge. Who knows what might happen to someone who produced a string that wasn't actually *theirs*?

Jack was clearly out of his mind to propose something so ludicrous, Javi thought.

And yet . . . Jack *did* make a good point about all the time and effort that Javi had already put in, the nights when he sacrificed sleep to study, the days when he could taste the salty sweat and metallic blood in his mouth.

Javi had *earned* his shot. And now he had only a few years left to take it.

Javier's feet felt weightless, carrying him forward, the endorphins pumping in his body. He knew that he would never be satisfied with the staid desk job that appealed to Jack. But without having a long string—or, at least, the *appearance* of one—that was all Javier would get.

He wondered what his parents would say to him now, if they knew what he was considering. That lying is a sin, no matter the motive? That they didn't work this hard just to raise a criminal?

Or would they speak the same words as his graduation toast? *We're so proud of you, Javier.*

By the time they had reached their front door, Javi still hadn't spoken, and Jack nervously shattered the silence. "Obviously you should do whatever you want to do," he said, still huffing from the final sprint. "It's completely *your* choice. But I just wanted you to know you have options."

Except Javi didn't feel like he had options, he felt like he had a time bomb that Jack had thrown into his lap. There was less than a week left now before Javier's appointment. Only three days to make a decision that his entire future hinged upon.

Javi shoved his key into the lock. "I need to sleep on it," he said.

But he didn't sleep.

He closed his eyes, wept into his pillowcase, stared at the ceiling, lay flat on his stomach, and flipped from side to side, but sleep never came. What did come were drowsy and delirious visions, fed by the echoing of Jack's offer in his mind.

The worst was when Javi imagined his own funeral. The colors of the American flag draped across his coffin appeared even more vivid against the black of the mourners' outfits. The flag would be the only consolation for his parents that day.

Of course, there would be talk about how he died. Perhaps the priest would tell the story if his parents couldn't form the words. That was the part that Javi found himself rewinding and replaying as he shut his eyes and begged for sleep.

"The car came out of nowhere," the priest said, shaking his head sadly.

Rewind.

"In the end, he lost his battle against the illness." The same sad shaking.

Rewind.

"He was a good swimmer, but the waves were too big."

Rewind.

"He was just sitting at his desk when the bomb went off."

Rewind.

"He was a true American hero, until his last breath," the priest said firmly.

For the first time, he didn't shake his head.

BEN

The air-conditioning in Room 204 was temporarily broken, so Carl pried open all the windows to let in a breeze. But the summer night was still, too still, and the motionless warmth that filled the classroom seemed to lull the group into a more ruminant state than usual.

"I'm curious," said Sean, "who still hasn't told their family members?"

Ben raised his hand timidly, somewhat embarrassed, while Hank casually lifted his index finger, as if motioning for the check.

"That's okay," said Sean. "Everyone moves on their own timeline."

"I actually told my parents this week," said Nihal.

He had just returned from a visit to Chicago, where his parents had lived for the past three decades, ever since Nihal's father was accepted into a doctoral program at Northwestern and the newlyweds emigrated from India.

"How was it?" Lea asked.

"Honestly? Tough." Nihal sighed. "But they both believe that our bodies are temporary vessels for our souls, and that these strings only apply to our current bodies, so my soul will be reborn after this, presumably with a brand-new string. Another chance."

"And you don't share those beliefs?" Sean asked.

"Look, I love my religion. It has so much . . . *joy* in it. And freedom. We're not bogged down by all the rules, all the fire and brimstone," Nihal said. "And until the strings, I didn't even spend that much time really thinking about rebirth. It was always just there in the background, while I focused on school or other things. And I know that my parents are only trying to help me, but now . . . I want more time in *this* life, not some *new* life, surrounded by new people."

A few of the group members nodded, understanding.

"My parents think it's part of this larger pattern of me turning away from my heritage," Nihal explained. "And yeah, sometimes I resented my parents when somebody stumbled over pronouncing my last name or commented on the food I brought to school. But I've *always* been proud to be their son."

"I'm sure they know that," said Hank.

"But I hate fighting with them, because I actually *wish* I could see it the way they do," Nihal said. "Maybe it would make things easier, being certain that this wasn't our only chance at life."

Listening to Nihal, Ben was reminded of his boss, one of the senior architects at the firm, who liked to say that buildings had "multiple lives," perhaps as a way to cushion the news whenever a beloved building lost the bid for preservation and was slated to be redone. It was his boss's theory of architectural reincarnation that inspired Ben's own habit of including some homage to the former building—perhaps a pattern in the stone or a shape of a window—within his designs for any replacement. He liked the notion that even buildings could have memories, and could, in turn, be remembered.

"I just feel like my parents did everything right," Nihal said. "They came to this country and built a life for themselves. And I listened to them, I worked my ass off to get into Princeton, and then I kept on studying while I was there, even when half of my classmates seemed to major in beer pong. I thought *I* did everything right, too."

"And your string doesn't negate that," said Sean. "Do you think I did something to put myself in this chair? Or any of the people in this room did something to shorten their strings?"

"No, of course not," said Nihal.

"Then why should you view yourself with any less compassion?"

Several groups concluded at the same time that night, their respective members spilling out onto the sidewalk in front of the school. Hank, Maura, and Ben lingered together on the corner.

"Well, that was a pretty heavy session," Hank said.

"It's been a pretty heavy year," said Maura.

"What do you normally do to cope with things?" he asked.

"Um . . . I don't really know." Maura shrugged. "I guess I just keep living my life."

"Do either of you have any sort of outlet? A way to blow off steam?"

"Isn't that what this group is supposed to be?" asked Ben.

"Well, yeah, but talking can only go so far," Hank said. "Maybe it's because I'm used to working with my hands, but I've always needed something . . . *physical,* as well." An idea seemed to dart across Hank's face. "Why don't you two join me the next time I go?"

"Go where?" Ben asked.

"Just trust me." Hank smiled. "Next weekend. It's best when you time it around sunset."

The following Saturday, Ben waited at the address that Hank had texted him, a massive sporting facility that sprawled along the banks of the Hudson River.

In the lobby, a television screen was filled with flames, the reporter covering the Midsummer bonfires currently being lit throughout Europe. The typical late June tradition had been co-opted this year by a movement across the Continent, encouraging people to throw their boxes and strings into the fires. Since neither could truly be destroyed, the gesture was more symbolic than practical, but thousands had heeded the call nonetheless.

Ben was mesmerized by the footage of crowded beaches in Croatia and Denmark and Finland, hundreds of young people jumping barefoot in the sand as the fires engulfed their boxes. Their rejection of the strings felt even more defiant in light of America's recent move to ban short-stringers from certain posts of authority. While some buckled under the frightening power of the strings, Ben thought, others set them ablaze.

"I gotta say, I was not expecting to meet *here,*" said Maura, suddenly appearing next to Ben. "Oh god, do you think Hank's going to make us rock-climb? Like some metaphor for overcoming obstacles?"

Ben laughed, but just then Hank arrived, carrying three golf clubs instead.

"Oh, I've never golfed before," Maura said warily.

"Me neither," said Ben.

"Well, I used to save lives for a living," said Hank, "so I think I should be capable of teaching you both how to swing a club."

"Okay, Doc," Maura conceded. "But I've gotta say, I hadn't pegged you for having such a bougie hobby."

"I know it *feels* very prim and proper." Hank smiled. "But it's actually a pretty good release. I used to come here after rough days in the ER. And then, this is actually where I came after opening my box."

For a second Ben wondered if Hank would tell Maura the truth about his string. But Hank led them to the elevator without adding a word.

The driving range floated atop the Hudson River, surrounded by netting to stop stray balls from splashing into the water. Ben, Hank, and Maura took the elevator three stories up to the highest floor, and when Ben stepped out onto the elevated platform, cantilevered above the fairway, the first thing he saw was the vibrant layers of color blanketing the sky. Hank was right about the sunset, the clouds gradually blending from indigo to peach to the brightest shades of orange.

Hank gave them both a quick tutorial, then they each approached their own tee.

Maura proved surprisingly adept, hitting the ball straight down the middle of the range.

"Maybe my mom had an affair with Tiger Woods," she mused.

Ben's first swing was an awkward miss, and when he finally made contact with the ball, it shot out sideways and into the netting.

"You'll get the hang of it," said Hank. "Just think of it as therapy, not golf."

Maura began hitting ball after ball, her cathartic monologue playing like a track overlaid atop the whoosh of each swing and the crack of the club against plastic.

"*This* ball is for the fact that I never used to get jealous of anyone. Ever," she said. "And now I'm jealous of every fucking person that walks down the street."

Crack.

"And *this* ball is for the fact that I can't even get angry about it, because being angry all the time will only ruin whatever's left of my life."

Crack.

"And that makes me really fucking angry!"

Crack.

Ben was still struggling to connect his mind with his movements.

Hank suddenly appeared at Ben's side and put his arm on his shoulder. "This isn't the Masters, Ben. Who cares where the ball goes? This is about *you*, and whatever you're feeling now, and channeling that through your arm and down into the ball and out of your body."

"You sound like Sean now," Maura teased.

"Got it?" Hank asked Ben.

"I think so."

Hank took a few steps backward, leaving Ben alone on the platform.

Ben readjusted his grip on the club, his back slightly hunched, and he realized that the last time he had posed in this very position was on his second date with Claire, playing mini-golf on Governors Island, inadvertently crashing a nine-year-old's birthday. On the ferry ride back to Manhattan, Claire's wind-whipped hair kept sticking to her lip balm, and Ben kissed her for the first time during the brief interval when her lips were free.

But that was a long time ago. Before she spoiled everything.

Ben could still hear Maura whacking her golf balls, but his mind was elsewhere now.

It was sitting at the kitchen table. Around seven P.M. A month after the boxes arrived.

You didn't need to die and be reborn in order to shift from one life to the next, Ben thought. That night in the kitchen was the moment that his very existence seemed to splinter, his old life ending and his new one beginning.

It happened while they were eating takeout, which now struck Ben as a ridiculous detail. But the memory always began with Claire fidgeting in her seat as Ben unpacked the chopsticks.

She let him start eating. Why did she let him start eating? Why didn't she just come out and say it?

Claire pushed a dumpling back and forth on her plate.

"How was work today?" Ben asked.

"I have something I need to say, but I don't know how to say it." Claire's face was serious, worrying.

"Okay." Ben wiped his mouth with a paper napkin and straightened his back, bracing.

"I don't think we should stay together."

Her words landed in the space between them, splayed across the kitchen table, and Ben let them settle for a moment, deciding how to react.

"Are you sure?" he asked. He immediately regretted it, what a stupid thing to say. He wished he could take it back.

But then Claire's lips started to quiver, and soon she was crying, and Ben could feel his face burning up.

"What happened?" Ben managed to ask.

His mind flashed through all of their biggest fights from the past year and a half, culminating with the prior week's argument, when they had listened to the president declare that the strings were real, and Claire insisted they look in their boxes together. Ben told her that he wasn't ready.

"I opened my box," Claire said, her face wet with tears.

The sentence was a bullet to his gut. She had opened her box. Without him.

Ben saw her tears and assumed that she was crying for herself. That she had seen her own short string.

"Oh no, Claire, no."

Then came the worst.

"It wasn't mine," she said, barely louder than a whisper.

"What do you mean?"

"Mine was long," she said. "It was yours that . . ." Claire's words melted into heavy sobs.

"Wait . . . let me get this straight." Ben's mind was spinning as he spoke. What exactly did she do? She had looked at her string, that much was clear. But she said that hers was long.

It was *his* that made her cry.

"Oh god." He thought he might vomit.

"Please don't be mad at me," Claire whimpered. "When I saw that mine was long, I just assumed that yours would be, too! I honestly didn't even think it was possible that it wasn't."

Ben shut his eyes and tried to breathe steadily, but he was choking on the air.

"How the hell could you do that?" he shouted. He didn't realize his voice could hold so much anger. "It's one thing to look at yours, but you had no right to look at mine!"

"I know," she said. "I'm so sorry."

Ben stayed silent for several minutes, while Claire cried in the chair across from him, hugging herself tightly. There was simply too much happening, there were too many blows for him to process.

He was trying to focus on her betrayal.

That was safer ground than thinking about what she had seen.

"I wanted so badly for them to be the same. For us to share our lives together," Claire said. "I hope you know that."

He finally had to ask. "How short was it?"

"Mid-forties," she said, her voice hoarse and cracking. "That new website isn't perfectly . . . exact."

Mid-forties.

That gave him fourteen, maybe fifteen more years.

But he would think about that later. Run the calculations later.

For now, he needed to deal with the present crisis, his relationship rupturing right in front of him.

"If you really love me, then why are you leaving? Especially now?" Ben asked.

"Please . . ." Claire hid her face behind her hands.

Ben stared at her, his vision blurring. "Don't you owe me that much?"

Claire took a breath, trying to regain her composure. "I just can't do it," she said. "I can't stay with you and have a countdown clock ticking away the whole time. I'll go crazy." She peered at him, her eyes anguished. "I know I don't deserve your forgiveness, but I'm truly sorry, Ben."

He felt like a tiny sailboat in the middle of a storm surge, and he needed something solid, some anchor for his mind to latch on to, if only for a moment. Ben looked down at Claire's trembling hands on the table. He had held them so many times in the past year and a half, on long walks and in bed, their fingers easily interlaced. He recognized the chipped purple nail polish as one of her favorites. Lucky Lavender, or maybe Lucky Lilac. It was one of the two.

Claire must have noticed him watching her fingers, because she looked down at them, too. And they both kept looking at her shaking hands, because they couldn't look at each other.

But now Ben was staring at his own hands, wrapped around the grip of the club.

"You okay there, Ben?" Maura called over her shoulder.

Another man might have imagined Claire's face on the golf ball and struck it with all his strength. But Ben didn't want to do that. He didn't want to hurt Claire.

He could blame her for betraying him, for not allowing him the chance to choose for himself. But he couldn't really blame her for leaving.

Claire had said it herself, she wasn't strong enough. She needed security, stability. A lifetime guarantee. It was just who she was, and plenty of other people would have reacted the same. Perhaps *most* people would have. That didn't make them bad people. And spending the rest of his life simmering in bitterness and spite wouldn't do anyone any good.

Ben needed to look forward now, not behind.

He squinted at the darkening horizon, where the last slivers of the sun were burning off in a small swirl of fire above the Hudson, like the bonfires on the beaches in Europe, swallowing the strings in their flames.

Then Ben squared his shoulders, swung his arms, and sent the ball soaring toward the river.

HANK

After he had shown Ben and Maura the basics, Hank didn't feel quite as interested in teeing up himself. So he took a seat on one of the benches with a view of the range, watching the tiny white dots dash across the green like shooting stars. The sunset coated everything with a mystical tint, and even the Hudson River below, so often derided by locals, struck Hank as quite beautiful now, its dark ripples tinted pink.

The water reminded Hank of a young woman he had once seen at New York Memorial, sitting on a bed in one of the pre-op rooms. The tips of her long black hair were dyed bright pink, the way that a few of the girls on Hank's block growing up used to dip their hair in Kool-Aid.

"She's waiting for a transplant," Anika said, coming up behind him and offering him a coffee.

It was late May, one of his final days at the hospital and the first that felt like a return to normalcy after the shooting on the fifteenth. The ER had remained vacant for several days after, even once the police had finished their sweep, most patients preferring to travel a few minutes farther to a hospital that wasn't a crime scene. But the city's memory proved remarkably short, and the waiting room was back to capacity by the end of the month, Hank finding only a brief interlude to visit Anika upstairs.

"She's not at the top of the list yet," Anika explained, "but she happened to be here for a checkup when we got the call about a lung that *might* be a match."

"That's great luck," Hank said. "I hope it works out."

"How are *you* doing?" Anika asked, just as the pager at her hip began to sound. "Shit, I've got to handle this. You can have mine, too." Anika handed him her own coffee, the lid still unopened.

"I don't need this much caffeine!" Hank said with a smile, but she was already speeding away.

"I'll take it, if you don't want it."

Hank turned around to see an older woman gesturing toward his spare cup.

"Oh sure, of course." He passed it over.

"Thanks, it's been quite the morning," the woman exhaled, turning her face toward the warmth of the steam. "That's my daughter in there, waiting to hear about the lung."

"I can't even imagine," Hank said. "But it sounds like it might be good news today."

"If this were happening a few months ago, the nerves would have wrecked me," the woman said. She leaned in closer to Hank. "But I know something's going to work out. If not this one, then the next."

Hank was slightly confused, but he admired her faith. He just hoped she was capable of bearing disappointment.

"My daughter hasn't looked at her string. And she made us all promise we wouldn't look, either, but . . . I needed to prepare myself," the woman said, glancing back at her daughter, who was leaning against the pillows of the hospital bed and reading a book. "It was long." The woman smiled. "My baby's string is long."

"That's amazing," Hank said. "Truly."

"Just don't tell her I told you!" The woman took a sip of her coffee.

"Wait, you haven't told your daughter that her string is long?"

"She made me *swear* not to look." The woman shook her head ominously. "She'll hate me if she learns that I did."

Hank thought for a moment about Anika peeking at his string in the kitchen, how briefly betrayed he had felt. And Hank had privately theorized, from the way Ben spoke about his own experience—always "when my box was opened," and never "when I opened my box"—that perhaps an even greater betrayal had befallen him.

"I'm sure your daughter would forgive you," Hank said. "Especially once she heard the great news."

"You don't know her," the woman said. "When she puts her mind to something, she can do anything. Even holding a grudge. She'll have her new lease on life soon enough. She never needs to know that I looked behind her back. All that matters now is that she's going to live."

What a peculiar new world these strings had fashioned, Hank thought. For all the sadness, and deceit, and broken trust, for all the times that Hank had watched someone arriving at the hospital, gripping their box in fear, at least there was this: Hope for the mother of an ailing child. The grace in knowing that prayers would be answered.

Hank had followed up with Anika a few days later, asking if the daughter's surgery went through.

"Unfortunately, we heard from the donor's sister that he was treated for cancer last year," she said. "We couldn't use the lung."

And yet, there was no need for despair. Hank could hear the mother's words. If not this one, then the next.

He leaned his body weight into the bench, soothed by the staccato rhythm of the clubs striking the tees. How strange, Hank thought, to be the woman with the pink-tipped hair, anxiously unaware of the salvation, the gift, awaiting her.

But Hank noticed, then, that Ben was still struggling at his tee. So he stood up and approached Ben from the side, careful to avoid his swinging club, and rested an arm on his shoulder, ready to offer some reassurance.

JACK

Jack usually didn't remember his dreams, but the morning after he proposed the switch, he woke up, groggy and fatigued, having dreamt of his grandfather.

Grandpa Cal was the only member of Jack's family who never made him feel like an outsider, who had treated both Jack *and* Javier with the respect of a fellow soldier.

Jack had introduced them at a football game during freshman year, when Cal had the wispy white hair and arched back of any man in his early nineties, but still boasted the mental clarity of someone years younger. Jack listened as his grandfather recounted the familiar tale of lying about his age so he could enlist in the Second World War, when he was an impressively tall but still-pimpled teenager.

"What you boys are doing is a noble calling," Cal told Jack and Javi, the three of them huddled close against the wind ripping through the bleachers before kickoff. "We tend to only hear stories about the bad ones, but the men I met in the service were some of the finest people I've ever known."

Jack had heard it all before, at nearly every family gathering, but he was pleased to see Javi so engrossed.

"Before we could do any fighting," Cal continued, "we spent sixteen weeks training up in New England, and a couple of the older guys sort of adopted me into their group. They snuck me some of their cigars and took me to movies on our nights off. This one boy in particular, Simon

Starr, he really took me under his wing. Never let anybody say a mean word to me.

"But when they eventually gave us our assignments, it turned out that I was heading to the Pacific, while those older guys were being sent to Europe. And I'm sure Jack has told you that most of the men in my family have served in some way or another, so it was always expected that I would enlist at some point, but the war pulled me in at a much younger age than any of us could have anticipated, and no matter how prepared you may think you are, you can't help but be afraid before shipping off."

Javi nodded silently.

"Well, Simon could see that I was pretty upset about being separated from the group, so he pulled me aside and dug into his pocket for a little prayer card that he always carried around with him. He said it was the Hashkiveinu, a Jewish prayer asking God to protect you through the night. His fiancée back home had given it to him. And would you believe that he gave that prayer card to me? He told me it would keep me safe."

Cal was shaking his head, as if he still couldn't believe what had happened all those decades ago. "And I'm a Christian man myself, but I kept that prayer tucked inside my uniform every day, and Simon was right. It kept me safe."

"Did you stay in touch with Simon and the others after the war?" Javi asked.

Whenever his grandfather reached this part, Jack could see the shame on his face, the remorse. Grandpa Cal's story—of his panic before heading out alone overseas and his regret of what came after—was one of the few times that Jack had ever seen a Hunter willingly drop the steely familial facade and expose themselves as vulnerable.

"I'm not proud to admit this," Cal said, "but I don't actually know what happened to Simon, or any of the others. I wanted to look them up when I finally got home, but truthfully, I was scared. As long as I don't know what happened, I can picture each of them old and wrinkled like myself, surrounded by kids and grandkids. Hell, I can even picture them in these very bleachers, cheering on our team today. And I'd like to think that's why none of them ever came looking for me, either."

Jack and Javier were both quiet as Cal surveyed the stands.

"Look, boys, I'm old, but I'm not blind," Cal said. "I know things are different now. I knew times had changed when I saw how terribly we treated those men who came back from Vietnam. But, to me, there's no finer way you can dedicate your life. And I consider it an honor and a privilege to have served alongside my fellow soldiers. I believe that I owe my life and my good fortune to God. But I also owe it to those men."

Jack and Javi knew exactly what he meant. They couldn't even count the number of times they had stayed up late quizzing one another for exams or cheered each other on through mud and rain. It was the only way they made it through.

In the backseat of a black van, on the way to Cal's funeral the following summer, Jack's father had handed him a small envelope. *For my grandson* was written on the front. Jack turned his face to the side to keep his father from seeing his tears.

Not wanting to get up just yet, Jack rolled over in bed and lay on his chest. In a strange way, he was thankful that Grandpa Cal hadn't lived to see the strings. Even after all the horrors he must have witnessed in the war, Cal was a man of such pure faith—faith in his God, faith in his country. Who knows how this maddening new world might have affected him?

Jack sighed and turned his head on the pillow, staring at the thin ray of sunlight circumventing the window shade and striking his dresser, where an old and faded Hashkiveinu prayer card sat tucked inside the top drawer.

Of course, Jack was even more grateful that his grandfather wasn't around to learn that he, too, was planning to lie to the army—only Jack's lie was meant to get himself *out* of battle.

JAVIER

Javier woke up and stared at the date on his alarm clock. Only two days left to decide.

He squeezed his eyes shut, wondering if he should pray on it, until they floated back to him in the darkness, the apparitions of the night before. The visions that had played and replayed while he straddled the border between sleep and consciousness, while his mind tried to process Jack's offer.

The flag and the priest and his sad, shaking head.

He was a true American hero, until his last breath.

"What about your dad?" Javi asked Jack. "You'll have to tell him we switched strings, or he'll think . . ."

"I know," Jack said.

He decided to tell his father that the switch was Javi's idea, that he had only agreed in order to help a brother in arms. His dad would hate that they were deceiving the army, but hopefully he would respect his son's loyalty to a friend.

Jack's dad was the only person who would hear about the switch. Nobody else could know. Especially not his aunt Katherine, who was somewhere in Middle America, or maybe Florida by now, trying to convince a county of swing voters to donate to his uncle's campaign. It was certainly not the time for a family scandal. They would simply have to believe that Jack's string was *truly* short.

"And what about . . . after?" Javi asked. "Won't everyone be confused?"

"I guess we've still got a few years to figure that out," Jack said. While he had planned what he would tell his father, Jack hadn't plotted much further than that. "And who knows, maybe the strings won't be such a big deal by then anyway."

Javier was hesitant. Plunging headlong into such a tangled situation, without an exit strategy, felt like everything the academy had taught them *not* to do.

But they had also been trained to be brave, even in the face of uncertainty.

"Okay," Javi said. "I'm in."

Dear B,

When I walk through my neighborhood, I often pass by this spectacular apartment building called the Van Woolsey. I'm sure you've seen it—it's gorgeous and spans an entire block along Broadway. The entrance is guarded not only by a massive iron gate with its name in gold lettering, but also by an actual security guard in a small gatehouse, so only those fortunate enough to live there can get in. Like Buckingham Palace on the Upper West Side. From the sidewalk, you can peek between the bars of the front gate and see the center courtyard, a mini park with perfectly trimmed hedges and white stone benches surrounding a tiered fountain.

I suppose everyone in New York has some place that becomes a symbol of their alternate life, their dream life. Maybe it's the theater in Times Square where you're desperate to perform, or the Brooklyn dive bar you're saving up to buy. The Van Woolsey is mine.

Whenever I walk past the building, I imagine what it would be like to live there, in one of those multimillion-dollar apartments I could never afford on my teacher's salary. And I could sit on the bench by the fountain and reminisce about all the fantastic places I've traveled and the people I've met and the books I've read and the students I've taught. And I could look up from the bench and see into my apartment, a few floors up, where my imaginary husband and children are cooking a dinner together that I can smell when the breeze is just right, carrying the aromas from the open window.

I feel foolish and shallow whenever I think about it, especially now that everything's changed and the future seems so much more fragile. And I know it's really such a boring dream, not particularly unique. But it's not really about the money or the opulence or the appearance of success. That version of myself who lives in the Van Woolsey has everything settled on the inside, too. She looks at her life and simply feels satisfied. She doesn't need to spend time on fantasies anymore, because she's already living in one.

And I suppose that's why I can't look at my string, because as long as I haven't looked, then I can still imagine the day when I'll be that woman on the bench in the courtyard of the Van Woolsey. Any of the daydreams might still come true.

—A

NINA

On Sunday night, while Maura was attending her weekly group, Nina asked Amie to join her for dinner at a new restaurant downtown.

Her sister was running late, so Nina settled at a table by herself. She had read about the restaurant's opening, a few days prior, and recognized the story: the short-stringer chef who had been denied a loan, and the sibling who crowdsourced the money. She had seen it first on String Theory, back when she was checking the website regularly.

Nina hadn't visited the site in quite some time, nor had she read any of the other blogs or forums, despite new ones cropping up daily. She had stopped her searching rather abruptly after her fight with Maura, fending off the pull of the online sirens.

Nina noticed a paper flyer taped to the menu at her table, advertising for an open mic night next week, and in the back of the dining room she spotted a small platform and a microphone stand. She couldn't help but imagine Maura up on that stage, her face partially obscured by the microphone though still obviously beautiful, performing an enthusiastic, if slightly sharp, homage to Amy Winehouse. It was hard to believe that more than two years had passed since Nina was sitting at the bar with Sarah, her college roommate, and first spotted Maura.

The karaoke bar had been Sarah's idea. Whenever she visited New York, she liked to relive the musical theater days of her youth—when her crowning achievement was being cast as Adelaide in her high school's *Guys and Dolls*—by attending a Broadway show and singing karaoke downtown.

After Maura bowed off the stage, Sarah insisted that Nina introduce herself. "You should go talk to her. She's pretty."

"I can't do that," Nina demurred.

"Why not?" Sarah asked.

"Well, for one thing, I don't even know if she's gay."

"Oh please, only lesbians sing 'Valerie.'"

"That's ridiculous," said Nina. "It's just a crowd-pleaser. And it was originally written by a *man*."

Sarah just rolled her eyes. "You don't need to fact-check everything."

"Well, even if she *is* gay," Nina said, "I don't go up to strangers at bars like you do."

"Are you saying I'm a slut?" Sarah feigned offense.

"No! I'm saying you have confidence. Something I've always had less of."

"You're confident enough to tear apart any piece of writing with that red pen of yours. You certainly did it to my papers often enough."

"That's different. It's work."

"This is work, too," Sarah said. "And eighty percent of success is showing up." A sip of her vodka cranberry punctuated the thought.

Though they hadn't seen each other in six months, since Sarah's last trip in from Los Angeles, they easily fell into their old rhythm, with Sarah doling out romantic advice and Nina wondering whether to listen.

When they were randomly assigned as roommates their freshman year, Nina never thought that she would befriend Sarah, a bubbly blonde whose hair possessed the preternatural power to dry in smooth, shiny ringlets. But during their third week of sharing bunkbeds, Nina divulged that she was gay, and Sarah, happy that there was one less girl competing for the top guys on campus, decided to take the quiet Nina under her J.Crew-clad wing.

For Sarah, dating was a game, flirtation a means of piquing a man's interest and tempting him with a challenge. She shared her method with Nina: Strike up a conversation, dangle your attentions, but always, always, make *him* ask you out. And Nina grasped at that rule like a shield. If she let the other women take the lead, then she never had to put herself *too* far out there. She never had to feel vulnerable.

And just looking at Maura onstage—her confidence, her radiance, the way she captivated an entire audience without even being *that* skilled as a singer—made Nina feel particularly vulnerable. She felt utterly dull in comparison.

By the time Nina had worked up the courage to speak, Maura had already retreated to the bar, taking a seat among a group of what looked like coworkers, still in their slacks and skirts. Luckily, she was perched on a stool near the edge of the group, easy to approach.

Just do it, Nina told herself. She hadn't gone on a date in over a year—working overtime to earn a promotion was the excuse she gave whenever Amie or their mother probed—and a push from Sarah was probably her best chance to get one.

Nina cleared her throat. "That was a great performance up there."

"Oh, thanks!" The singer tilted her head and smiled. "Are you planning to serenade us tonight, too?"

"Oh no, I have crippling stage fright."

"Well, the night's still young. You have time to get over that."

"I'm Nina."

The woman laughed when Nina stuck out her hand for a formal shake. "Maura."

"Are you here with your coworkers?"

Maura nodded. "We're celebrating. I work at a publishing house, and we just won a vicious bidding war for a big YA series. Basically the next *Harry Potter*."

"Oh wow, congratulations! Which publisher do you work for?"

"Now, *that* I can't tell you," Maura said coyly. "Technically I'm not allowed to say anything until the press release is out."

"Well, that's probably best, since I do work for a magazine."

"Oh shit! I probably shouldn't have said anything at all." Maura laughed again.

"It's okay." Nina smiled. "I promise to keep your secret."

With Maura, things were instantly different. Nina found herself, for the first time, wanting to be the pursuer instead of waiting to be pursued, Sarah's advice be damned. She may have been willing to risk her prior relations for the sake of maintaining her shield, but she felt in her gut that something had changed. Nina was stunned that a woman like Maura, bold and proud and unafraid, would ever take an interest in someone as plain and anxious as she was. So she traded her lonely apartment for concerts in Brooklyn, hot yoga classes, wine tastings, book-launch parties.

On her dates with the women before Maura, Nina always made sure that she was the second one to arrive, never wanting to wait around nervously or appear too eager.

But with Maura, she showed up early.

"I'm *so* sorry I'm late!" Amie apologized, clumsily dropping down in the chair across from her sister. "I missed my stop again."

"What were you reading this time?" Nina asked.

"*Lady Susan*," Amie confessed. "I was in the mood for an epistolary novel, since I've, well, it doesn't matter . . . but then I realized it's my final Austen, which is quite sad."

Nina smiled, remembering the time during college that she sent Amie a copy of *Northanger Abbey* with a mock warning label taped to the cover: *See where all your wild fantasies might lead?!*

Amie looked up from the menu. "Did you hear about that crazy database?" she asked. "My neighbors were talking about it in the laundry room."

"What database?"

"Apparently it's some massive Google spreadsheet that claims to be tracking the string length of everyone in New York," Amie explained. "And it's like Wikipedia, so anyone can edit it with whatever information they have, about themselves, or . . . someone else. Supposedly they hit sixty thousand names yesterday."

"Oh my god." Nina's voice shriveled to a whisper. "That's . . ."

"Terrifying," Amie finished for her. "I think the police are trying to find the original creator, but it's taken on a life of its own. My neighbor showed it to me on his phone. Gave me chills."

"It's such an invasion of privacy," Nina said. "What if you didn't know that someone put your name down? Exposed something so personal about you?"

An uneasy tremor slithered through Nina's body, reminding her of the day she was outed at school. She was almost too afraid to ask Amie the question, but she needed to hear the answer. "Do you know if Maura . . ."

Amie understood. "I did a name search of the document on his phone and didn't see anyone I know."

"Oh thank god," Nina said. Then she desperately wanted to change the subject. She wanted just one night that wasn't laden with stress and sadness. A fun dinner with her sister, just like old times.

Nina steeled herself with a cleansing breath. "Well, on a brighter note, this would be a pretty good date spot, right? Sharing tapas is very romantic." Nina nudged her sister with her eyebrows. "Maybe you can bring someone here, and then Mom will stop pestering *me* about your lack of love life."

Amie shook her head in mock frustration while reaching for a piece of bread. "She has *no* idea how weird it is to date now. As if it weren't hard enough before! It's like there's this string-size elephant in the room the entire time."

Nina just nodded. The old times were gone, and she was foolish to want otherwise.

"So, I'm guessing there isn't anyone special right now?" Nina asked.

"Only you, my dear sister." Amie grinned as she bit into the slice of bread.

"Well, maybe if you stopped hogging the bread basket and learned to share . . ." Nina teased, pulling the dish closer to her.

"Hey!" Amie dipped two fingertips in her glass of water and flicked a drop at her sister, like they were two kids back in their parents' kitchen, fighting over the last french fry on the plate.

"Don't embarrass me!" Nina smiled. "This is a nice restaurant."

Amie laughed. "Okay, Mom."

The old times *were* gone, Nina thought. But at least this remained.

JACK

Jack missed the old times. Before graduation, before the strings, before he and Javi were forced to open their boxes and reveal their strings to the army. Before his uncle became a household name.

Anthony was never supposed to get this famous. He was never supposed to have this many fans—and a worrisome number of opponents. After the strings arrived, Jack assumed that Anthony's limp campaign would barely last through spring. But here he was, in August now, less than a year out from the conventions and only gaining momentum.

Ever since the June debate, Anthony's speeches earned more and more attention, and Katherine kept pressuring Jack to attend their events. (Apparently it was crucial, in the wake of the controversial STAR Initiative, to showcase Anthony's military support.)

Katherine had just invited Jack to join them at a massive rally in Manhattan, but he was still deciding whether or not to go. He hadn't yet told his aunt and uncle about his "short string," and he wasn't sure how much longer he could stall. Eventually someone would ask.

Jack was trying to delay that talk as long as possible. He had already suffered through one false admission, last month at the army recruiting office, the memory of which continued to haunt him: Jack sitting in the chair across from Major Riggs, his thighs starting to sweat, worrying that the droplets might seep through his pants and expose him as a hideous imposter. He had tried to lift his legs up slightly, imperceptibly, so they wouldn't press quite as closely against the seat.

"Have you already opened the box yourself?" the major asked.

"Yes, sir."

"And?"

"It's quite short, sir. Five or six more years, at most."

Major Riggs noiselessly slid the box toward himself—the chest bearing Jack Hunter's name, holding Javier García's fate—and measured the string for himself, his lips pursed tightly, his focus intent. He didn't seem to enjoy this particular assignment, invading the lives of his fellow soldiers. But he wore a tough face.

"I'm very sorry about that," said the major, recording the official length for his notes. And Jack realized, then, that it didn't matter if he was visibly anxious. It didn't even matter that the pen had nearly slipped out of his hand as he struggled to sign the affidavit. Major Riggs would simply assume that he was upset about his string.

Jack turned on the TV in his apartment, desperate for a distraction from thoughts of his uncle and memories of Major Riggs, and happily landed on the Nationals game. But the fourth inning had barely begun when the game cut to commercial and a new "Rollins for America" ad started playing.

The face of a petite blonde woman filled the screen.

"My name is Louisa," the woman said, "and I was walking near the Capitol on the morning of June tenth, when the bomb went off. When a short-stringer set off the explosive that he had spent weeks building."

The camera pulled back to reveal that the woman was seated, missing one of her legs.

"I understand the pain this man must have felt after seeing his short string. But why did he have to thrust that same pain onto so many others?" Louisa's eyes glistened as she spoke. "I trust Congressman Anthony Rollins to keep our cities safe, so no other innocent bystanders will have to suffer what I went through."

Anthony was really laying it on thick, Jack thought. What happened to that woman was undeniably terrible, but it wasn't exactly a daily occurrence. Nor had the country been some bastion of peace *before* the strings arrived.

Toward the end of the ad, Anthony himself appeared. "That's why I'm a proud member of the presidential task force created in response to the strings, as well as an original supporter of the STAR Initiative and future legislation that will protect all Americans, like Louisa, from further violence," he said. "I'm Anthony Rollins, and I approve this message."

Jack was shocked. *Anthony* was a part of the president's task force? *Anthony* helped create the STAR Initiative?

"Shit!" Jack shouted.

His own uncle was the reason why Jack and Javi had to look inside their boxes. The reason they had to switch their strings and lie to everyone around them. The reason Jack had to sign his name, willfully perjuring himself, under the pitying gaze of Major Riggs.

Jack grabbed his water bottle from the cushion next to him and hurled it toward Anthony's face. "Shit! Shit!"

The plastic bottle bounced loudly off the screen, spraying its remaining droplets into the air just as the baseball game resumed.

Thank god Javi wasn't around to see this ad, Jack thought, to realize just how culpable Anthony was—along with the rest of Jack's family, who stood behind him.

And now Anthony wanted Jack to join him in New York, to stand there stupidly onstage, while his uncle bragged about drafting the very decree that had fucked up Jack's and Javi's lives forever.

Families support each other, Jack heard his father's voice. *Especially ones like ours.*

ANTHONY

Anthony was ready.

His speech sat in bulleted form on a series of note cards in his lap, and he leaned back in his cushioned beige seat as his campaign bus, with "Rollins for America" splayed across its side paneling, steadily made its way from D.C. to a park in downtown Manhattan, where a sizable crowd was gathering to hear Anthony speak and an equally sizable crowd was gathering in protest.

Anthony's campaign manager had warned them about the demonstrators.

"Should we be worried?" Katherine asked.

"There'll be plenty of security," said the manager. "And the bomb dogs have already sniffed the place."

"I meant about the optics." Katherine frowned.

"Well, we knew this was a possibility when we decided to use the strings as a talking point," said the manager. "But honestly, I take it as a sign that your husband's star is rising. People wouldn't show up for just anybody."

"Maybe we'll even get lucky and some crazy protesters will throw a few punches," Anthony mused. "Nobody likes an angry mob."

And as the bus rolled up to the congested park, it was indeed difficult for Anthony and Katherine to discern which of the clamorous hordes comprised their supporters and which might be there to cause trouble.

HANK

Hank was ready.

He was about to meet some friends from the support group at the protest downtown, where Anthony Rollins was due to speak, and he felt like he was finally *doing* something, for the first time since leaving the hospital.

As he finished his coffee, he turned on the news, where reporters were still covering the past week of demonstrations in China.

"For any viewers just tuning in, we're following the fourth day of protests under way in Beijing," the anchor announced. Video footage showed several thousand people blockading the streets in the city's central business district.

"A few months ago, the Chinese government called upon all citizens to report their string length as part of a national data registry, claiming it was for the public's protection and official recordkeeping," the anchor explained. "And while there was some international outcry surrounding the ambiguity of those motives, most notably within the EU and the U.S., it was the sudden arrests, earlier this month, of three Beijing residents who refused to comply with the order that inspired these larger protests we're seeing now."

Hank assumed that the ongoing coverage of Beijing had partly inspired the crowds expected today in New York. It was hard to hear Anthony Rollins's speeches and not worry that America was treading closer and closer to China's sweeping mandates.

It was rumored that Anthony Rollins was among the key forces behind the government's latest policies, and his stunt at the June debate was viewed by many as the spark that ignited the current discrimination against short-stringers, spreading from Congress into nearly every community. According to the event page on Facebook, nearly twelve thousand participants planned to converge on the small Manhattan park where Anthony's rally was being held, bearing posters and megaphones and flags to voice their outrage.

Hank remembered when Anika had dragged him to the March for Science. He hadn't wanted to go at first. He wasn't convinced it would have any impact.

"Maybe it won't," Anika said. "But I'll tell you the same thing I told my friends at the Women's March. We don't *just* march because we hope it will trigger change. We march to remind them of our numbers. To remind them that they can't forget about us."

Hank turned off the TV and set out.

Inside the park, Hank was surrounded by signs. "Short-Stringers Stand Together!" "A Long String Is Overcompensating." "Equality for All." "We Are More Than Our Strings!"

He was surprised by how overwhelmed he felt. It was a beautiful sight, this kaleidoscope of neon posters, of words both snarky and sincere.

The feeling that overtook Hank in that moment transported him to another time and place, some two decades ago, when his old girlfriend Lucy took him by the hand and led him to the maternity ward during their first week of training at the hospital, and the two of them gazed through the glass at the rows of newborns—sleeping, squirming, yawning, crying. Lucy's eyes grew teary, but Hank didn't want to cry in front of the girl he was still trying to impress. So he just stood there, staring at the future. At a dozen blank canvases in bassinets, still unmarred by the world outside the ward. A dozen reasons to have hope.

Many of Hank's classmates said they wanted to become doctors to be a part of something bigger than themselves. Hank had always nodded along when they spoke, but he never really understood what they meant. He just wanted to help people.

But here, amid the crowd, as his gaze swept from face to face, he understood.

In the background, Hank could hear Rollins arriving onstage to a mixture of cheers and heckling, but he didn't want to turn around just yet. He wanted to watch the field of protesters for just another moment.

Until Hank's roaming eye came into focus.

An auburn-haired woman was moving swiftly through the crowd, bumping into people and hastily brushing them off as she moved toward the front, her right hand tucked inside her jacket, like she was holding on to something.

Fuck. Hank felt it in his stomach. The same gut response, the same nauseating sense of assuredness that he could feel when a patient was brought into the ER with barely a chance of survival. His body had a knack for knowing when something awful was about to happen.

Someone was introducing Rollins at the microphone behind him, heralding the congressman's courage and conviction and faith, but Hank could hardly hear it. He was following the woman, inching closer and closer to her, trying to figure out what she was planning. Maybe it was just a particularly pointed sign, or a bottle of pig's blood. Whatever it was, she was determined.

He was only a few feet away from her when she finally pulled out a gun.

Hank had been driven by an instinctive impulse his entire life—it allowed him to stay alert during twelve-hour shifts, to stick his hand inside a gushing wound and pinch the artery with his fingers, to run toward the gunshots that morning in May at New York Memorial Hospital. It was that same impulse that pushed him now.

He didn't think about the obvious danger to himself. He didn't think about his string. He thought only of this moment, of the people in peril around him.

He couldn't save his ER from the shooter in May. This time would be different.

Hank saw the woman's hand on the grip.

Her fingers quivered slightly, two full seconds of hesitation. Enough time for Hank to jump in front of the gun, just as she made her decision to pull the trigger.

ANTHONY

Anthony had only just registered the sound of a gun firing when he was suddenly crushed under a swarm of security guards and cops and pulled from the stage to an awaiting van. The panicked shrieks of the crowd were instantly silenced as the bulletproof door slammed behind him.

"What happened?" he asked the driver.

"We're not sure yet."

"Where's Katherine?"

"She's secure. They've got her in the next car."

Anthony nodded and looked down at his suit, which had been crumpled during his chaotic exit.

He was safe.

Katherine was safe.

He had just survived what was, in all likelihood, a targeted shooting. An assassination attempt. On *his* life.

Holy shit, Anthony thought. Somebody out there wanted to kill him.

He had always had a few enemies: the rival frat brothers in college, an obnoxious law school nemesis, a colleague at the DA's office angling for the same promotions. But this was different. This was dangerous.

For a moment Anthony was truly scared.

But then he remembered his long string, and the three more decades it promised him, and the fact that, despite his wrinkled Armani, he was totally unscathed.

A second thought followed soon after.

This was, quite possibly, the best thing to happen to his campaign.

People would sympathize with him, be inspired by him, see him as a triumphant survivor. How many political leaders had defied plots to take them out? Teddy Roosevelt, Richard Nixon, Ronald Reagan. And he, Anthony Rollins, Virginia congressman, had just joined their elite ranks. Thanks to a gunman with horrible aim, he was that much closer to the Oval Office.

In the coming days, he would surely craft a poignant speech condemning the violence and hatred that sought to strike him down, grieving any tragic casualties, and calling upon his fellow Americans to march on in the face of fear.

They'll eat it up, Anthony thought. *I'll be a goddamn hero.*

HANK

The woman was trying to help him, that much he could tell. She had shot him, and now she wanted to save him.

"No no no no no no," she begged over and over. "I wasn't aiming for you!"

The shooter pressed her hands firmly against the hole in his stomach, her tears falling hard and fast. Her face was so close to Hank's that he could see the water streaking down her cheeks and the bubbles forming in her nostrils. Loose strands of auburn hair were grazing Hank's nose.

"I'm sorry," she sobbed. "I'm so sorry."

Her arms were still stretched out toward him as a few brave bystanders descended, pulling her up and away.

The woman was replaced by more familiar faces, Lea and Terrell, kneeling down to take over and apply pressure to Hank's wound, which suddenly hurt like a motherfucker, the adrenaline starting to wear off, his skin burning and his ears ringing.

"You're gonna be okay," Lea whispered.

"It's fine, he's gonna be fine!" Terrell was shouting, trying to calm everyone down. "He's still got a few years left like the rest of us."

Hank tilted his head and caught a glimpse of Ben, his body shuddering as he gripped Maura's hand. Ben would have to explain to them all.

Then a third set of faces arrived. EMTs with a stretcher and an oxygen mask.

As a doctor, Hank had witnessed the final moments of 129 patients.

Each one he remembered more vividly than any of his memories with Lucy and Anika, or with his parents while he was growing up. The peaceful moments, and the violent ones. The expected, and the shocking. He could picture every flatline on the monitor. A string spread taut across the screen.

Hank had always wanted his own moment to be quiet, but the commotion of the crowd and the sirens of the ambulance ensured that it would not be.

As the rubber straps of the oxygen mask were pulled over his head, Hank wondered what was coming. He was terrified as hell, and he had only hope to hold on to. Hope that it was somewhere nice. Hope that his father would be there, waiting. Hope that his mother would be okay and that, in time, she would be there, too.

Ben's was the last face that Hank saw before shutting his eyes. Ben had evidently run after the EMTs and alongside the stretcher, managing to reach Hank just before they loaded him into the ambulance.

"All those people with the long strings who you thought you saved," Ben said, "you *did* save them. Their strings were long because you were *meant* to save them. Their strings were long because of *you*."

Ben's face quickly receded into the distance, locked away behind the ambulance door, and Hank closed his eyes, alone with his hope.

JACK

Jack was supposed to be at that rally in Manhattan. Katherine had urged him to attend, but Jack lied and said he was sick.

Thank god he hadn't been there to witness it. To see an innocent man *killed* at his uncle's event, his body ripped by the bullet meant for Anthony. He couldn't understand how things had come to this point, how his family's actions had turned fatal. How, on a hot day at the end of August, Jack found himself staring at the photo of the man who had died, mere feet from his aunt and uncle.

In the picture, the doctor had short black hair, deep lines around his grin, the lightest shadow of stubble on his cheeks, a stethoscope resting around his neck. It was probably his official headshot, Jack thought, the portrait from the hospital directory.

Jack asked his father how Anthony and Katherine were holding up.

"Your aunt's obviously shaken that they were targeted by this maniac," his father said. "But overall, I think they're doing remarkably well. Your uncle's polling even higher since the attack."

Doing remarkably well? Back to focusing on polls? Hadn't they watched a man get shot?

Jack didn't want to believe that his own family could have caused this man's death. Sure, many of his relatives had fought in wars, but this was different. This was a park in Manhattan, not a combat zone. And, until that summer, Jack honestly believed that his family's greatest transgressions had been committed against their own, against the members like

Jack and his mother, who couldn't fit the mold handcrafted by their ancestors.

Jack knew, in many ways, that he was lucky to be a Hunter, with all
their comforts and connections. But Anthony's campaign had unleashed
something new, something darker, something that made all the other
family faults seem trivial.

Most reports on the shooting exclaimed that the doctor had "saved"
Congressman Rollins's life, but Jack read one article online in which a
friend explained that the victim, Hank, had actually been attending the
anti-Rollins protest.

Was it really Hank's hatred for Anthony that led to his death? His
passion for the short-stringers' cause? Jack wanted to pinpoint the ra-
tionale, the motivation that Hank apparently felt was worth jumping
in front of a gun for. As hard as he tried—and, indeed, at the academy
he tried over and over—Jack still couldn't imagine feeling *anything* so
strongly that he would willingly risk his life for it. He had seen that
commitment in his fellow cadets, and he saw it in Javier, who was still
zealously pursuing his path of service even after receiving his string.
Jack wondered what it would feel like to be so certain, so devoted. To
feel that nothing about you was a mistake.

Jack pulled up in front of his aunt and uncle's house, inhaling deeply.
He had to do it today. No matter how many hours he spent ruminating
over his family's flaws, they were still his family. He couldn't hide from
them forever. And he already told the army about his "short string," so
he needed to make it look real.

But he had consciously chosen the afternoon, when Anthony would
be at work, and he would only have to face his aunt.

"Thank goodness you weren't at the rally with that horrible protest," Katherine said, pulling her nephew into her arms. Jack's father
winced at anything too physically intimate, but Katherine was always
a hugger.

"I know it's been a crazy time for you and Uncle Anthony, but I, uh,
I came because I have to tell you something," Jack said, as Katherine
poured him a cup of coffee. "I'm sure you know that I had to complete

a string disclosure for the army, so I wanted you to hear it from me that . . . it's short."

Katherine's hand trembled as she put down the pot. "How short?" she whispered.

"It seems to end somewhere between twenty-six and twenty-eight," he said. (Jack always referred to the short string as *it*, fully detached from himself. He could never quite utter the words *I* or *my*.)

"Oh, Jack, no, I don't know what to say. I'm so sorry." Katherine's voice broke with tears.

"It's okay. Please don't cry for me," Jack pleaded, suddenly uncomfortable with her reaction. But what else had he expected? He knew his aunt could be just as blindly ambitious as his uncle, standing beside him no matter what. But she was still the one who had given Jack those G.I. Joe and Captain America action figures as a kid, who carried frozen meals to his house in the wake of his mom's departure. Of course she would cry at the news.

He just didn't deserve her tears.

"Really, I'm doing okay," he assured her, though he couldn't help but think that his whole dilemma was her own husband's doing. If only he could say something on behalf of Javier, perhaps even trust her with the truth.

After his mother abandoned him, Jack had looked to his aunt, his father's little sister, to fill the empty space. And, sometimes, she managed to do so. But she never wanted to be Jack's mother. She wanted to be Mrs. Rollins.

She wanted the picture-perfect marriage, the coveted social status, reigning over dinner parties and fundraisers and yacht clubs and maybe, someday, the whole country. And Hunters always got what they wanted.

"You're very brave," Katherine finally said. "The whole family would be proud."

And that might have been worse than the tears.

A weak, "Thanks," was all Jack could muster. "But I should probably be heading back," he said. "Try to beat the traffic."

"Well, I'm here if you need me," Katherine added. "Your uncle is, too."

Somehow, Jack doubted that last part.

Katherine smiled at him as she opened the door, and Jack slid out of the house and into his car, relieved to be alone.

Back at his apartment, Jack flopped onto the bed, exhausted and queasy with guilt.

The lying was hard enough; did his aunt have to praise his stoic courage? His classic Hunter bravery? Making the family proud?

He hadn't earned her admiration, and he certainly didn't deserve her pity. It made Jack sick to think that she was crying for him, for the short string she thought he had, while there was nobody crying for Javier. *He* was the one who was truly brave, not Jack.

When Jack sat up, he stared straight into his closet, the door ajar and exposing the sloppy piles of clothes on the floor, the jackets slouching on hangers. The army never would have tolerated this mess. And they certainly wouldn't have tolerated the lies he told his aunt, falsehoods formed out of fear.

When Jack spotted his uniform hanging in the back, freshly pressed and still protected by the plastic dry-cleaning bag, something set off inside of him. He ran over to the closet and started clawing at the pieces—sweatshirts on hangers, T-shirts on shelves, a folded pair of sweatpants—anything from the academy or the army, any proof that he once tried to fit in. Then he gathered all the offending items into a rumpled heap in his arms, turned back toward his room, and shoved the whole lot of them under his bed.

ANTHONY

It was just as Anthony expected, his numbers skyrocketed after the rally. His message was resonating. The people were scared. And they were looking to him for help.

Just when Anthony thought it couldn't get any better, the police found a box with a short string while searching the apartment of his would-be assassin, revealing she had only a few years left. She must have been driven mad, the public concluded. Yet another reason why short-stringers couldn't be trusted, why Anthony was right all along.

The news set Twitter ablaze.

Another pyscho short-stringer!! No surprise there!

The hospital, the mall, the bombing, now this. We can't let these people keep terrorizing our country!

My child's fourth-grade teacher has a short string. Should I be worried for her safety at school?

To everyone who keeps defending the shooter and blaming Congressman Rollins: Shame on you! A short string shouldn't excuse murder.

What dumbass let that feminazi short-stringer get her hands on a gun anyway??

Anthony didn't much care what the peons of the Internet were arguing about, but his campaign manager was particularly pleased. The national discussion seemed to be shifting further in their favor.

The strings were still a relatively new phenomenon, so any violence spawned by their arrival was a *new* kind of violence. The fact that the rally shooter turned out to be a woman only helped Anthony's cause. Before the strings, it was rare for the country to see female assailants, but now *anyone* with a short string could be viewed as a potential threat. The old methods of law-and-order simply wouldn't cut it anymore. And Anthony was the only candidate positioning himself as a fighter equipped for the battle.

Though Wes Johnson was still attempting his appeal to the better angels, most of the other candidates had been hampered by some stereotype: The Ivy League professor was too out-of-touch, the brash governor too uncouth, the conservative congresswoman too maternal. Anthony had been smart to latch on to the strings, to associate himself with the most salient issue before anyone could label *him*, or, worse, deem him irrelevant.

It only took a few days before people started demanding that short-stringers be barred from purchasing guns, and Anthony took it upon himself to begin drafting the legislation. Even the science seemed to be on his side. The same week that Anthony set to work on his bill, a team of Japanese and American scientists dropped a bombshell on the world: an updated version of their string measurement site. No more windows of several years, no more estimates or ranges. Now there was a single number. A specific age for everyone's death.

Thanks to the addition of the last six months of data, people could now measure the length of their strings down to the very month.

The more precise the technology, Anthony thought, the more easily the short-stringers could be regulated.

"What a great day it's been." Anthony smiled as he slipped off his blazer. He didn't notice his wife right away. "This new ban on short-stringers buying guns might be the first piece of gun legislation to actually get through Congress in years. It's unbelievable."

"I'm not so sure that we should keep going after them," Katherine said, her voice carrying into the hall.

"Going after who?"

"Short-stringers."

Anthony was taken aback. He stepped into the living room to see his wife, seated dolefully on the antique sofa. "Where is this coming from?" he asked.

"Well, it almost got you shot recently, and I just don't think we've thought through all the consequences."

Anthony knew the shooting had unnerved her, despite the fact that the bullet never came close to either of them. Perhaps he hadn't realized just how much she worried.

"We both have very long strings," he said, trying his best to sound soothing. "We'll be fine. The strings are proof."

"That's not nearly as comforting as you seem to think it is," Katherine said. "That only means we won't be *killed*. There are plenty of other bad things that can happen to a person."

"We both chose a life in politics," he said. "We knew what we were getting into."

"Well, maybe this particular route . . . using the strings . . . isn't the way anymore."

"Are you forgetting that it was *your* idea to go after Wes Johnson's string in the first place? *I've* just been following through. And why are you questioning something that's been working so well for us?"

"Jack came to visit today," Katherine finally said. "He told me he has a short string."

Anthony sighed and sat next to his wife, taking her hand gently. "That's terrible. He's a good kid."

"I know he is, which is why I can't understand why this would happen to him! Or to my brother. Our family has only ever done good things for this country, and this is how we're repaid? My brother has to lose his only child? After that hippie already abandoned him to raise Jack alone! And, after all those years of hard work of carrying on my father's legacy, Jack gets relegated to some pathetic corner of the military until he dies before he even turns thirty? How is any of that fair?"

Anthony let his wife cry for a minute, while he figured out what to say.

He couldn't let this derail them, especially now, when his momentum was reaching its crest. He needed Katherine by his side. Ever since they met in college, when he was a senior with his sights set on law school and she was just a sophomore, he knew that she was his match. She shared his dreams and ambition, and her background was truly unsurpassed. Her family could trace its lineage back to the American Revolution, for fuck's sake! It's why he tolerated her initial prudishness, her occasionally overbearing self-righteousness. She had all the necessary pedigree and social graces to succeed, plus the stomach to do what it takes. After she "accidentally" spilled her coffee on his opponent two minutes before the college debate finals, he told her that he loved her.

Katherine believed in him. She believed in *them*. She had always been an asset. Anthony wouldn't let her become a liability now.

"Your family is very strong," he said. "You'll get through this."

Katherine reached for a tissue to wipe her nose. "But what if it's a sign that we should . . . reevaluate things?"

"You're just upset right now. And understandably so," Anthony continued calmly. "But this doesn't change anything. We're so close to the White House, I can taste it. We deserve this. *Both* of us."

"And you think Jack *deserves* what's happening to him?" Katherine asked, disturbed by his seeming indifference.

"No, of course not." Anthony shook his head. "But I do believe that we've earned *our* success. We're protecting the future of this country. Giving the people what they want. Do you remember our first date at the café on campus? I told you it was my dream to be president, and you just said, 'Okay. We can do that.' And then went back to sipping your latte like it was nothing. I couldn't tell if you were crazy, or joking, or what. But you weren't. You were serious." Anthony smiled.

"I remember."

"You had so much faith in us, even then, when we were just two kids." Anthony touched his wife's cheek, the skin soft and damp under his thumb. He looked straight into her eyes. "Do you have faith in us now?"

"You know I do," she said.

"And do you have faith that God wants this for us?"

"I do."

"Well, so do I. We're *meant* to do this." Anthony wrapped his arm around his wife's shoulders, and Katherine leaned her head against his chest, relaxing into the familiar comfort of his solid form.

"The path we're on now—I know it's a difficult one," Anthony said, stroking his wife's hair. "But it's the only way we're going to win."

It was only after Katherine had fallen asleep that Anthony actually thought about Jack.

Anthony and his wife had never wanted children. Kids would certainly not have fit into either of their schedules, and Katherine seemed perfectly content to play the doting aunt at birthdays and graduations, to help out whenever her brother was particularly burdened, and then return to the thrilling life she was building with Anthony.

Of course, Anthony felt sorry for his short-stringer nephew. He always thought Jack seemed a little out of place, the scrawny kid at family reunions, usually picked last as a partner for the three-legged race. He never had the same sense of fight in him, Anthony thought. Probably inherited too much from his flaky mother, who ran off to Europe like some socialist. Anthony just hoped that Jack's short string wouldn't lead him to do anything rash, anything that could taint his and Katherine's good names.

And then it hit him. The protests and the shooting had made it alarmingly, if unsurprisingly, obvious that Anthony had a popularity issue among short-string voters. Perhaps Jack had just given him a solution.

MAURA

Coverage of the shooting lasted for days: "Local Doctor Remembered as a Hero." The anchors mourned the martyrdom of a dedicated physician who saved a congressman and a crowd of spectators from a potential rampage. Few reports mentioned that Hank was only at the rally in order to protest the congressman's actions.

In the days and weeks that followed his death, Maura felt anxious, unmoored. But she still had to set her alarm each morning and ride the subway to work and sit inside her cubicle, staring at a spreadsheet, listening to the smack of her coworker's gum. Maura's department was scaling back, every team had to trim their budgets, and though Maura never let any of her jobs define her, she had always liked her role in publishing—crafting clever captions for social media posts, brainstorming new publicity strategies, all the interesting gatherings of creative minds—until now. Hank was dead, her own life tumbled by, the whole *world* seemed set on fire, and yet she was expected to keep sending press releases and finding excess expenses to cut, as though nothing at all had changed?

Of course, Maura needed a paycheck. She couldn't just quit because of her string. And she couldn't even contemplate *any* moves without hearing the warnings on loop: *You're a short-stringer. Your options are limited. Your time is valuable. Choose wisely.*

That's when Maura realized why Hank's death had been so unsettling. It wasn't just the profound loss, or the shocking violence. It was the fact that Hank was the first.

Not the first person that Maura knew who had died, of course, but the first *short-stringer* that Maura knew who had reached the end of their string. Who had run out of options, out of time.

And it made Maura wonder about how it might happen to her. The scissor that would snip the strand.

Nina, with her gloriously long string, had actually been given two gifts: A lengthy life *and* the ability to assume that death would catch up to her naturally, perhaps in her sleep, when she was old and tired and ready. The peaceful ending that we all deserved, yet only the lucky few got.

Maura was not so lucky.

The science was sharpening quickly, measurements growing more exact. The window in which your life would end was tightening by the minute, and both short- and long-stringers had gone back to the updated website to amend their expectations. But the precision only fueled the fear, as what was once a handful of years became a season, became a month.

And Maura heard the stories of short-stringers approaching the end, with no obvious illness, stalked by dread and uncertainty, hesitating before crossing the street, standing far from the subway tracks. It sounded unbelievably stressful. An awful, powerless feeling. Maura wasn't surprised that some short-stringers had apparently formed a network for obtaining special pills, either from sympathetic doctors or dealers abroad, choosing to slip away gently, with their favorite people by their side, rather than wait a few more days for a potentially painful accident. It was quite a complex issue—Nina's magazine had just covered the trend—since these short-stringers were seemingly healthy, their actions still illegal. But did they not share the same rights as the terminally ill? Maura wondered. The chance to exert their power, their freedom, in the final hour of their life?

Maura chose not to return to the website and remeasure a more accurate time frame.

She already knew enough.

And that particular gnawing question—the one thing she *didn't* know—she tried to shove deep inside of herself, pushing it down as best she could. But still it emerged, every once in a while, and on the rare occasion when she let herself succumb, she tried to focus instead on the outcomes that would surely never occur.

Shark attack. Broken parachute. These, at least, she could rule out. And wasn't there comfort in that?

Venomous snake. Lightning strike. Malnutrition. All improbable.

And yet, Hank's death—gunned down at a protest—seemed exceedingly rare in itself. One year ago, if someone had told Hank that he would die at a "short-stringer rally," he wouldn't have even understood the phrase. Who would have guessed that he would be shot by a woman aiming for the corrupt politician behind him?

Or perhaps it was obvious, Maura finally realized, that he would die the same way he lived, according to his oath—saving the lives of others, even those who seemed unworthy.

When Maura arrived at the school on Sunday night, Chelsea was sitting on the steps of the entrance, languidly smoking a cigarette, sweating in the muggy summer heat that barely relented after sundown. There were still a few minutes before their session started, so Maura took a seat next to her.

Chelsea held out the cigarette as an offering. "You smoke?"

"Just a few times, in college," Maura said. "Of course, that was *pot* . . ."

Chelsea laughed before taking another drag.

"You know, if Doc were here now, he'd probably yell at me for not quitting," she said. "But sometimes it feels like the *only* good thing about having a short string is that I get to smoke freely again. Whatever's gonna get me is already coming, whether it's lung cancer or something else."

In the earlier sessions, back in April, Maura had stared at Chelsea and wondered about her, the natural orange tints in her hair matching her quite unnatural orange tan. It fascinated Maura that, even after receiving her short string, Chelsea continued to prioritize her biweekly spray tans. But there, on the stoop, watching Chelsea savor the final puffs of her cigarette, Maura actually admired her dedication. So what if she had a short string? She still wanted to live her life. She still wanted to look tan.

"So, did you look again?" Chelsea asked. "At the new website?"

Maura shook her head.

"That was probably the right idea," Chelsea said. "It's a lot easier to freak out when it's so much more specific. At least Hank didn't have to wake up that morning and think, *This could* really *be it*."

Chelsea dropped the butt of her cigarette onto the ground, smothering its glowing tip under the heel of her wedge sandal, and slowly stood up. "Shall we?"

When the two women walked into the classroom, the rest of the group was already talking.

"He should have told us the truth about his string," Lea said.

It was the first session after Hank's funeral.

"That Dr. Singh gave a nice eulogy," Terrell remarked. "Saying that Hank inspired her to join Doctors Without Borders? I doubt any of my exes would be that kind."

"Did they find out anything more about the shooter?" Sean asked.

"It sounds like she *was* aiming for Rollins," said Ben. "So it probably wasn't going to be some mass attack."

"Only one thing's really for sure," said Nihal. "Her string is almost up."

Chelsea groaned audibly. "First, she murders our friend, and now she's giving *all* of us a bad rap."

But it was *Anthony* who had actually linked the shooting to the woman's box, Maura thought, painting her motivation as a short-stringer's fury. Very few details had surfaced about the shooter herself. She was in her early forties, unmarried, no children. No family or friends came forward publicly, neither to defend her nor to express their shock.

But the shooting—like the other acts of violence before it—would undoubtedly feed the unconscious bias simmering in so many brains, Maura was certain of that. The next time somebody met a short-stringer, would they pause, for just a moment? Would they wonder, *Can I trust this person? With everything they're going through? All that pain? All that baggage?*

How could they possibly be . . . normal?

FALL

AMIE

Some students didn't return that fall.

A few parents moved their children out of private school, unable to justify the additional expense when a shorter string foretold a future loss of income. Several families fled Manhattan, now acutely aware that life was short and wondering if its quality might improve outside the city. A handful left the country altogether.

In fact, by September, six months after the strings' first appearance, the *Times* had collected enough data to reveal that a very small but statistically significant percentage of the American population had departed since the boxes arrived. Many of the emigrants simply crossed into Canada, while some journeyed even farther north to Scandinavia, where the years of good press—ranking among the happiest regions in the world and the most dedicated to promoting equality—seemed to outweigh any fears of the endless winter.

Even long before the strings, Amie herself had toyed with the notion of moving, finding a new home where the everyday aspects of living were just a little less expensive and a little less difficult. But the city always managed to change Amie's mind, pull her back in. For every matted brown rat that scurried past her feet, there was a neighborhood garden sprouting with color. For every late-night mugging on the news, there was a late-afternoon stroll in the park, where musicians and singers on every corner composed a different score. Some things even the strings couldn't change.

If only her school were one of them.

Back in August, a week after the shooting at the congressman's rally, the principal had sent a staff-wide email lamenting the ongoing violence across the country and offering his condolences to anyone who had been adversely affected by the strings' arrival.

"I understand the compulsion that many teachers must feel to provide guidance for their students during this difficult era in our lives," the principal had written. "However, given the increasingly incendiary nature of the topic and recent developments in our string measurement abilities, I am advising all teachers to refrain from any in-depth discussion of the strings in their classrooms this coming fall."

The Parent-Teacher Association had apparently come to the conclusion that such a sensitive subject should be reserved for the parents alone.

Amie understood the challenges facing families, but she had never agreed with the new mandate, sidelining the teachers so completely. She believed the school had a real chance to add value by addressing the strings head-on, filling her syllabus with books on mortality and loss, on empathy and prejudice. Amie had even been planning to create a pen pal program between her students and a local nursing home, inspired by her own correspondence with "B." She hoped that hearing from people who had survived so many decades of a changing world might provide a useful perspective for those coming of age now, but she feared the experience would feel stilted without any mention of the strings.

She had laid out her concerns to the principal at the end of the summer, to no avail.

"Do you have children, Ms. Wilson?" he asked her.

"Well, no, I don't," she said.

"Then, as much as I admire your idealism, I'm afraid you can't appreciate how our parents feel. You know, I receive two dozen calls *every* year about our sex-ed class, some saying it's coming too soon for the students, some saying it's coming too late, and others taking issue with the content of the course itself. There's no such thing as pleasing everyone. But the *parents* are the ones paying tuition. They need to decide when and where and how they discuss the strings with their own children."

The principal paused for a moment. "When *you're* a mother, I'm sure you'll understand."

Amie had simply nodded along, insulted, though not surprised.

A few weeks later, the numbers came out. The drop in enrollment was shocking.

And then, only four days into the fall semester, the first teacher was officially fired.

Amie arrived at the Connelly Academy that morning to see a group of her colleagues and a few displeased parents already gathered outside the principal's office.

"This was a very difficult choice," said the principal, trying to settle the crowd. "But we must abide by the new code of conduct that was agreed upon in August."

"What happened?" Amie asked.

"It's Susan Ford," a colleague answered. "Apparently she made this whole presentation about the strings yesterday, totally off-book, telling the seniors that they shouldn't be afraid of getting a short string . . . and that they shouldn't be afraid of short-stringers."

"That's not exactly a bad message," Amie said.

"Yeah, but . . . some parents were pissed. This is pretty touchy stuff."

When Mrs. Ford somberly exited the office, tossing a box of posters unceremoniously into the trash, the crowd turned irate.

"This is ridiculous!" shouted one of the parents. "We don't pay to send our children to school in a dictatorship! We should be *encouraging* discussion, not silencing it."

"The board and the PTA have already made their decision," said the principal. "We can reopen the conversation at our meeting next month."

The clock struck eight A.M., and the first streams of pupils started to enter the building, forcing the group to begrudgingly disperse rather than alarm the students. Two of the protesting moms took Mrs. Ford by the arm, comforting her as if she were one of their children, rather than a fully grown woman.

And Amie stared sadly at the trash can outside of the principal's office, the corners of Mrs. Ford's crinkled posters poking out of the bin, trying in vain to escape.

MAURA

On Sunday night, Maura made her way to the school, scrolling mind-lessly through Facebook on her phone, skimming post after post of bad news. She could barely tolerate one more story about Anthony Rollins's booming campaign, or the reasons why so-and-so billionaire believed we should relocate to Mars and leave the strings here on Earth, but she paused at an unfamiliar headline: "Fake String Website Busted, Owner Arrested." Some man in Nevada had apparently been making replica short strings in his garage and selling them online. Before he could be stopped, hundreds of people had purchased the fabricated strings to pull off obscenely cruel pranks, swapping out someone's real string with a counterfeit short one. As if that were the worst fate imaginable. The butt of the world's best joke.

She nearly smashed her phone on the sidewalk.

A few members of the group were discussing the news as Maura en-tered the classroom.

"Did anyone else see that story about the fake strings?" Nihal asked. "The guy really had nothing better to do?"

"First we get that fucked-up Google doc collecting people's string lengths, and now this?" Carl complained.

"Don't forget the new gun law," added Terrell. "This country used to let anybody walk around with an assault rifle and nobody cared who got killed, but now, after years of debate, they're suddenly drawing the line with short-stringers?"

"Honestly, it pales compared to what my dad told me," said Chelsea. "A woman in his office is trying to sue for full custody of her kids on the grounds that her ex-husband is a short-stringer. I guess she's made up some bogus claims about his emotional stability, or protecting the kids from unnecessary trauma."

"Oh god," Terrell grumbled.

"Well, I hope the dad fights for them," said Ben. "Even if they have to lose him, at least they'll know he didn't want to let them go."

"And I'm sure there'll be more protests if this custody battle turns into a bigger issue," Nihal added.

"Aren't you all getting sick of this?" Maura suddenly shouted. "It's not fair that *we* have to do everything."

"What do you mean?" asked Sean.

"It just feels like we're caught in this cycle of proving ourselves. Proving that we're not dangerous or crazy. Proving that we're exactly the same people that we've *always* been, before the strings got here and everyone started looking at us like pariahs," Maura said, her voice cracking with frustration. "We've all been to the protests. We know what it's like. Why do *we* have to be responsible for making a change? Don't short-stringers have enough to deal with already? How can *we* be the only ones fighting?"

When Maura returned to her apartment that night, she could instantly sense Nina's concern.

"Everything go okay?" Nina asked.

"Yeah, I'm just . . . tired," Maura said. "It's been a long six months."

"Do you want to talk about it?"

Maura sighed. "You already know that I was feeling like all these doors were closing in front of me . . . and feeling stuck at work . . . and now the news just keeps getting worse, and people keep doing really shitty things, and I wonder if maybe I should be spending all my time fighting *that*, instead of sitting in an office," Maura said. "But even being forced to keep fighting for myself, over and over again, feels like its own form of being . . . trapped."

"I'm so sorry," Nina said, her face pinched with pain. "Is there anything I can do?"

Maura closed her eyes and took a breath. "Will you lie next to me while I fall asleep?"

The two women quietly climbed into bed, and a few minutes passed in silence, neither one yet asleep, before Nina turned and whispered, "Why don't we go somewhere?"

Maura turned to face her, slightly confused. "I didn't think you were that much of a night owl."

"Not *now*." Nina smiled. "But soon. Somewhere far away. Where neither of us have been."

Maura was surprised. "Are you being serious?"

"If you're feeling trapped," Nina said, "then maybe it's time we get out."

"I mean, that *sounds* great, but . . . can we afford it?" Maura asked.

"We hardly ever leave New York, we deserve to splurge, for once. Especially on something important."

"Okay." Maura decided to humor her. "Where would we go?"

"I don't know, anywhere! Maybe someplace romantic, like France or Italy."

"Well, I did take a year of Italian in college that I never use . . ." Maura said. But then she paused. "You don't need to do this for *me*."

"Are you kidding? You know how much I love planning. I'm excited just *thinking* about all the hours I could spend on Tripadvisor."

Maura laughed. "I just meant . . . I know things sound really bleak, sometimes, but . . . I'll be fine."

"I have no doubt about that," Nina said. "You're the strongest person I know."

Maura kissed Nina's forehead lightly. "Okay," she said. "We can start brainstorming in the morning."

Maura nuzzled her cheek into the pillow, as all the darkness of the day—the man selling fake strings, the woman suing her husband—retreated into the distance. Instead, she found herself thinking about a poster she had discovered at the school, its edges sticking out of a trash can yet to be cleared. Maura had spotted it on her way out of that night's session, and when nobody else was looking, she stealthily lifted it from the bin.

The poster was covered with wrinkled photos of famous figures, all of whom had passed prematurely: Selena Quintanilla, Kobe Bryant, Princess Diana, Chadwick Boseman. *A meaningful life, at any length* was written across the top in cursive lettering.

Maura had no idea who had crafted the poster, or why, but, holding it in her hands, she felt, somehow, less alone. *Somebody* was on her side. Somebody saw the value in her life, in all the short-stringers' lives. Perhaps she wasn't the only one fighting.

It was then, in the final seconds before sleep pulled her under, that Maura decided where she wanted to go.

She could still see the photos from Italian class.

The canals, the gondolas, the dazzling masks.

The dire warnings, year after year, that the city was sinking.

The odds are against it, the water always rising. *But still it stands,* Maura thought.

A fighter.

JAVIER

Javi was hoping to see a fight.

The September primary debate had been advertised as a rematch between the divisive Anthony Rollins, whose aggressive targeting of short-stringers had made him a household name overnight, and the emotional orator Wes Johnson, whose speech at the first debate had moved many but failed to keep Rollins at bay. Javi was itching for Johnson to pull ahead somehow, never anticipating the next moves that both candidates would make.

Jack was away visiting his father, so Javi was alone in their apartment, streaming the debate on his laptop.

"I would like to use my opening statement to address the rumors that have been circling my campaign since June," Senator Johnson began.

And then he said it.

"I am not ashamed to say that I received a shorter string."

Johnson continued speaking atop the murmurs in the crowd and Javier's own surprise.

"Some people will use this fact to question my fitness for this role," he said. "I would like to remind them that *eight* of our presidents died while holding office, including some of the finest leaders that our world has ever seen. It is in their honor that I continue my campaign."

The senator paused for a moment and drew a breath. "I would also like to speak directly to my brothers and sisters with short strings who are listening tonight. The great American writer Ralph Waldo Emerson wrote, 'It is not the length of life, but the depth of life.' You don't need a long lifetime to make an impact on this world. You just need the *will* to do so."

The rapturous cheers of the audience reverberated within Javier. For the first time since he agreed to the switch with Jack, he felt convinced that he had made the right choice. He would make his impact on the world. He had the will, like Johnson said, and Jack's string would pave the way.

The moderator turned to Congressman Rollins, and Javi frowned at the sight of Jack's uncle, his hair stiffly parted and glistening under the stage lights, a phony grin chiseled into his smoothly shaven face—right down to the dimple. A man had been killed at Anthony's rally in New York, and it hardly seemed to affect him.

"Well, I would first like to applaud Senator Johnson on the courage and . . . *vulnerability* . . . he showed tonight," Anthony said. "I know that some people have been critical of my response to the recent violence plaguing our country and believe that I am acting unfairly toward short-stringers. But this is *not* a matter of fairness; it is a matter of national security. As the target of a thwarted attack myself, I will do whatever it takes to keep America safe. As our string-measuring capabilities become even more precise, this task becomes even more urgent. But to those who claim that I don't have any sympathy for short-stringers, you couldn't be more wrong. My nephew is a second lieutenant in the U.S. Army, and I am proud to be his uncle. He also has a short string. When I am president, I will lead not only with the strength of someone who will protect our nation, but also with the compassion of someone who has felt the impact of the strings in my very own family."

As the audience clapped for Rollins, Javier sat dumbfounded on his bed, the uplift of Johnson's speech instantly swept away.

Jack's uncle was parading around Jack's short string—which was actually *Javi's* short string—for his own political benefit.

Javi felt sick. His personal misfortune had been corrupted into something that might actually bring to power this greedy, selfish man.

Had *Jack* known about Anthony's plan tonight?

Jack had barely mentioned his aunt and uncle in recent weeks, but

Javi knew that he had finally started telling his family about his "short string," which Javi assumed was the reason why Jack had been spending more and more time sitting somberly on the couch, nursing a beer, lethargically eating barbecue chips. Clearly, he had shared the news with Anthony before tonight. But did Jack know that his uncle was going to use him like a fucking pawn on national television?

Javier was too angry to keep watching the debate, so he shut his laptop, pulled on his sneakers, and set off on a run, darting out of his building and across the neighborhood. He kept on running until he reached Georgetown, where his body dropped, tired and panting, on the steps outside Dahlgren Chapel.

Javi gazed at the students conversing and studying and flirting on the lawns around him, the red-brick campus humming with the early autumn energy that can only be felt at a school. Many colleges had apparently doubled the number of on-campus counselors for the coming year, including some specially trained to help students navigate their twenty-second birthdays. Javi heard that plenty of college seniors had vowed not to open their boxes when they arrived, the hashtag #KeepItClosed briefly trending online. But it was easier tweeted than done, Javi thought. Even after four years of training, Javi knew it was impossible to predict exactly how he might react in a high-stress situation. No matter how committed these college kids may feel, the true test was coming face-to-face with the box.

Javi wiped the sweat off his chin, then turned around to look at the small chapel behind him, squinting against the sunset.

He was slightly embarrassed to think that he hadn't gone to Mass that whole summer. When he was growing up, his parents brought him to church every Sunday, and his mother would slip him little tamarind candies to keep him from squirming in the pew. At the academy, he still attended most major holiday services, but gradually he started forgetting to go.

The strings had apparently sparked a resurgence in faith for many lapsed followers like himself. Javi recalled seeing multiple news reports that worship across all religions had increased in the months after the boxes arrived, accompanied by photos of packed churches and synagogues. His own parents had even remarked that their parish was more crowded than ever, a welcome reversal after years of shrinking patronage.

Javi had spent his childhood steeped in religion. He understood why attendance would be rising now, why people would turn here for help. For many, the strings were either proof of predestination, or just another reminder of the stark randomness of life, the inequities of luck. But surely the chaos didn't feel so chaotic if you believed it was part of God's plan.

Yet Javi wasn't convinced that there *was* a plan, and he wanted to believe that humans had more agency than mere cars on a track assembled by God. But he couldn't deny the consolation that came with faith, the clandestine relief of the confessional stall, of absolution at the hands of the priest. Javi wondered now if he should confess to the switch, to the lies he shared with Jack, seizing his mind at all times. Perhaps it would ease his conscience. Truthfully, though, Javi was much more worried about his potential punishment on earth than about any divine repercussions. Military discipline was all too real, the standards notoriously scrupulous. Javi could still recall his third month at the academy, when seven cadets were expelled for cheating, and he watched the boy in the neighboring dorm room shamefully pack his belongings.

Javier sighed and stood up slowly, examining the wooden door to the chapel. His legs were still wobbly from sprinting down the cobblestone streets and forgetting to stretch, distracted by his anger. No matter how hard he trained, how sturdy his muscles, his body still had its limits.

"God never gives us more than we can handle," Javi's mother often recited.

Was that what she would say now, if Javi told his parents the truth about his string? That Javi was strong enough to handle this? That *they* could handle this?

Javi suddenly felt compelled to reach out his hand and tug at the door, slightly surprised to find it unlocked, and he entered the chapel, just as the final rays of sunlight streamed through the royal blue and crimson red panes of the stained-glass windows above the altar. But he didn't want to step much farther inside, so he lingered in the back, near a rack of votive candles, wondering if he had any right to be here, given his current feelings.

He was angry at God, of course he was. Hadn't God given him his short string?

A solitary nun arrived just behind Javier, offering him a nod and a restrained smile as she walked past, before sitting down in one of the rows of chairs. The creases across her tan skin, the cheerful crinkles by her eyes, the pair of spectacles slipping down her nose—almost everything about the woman reminded Javi of his grandmother, who had lived with Javier's family in his infancy, but whose early passing meant that most of Javi's memory of her appearance stemmed from the photo on his mother's nightstand.

"That's your *abuela,*" his mother would say, holding the picture before him, desperate for her son to remember what he was simply too young to recall.

"She used to live here, with us, but now she lives in Heaven, with God," Javi's mother explained. "Which means that, someday, we'll both see her again."

Javi leaned against the wall behind him, his eyes beginning to sting.

He knew that other religions had their own theories about the afterlife—the belief in rebirth, in karmic rewards and second chances, seemed like a particularly appealing alternative to him—but Javi had always found Heaven, much like the act of confession, to be a remarkable comfort. To die was still frightening, of course, but so much less dreadful with the faith that there was *something* beyond this world. The end of his string didn't have to be an *ending* if it was the start of something else, something eternal. His father and mother and grandmother certainly believed it to be. Perhaps, when Javi left home, when he stopped attending Mass, when he was surrounded instead by stoic soldiers, he had forgotten that he, too, believed.

All at once, Javi missed his family fiercely, much more than he ever had during his years at the academy, with his goals and his drive and his best friend to guide him. He had just watched Anthony Rollins twist his short string into some devious political ploy, using Javier's fate as an anonymous prop in his campaign of fear and hatred, and Javi had never felt so alone.

He stared at the back of the nun's habit as she bowed her head in worship, and without even thinking, Javi turned to the small altar beside him, adorned with a few low-burning candles, and knelt down.

When he laced his fingers together, he realized that he hadn't prayed in quite some time, not since the boxes had arrived. The last time Javi had prayed, he had asked for a long string.

"Dear God," Javi said quietly, "I know it's too late to change things for me, but I *need* to know that my family will be okay. That you'll guide my parents through this." He felt his voice quiver, weighted down by desperation. "Please help them, God. Don't let them fall apart."

Javi's body slid even farther toward the cold floor beneath him. "And please give me *strength*," he said.

His toes began to tingle with numbness, his legs folded beneath his bent-over frame. Javi hurriedly rubbed the sleeve of his sweatshirt against his nose, despite the fact that the only potential witness to his tears was an elderly nun with her back turned against him.

"And please help the other short-stringers," he begged. "Don't let things get worse."

He could hear the nun rise to her feet, steadying herself against the back of her chair. Javi closed his eyes tightly.

"And please, *please,* when the time comes, let my *abuela* be waiting for me. And all the other family who I knew, and all those I never got to know, please let them be there," Javi asked. "So I won't be alone."

He paused, at the end, to collect himself before the amber glow of the flames. Then Javi stood up from the floor and silently left the chapel.

The sky had begun to darken by now, and on the edge of campus Javi passed by the light of a ground-floor window, where a few dozen students had gathered in a common room to view the evening's debate, just now reaching its end. Javi paused outside the open window when Wes Johnson appeared on the screen to deliver his closing statement.

"If I could go back to March, maybe I would tell myself not to look,"

Johnson said. "Maybe I would tell everyone not to look. But we can't go back. We have to accept that these strings are a part of life. But we *don't* have to accept what's happening now. I hear stories of people losing their jobs, losing health coverage, losing loans, all because of their strings. And I'm not willing to simply toe the party line and keep quiet. I see what Congressman Rollins and our current administration are doing— forcing members of certain professions to look at their strings when they had chosen not to, questioning people's ability to serve their country, and treating people differently based on a mere accident of fate. But *I* believe in the freedom of choice. I believe in equality. The civil rights activists and women's rights activists and gay rights activists have all been fighting this fight for generations. And while those of us with short strings may not measure as large in number as those communities, we are not insignificant. And we will not stop fighting, either."

MAURA

It was nine P.M., and Maura was alone. The candidates had finished their closing statements and waved their way offstage, and Nina was staying late in her office to help with the debate coverage, so Maura reached for her phone.

Want to get a drink? she texted Ben.

By nine thirty, they were sitting behind the dark wooden bar in a quiet neighborhood joint.

Maura had arrived a few minutes late, sneaking up on Ben while he was doodling his own impression of the bar on a flimsy paper napkin.

"I forgot how good you are!" Maura smiled, examining his tiny sketch as if it were mounted in a gallery. Then she gestured at the bartender to bring her a beer.

"Do you really think Rollins has a short-stringer nephew?" Maura asked. "I wouldn't put it past him to make something like that up."

"Perhaps in a time before fact-checkers." Ben laughed. "But not nowadays."

"Well, at least the ACLU has filed a suit against his bullshit STAR Initiative, so maybe that's a bright spot. Plus, Johnson's still in the race. Though I can't believe he was so hounded by rumors that he had to come out and say it, like a gay candidate being shoved out of the closet," Maura said. "People are guessing that his string ends around age fifty, so he's officially a 'short-stringer' now."

Ben nodded slowly. "It's weird, because I certainly wouldn't wish for *anyone* to have a short string," he said, "but I think maybe there was a part of me that hoped the rumors were true? That somebody up on that stage might be . . . one of us."

Maura tucked her hands into the front pocket of her threadbare CBGB sweatshirt and tilted her head curiously. "Are you seeing anyone?"

Ben nearly coughed on his beer. "That's quite a change of subject. Plus, I thought you were gay." He smiled.

"And if I weren't, then *obviously* I'd be interested," Maura teased, "but it's what you said. That Wes Johnson is 'one of us.' That's a whole debate on its own, right? Whether people *like us* should be dating people who aren't?"

"Well, actually, I *was* seeing someone, when the strings arrived. But we're not together anymore."

"What happened?"

Ben stared at the neck of his beer bottle, spinning it gently with two fingers. "She opened my box," he said, the words steady and deliberate. "Before I had decided what *I* wanted to do. And then she broke up with me after she saw my short string."

"Oh shit." Maura was shocked. "I'm so sorry."

"Thanks," Ben said quietly.

"Why haven't you talked about this with the group?" Maura asked.

"I guess I just wanted to move on with my life," Ben said. "And I *have*, really. I've forgiven her for breaking up with me. I know that not everyone could stick it out in such challenging circumstances, so I can't really be mad at her for that. But I guess now I'm worried that the *next* girl, and the *next* girl, still won't be the right type, either. It's probably why I haven't even tried dating since the breakup."

Even though she knew Ben's string was longer than hers, Maura felt sorry for him, in this moment. All he wanted was for someone to say to him what Nina had said to her: *I would never leave you.*

Maura leaned back on her stool, feeling the chill of the beer bottle against her skin. A newspaper had been left on the seat next to hers, and she held it up for Ben.

"Did you see this?" Maura asked, pointing to the front-page headline. It was yesterday's lead story, tracking the proliferation of new "mind-uploading" companies, hoping to discover a means of scanning the human brain into a computer for perpetual preservation. Anything to satiate the spike in interest among short-stringers looking to extend their lives, in this generation or the next.

Ben scanned the page in Maura's hands. "There's never been more demand for this research," one of the founders was quoted. "Before, very few of us knew when our time was limited, and now, of course, it's possible to know. But, if we can find a technological solution, then perhaps the strings become irrelevant. We can offer an escape from the timeline dictated by the physical body, by your string."

The article had interviewed two eager candidates, each at the end of their string—a scientist who dreamt of seeing the distant future and a fifty-five-year-old mother willing to leave her daughter now in the hope of returning, one day, to meet her grandchildren.

"The science has moved remarkably fast when it comes to string measurements," said one of the candidates. "We've already narrowed our projections from the span of a few years all the way down to a single month. Who says the science can't move quickly here, too?"

"People have been working in this field for a while," Ben said. "Some companies are trying to freeze your body in a cryonic chamber; I guess these folks want to remove your body altogether." He paused. "I don't really think it's for me."

"I just wanted to make sure you weren't secretly planning to digitize your brain and leave me all alone in the group." Maura smiled.

"Look, it's an exciting dream," said Ben. "But it doesn't really help us right now."

"It's kind of crazy that we already have so much technology at our disposal, and even more coming down the pike. All these brilliant minds fixated on *solving* the strings, if that's even possible. But then there are these huge swaths of the world population without any of it," Maura said. "My girlfriend, Nina, was just working on this article about people living in places with no Internet. No at-home measurement websites, no way to learn what's going on in other countries."

"Whole communities where nobody knows what the length of their string really means?" Ben asked.

"Well, they can still do simple comparisons, see whose string is the longest," said Maura. "And apparently some groups have been forming their own makeshift data sets, like recording the age at which someone dies and then using that person's string as a benchmark. Humans always find a way to adapt, right? But there are lots of people who aren't even doing that. They're just . . . continuing on, like before."

Ben nodded, taking a sip of his beer. "How has Nina been through all of this?"

Maura silently recalled their heated dispute over Nina's search obsession, then their quiet acceptance of not having kids. All the times that Nina had said, "I love you," after the strings arrived.

"We've had a couple rough moments, of course, but . . . she's never once wavered when it comes to *us*," Maura said. "She even planned this whole getaway for the two of us next month. To Venice."

"Wow, that sounds great." Ben smiled.

"I think we both just needed to go somewhere that we've never gone before. To get out of our apartment and have a little adventure. It's like Wes Johnson said tonight, we can't go back. But at least we can go anywhere else."

ANTHONY

Anthony was quite pleased with the September debate, the voters responding favorably to his story about Jack and decidedly *unfavorably* to Johnson's admission.

He grinned, staring at a copy of the day's top headline: "Johnson Slumps after Short String Reveal."

"Obviously I feel badly for Senator Johnson," an anonymous voter was quoted, "but I don't feel comfortable electing someone who can't commit to a full term."

"I really admire Johnson's talents," said another, "but I worry that having a short-stringer lead our country might make us look weak in front of other nations. Especially one who won't even say the exact time he has left."

A third phrased it most bluntly: "Sympathy doesn't get you votes. Strength does. And we've seen that in Congressman Rollins."

Even now, the shooting at the August rally remained a boon for Anthony's campaign, his image a paragon of fortitude. After the incident, a brief flurry of rumors had attempted to offer a motive for the attack, short-stringers and their advocates desperately searching for something to explain the woman's rage that *wasn't* the string in her box. But most theories quickly evaporated, met with silence from the subject herself.

Which was why Anthony never expected the emergency meeting called by his campaign manager and head of oppo research.

"We found something," they said. "About the shooter."

One of the men slid a folder of papers in front of Anthony: two birth certificates, one death certificate, and a copy of a scanned article from Anthony's college newspaper about the night that a boy died at a frat.

"But they have different last names," Anthony said. "You're telling me the shooter and this boy were related?"

"Her half brother, apparently."

Fuck.

Anthony thought that night was behind him. It was three *decades* ago, after all.

"Give me a minute," Anthony said, holding the scanned article closely.

Of course Anthony remembered the boy. He was one of a handful recruited by Anthony's fraternity simply for the fun of it, dragged along in the pledging process with no real prospect of becoming a brother. And yet, the pledges *always* believed it was genuine, Anthony recalled. That was what made it funny.

Anthony was president of the frat at the time, but he hadn't picked the boys. That was the pledge master's forte. Anthony couldn't remember exactly why that year's crop had been chosen, though they were usually plucked from the poor kids on Pell grants or other government aid, boys who could never afford the dues, who couldn't dream of fitting in with the sons of the captains of industry.

Anthony's recollections of that particular night were sparse and disjointed and jagged, pieces of shattered glass: He remembered that someone kicked the boy's dirty sneakers, trying to rouse him. He remembered that someone else vomited on his own brand-new loafers, after realizing what had happened. He remembered the back of the boy's head, a mop of thick, dark hair, thankfully turned away from Anthony as the boy lay on the floor, inert. He remembered the sharp, stabbing panic, leaving him dizzy and breathless.

But Anthony didn't remember much of what came after, when a group of the boys' fathers—Anthony's included—rushed out to campus in the middle of the night and huddled in the office of the college president for nearly two hours before phoning the local police.

The boy had simply been a party guest, it was decided. The boy drank too much, of his own accord. The cause of death was alcohol poisoning, and the death was ruled an accident.

As fraternity president, Anthony was called upon to provide a public statement, with the help of his family lawyer, mourning the tragic loss of life and offering up his thoughts and prayers. He looked like a true leader, everyone said, someone who would do great things.

And Anthony's life marched forward.

The shooter's, apparently, had not.

"But she hasn't said anything? About her . . . brother?" Anthony asked.

"She's been totally mute since the arrest. They think she might have some sort of PTSD from killing that doctor."

"Then let's keep it that way," said Anthony. "This story was buried once before."

After his colleagues left, Anthony downed two glasses of scotch, trying to numb his nerves. He decided not to tell Katherine. She would surely overreact.

The boy could have left at any time, Anthony reminded himself. That's what the brothers had said back then. They may have *told* the boy to drink, yelled at him even, and maybe, yes, a few of the more aggressive brothers had poured liquor into the open mouths of the pledges, and perhaps some dull objects (footballs or basketballs, most likely) had been thrown at them, too. But, technically, the door was never locked. The exit always an option.

And now, Anthony realized, there was something else. Something they hadn't known at the time. The boy was a short-stringer, before there *was* such a thing. And, that night in the frat house, his string had reached its end. If the alcohol hadn't killed him, then something *else* would have, right?

As long as the boy's string was short—had *always* been short—then Anthony wasn't to blame. He couldn't think of it any other way. He couldn't entertain the possibility that there was a particular *reason* the boy's string was short. Anthony believed in God, of course, but he couldn't let himself believe that God had seen the future, seen that Anthony and his brothers would coax the boy into their midst, pretend he had a chance, physically and verbally taunt him until he imbibed so much he could barely stand.

And Anthony allowed himself to forget about the boy as the scotch seeped into his bloodstream, his attention span already shrinking, his brain slowing down just a tad. He poured himself one final glass for the night.

In the morning, his life would march forward.

Dear A,

I knew a guy in college who took a job as an investment banker, and he was so worried that he would end up hating the job but sticking around for the money, that he set an alert on his phone to send himself the same message every year on his birthday: "Sit down and ask yourself: Are you happy?"

We haven't spoken in a few years now, but yesterday was his 30th birthday, and I wonder if he still asked himself the same question. Am I happy?

I think we're raised to believe that happiness is something we've been promised. That we all deserve to be happy. Which is why this really fucked-up thing that's happening to some of us is so hard to accept. Because we're supposed to be happy. But then this box arrived at our doorstep, saying that we don't get the same happy ending as the people we pass on the sidewalk, at the movies, at the grocery store. They get to keep on living, and we don't, and there's just no reason why.

And now the government and so many others are only making it worse, agreeing that we deserve less than everyone else. I haven't even heard from most of my long-string friends in weeks. I think that maybe long-stringers feel a need to disassociate from us, to put us in a different category than themselves, because they were also raised to believe that they deserve happiness. And now they want to enjoy that happiness from a comfortable distance, where they don't need to feel so guilty about it whenever they look at us. Where our bad luck can't rub off on them.

Well, that, plus the fact that they've been told to be afraid of us. The wild, unhinged short-stringers.

I'm sorry to bombard you with such negative thoughts, but a friend of mine died last month, and sometimes it feels like everything is barreling downhill, and even though I've joined a group where I'm encouraged to speak these thoughts aloud, it feels easier, somehow, to write it all down.

—B

AMIE

Amie still had the letter from last week. She'd read it over and over a dozen times by now, but she didn't know what to write back.

She held the paper in her lap, sitting on the couch in the teachers' lounge, thinking that "B" was right. A chasm had opened between the long and the short, one that only a few people, like Nina and Maura, had somehow managed to bridge.

Amie worried, for the first time, that she had made a mistake by responding to the first letter that spring. She had known, then, or at least suspected, that the writer had a short string. And now their exchanges grew deeper, more intimate. How could Amie be sure that she was saying the right thing? Or, god forbid, saying the wrong thing?

She was staring at the letter when it hit her.

She was doing it, too.

Everything the writer had said.

Making assumptions about them. Tiptoeing around them. Wondering if this friendship was too much to handle, too fraught. Fearing that— because of their string—they were breakable, delicate, *different*.

The letter was sitting inside her purse, still awaiting a response, when Amie met Nina for a walk in the West Village, before she and Maura set off on their trip.

The two sisters strolled through Washington Square Park, which was teeming on the warm evening with skateboarders and dog walkers, families and lovers, and at least two drug dealers in opposite corners of the park, thanks to the heightened demand among long-stringers looking to celebrate and short-stringers seeking escape.

Amie and Nina crossed under the massive marble arch at the entrance to the park, where someone had spray-painted along one of the two white columns: "What if YOU had a short string?"

Normally, Amie relished all the "what ifs," she dreamt in the conditional mood. But this was one question she couldn't invite, one box she just couldn't open. Whether the answer was fifty or ninety, she didn't want *any* number in her head. Amie's refuge was found in her fantasies, in her musings about the future. A number would destroy all of that. It would ground her. She simply *had* to live her life in oblivion, as if her string were somehow infinite. It was the only way she knew how.

And she honestly had trouble understanding how so many people—Nina and Maura and the author of her letters—had the ability to live any other way.

"Sometimes, I think about everything you and Maura have to contend with," Amie said, "and I don't know how you deal with it all."

Nina thought about it for a moment. "I guess I just try to remember, as hard as it is for me, it's so much harder for Maura. That's why I planned this whole trip for us."

"Well, maybe I'm not as strong as either of you are." Amie sighed.

"You mean because you haven't looked?"

"No, not just that . . ." Amie thought about the unanswered note in her purse. "I'm sort of a pen pal for a short-stringer, and it's getting difficult for me to keep writing back when I know they're going through something so awful."

Nina looked confused. "Who are they?"

"Well, the thing is," Amie said hesitantly, "I don't actually know. We've never exchanged names."

"How did this start? When?"

"It started through school," Amie said. It felt too strange to explain in depth. "Back in the spring. And I thought it might taper off during the summer, but every week that I checked on my classroom, there was another letter."

"Do you know how long this person has left?"

"About fourteen years, I think."

"And how old are they now?"

"Well, that's something else I don't know. But I think around our age. They mentioned a friend who turned thirty. And I know I'm not *technically* a long-stringer, since I haven't looked," Amie said, "but I still feel guilty. And so sad for them."

They passed by a couple curled together on a bench, folded into one another, and Nina looked at Amie's anxious face.

"Would you date a short-stringer?" Nina suddenly asked.

"Um, yeah, I'm sure I would date them," Amie answered, though she hadn't dated anyone since the time before the strings.

Amie's tendency toward daydreams led to an unfortunate habit of picturing her wedding by only the second or third date, and her imagination had a knack for exaggerating even a man's most minor flaws. In her visions, the guy who cut her off in conversation was now interrupting her vows at the altar, and the man who seemed uncomfortable around mothers breastfeeding in public now refused to take care of their own fictive baby.

And sometimes, as hard as she tried, she simply *couldn't* see the future with a particular man. The images just wouldn't take shape in her mind, or they showed up fuzzy and dark, blurring the poor man's face. That was even less promising than the bad ones.

Only two men had managed to pass muster so far, Amie's exboyfriends from her early twenties: a lawyer who didn't have time to commit and a poet more fanciful than Amie.

"So maybe you would *date* a short-stringer, but would you *marry* them?" Nina asked.

"Honestly, I don't know," Amie said slowly. It wasn't the first time she had considered the question. "I'm sure it would be different if I were *already* in love with the person, like you and Maura, but if we were just starting out? I mean, I know you guys don't want kids, but I'm pretty sure I do, so it wouldn't just be about *me*. I'd be knowingly putting my family through such a horrible loss. Choosing to give them a future without their father."

"I understand," Nina said.

"It's just that life is already hard enough, and that would bring even more sadness into it," Amie said. She turned to face her sister directly. "Do you think that makes me a terrible person?"

"I think it just means that you don't know what you're capable of," Nina said. Nearby, a troupe of street performers, a jazz quartet, struck up a tune.

"Do you remember when 'the strings' just referred to the string section of an orchestra?" Amie asked, as if the gap between then and now spanned many years, instead of months.

"Maura never lets me walk past a performance without stopping to listen, just for a minute," Nina said. A small audience had already gathered around the musicians, swaying and tapping their feet to the score.

"What about dancing?" Amie smiled, beginning to roll her shoulders and swing her hips subtly.

Nina instinctively tensed, her arms crossed in front of her. "No, thank you," she said.

"Come on," Amie begged. She tugged gently at her sister's arms until Nina relented, her body slackening, easing its way into an uncoordinated groove, still somewhat inhibited but a great improvement.

And the two sisters rocked back and forth within the crowd of dancing spectators, all of whom were briefly grateful to be transported to a time when the strings really were just a group of beautiful instruments.

JAVIER

After the September debate, Javier hoped that Jack would bring it up himself: the fact that his uncle had touted the sob story of his short-string soldier nephew on the national stage. As if it were something to brag about. As if it were *his* story to tell.

But Jack returned to their apartment the day after the debate, and he never even mentioned it. Javi wanted to believe that Jack was simply preparing to discuss it, perhaps even conferring with his family about Anthony's behavior before approaching Javi with a solution. But after several days of skirting the subject, Javier was fed up with the silence.

He decided to ask while he and Jack were at the boxing studio. Though Jack had stopped most of his combat training after revealing his "short string" to the army, he still suited up in gloves and headgear each week to help Javi as a sparring partner.

Javi was practicing his punches against the strike shield Jack held up. "Are we ever gonna talk about what your uncle did at the debate last week?" he asked.

"Yeah, that was a real dick move," Jack responded in between jabs. "Even for him."

Javi waited for Jack to say more, but the gym was quiet, save for the smacking of Javi's gloves against the padding.

"Well, did you talk to him after?" Javi asked.

"He's not exactly easy to get ahold of right now."

"Then what about your aunt? Or your dad?"

"I guess I just didn't want to make a big deal about it." Jack shrugged from behind the shield.

"But it *is* a big deal!" Javi said. "I wish you would take this more seriously."

"Well, I'd rather not call any *extra* attention to my string," said Jack. "For obvious reasons."

"I just don't want your uncle using *my* string to get himself elected," Javi said, beating his own chest with his glove. "That's *my* life. He has no right to use it."

Jack sighed, nodding. "I know, Javi. You're right. He shouldn't have done it. And I'm sorry that I haven't had a chance to talk to my family about it," he said. "I've just been dealing with everyone texting me and calling me, asking if *I* was the short-stringer he was referring to that night. And now everybody wants to talk to me about it, but I *really* don't want to talk to any of them."

Javi couldn't believe how self-centered he sounded. Jack hadn't been the one on the floor of the chapel, worrying about his family, praying to God through tears.

"Wow, I'm sorry, man. I had no idea you were dealing with so much shit," Javi said bitterly. "It must really suck to be a short-stringer."

Jack shook his head. "You *know* that's not how I meant it. The only reason I hate talking to these people is because it makes me feel like such a fucking fraud!" Jack threw his strike pad against the wall, startling a few other boxers across the room and reminding them both to lower their voices for fear of being overheard.

Javi knew that his friend had been struggling with the switch. That morning Jack was wearing a T-shirt with his high school mascot on the front, and Javi realized that it had been a while since he had last seen Jack wear anything with the army logo. Javi was glad that Jack was at least *feeling* something, that their actions weighed on him, too. But Javi still wanted to shake Jack's shoulders, snap him out of his funk, make him realize there was so much more he could be doing with his time.

"I just don't see why you're letting your uncle get away with this," Javi said. "With everything. All of his anti-short-stringer crap."

Javi was struggling to fend off his anger, until he remembered what he had recently seen online, a few tweets that confirmed Anthony Rollins was in the room when the STAR Initiative was born.

Something that Jack, assuming he knew, had conveniently forgotten to share.

"It's your uncle's fault that we even had to lie about all of this in the first place!" Javi hissed.

"You think I don't know that? When I found out that *he* was basically the one behind all of this, it made me feel like shit! But there's nothing I can do, Javi. It's not like the guy ever talks to me, unless he's asking for a favor. And even if we did talk, he wouldn't listen to me."

"But you're still his family! There's got to be something you can do."

"He *is* my family," Jack said. "Which is why I can't exactly tell him to stop running for president, when everyone else in the family is out actively campaigning for him."

"Well, you can at least tell him to stop making life harder for people who are *already* suffering," Javi urged.

"Look, I know that he seems like the ringleader here, but clearly he's not the only one who feels this way," Jack said quietly. "I'm not trying to excuse him, but . . . maybe he's just tapping into something bigger."

"Then he should be using his platform to change people's minds! Not pouring fuel on the fire," Javi said. He couldn't understand why Jack wasn't equally furious. "Unless you actually *agree* with him?"

"Jesus, man, of course I don't agree with him!" Jack exclaimed, raising his hands defensively. "I just don't really see the point of going up against my uncle. He's gonna do whatever he wants, no matter what you or I say."

Jack's pathetic acceptance, his resignation, was making Javi even angrier.

"But don't you care that actual *lives* are at stake here? That doctor who got shot in New York is only dead because of your uncle!"

Javi could tell from Jack's face that his comment struck a nerve.

"What happened to that doctor is horrible," Jack said. "But if I start criticizing my uncle now, I could get myself disowned by the entire family. *Who* do you think they'll side with? The kid who barely made it through the academy, or the man who might be president? And I don't see why he's *my* responsibility to fix. I didn't ask for him to be my uncle, he's just an egomaniac who married into our family. His fuckups shouldn't be my problem."

"Well, they became your problem when he stood on that stage and told the whole world about you," Javi said harshly. "About *us*."

The gym manager was walking toward them now, keys jingling in his pockets. "Everything okay here, boys? We've had a few complaints."

"Yeah, don't worry," Jack said. "I'm leaving anyway." He spit his mouth guard into his hand, then stormed off toward the locker room. And Javi watched as the door swung shut behind Jack, the final punctuation on their first real fight in more than four years of friendship.

Despite Jack's wealth and connections, Javi always felt a bit sorry for him, knowing that his childhood hadn't held the same happiness as Javier's own, that he had grown up feeling lost and abandoned. Javi knew that Jack's family was demanding, that he carried his last name like a burden, always laboring to live up to their expectations. So Javi couldn't understand *why*, in this crucial moment, Jack would side with *them* over his best friend.

Was he that afraid of their reproach? That desperate for their approval?

Or was he just that good at compartmentalizing, that he could somehow separate the people he loved from the pain they had caused?

Perhaps there was something else entirely, something Javier was missing.

Javi was about to leave the gym himself when he spotted a tall punching bag hanging alone in the corner, and struck it angrily with his clenched fist, sending the bag flying into the wall behind it.

Dear B,

I think you're right about long-stringers. Some of them may not even realize what they're doing. They just want to distance themselves from sadness, or from guilt, or from any reminders of their own mortality. No matter how much time they may have left, nobody wants to think about the end.

It's strange, because society used to be so much more comfortable with death. In our unit on the Victorian era, I explain to my students that people back then were surrounded by death. They wore lockets with dead relatives' hair, they kept the casket in their living rooms during a wake, they even took photos with deceased loved ones to keep as remembrances. Nowadays, we want to avoid the idea of death as much as possible. We don't like to talk about illness, we isolate our dying community members in hospitals and nursing homes, we relegate cemeteries to remote stretches along the highway. I suppose short-stringers are the latest group to suffer from our death-averse ways, and perhaps more than any before.

But you asked if everyone deserves happiness. I certainly think so. And I don't think having a short string should make that impossible. If I've learned anything from all the stories I've read—of love and friendship, adventure and bravery—it's that living long is not the same as living well.

Last night, I looked at my own box for the first time in months. I didn't open it, but I reread the inscription. The measure of your life lies within.

Sure, it's pointing to the string inside, but maybe that's not the only measure we have. Maybe there are thousands of other ways we could measure our lives—the true quality of our lives—that lie within us, not within some box.

And, by your own measure, you can still be happy.

You can live well.

—A

MAURA

It was a relief to land in Venice, after the madness at the airport.

The international terminal had been more crowded than Maura could ever recall. While she waited outside the newsstand for Nina, three tour groups walked past, led by guides in branded windbreakers. Hundreds of prepackaged "bucket list" trips had been gaining popularity among short- and long-stringers alike, anyone who felt like the sun was setting on their chance to see the world.

A motley assortment of backpackers had lingered across from her, overstuffed duffels strapped to their bodies, sleeping bags and yoga mats rolled under their arms. A few overheard morsels led Maura to believe they were heading to the Himalayas, which wasn't so surprising. Droves of Westerners had reportedly been drawn to the same corners of Asia since the boxes' earliest arrival.

Back in April, when the crisis was fresh, a few Buddhist monasteries opened their doors to foreign visitors seeking guidance, but they underestimated the sheer number of souls searching for enlightenment. By the summer, some regions of Bhutan and India were so overrun that the governments imposed new limits on the number of travelers they could accept. Areas that once lay undisturbed were now covered in tourists' prayer flags, entire Tibetan fields crisscrossed with lines of mesmerizing rainbow cloths.

And many of the world's most holy places were drawing millions more than usual, pilgrims carrying their boxes and strings to the Western

Wall in Jerusalem, to the Kaaba in Mecca, to the Grotto of Massabielle in Lourdes, some pursuing a return to their spiritual origins in a time of immense confusion, others praying for a miracle.

Maura had attended plenty of climate rallies and protested overtourism. But she couldn't really blame these nomads for wishing to explore while they still could. For wondering if some far-off land might hold the answers they couldn't find at home.

Like those sacred sites, Venice, too, was rife with visitors, but as soon as Nina and Maura boarded the airport ferry, watching the city rise from the waters around them, and then as they struggled to roll their luggage along the bumps in the street, up and down the small bridges that spanned the canals, they could feel it in each breath they took, their lungs filling with the exhilaration of being someplace new. Their minds gleefully tried to accomplish a thousand tasks at once, taking in the sights and sounds and scents, every element of awareness heightened, knowing that this was special, a bold and bracketed moment in time, something that must be remembered.

Though it was October, and the infamous summer crowds had already dispersed, families and large clusters of tourists still filled the wide piazzas, baking under the heat of the sun, so by their second day Maura and Nina had learned to turn away from the main squares and venture down the narrower, shaded alleys, some the width of just two pairs of shoulders, following the maze of the city with no particular end point in mind.

Flanked by crumbling stone walls, these smaller lanes were surprisingly insulated from the surrounding noise. Nearly everywhere else they had walked, the echoes of jackhammers and faint clanging sounds served as constant reminders of the city's fragility, its inevitable demise. Venice, it seemed, was perpetually repairing itself—attempting to ward off its fate.

One afternoon, Nina and Maura stumbled upon a particularly scenic juncture, where one of the empty alleys gave way to a wooden pier by a thin canal, far from the larger waterways where pricey gondolas ferried tourists.

Maura walked down to the dock, wanting to dip her toes in the water, but Nina objected, citing an article she read about the pollution in the canals and the infrequency with which they were cleaned. So they settled for simply sitting alongside the softly lapping water, Maura resting her head on Nina's shoulder.

Maura looked down at the water below, green and opaque as it drifted slowly past. It looked cloudier than she had expected, as if a painter had just rinsed off his brushes in the canal.

"We're lucky we got to see it while it still looks like this," she said. "A part of me can't even believe they built this city. A world on top of the water."

"I read an article about it on the plane," Nina said. "They actually dug wooden stakes into the mud and clay under the water, and then built wooden platforms on top of the stakes, and then stone platforms on top of that, and then finally the buildings themselves."

"But the wood didn't rot?" Maura asked.

"The wood they used was water-resistant, and since it was underwater and not exposed to the air, it never decayed," Nina said. "It's been standing for all these centuries."

Though the streets occasionally smelled like a fishing port, the city was bewitching, unlike any other place they had seen. The colorful pastel buildings, whose Gothic arches melted into the scintillating water, and the rows of gondolas out front, bobbing in wait, looked exactly the way they appeared on postcards and in daydreams.

Particularly amusing were the curious faces they encountered around every corner. Sculptures perched on rooftops, figures painted in ceiling frescoes, facades adorned with small busts, even doorknobs carved in the shape of heads—everywhere they went in the city, the eyes of saints and artists peered back at them.

Once, Maura almost jumped at the sight of a dozen painted faces staring at her through haunting, empty eyes from the window of a small shop.

Nina followed her inside, where every inch of the walls and ceiling was covered with traditional Venetian masks, hundreds of porcelain visages, each with their own personalities. There was the jester, with his fool's cap and bells. The ominous plague doctor, with his lengthy beak. There were masks in every color of the artist's palette. Some had ribbons and feathers and intricate gold leafing. Others wore pained expressions or mischievous grins. Maura stepped closer to admire a white mask adorned with delicate music notes.

A woman soon emerged from the shop's back room, one arm leaning on a mahogany cane, and nodded at Nina and Maura. Her dark, wavy hair, bestrewn with strands of gray, was twisted into a loose bun, and she wore her red-rimmed glasses like a necklace.

"Ciao," she said. "Where are you visiting from?"

"New York," Nina answered.

"Ah, the Big Apple," the woman said with a laugh. Her English sounded well practiced, if heavily accented. "Do you know about the history of our masks?"

Both Nina and Maura shook their heads.

"Well, everybody knows that we wear masks during the famous Carnival, but there was also a time before, when the people of Venezia wore masks *ogni giorno*, every day. Not only for celebrations."

With her free hand, the woman gestured to the world outside the window. "If you were just outside walking on the street, you could wear a mask, and nobody would know who you were."

"It sounds very . . . freeing," said Maura.

"Freedom. *Sì*." The woman said solemnly. "In Venezia, the old social classes were very strict. But with the mask, you could be . . . anyone. Man, woman, rich, poor. It's a bit like your New York, yes? You go there to be anyone you want."

Nina nodded in agreement. "Then why did people stop wearing them?"

"Well, what's the word . . . anonymous? *Sì*. Being anonymous has a price. You feel like you can do anything. You drink, you cheat, you gamble . . ."

The woman tipped her head back toward the ceiling, smiling at the rows of endless faces gazing down upon her. "At least we kept the Carnival."

Maura wanted to pick out a mask to hang in their apartment, and Nina modeled a handful of different options before her, each more flamboyant than the last. It was almost shocking how every mask rendered her unrecognizable, and Maura found herself thinking about what the shop owner had said, about the freedom that masks afforded the wearer. The sense of invincibility. Perhaps that was how long-stringers felt, she realized.

And although their time in Italy had been beautiful thus far, a distraction from life back at home, Maura couldn't help but wonder about the chance to don a mask, to become someone new temporarily, someone with a different string. To feel that relief, that peace, for one day.

Maura watched the shop owner daintily lift a mask off Nina's face. "What happened here in Italy when the boxes came?" she suddenly asked. "Did most people look?"

The woman nodded, like she had been expecting the question.

"Some did, but I think most did not. My sister, she is very traditional Catholic. She did not look, because she says she will go whenever God calls her back. And I did not look because . . . I am happy with my life." The woman shrugged. "I hear of these Americans, they say the strings have made them think again about their lives. How do you say, their . . ."

"Priorities?" Maura offered.

"*Sì, sì.* Their priorities. But, in Italy, I think we already knew. We already put the art first, the food first, the passion first," she explained, a sweep of her arm encompassing the entire shop. "And we already put the *family* first. We did not need the strings to tell us what is most important."

JACK

The last of Javier's duffels had been dragged to the front hall, ready to be loaded into his father's van and begin the fourteen-hour drive to the army post in Alabama, where he was due to start his training in aviation. But Mr. and Mrs. García were still a half hour away, so Javi was sitting atop his suitcase, waiting.

He wasn't supposed to be leaving this early. He and Jack were supposed to spend their last week together. But after their fight, Javi decided to spend his remaining time with his parents.

Of course Javi wanted to be with his family, Jack thought. He actually *liked* his family. As far as Jack knew, the only lie that Javi had ever told his parents was about his string. And he spared them that truth out of love.

Jack had never been that honest with his own family, at least not when it mattered most. After his wife left, Jack's father became utterly devoted to his career, overseeing Department of Defense contracts. He dated a few well-heeled, well-bred women, at his sister Katherine's request, but his work stole all his attention. Jack could sense that his father *needed* to succeed in order to maintain their status in the family, to erase the stain that his mother had inflicted—and needed Jack to succeed, too.

Grandpa Cal was perhaps the only one who might have understood Jack, who wouldn't have mocked or berated him for speaking his mind. But there was just no way that Jack could have walked into his grandfather's oak-paneled living room, where three of his ancestors' nineteenth century muskets were mounted on the wall, alongside a framed Bronze Star, and confessed that he couldn't do what so many Hunters had done.

He simply couldn't admit that maybe there was another path for him, one that wouldn't give him chills in the middle of the night or tension headaches when he thought of the future. And he certainly couldn't say it without proposing an alternative, something respectable like law or politics. Yet as much as Jack knew that he *wasn't* meant for the army, he didn't know *what* he was meant for. He had no real passion, no sense of direction (outside of where his family had steered him). He wasn't like everyone else—Grandpa Cal, Javier, the rest of the army, that doctor who died at the protest. Even Anthony and Katherine had a goal, albeit misguided. And now, after his "short string" had effectively demoted Jack to a low-level desk job in D.C., he felt more aimless than ever, his uniform merely an ill-fitting costume.

Jack had to remind himself that it wasn't such a crime to feel lost—he was only twenty-two, after all. Wasn't this the time in your life when you were allowed to feel adrift?

And hadn't the arrival of the boxes sent so many people astray, a gust that blew them off course?

But the uncomfortable irony wasn't lost on Jack that *he* had been given a long string, a long life, and yet he didn't know how to spend it, while Javi was the one with purpose.

Jack already felt like a failure in so many ways—as a soldier, a son, a productive member of society. He didn't want to fail as a friend, too.

Jack needed to show Javi how sorry he was and how grateful he felt for their friendship, from the very first day at the academy to the night that Javi agreed to his plan.

Their friendship was the only part of Jack's life that he'd ever felt certain about.

When Jack stepped out of his room, Javier was still seated pensively on his luggage.

"I know I'm probably the last person you want to see right now, but I couldn't let you leave without saying goodbye," Jack said. "And apologizing."

Javi just nodded quietly.

"I know I've been a shitty friend ever since the switch, and you don't deserve to be punished for *my* issues," Jack said. "I hope you know that I'm really proud of you, Javi. You're twice the man I'll ever be."

Javier looked up at his friend, appearing touched by the tribute.

Jack's eyes were swollen, his face shaded with ungroomed stubble, yet Javi still looked the same as their first day as roommates, when Jack had met Javi's parents and noticed how nervous they seemed, hesitant to leave their son. Jack had given them his word, then, that he would look out for Javi. They were in it together.

"Thanks for saying that," said Javi.

Jack smiled and gestured toward the foosball table. "Wanna play one last game?"

"I think I just need to be alone, if that's all right. Keep my head clear."

"Okay, yeah. No problem," said Jack. Evidently he was wrong to think one small apology would suffice. "I, uh, I just wanted to give this to you before you go."

Jack handed Javi a thin white envelope. *For my best friend* was written on the front. Javi slid his finger under the seal, and a weathered prayer card, worn at the edges from so many decades of clutching, slipped out and into his palm.

"I can't take this," Javi said.

"Of course you can. You deserve it more than I do."

Javi shook his head. "Really, Jack, I can't."

"I know you're Catholic, and this is a Jewish blessing, but . . . it's all the same God, right?"

"It's not that," Javi said, placing the card on the bookshelf near him. "That's *your* family legacy. Not mine."

It hurt Jack to hear him say it like that. Javi had been more of a brother to him than any of his actual kin. Javi was the only one who knew how Jack truly felt about the Hunters, about the army, about everything.

"You *are* my family," Jack said.

Javi was silent for a moment, only the muted sounds of the traffic outside filling their apartment. "I appreciate that, Jack. But I've been doing some . . . reflecting . . . and I think I just need some time to myself right now, with *my* family, away from all the Hunter-Rollins drama. No offense, but . . . they cast a wide shadow."

Jack sighed. He couldn't argue with that.

"You know, the *only* Hunter who ever owned that card was my grandfather," Jack said. "And it was given to him by his friend Simon, to keep him safe. That's all I was trying to do."

"And it's a nice gesture, Jack. But I don't really want to talk about it anymore."

Jack could sense the quiet frustration in Javier's voice. He had dropped the biting tone of their earlier fight, replaced his ire with something more like sadness. As if Jack were no longer worth yelling at. A hopeless cause.

"Okay, then, I guess I'll get out of your way," said Jack, awkwardly shuffling toward the door. "But I'll leave the card there, in case you change your mind."

Javi turned his face away, and as Jack stood in the threshold, he took a long look at his friend. His gaze landed atop the knotted laces on Javier's sneakers—two strings tied together, like his and Javi's would forever be.

Jack was truly grateful that giving Javi his string would allow his friend to achieve what he had worked so hard to earn. But they both knew that Javi's dream was only part of why Jack had suggested the switch—and a small part, at that.

Jack gave Javier his string to save himself. And Javi never called him out on that, never once made him feel like a coward. That was all Jack's own doing.

Javi didn't want some old, washed-out prayer card that never belonged to him. He told Jack *exactly* what he wanted, during their fight at the boxing studio, and yet Jack couldn't give it to him. He couldn't confront his uncle, the way he could never confront anyone in his family. And now Anthony was the heir apparent, the potential president, while Jack was the same as he had always been. The last teammate chosen at the annual Hunter picnic. The son abandoned by his own blood.

What the hell was Jack doing? Allowing the family that never truly understood him to drive away the only person who did?

Jack thought that he knew what loneliness felt like, a perpetual out-sider among his kin, a mistake. But that was always the *absence* of love. Here, with Javi, it was the *loss*.

And losing something felt so much harder, so much lonelier, than sim-ply going without.

Jack couldn't lose Javi. Not now. Not years before he had to. And cer-tainly not when his own weakness and fear were to blame.

Jack looked at his friend and former roommate, tearing up against his will.

"I promise I'll find a way to make it up to you, Javi, to earn your for-giveness. And your respect. Because I have so much respect for you," he said. "I know you'll make the army proud."

BEN

When Ben met Maura for drinks in September, she had asked him for a favor, setting up a surprise for her girlfriend while they were away in Italy.

So, once they had left for their trip, Ben took the subway to their building, walked up three flights of stairs, and pulled out the spare key that Maura had given him at the previous support group session.

He was expecting an empty apartment.

But as he opened the door and stepped into the living room, he nearly crashed into a woman, gripping a potted plant above her head.

"Oh shit!" Ben jumped back, fumbling his keys in surprise.

"Who are you?" the woman exclaimed, looking just as startled as he was.

"I'm a friend of Maura's," Ben explained. "She gave me the key."

"Oh," the woman said, suddenly aware of her defensive stance. "I'm sorry, I heard you coming in, and I knew you couldn't be Nina or Maura, so I just grabbed the first weapon I could find."

Ben glanced at the row of bright green plants behind her. "The cactus might have been a better choice," he said. "Extra-painful."

At that, the woman smiled, her shoulders relaxed. She placed the pot gently back on the shelf.

"I'm Nina's sister," she said. "Amie."

"Nice to meet you," he said. "I'm Ben."

• • •

Both Amie and Ben had apparently been tasked with assignments during the trip: Nina had asked Amie to water the plants and bring in the mail, while Maura had commissioned Ben for an art project.

Ben pulled out a handful of papers from the poster tube under his arm, spreading them out on the coffee table.

"You drew all of these?" Amie asked in amazement.

She leaned in closely to examine the series of sketches—a divey downtown karaoke bar, a café patio bedecked with string lights, the greenhouse dome at the Brooklyn Botanic Garden.

"Maura's seen me doodling a bunch of times, and apparently she liked what she saw." Ben laughed. "But I tried to make *these* slightly more professional-looking. I was coming in today to take some measurements on the wall, so I can get them framed."

Amie nodded, piecing the story together. "So, that's where they met, and that's where Nina said, 'I love you.' I just don't recognize the place in the middle."

"First date," Ben answered. "Maura wanted all the milestone places."

"It's a beautiful gift," Amie said. "And the *drawings* are beautiful. Are you an artist?"

"An architect," he said.

"So, an artist who's good at math." Amie smiled.

"What about you?

"Oh, I'm terrible at math," she said.

Ben laughed. "I meant, what do you *do?*"

"I'm an English teacher," she said. "No numbers, just novels."

Ben was about to ask which school she taught at when he heard a frantic knocking at the door. "Nina! Maura!" called a panicked voice.

Ben quickly opened the door to reveal an elderly man, his frail frame covered by sopping clothes.

"Who are *you?*" the man asked. "Where are Nina and Maura?"

"Uh, they're away," Ben said. "We're their friends. Can we help you?"

"I don't know, I didn't know where to go. Maura and Nina are usually here to give me a hand," the man rambled anxiously. "Something happened, I think a pipe must have burst. There's water everywhere." He looked as if he might cry.

"Okay, sir, why don't you come inside and sit down," Ben said gently, while Amie helped the man onto the couch.

"Where did the pipe burst?" Ben asked.

"Down the hall, Apartment 3B."

"I'll grab some towels," Amie said, as Ben ran off to 3B.

When he entered the cramped galley kitchen, he nearly slid across the floor. A pipe was indeed spewing water, and a thin layer already flowed across the black-and-white tiles, a liquid phalanx marching fast, invading the hardwood floor in the hall, threatening the carpet ahead. Ben squinted against the spray as he crouched beneath the sink, his fingers feeling around for the shutoff valve.

He found it and successfully stopped the spurting just as Amie rushed in, her arms filled with bath towels. If Ben hadn't been so blinded by water and adrenaline, he would have felt grateful that he had managed to solve the crisis just in time to impress her.

"A plumber is on his way," she said, tossing a few towels to Ben, who wrapped one tightly around the leaking pipe. The elderly neighbor had followed Amie in, standing cautiously by the threshold while Ben and Amie knelt down and began to mop up the water.

"I'm so sorry, you shouldn't have to do this," the man said, clearly ashamed of his need. "I would've done it all myself, but . . . I was afraid I might slip and fall."

"It's really no problem," Amie said kindly. Then she glanced at Ben, stifling a laugh.

"What?" he asked.

"You're just . . . you're very wet," she said.

"Well, you timed *your* entrance well." Ben smiled, attempting to fling his damp hair from his face. "You missed the part when I was headfirst in a geyser."

After the plumber arrived, the old man walked Ben and Amie into the hall and thanked them again profusely.

"That was very heroic," Amie told Ben, as they carried the pile of dirty towels to the laundry room.

"We mathematicians are known for our bravery," he joked.

"I hope you're also known for your discretion," she said, "because we can never tell Nina that we used her fancy guest towels to clean up a flood. She gets nervous if I even drink water too close to the couch."

"The secret's safe with me." Ben smiled.

"Well, I'm assuming you'd like to go home and change your clothes," Amie offered.

But Ben didn't want to part just yet. Something inside him told him to stay.

"Actually . . . what I'd really like is a drink," said Ben. "And maybe some company?"

Drinks blended into dinner at a trattoria around the corner, which Amie suggested to pretend that they, too, were in Italy.

"I asked Nina to bring back gondola key chains for all my students," she explained, after they'd polished off their food.

"That's really nice," said Ben. "Sounds like something my mom would've done. She and my dad were both teachers, too."

"So, I remind you of your mother?" Amie teased, just as the waiter arrived with two steaming cappuccinos. "Girls *love* that."

Ben thought that he and Amie had been toeing the line between friendliness and flirtation. Had Amie just intentionally crossed it?

Was this what a first date felt like? It had been so long that Ben had nearly forgotten.

Suddenly he was nervous that he might spill his drink or get cappuccino foam stuck on his lip. Was he crunching the biscotti too loudly? All these trifling little worries of the time before, the nagging insecurities.

It was almost a luxury to feel them again.

As Nina and Maura enjoyed their journey abroad, Ben stumbled into something of an adventure himself, a whirl of outings with Amie.

They met again at Nina and Maura's apartment, so Ben could finish taking his measurements, then Amie accompanied him to the frame shop, helping him pick something her sister would like.

In the span of just over a week, there were dinners and walks in the park. Morning bagels and evening drinks. And after Ben leaned in to kiss her one night, Amie asked if the date *had* to end. In an incredible feat of willpower, Ben invited her to a nearby café instead of back to his apartment. He couldn't take that next step yet, at least not without feeling guilty.

Not when Amie still didn't know.

But they had spent all this time together, and the topic of the strings had never come up. Amie seemed content to avoid the subject, and Ben didn't know how to address it.

Over coffee that night, Amie pulled out her phone, scrolling through the recent messages, while Ben's eyes traced the curve of her profile. As an architect, he strove for symmetry, but he was oddly delighted by the fact that she had a small constellation of freckles on her right cheek, and none on her left.

"Look at this," she said, holding up a photo of the Italian countryside. "Nina just sent it to me. Isn't it gorgeous?" Then she cupped her hands around her mug and let out a contented sigh. "Do you ever think about moving to some small village in Europe? Like, just leaving the frenzy of New York and living in a cottage, where you can bike into town, and everybody knows everybody else, and you can eat fresh breads and jams and cheeses for the rest of your life?"

"Honestly, not very often." Ben laughed. "But it does sound nice when you describe it."

"I'm sure the fantasy is nicer than the reality," Amie said with a shrug. "It's strange, because people often talk about that dream of 'the simple life,' or focusing on 'the simple things.' But just because you live in the country, away from all the superficial stuff, I guess that doesn't really make *life* any less complicated."

Ben nodded knowingly. "At least you get to face it while eating fresh breads and cheeses."

Amie smiled. "Nina and Maura are going to Verona tomorrow, for their last day," she said. "And I keep thinking about *Romeo and Juliet*. Did you know there's actually this tradition in Verona of writing letters to Juliet?"

"The fictional character?"

"Well, sort of," Amie explained. "Each year, thousands of people send a letter addressed to Juliet, asking for her guidance in their love lives. And there's a group of people who live in Verona, they call themselves Juliet's secretaries, and they answer each letter on her behalf. By hand."

"That sounds like a big responsibility."

"I know. I certainly don't think *my* advice could be trusted when it comes to romance," she said. Then an odd look of entrancement settled upon her face. An idea, or perhaps a memory, visibly dancing across her mind.

"You look like you're lost in thought," Ben said.

"Oh, I'm sorry, I do that sometimes." Amie smiled, looking slightly embarrassed. "I was just remembering this woman who could have really used Juliet's counsel."

"A friend of yours?" Ben asked.

"No, not at all. Just someone whose story intrigued me once. Funny enough, I actually read about her in a letter. This woman named Gertrude."

The word nearly knocked Ben off his chair, the name an electric jolt. *Gertrude*.

Those simple syllables awakened every other recognition, as if the similarities between Amie and the mysterious "A" had been slowly piling up since they'd met, at last standing tall enough to be viewed in full. Both were English teachers in Manhattan, both lived on the Upper West Side. And this letter about Gertrude, it had to be *his* letter, right?

Ben's heartbeat started to accelerate. It couldn't be. Absolutely not. *Could it?*

"I just realized," Ben said, "I've never asked you what school you teach at?"

"Oh, it's called the Connelly Academy, on the Upper East Side," Amie answered. "I know, it's *much* more posh than I am."

Ben opened his mouth to say something, anything, but no words came out, so he quickly lifted his cup to cover his face, to give him just one moment to compose himself. But he nearly choked on his coffee.

Amie taught at the same school where Ben sat every Sunday night, where he left his letters each week. It *had* to be her, he thought. He could feel it in his bones, if that were even possible.

He *knew*, in the rational part of his brain, that there might still be another answer, but he *felt* that there was simply no alternative. It had to be her.

NINA

On their final day in Italy, Nina and Maura boarded the hour-long train from Venice to Verona.

The day trip was Amie's recommendation, and both Nina and Maura had agreed that the literary city was worth a stop. Verona was also far less crowded than Venice, except for one corner off the main piazza, where lovers and bookworms and tourists alike all made the pilgrimage to the Casa di Giulietta.

As the women made their way to Juliet's courtyard, they passed beneath an archway at the entrance. The inner walls of the arch were completely covered with layers of names scrawled on top of each other, accumulating year after year. From afar, it looked like a chaotic web of graffiti, illegible scribbles in thick black Sharpies and pens of every color, filling the entire wall with markings. But, upon leaning in more closely, they could untangle individual names and signatures: *Marko and Amin. Giuli & Simo. Angela + Sam. Manuel and Grace. Nick & Ron. M+L. Teddy was here.*

Maura glanced at Nina, who could always be trusted to carry a pen, and they each signed their initials on the wall, wherever they could find some blank space. Then they emerged from the walkway onto a patio, where a few dozen visitors had gathered to gaze at the storied stone balcony above and take photos with the bronze statue of Juliet, standing demurely in the center.

The couple was rather disheartened to learn, almost immediately, that another popular custom was to rub the young girl's breasts, the way other statues' toes or shoes are touched for good fortune.

"*Mi scusi.*" Maura caught the attention of a woman near them. "*Perché la toccano?*" She gestured toward the tourist with a hand on Juliet's chest.

The woman turned out to be a fellow American. "Are you asking me why they grab her boobs? I think it's supposed to bring you good luck in your love life."

"Because Juliet was so lucky in that department," Nina whispered skeptically.

"Well, this is just upsetting." Maura winced, watching two teenage boys who seemed desperate for love.

So the two of them sidestepped the crowd waiting in line for their turn with the statue and headed to the wall behind Juliet, filled with hundreds of messages written on small Post-it notes and jagged-edged pages ripped from journals, as each new visitor partook in the time-honored tradition of leaving a letter for the tragic heroine.

"This one's cute," said Maura. "'Your name is Taylor, but you're my Giuletta. We're in Verona, let's never forgetta.'"

"Can you tell what this one means?" Nina pointed to another sticker. Maura studied the yellow paper under Nina's finger.

Se il per sempre non esiste lo inventeremo noi.

Her forehead scrunched, her brain searching for the words. "If forever doesn't exist," she said, "we'll invent it ourselves."

In the afternoon, Nina and Maura wandered along the edge of the Adige River, wending their way toward the Ponte Pietra, the main bridge in Verona. The Roman-era overpass had been built with a combination of red bricks and limestone, and Nina thought that the blending of the two different materials managed to appear both messy and beautiful at the same time.

The wind was whipping hard off the water, and a few passersby clutched their hats. The river's current looked surprisingly rough, white-caps passing beneath the bridge.

"It's Juliet's spirit," Maura theorized, "come to exact her revenge on all who groped her statue."

They saw a small gathering of people near the end of the bridge, where a makeshift shrine of flowers, candles, and a few stuffed bears had been erected.

"It looks like a memorial," said Nina.

As they approached, Nina recognized the man and woman in one of the framed photographs. The newlyweds who had jumped off the bridge that spring.

"Let's keep walking," Nina said, hoping not to dwell in sadness. But whenever she glanced back at the water, she couldn't help but think about the couple who had leapt in together, and the short-string bride who had drowned. At least she had known a great love in her life. What were the words that Maura had read on that Post-it? *Maybe we can invent our own forever.*

"What are you thinking about?" Maura asked. "You're so quiet."

"The note you read in Italian," she answered. "*Si siempre no existe . . . ?*"

Maura laughed. "I think that's Spanish."

Another burst of wind blew past, and Nina felt a strange sense of energy lifting her up. She stopped walking and turned to face Maura, her expression suddenly serious.

"You know, for the first few weeks we were dating, I kept waiting for you to break up with me," Nina said. "I couldn't imagine that someone so special, so . . . unforgettable . . . would even remember my name." She paused. "And here we are, two years later, facing the fact that forever doesn't exist. For anyone. But I still want to invent it with you."

Rarely had Maura been rendered speechless, but in that instant, she seemed to be.

"I'm asking you to marry me," Nina clarified nervously.

"I know," Maura finally said. "And the thing is . . . I would have said yes, if the proposal hadn't been so cheesy."

Nina let out a laugh of pleasure and relief. "Will you give me a second chance, then?"

Maura smiled at her. "Yes."

BEN

Ben's parents had kept a storage unit in lower Manhattan ever since they sold their family home in New Jersey and moved into their apartment, but in her newfound retirement, Ben's mother had read one too many books on downsizing and decluttering, and she was convinced that at least half of their stored items were now unnecessary. So, on Saturday afternoon, Ben headed downtown to help his parents clear out the unit.

When he arrived, his parents were already rummaging through towers of sealed brown boxes and tossing items into huge black trash bags.

"Just throw away or donate anything you don't want to keep," his mother said.

"Anything that doesn't spark joy?" Ben teased.

His mom playfully mussed her son's hair with her fingers, the way she often did when he was younger. Back then he found it annoying and babyish, but now Ben didn't mind so much.

"I think you need a haircut," she said, unable to control her motherly impulse.

"Let's just focus on the boxes, shall we?"

Ben sat down atop an unopened trunk and started combing through cases of old clothing, separating the pieces that would go to Goodwill from those in too rough a condition to salvage. The methodical task allowed his mind to roam untethered, and it didn't take long for him to think of Amie, of all the truths still untold—about his string, about their letters.

But there was just no obvious answer. Ben liked Amie. He liked her broad smile and her asymmetric freckles, her passion for her job, and the fact that everything just felt so easy between them, as easy in person as it was on the page. And, of course, what Ben *truly* liked about Amie were the thoughts and fears and dreams that lay beneath the surface. The ones she revealed in writing.

And Ben thought that Amie might like him, too. But what if she only liked the part of Ben that she met this week, the hero who helped a neighbor in need, and not the sad, self-pitying short-stringer who was also, inextricably, a part of Ben?

He looked up at his parents, both in their early sixties now, sorting through the records of their shared life, of decades spent side by side. How could Ben ask any woman to choose *him*, when he couldn't give her that?

His last few months with Claire, around his thirtieth birthday, were the first time that Ben actually contemplated marriage and fatherhood in a real, palpable sense, rather than some elusive hypotheticals. And after Claire left him, after he learned about his string, suddenly all of the future steps that he'd always taken for granted—getting married, raising a family, watching his kids grow up as he aged with his wife—were no longer guaranteed.

It was painful for Ben to think that if the strings had never arrived, or if Claire had never opened his box, then he simply would have pursued those steps, no questions asked, no second thoughts. But now those second thoughts tortured his mind.

"Oh gosh, look at this!" His mother lifted a pint-size pumpkin costume from the box labeled *Halloween*.

Ben leaned over to examine the ensembles in the box: Woody's cowboy hat, a retractable lightsaber, even the matted faux-beard from his yearlong obsession with Antoni Gaudí after a family trip to Spain.

"These will make some little kids so happy." His mom smiled, placing everything in the donation bin.

His dad was about to crush the empty box when Ben spotted a small Hallmark card stuck to the bottom. On the front of the card was a cartoon ghost shouting *Boo!* and on the inside, his parents had written, *Don't be scared! We're always watching out for you.*

"I guess we used to be a little schmaltzy," said Ben's father.

"*Used* to be?" Ben joked.

But his mother elbowed her husband gently. "Hey, that was a nice card," she said. "And we meant it."

As his parents returned to their respective piles, Ben looked down at the open card in his lap, the joke scrawled in his mother's cursive, and he felt a strange twinge in his eye.

His mom was right. Ben couldn't even remember a time when he was with his parents and still felt scared. He had only ever felt protected.

Even after he flipped off his bike as a reckless teenager and was lying in the hospital bed, anxiously awaiting his X-ray results, just the sight of his parents, running into the ER, had instantly steadied his nerves. It didn't matter that they would spend the next hour chiding him for his carelessness. When he saw them coming, he simply felt safe.

So how could he not turn to them now, in the most frightening hour of his life, when he needed their comfort the most?

Yes, the truth would hurt them, Ben thought, but wouldn't it hurt them more to find out later? To think their son hadn't trusted them enough? After all the times they had been there?

"There's something I need to tell you both," said Ben. "I know about my string. It's the real reason why Claire and I broke up. And . . . it has about fourteen more years. A decade and a half." He smiled thinly. "It sounds a bit better that way."

There was a brief pause then, a gap in time when nobody spoke or moved, and Ben worried that something in his parents had irrevocably cracked, shattered in one small instant.

Until his mother leaned forward and pulled him toward her and hugged him with the fierceness, the almost-otherworldly intensity, that can only be reached by a particular person in a particular moment: a parent sheltering their child. Ben was taller and broader than his mother, he had been since college, but somehow, now, her body seemed to wrap around Ben's, engulfing him like he was a little boy, swaddling him with her whole self. And Ben's father placed his hand atop his son's shoulder, warm and heavy, exerting just enough pressure to keep Ben from folding over.

Ben realized, then, that Claire never once touched him when she told him the truth that night. It was quite shocking, in retrospect. She had squeezed her arms around *herself*, trying to hold *herself* steady. But Ben's parents didn't care about themselves, not right now. They cared only about their son.

So Ben sat there, on top of a storage trunk, in the arms of his mother, under the hand of his father, and everything that needed to be said was said in the silence, in their touch.

JACK

A few weeks after Javier left, Jack needed to escape their apartment, the entire place a reminder of their strained friendship. They had hardly spoken since their fight, and Jack finally understood why his father made them move to a new house when his mother left, the way that memories can tarnish a room.

So, on a Friday night, after a week of cybersecurity training for his new role in D.C., Jack walked straight to Union Station and boarded the next train to New York.

He took a seat in the rear car and looked out the window, foggy with years of fingerprint smudges and strangers' breaths. He couldn't wait to get to New York. He had only visited the city a few times before, but he knew that it was the only place in the world where there was always a crowd, no matter where you went or what time it was. The only place where his anonymity, an almost-normal life, was all but guaranteed.

Jack spent two days roaming the streets of Manhattan, sleeping on a buddy's shabby gray futon, drinking and playing pool at a dive bar, trying to decipher the unintelligible announcements on the subway, slipping past unrecognized by anyone around him. But still he thought of Javier.

Every helicopter that rumbled overhead made him think of his friend, the pilot-in-training. Though he slept in the living room with the windows open, hearing every siren and shout and shattering of glass in the trash bags dragged to the curb, Jack's mind was back in D.C., or their dorm room at the academy. Even New York couldn't free him. The distractions of the city just weren't enough to outweigh the guilt that nagged him, reminding Jack that he had yet to make good on his promise to Javier. To be worthy of his forgiveness.

By the end of the weekend, Jack was walking down the street, hands sunk in his pockets, depressed by his failed attempt at diversion. It wasn't yet eight P.M., but the sidewalk was quiet, just a handful of pedestrians skimming past, a political canvasser shyly asking for signatures, a drummer tapping on overturned buckets.

Jack could see the two teenage boys approaching the activist, a short man with glasses clutching a clipboard. There was something about the way the boys carried their bodies, aggressive and arrogant, consuming more space than they possibly needed, that reminded Jack of his academy tormentors. As the boys swaggered closer to the oblivious canvasser, Jack picked up his pace.

The man actually tried offering the boys his pitch, flashing an innocent smile. "Do you have a minute to support Wes Johnson?" he asked.

One of the boys cocked his head. "You mean that *short-stringer?*"

"Senator Johnson has proven that he'll be an advocate for *all* Americans, which includes those with short strings," answered the activist.

"Why would I want to waste my vote on someone who's just gonna kick the bucket? He should get his sad short-stringer ass out of the way. He's a fuckin' embarrassment."

One of the boys grabbed the clipboard out of the activist's hands and greedily scanned the names. "Who the hell even likes this guy?"

A passing mother, noticing the scene, nervously gripped her child's hand, leading her away from the tense trio of men, while Jack hovered nearby, waiting.

"Please return that," the canvasser pleaded.

The boy smiled crookedly, then hurled the clipboard onto the sidewalk, the plastic striking the pavement with a single smack. The drummer nearby stopped playing.

Jack could see the agony on the canvasser's face, trying to calculate the safest move. If he stooped down to pick up the clipboard, he'd be taking his eyes off the boys and, more crucially, the table with the box of donations.

Jack glanced around. The next closest witness was a young pregnant woman hanging farther back, her right hand clenching her phone, fingers presumably poised to dial 911 should the situation escalate. Where was the crowd when you needed it most? Jack thought. He nodded at the woman, and she tipped her head back in response, the instant kinship of mutual concern.

"Aren't you going to pick that up?" the boy asked the activist, while his friend inched closer to the table.

Aren't you going to hit him back? Jack could still hear the taunts from the sidelines at school. *Too bad your family isn't here. Too bad your uncle isn't here. Too bad you're just not as strong as they are.*

Suddenly Jack's anger burst.

"Why don't you just leave the man alone, and we can all get back to our evenings?" Jack said firmly, stepping forward and offering the man a brief window to snatch his clipboard from the sidewalk.

"Why don't *you* just mind your own business, asshole!"

"I'm not looking for a fight," said Jack.

"Then back the fuck off."

"Not until you let this man return to his job in peace," said Jack.

The boy snickered. "You're probably one of them. The both of you. *Short-stringers,*" he said, his words drenched in malice.

When Jack refused to respond or step away, the boy turned his head slightly, as if about to back down, before swiftly pivoting back, fist flying toward Jack's chin.

Incredibly, Jack blocked the punch.

The boy's friend then swung at him from the side, but Jack managed to shield himself again.

Stunned and angered, the two boys each tried another maneuver, but still Jack fended them off. What the frustrated boys couldn't have known was that Jack wasn't on the streets of New York anymore. He was back in the ring with Javier. Sparring against his best friend, his brother. Subliminally memorizing Javier's moves, and how to defend against them.

Jack really didn't want to hit the kids, but he figured it was his only way out, so he landed a jab in each boy's stomach, nothing too hard, just enough to send the message that the battle was over.

And when the boys both staggered back, and Jack realized what had happened, he smiled to himself. Even when he wasn't around, Javi always had his six.

After the boys had fled in defeat, a police officer arrived. He was taking the canvasser's statement when the young pregnant woman, who must have called the cops, walked over to Jack.

"You're quite the fighter," she said.

Jack's body was still trembling with adrenaline, and his wrists were sore, but it was nothing compared to the pain of that brutal fistfight during freshman year, when he had been knocked clean on his ass in front of all his new classmates, and Javi had to steal ice from the kitchen to keep his face from swelling.

"Thanks," Jack said. "I'm normally not that . . . capable."

"I'm Lea." The woman smiled.

"Jack."

"Well, Jack, I'm on my way to a discussion group tonight. So, thank you for giving me a good story to share."

Jack noticed, then, that the girl was wearing a gold pin on her sweater, with a design he had never seen before: two curving lines intertwined, like the snakes twisted around Hermes's caduceus, only these lines were of two different lengths.

Lea spotted his curiosity. "It's two strings," she explained. "One long and one short. For solidarity."

"Did you make that?" Jack asked.

"My brother gave it to me," she explained. "I think someone just started selling them on Etsy, but apparently they're catching on pretty fast. Wes Johnson even wore one last week."

Something his uncle would surely hate, Jack thought.

"Do you think that's *really* why they were so cruel?" Lea asked. "Because the man was working for Johnson?"

Jack shrugged.

"I can't believe the stuff they said about short-stringers." Lea shuddered.

"Well, hopefully now they'll think twice before saying something like that again."

"Thank you," Lea said solemnly.

The gravity of her tone struck Jack. "It was just two bullies looking for kicks, maybe some cash," he said. "It was really nothing."

"You saw something *wrong*, and you didn't look away," said Lea. "That's not nothing."

Jack remembered what Javi had said during their argument. That it wasn't just about Anthony's ego, not anymore. People's lives were at stake now. People who had been dealt a hand far worse than Jack's, no matter how many times he complained about his family, wishing his life were different. Javi tried to tell him that, to pull him out of his self-absorption.

As usual, Jack had failed to see it, and Javier was right.

Jack wasn't sure what had come over him, pushing him to intervene on the street, but he couldn't help heading back to D.C. that night with the feeling that maybe he wasn't so weak, after all. Maybe he just needed the right moment, away from his family, away from the cameras, away from the army, away from anyone he had ever lied to, or tried too hard to impress. Maybe, after all those years living with Javier, he had learned more from his friend than just boxing.

It was exhilarating, this feeling of having done something meaningful, even if just for a moment. All his life, Jack had limply followed orders, shrunken into himself. He felt like he had always done nothing.

But this, at last, was not nothing.

Jack knew that it was only a matter of days now before the next invitation to join Anthony and Katherine onstage. And maybe, this time, he wouldn't be so afraid.

BEN

On Sunday morning, the day after he told his parents the truth, Ben woke up and realized that he still hadn't written a letter. He hadn't yet decided what to say to Amie, and tonight was another meeting, another session in *her* classroom. His last chance to leave the usual letter behind, to pretend that nothing had changed.

But before he could think any further, Ben glanced at his phone, and the date caught his eye.

Two months ago, exactly.

Within an hour, he was on the subway, heading downtown. There was somewhere he needed to be.

He hadn't been there since that afternoon in August, when the park was packed with spectators, both adoring and enraged.

As he neared the park entrance, Ben noticed a small crowd gathered by the side of a building, a handful of people even snapping pictures. The question briefly crossed Ben's mind—were they here for the same reason he was?—before he realized they were photographing some sort of graffiti on the stone wall.

When the group moved aside, Ben saw what they had been looking at: a black-and-white mural of the mythical Pandora, crouched over her opened box. It was too late, the contents of the infamous chest—shadowy spirals and demonic faces—had already been released into the world, crawling upward along the edge of the wall. The image prickled Ben's skin, and he quickly turned away from it and walked into the park.

His memory seemed to lead his body instinctively toward the place where he had stood that day, and as Ben came closer, he was surprised to see a young woman standing motionless, almost meditative, in the middle of the busy walkway, the stillness of her body only broken by the hem of her long floral skirt dancing lightly around her ankles. The woman pulled a bouquet of flowers out of her bag and knelt down to rest them on the pavement.

She was several yards away from the spot where Hank had fallen, as though she had also been there that day—or perhaps was guided by the descriptions of the event in the news. Regardless, Ben felt sure of her intent, and he debated whether or not to approach her. He knew the rules of the city, the eyebrows raised at those who willingly spoke to strangers. And, if this woman were truly mourning Hank, was it rude to disturb her grieving?

As he walked slowly toward her, Ben tried to deduce who she might be. Hank didn't have any sisters, and this wasn't the woman who had eulogized him, Dr. Anika Singh. Perhaps a cousin, a colleague, another ex.

"I'm sorry to bother you," Ben said delicately, "but are those for Hank?"

The woman was startled by his voice. "Oh yes, they are," she said. "Did you know him?"

"I did." Ben nodded. "Though only recently, I suppose."

The woman paused for a moment, her head slanted in thought. "What was he like?" she asked.

Ben was surprised. He had assumed that this woman knew Hank. But she was hardly an acquaintance, it seemed. Some obsessive admirer who heard Hank's story?

"Uh, well, he was one of the most interesting people I've known," said Ben. His initial caution melted away, as he saw the woman's intrigue. "I got the sense that he never wanted to be a burden, or let people feel sorry for him. He always wanted to be the hero." Ben smiled. "And lucky for him, he usually was."

"That's why I wanted to come," the woman said. "To thank him."

Of course, Ben thought. A patient who only knew Hank the physician, not the man outside the ER.

"He was your doctor, then?" Ben asked her.

"Actually, no," she said, just as the breeze lifted the edges of her long black hair, the ends dyed a vibrant pink. "He . . . gave me my lungs."

For a moment, Ben felt his own lungs struggling for breath. He stared, blinking, at the woman in front of him, her chest expanding and filling with the autumn air.

Ben had no idea that Hank was an organ donor; nobody mentioned it at the funeral. But it made perfect sense, didn't it? A hero's final act.

"It's been two months, and this is the first time I've been able to visit. But I think of him all the time."

"I'm sure he would be very happy to know about you," said Ben.

He suddenly remembered a conversation with Maura, something about cryonics and mind-uploading, all the bargains and sacrifices that people made now in the hope of living on someday. But when Ben looked at the young woman before him, he thought about her string, and how every piece of the thread that extended beyond that afternoon in August was a portion gifted from Hank's string to hers, how this woman's life had been lengthened simply because Hank had been alive, and Ben realized that there was more than one way to live on.

"I still haven't looked at my string," she said, as if Ben had voiced his musings aloud. "At first, before I knew about the surgery, I was too afraid to look, and I made my whole family swear not to look, either. But now, no matter how long my string is, every day just feels so sacred. And I don't want to waste any time feeling sad or distracted. I just want to be grateful. To live as much life as possible."

The woman was speaking to Ben, but she wasn't looking at him anymore. She was watching the other people in the park—the couple discreetly sharing a bottle of wine on a blanket, the jogger curled over the water fountain, the teenager reading at the base of a tree.

The woman's phone suddenly rang in her purse, and she looked down at the screen.

"Oh shoot, I've got to run," she apologized. But then her lips unfurled in an unexpected grin, and she looked up at Ben. "You know, I used to only mean that as an expression, because I couldn't *actually* run, without literally gasping for air. But that phone call was from my friend," she explained. "Now that I'm two months post-op, we're going to start walking together, and then jogging. And then, next year, I'm going to run a half marathon."

Ben smiled at the girl's confidence in her own prediction. "Good luck," he told her.

After the woman walked away, Ben stared at the peach-colored roses she had placed on the ground. How many people would walk past them and wonder why they were here, who they were meant for? Perhaps some of them might actually know.

On his way out of the park and back to the subway, Ben passed by the same black-and-white mural as before, but this time he wasn't afraid to step closer. As he looked at Pandora's distraught face and the empty box in her hands, he noticed that something had been painted on top of the mural that he hadn't seen from farther away. It must have been added by a different artist, Ben reasoned, using bright blue paint and a thinner brush.

Only a small section of the box's interior had been left visible by the original muralist, but it was here, in a dark corner of the chest, that a second artist had come along and inscribed a single word, *Hope*.

AMIE

On Monday morning, Amie found the letter in her classroom.

She was stunned to see it addressed to her by name, rather than just her initial. She tried to recall if she had accidentally revealed her name in a previous note, but she didn't think she had, and when she flipped the page over to the other side, she saw that the author had signed with his name, too.

Dear Amie,

I once heard about this remote island in the Galápagos, where only a hundred people live nowadays, but back in the 18th century, some whalers set up an empty barrel on the shore to serve as a makeshift "post office." And they started this tradition where any ships passing through the island would take letters out of the barrel and carry them back to England or America or wherever they were coming from, essentially delivering the mail on behalf of their fellow sailors. To this day, visitors can still leave their own postcards or letters inside the barrel—no stamp required—in exchange for taking somebody else's letter out and promising to deliver it to its rightful recipient. I haven't seen any statistics, but supposedly the system works surprisingly well.

I'm not sure why I'm telling you this, other than maybe it makes me believe that even in the strangest of circumstances, a letter can find its way to the right person.

Somehow, months ago, my letter found its way to you.

And, as crazy as it sounds, we actually found our way to each other, and I realized that you worked at the very school where I've sat every Sunday night since April, in a support group for short-stringers. (This group is also where I met Maura, but I haven't told her about these letters, or about you.)

I spent most of my twenties worrying about how my boss would react to my designs, or whether I was making as much money as I should be, or if I finally had the life that would make my old classmates see me as someone bigger and stronger than the nerdy boy they had known. And of course, those things—building a career, making money—are still important, but they're not the only things that matter. The strings have made that clearer than ever.

I can see now, as an adult, that my parents gave me two wonderful gifts: They modeled what a true, loving partnership looks like, and they built me a childhood where I always felt safe and protected, never scared.

I think I could do that, too. Be a good partner to the person I love, and pass on to my kids the greatest legacy of my parents.

I'm sorry, Amie. I'm sorry for the shock that this letter will bring, and I'm sorry because you once asked me to write about little things, and this is perhaps the biggest thing of all. But you also said that we could each find our own measure of happiness.

A stranger recently told me that she didn't want to waste any time feeling sad. She just wanted to live as much life as possible. And I think that's as good a measure as any.

Thank you for everything,
Ben

Amie slowly released the letter, its edges dampened by her sweating hands.

Ben was the person writing, all this time. *Ben* was the one she had consoled and turned to herself for consolation.

Ben had a short string.

P.S.—In the interest of living well and chasing the things I want, I'd like to see you again. No more secrets.

Amie felt feverish and light-headed, blinking back the tears that had gathered as she read. She needed time to think, to untangle everything. Her last class had finished for the day, so she left school early and caught the first bus she saw.

Amie settled into a seat, trying to stay calm, but a wave of nausea shivered through her body. She shut her eyes for the rest of the route, the bus stuttering slowly through traffic, until it arrived at her stop, and she raced out of her seat and up the stairs of her building, grateful to be back in her apartment.

Amie had saved all of Ben's letters, before she knew they were his, and she pulled every page out of the drawer in her dresser, rereading each one in turn. She sat cross-legged on her bedroom floor, staring at the sheets of loose-leaf fanned across the carpet. Each page decorated with Ben's neat handwriting, always etched in dark blue ink.

Was it possible she had recognized something in Ben, something from these letters?

Perhaps that was why she had been so eager, so forward, in their time together. Why she had instantly felt the warmth of familiarity, which usually took so much longer to kindle. She had even pressed to go back to his apartment after just a few days, much faster than her typical pace.

Was *this* why Ben had wanted to wait, that night? So he could tell her the truth beforehand?

Amie knew that she was drawn to Ben. She had been drawn to him even when he was just a nameless shadow behind his words. But he only had fourteen years left. He had written that number once, and Amie never forgot it.

She needed to speak with Ben, but she wasn't ready yet. Her stomach was in knots, her organs warring with each other. She wanted to scream, and she wanted to cry, and she wished that "B" were still an anonymous voice whom she could write to, now, for help.

Looking at all the letters spread across the floor, Amie saw the original note that Ben had written to her. Except he hadn't *really* written to her, not that first time. He had simply sent a message into the universe, and she had chosen to respond.

Why *had* she responded, all those months ago? She couldn't explain it, then or now. Something had simply pulled her in, never letting go.

She stared at that first letter, then picked up her phone and found the number for the World War II Museum.

"Hi, my name is Amie Wilson, and I'm a teacher in New York, and, um, I was hoping to get some more information about a certain letter in your collection?"

"Sure, is this for a lesson?" the receptionist asked.

Amie hated to lie, but she didn't know how to tell the truth.

"Yes," she said. "I'm doing a unit on women during the war."

When she was connected to a curator, Amie described the letter. "It's the one where a soldier asks his mother to tell Gertrude, 'No matter what happens, I still feel the same.' And I'd love to know what ever happened to them."

"Yes, that's a beautiful one," the curator said in her soft Southern lilt. "Let me check something quickly. Do you mind if I put you on hold?"

So Amie waited a minute, and then another, unsure what she even wanted to hear. She simply felt like she couldn't make any decisions about her own life until she knew what had happened to Gertrude's.

"Hello, are you still there?" the curator asked. "I found the letter and . . . unfortunately, the soldier who wrote the message, Simon Starr, never came home. He was killed in France, in 1945. Gertrude Halpern was the woman he was betrothed to at the time, and she lived in Pennsylvania until she was eighty-six. It looks like she never married."

Amie exhaled.

"I have similar backgrounds on a dozen other letters," the curator said. "Would you like me to send some over to you to share with your students?"

Amie politely accepted, reciting her email address by rote, but her mind was elsewhere now, wondering if she should tell Ben the truth about Gertrude and her soldier.

After a sleepless night, Amie knew that she couldn't process everything on her own. She needed her sister's help. Amie had already texted Nina, back when she and Maura were away, gushing about the man she had met in their apartment, whom she hadn't stopped thinking about since.

Ben still consumed her thoughts now, but for a different reason.

Amie was wary of talking at Nina's place, for fear of Maura overhearing, but luckily, Nina called first that morning, asking if she could drop by Amie's after work.

When Nina arrived, she'd barely entered the apartment before Amie burst open.

"I can't wait to hear all about your trip," she said breathlessly, "but something truly crazy has happened. You'll never believe it. The person I've been writing letters to for the past few months, remember the one I told you about? Well, apparently it's Maura's friend, *Ben*. The one I met at your apartment. The guy I just started seeing."

Amie remained standing while Nina lowered herself onto a chair at the kitchen table, her forehead wrinkled in thought.

"The one who drew those sketches for us?" Nina asked. "I . . . uh . . . Are you sure? How do you know?"

"He told me himself," said Amie. "In a letter."

"Oh my god, really? How did this even happen?"

"His and Maura's support group," Amie said. "At my school."

Nina nodded slowly.

"You know, *you* could have told me that's how he and Maura met, when I first texted you about him." Amie's voice was tinged with accusation.

"All you said was that you ran into Maura's friend at the apartment and went out for drinks," Nina answered. "You didn't say that you had fallen in love with him!"

"I don't . . . I don't know if it's *love*," Amie said defensively, her arms crossed tightly. "It's just a bunch of letters."

"Look, even if I had known the whole story, it wasn't *my* truth to share," Nina said. "If I went around telling you that Ben had a short string, that would've made me no better than the girls who outed me in high school."

Amie's arms dropped to her side. "I hate it when you're right."

"Have you talked to *Ben* about all of this?"

Amie shook her head, leaning back against the counter. "I don't know what to say. I've been going crazy about it. What do *you* think I should do?"

"I can't tell you that."

"Ugh, come on, Nina! If we were still in school, and I came to you asking for advice, you would jump at the chance to tell me what to do."

"That was always about little things, like which gym class to avoid. This is . . . bigger."

"I know it's bigger!" Amie said, her arms flying up toward her face. She always lost control of her limbs when she was anxious. "Which is why I don't . . . I don't think I should keep talking to him," she said quietly. "Either in person, or the letters."

Nina's eyes widened. "Are you serious?"

Amie's gaze turned toward the floor, unable to meet Nina's.

"It's just that he said all this really heavy stuff in his last letter, about being a good partner and having kids . . ." Amie drew a slow breath. "And I *know* that I want those things, too, and . . . I like Ben," she said. "But I don't know if I can be the person he *needs*."

Nina pressed her forehead into her hands, rubbing her temples with her thumbs.

"Please say something," Amie begged her.

"I just wasn't expecting this right now," Nina said. "I actually came here because *I* have something to tell *you*."

"Oh," Amie said. "What is it?"

"Well, this isn't exactly the way I wanted to share it with you . . ." Nina's voice trailed off. The news of her impromptu proposal was supposed to be a happy surprise, but given Amie's current state, it suddenly felt like an aftershock.

"Maura and I are getting married," Nina said.

Amie was stunned. "You're *what?*"

"I proposed when we were in Verona, and we just decided that there's no point in waiting long," Nina explained. "So we're getting married in two months."

"Nina! Two months? That's *really* soon." Amie started pacing nervously. "Do Mom and Dad know?"

"I'm calling them tonight," Nina said. "I wanted to tell you first!"

"But . . . are you sure you've thought this all through?" Amie asked.

"I know it feels sudden, but this is what I want," Nina said. "What *we* want."

Amie looked pale and distressed. "You don't think you should slow down for a second?"

"What are you talking about?" Nina asked. "We've been together for over two years. Where did you think this was heading?"

"You never said you were planning to propose! And I didn't think Maura was planning to, either. Especially after the strings." Amie winced, knowing her words must have stung.

"It wasn't planned," Nina said coolly. "It just happened. But clearly you're already upset about Ben, so maybe this isn't the best time to discuss it."

"You know I love Maura, but this is all happening so fast," Amie said. "I just want to make sure that you've taken the time to think about things before jumping into marriage."

"This isn't some stranger I met in Vegas, Amie. This is the woman I love."

"And I'm not telling you to leave her!" Amie could see that her panicked pacing was starting to grate on Nina, so she finally stood still. "It's just that marriage is a big deal. And marrying someone who's about to die is a huge fucking deal!"

Amie bit her lip right after she said it. She rarely cursed, and she honestly didn't intend to swear, the word had just jumped out. But it felt like a slap across both sisters' faces.

"I know it's a big *fucking* deal," Nina fumed. "And she's not *about* to die. We could still have eight more years."

Amie knew that her sister was the rational one, the sense to her sensibility. And Amie desperately wanted to reason with her, to help Nina understand her fears.

"I'm just worried that you're so focused on the fact that it's still years away that it doesn't feel *real* to you right now," Amie explained. "You're not thinking about what it will actually be like when it happens, and you're a widow in your late thirties!"

Nina stared at her sister coldly. "I've thought about that every day since we opened our boxes."

"Okay, well, what about kids?" Amie asked.

"You know we don't want kids."

"I know you feel that way *now,* but you're only thirty, so you might change your mind. And by the time you're almost forty and alone . . ."

"That's *life!*" Nina shouted. "Before the strings arrived, that was the chance *anyone* took when they got married, or when they had kids. There was no guarantee. But you still vowed in sickness and in health, not knowing which one you'd get, and you still promised till death do us part, with no idea when that parting would occur." Nina paused. "But now that we have the strings, suddenly the risk that *every* couple used to accept has become so unimaginable?"

Nina was right, Amie knew it. And she knew she was making a mess of things, but she couldn't stand down now. She had fallen too deep into the pit of her own uncertainty, convinced that her sister needed her. "I'm just trying to protect you!" she insisted.

"Well, you don't have to do that," Nina said sternly. "I never asked you to."

"Come on, Nina! You're not the only one who gets to worry about people and want to protect them. You've always been that way with me, and god knows you've been that way with Maura, and sometimes *we* get to feel that way, too!" Amie was nearly out of breath.

"This is different," Nina said, staring harshly at her sister through glassy eyes. "And you know what? I don't even think this is about me. This is about *Ben,* and you being a fucking hypocrite. You spend months writing all these secret love letters to him, and then you actually start falling for him in *real* life, and now you won't even give him a chance! All because you're afraid of his string."

"That's not fair," Amie said softly. Nina was wrong, she thought. It wasn't about Ben. It couldn't be.

"I just don't want to watch you suffer," Amie said. "You're my sister!"

But Nina was done discussing. She hastily stood up from her seat, the legs of the chair screeching against the floor.

"Just because *you're* a coward who would rather protect herself than take a chance on someone, that doesn't mean I have to make the same selfish choice," Nina said bitterly. "I've made my decision."

Amie knew that the argument was over now. Nina was shutting down. Her voice was brusque, her face stony and grim.

"And if my marriage is so upsetting to you," Nina said, "then you don't have to be there."

She slammed the door behind her as she left.

Amie remained frozen for a minute, staring at the closed door, wondering if she should run after Nina. But she couldn't run. She could barely move. Her legs grew weak beneath her, and she sat down heavily in the chair that her sister had just left empty.

Then she finally started to cry.

WINTER

JACK

Jack was picking at a platter of crudités in the corner of a corporate hotel suite, surrounded by various shades of beige furnishings, trying to prepare himself.

His suit hung a little looser on his frame; he had lost a surprising amount of muscle mass in the months since he stopped training for combat. Through the window, he could see the swarm of protesters gathered outside the hotel, holding signs that read "Support Short-Stringers!" and "Stop Rollins!"

In a few minutes, Jack would be standing onstage, under the arch of red and blue balloons, while his uncle made a speech about the future of the nation and his aunt waved to the crowds that seemed to grow larger and louder at every stop. Tonight's event, the biggest to date, was being broadcast on national television.

Jack looked over at his father, who was reading in a nearby armchair, and smiled weakly at him.

"You better sharpen that grin before you're on camera," his father said, flipping to the next page in the newspaper. "And maybe you should just sit down and relax until we're needed. Stop hovering over the food."

When Jack's father first heard about Jack and Javier's switch, he was relieved and grateful, of course, to know that his child had a long life ahead. But he was also horrified by the boys' actions. He had railed against Jack for hours, shocked that his son would jeopardize the Hunter legacy and live in such deception. Until Jack reminded his father about

Grandpa Cal's stories from his time in the army. The most important part was always the brotherhood, the loyalty among comrades in uniform. Jack told his father that the switch was what Javier wanted more than anything, and that's why he agreed to it. His dad could never know the full truth.

But Jack knew that his father still had nightmares about the lie being exposed, putting the integrity of the whole family at risk.

"Only three people in the world know about this," Jack assured him, over and over. "Just me, you, and Javi. That's it. And none of us are going to tell."

Yet the spotlight kept shining brighter on Katherine and Anthony, so it was hard for Jack's father not to feel anxious. And he dreaded the day, in the not-so-distant future, when the truth would inevitably come out.

But Jack finally saw a purpose in his lonesome upbringing. He had been raised to take care of himself. So, when that day came, Jack would find a way to handle it.

All Jack had to do today was stand in a corner of the stage and act supportive. But he had another plan.

Jack knew that whatever he did now wouldn't negate his selfish motives for proposing the switch back in June, that whatever words he spoke tonight wouldn't erase his months of silence. But *maybe* it would still be enough to fulfill his promise to Javier.

A tall security guard in sunglasses poked his head inside the room. "Mr. Hunter, Jack, they're ready for you both."

Jack's father stood up from his chair. "How's my suit?" he asked Jack. "Any wrinkles?"

"No, sir," Jack said, and the pleasure he derived from hearing his father ask for his help, no matter how insignificant, almost made Jack question his plan, knowing that some of the blame might land on his dad. But he had come too far to back down.

In the elevator, Jack thought of the demonstrators outside the hotel, still chanting even now. He thought of the rally in August, where a man named Hank had laid down his life during the protest. And he thought of Javier's own inescapable death, as the soldier that he was always meant to be and yet was almost barred from becoming. Someday that would be an act of protest, too.

Jack had been given a long string, much longer than Hank's or Javier's. The least he could do was join them now. To see something wrong and refuse to look away. Like that woman, Lea, had told him. He had been so consumed by his fight with Javi that he hadn't seen beyond it. But the battle was bigger than Anthony, or Jack, or Javier, or Hank, or the man with the clipboard, or the boys in New York. It was bigger than all of them now.

Jack and his father stepped out of the elevator to join the awaiting stage manager, and Jack slipped his fingers into his pocket, furtively pulling out a small gold pin with two interlocked threads. He flipped it around in his sweaty palm as he followed the stage manager down the hall, finally pressing it onto his lapel just as the glaring lights of the stage overtook his vision.

Anthony was mere minutes into his stump speech when it happened.

Jack lunged forward, grabbing the microphone out of his uncle's hands, shocking everyone onstage and in the audience, even surprising himself a little. Once the microphone was in his grip, everything froze for an instant, two seconds of exquisite tension, of gasps swallowed by bated breath, in which the whole room waited and watched.

Anthony, too, seemed to be waiting. He and Katherine and Jack's father were all suspended in confusion, unsure how to react. And while their brains tried to process the action unfolding before them, Jack began to speak.

"I'm Anthony's nephew," he said. "The soldier with the short string that he told you all about."

Jack's sentences were tumbling rapidly out of his mouth, as he tried to cram in as many words as possible before someone inevitably shut him up. Anthony and Katherine were still staring at him, speechless. Perhaps they hoped to avoid a humiliating scene by letting him speak for just a minute, pretending that this wasn't a spontaneous coup.

"But the truth is that my uncle doesn't really care about me, or any of the short-stringers!" Jack said. "And it's time we were brave enough to stand up to him! Nobody is any different because of their string. No-body's life matters less. We're all *human*, aren't we?" Jack was practically pleading into the mic. "But Anthony Rollins only cares about winning! Don't let him scare you anymore! Don't let him corrupt—"

Jack's body was jerked away from the microphone stand, his arms practically ripped from their sockets, as a bodyguard pulled him offstage, while an oppressive hush hung over the audience, only broken by the squeaking of Jack's patent-leather shoes as they dragged across the pol-ished floor.

Twenty minutes later, Jack was sitting in a chair backstage, guarded by two members of Anthony's security team, like a child in detention.

On the monitor overhead, Jack had watched Anthony apologize for the interruption and finish his speech, then walk off the stage alongside his wife, mouthing, Thank you, to the audience.

Leaning sideways in his chair, Jack spotted his aunt and uncle arriving backstage, before they could see him. Jack's father trailed behind them.

Anthony's campaign manager greeted them with a strained smile. "You both looked great out there. The speech sounded great. You han-dled everything like a pro."

But as soon as Anthony had stepped away from the cameras, his face curled into a livid grimace. "Where the fuck is he?"

"We kept him backstage," said the manager.

Anthony turned sharply toward Katherine and his brother-in-law. "Did either of you know about this?"

"No, of course not!" Katherine protested. Jack's father shook his head vigorously.

"Is he out of his goddamn mind?" Anthony shouted.

"I don't, I don't know," Katherine stammered. "Maybe he just meant it as a way to identify with other short-stringers."

Anthony's eyes narrowed, and then he headed for Jack, with Kath-erine, Jack's father, and the campaign manager walking hurriedly to keep up.

Seeing his uncle approach, Jack stood up from his chair, the gold pin on his jacket glinting under the backstage lights.

Anthony beelined over to Jack, grabbed him by his lapel, and shook him violently. "What the fuck is wrong with you?" he screamed, spraying spit across Jack's face.

A cacophony of frightened shouts escaped from Katherine, Jack's father, and the manager, all at once.

"Anthony!"

"Leave him alone!"

"Please calm down, sir."

Only Jack remained silent, staring at his uncle's raging eyes, his heart pounding in his eardrums. He thought Anthony might even strike him, until Jack's father and aunt had pulled him off, trying to pacify him.

Jack's dad straightened his back until he was an inch taller than Anthony. "That's *my* son," he boomed.

"Well, his fucking speech could cost *me* the White House!" Anthony raged.

"And I shouldn't need to remind you of the role that we Hunters have played in trying to get you there," said Jack's father. "So, I'll ask you to keep your hands off *any* member of the family."

Anthony glared at Jack's dad, unwilling to feel belittled.

"Besides, we're probably all overreacting," Jack's father added. "The audience knows that Jack has a short string, and the stress of that can drive anyone a little crazy. I'm sure they'll understand."

Katherine placed a restraining hand on her husband's chest and looked at her nephew with a wounded expression. "Why did you say such horrible things, Jack?"

Jack knew, in that moment, his aunt had chosen her side, but he felt a surge of confidence. He stared defiantly at his uncle. "I thought you wanted the whole world to know that I'm a short-stringer."

The campaign manager deftly intervened before Anthony could respond. "Sir, we really need to get moving. We have three interviews lined up, and we're already running late."

"Fine." Anthony practically spat the word out, before scowling one last time at his nephew. "But I want him out of here. Now."

AMIE

Amie had never felt so alone.

Her fight with Nina was the worst they'd ever had, the longest they'd gone without speaking. A month had passed since that night in the kitchen, Nina's wedding creeping closer on the calendar, and Amie wished she could talk to someone, anyone, to explain her side of the story. But she was too ashamed to divulge the details, especially to her parents, who could look past the tragedy and see the gift they'd been given: their eldest child had found a great love and was loved greatly in return. Luckily, it seemed that Nina hadn't told anyone, either, since no family members asked Amie why she had been disinvited from the wedding. (Nina had spent Thanksgiving with Maura's parents that year, leaving Amie alone with their cousins.)

As she sat behind her desk at school, Amie kept hearing her sister's words. In the hours when she wasn't teaching, her classroom felt airless and claustrophobic, and she couldn't eat anything without her stomach lurching. She felt like something was gnawing at her from inside, and she wished that it were simply the remnants of anger from the fight, but she knew that it was more.

It was guilt.

Even after the insults they had hurled at each other, Nina was still her only sister, her oldest friend, her greatest confidant and adviser. And now she was getting married. And Amie wasn't going to be there.

How could she live with herself, knowing that she had missed one of the most important days in Nina's life? Knowing that she had *ruined* it with her words?

She remembered the day when Nina came home crying from school and locked herself in her bedroom with their mother, while Amie sat on the carpet outside the closed door, leaning her back against the wall, waiting for her sister to emerge. She had clenched her eyes shut, praying away Nina's pain, imagining revenge on all the girls who had hurt her.

When Nina finally calmed down that night, Amie told her that she didn't have to say anything.

"All that matters is that you're my sister, and I love you," Amie said. "This doesn't change anything between us. It just makes me sorry that you had to go through this alone, and that this might make life harder for you . . . I guess it already has."

Nina's skin was red and puffy, but her face looked composed, resolute. "Maybe it will be harder," she said. "But at least it'll be right."

It was so easy for Amie to support Nina then, to stand on her side without any doubt. Why couldn't she do that now?

Maybe Nina's accusations were right, and this wasn't *really* about her. Maybe the guilt that Amie was feeling had more to do with Ben.

She had let his final letter go unanswered for weeks now. Ben must hate her, she thought. She *wanted* to write to him, desperately, but she didn't yet know what to say, and she feared rushing her response, marring whatever connection they had.

Amie tried to remember all that she had demanded of Nina: Are you sure about this? Have you considered the pain? Is it *worth* it?

Perhaps there was a reason why the questions flew so quickly off her tongue.

She had already asked them all of herself, after reading Ben's confession.

But Amie couldn't even begin to make sense of her feelings for Ben while her fight with Nina still loomed so heavily, so painfully, in her mind.

In between classes, Amie opened her laptop and scrolled through her email, surprised to see that one of the teachers had forwarded a YouTube video to the entire staff: "21-Year-Old South African Student Gives Rousing Speech About Strings."

Amie wasn't sure, at first, if she should watch. The strings had already scrambled her life, threatened to divide her from her sister. But she clicked on the link and saw a young woman standing before a crowd on what appeared to be a campus. The clip had already garnered nearly three million views.

"Here in South Africa, and around the world," the girl said, "we have moved past the era of formal segregation and apartheid, but we have not shed our habits of prejudice and exclusion. Inequality has simply donned a new mask. Injustice has merely changed clothes. And, decade after decade, the pain feels the same. But what if we could break that cycle?

"In a few months, I will turn twenty-two, and I will receive my box. Many of you, my fellow classmates, still have years to wait. Look, or don't look. That is your choice. But it's not the *only* choice we are faced with.

"We have a chance, now, to make a change. The strings are still new. We are still learning how to react. Which means we can start fresh. Reject the patterns of history. Promise not to repeat old mistakes. We can lead with compassion and empathy. Fight back against those who look to divide us, or pit us against one another, or make anyone feel *less than*. It is up to *us*—the ones who have yet to receive our boxes—to decide what type of world we wish to inherit, no matter how much time our strings may give us."

The crowd of students whistled and clapped for the girl.

"A friend just showed me a video from America," she continued, "where a boy spoke up at a rally. He said that nobody is different because of their string, we are all still human. I challenge everyone to do the same, to stand up against the people in your life who are acting unjustly. Help them see that we are all the same, all connected. We are all strung together."

The girl was poised and passionate and eloquent, a striking combination of attributes for someone so young, Amie thought. The video was filmed closely enough that Amie could see some sort of broach or pin on the girl's dress, small and golden.

We can start fresh, Amie repeated.

Perhaps it wasn't too late to start over with Nina. She hadn't missed the wedding yet.

Now, more than ever, Amie needed to be the same girl who sat outside Nina's door for hours that night during high school, the same girl who read with Nina on the rug in the bookshop, who sent her novels across the country, filled with sticky notes inside. Amie needed to be her *sister*, the two of them strung together, always.

BEN

Ben was disappointed to return to the classroom yet again with still no response from Amie. But he couldn't lose faith. Not yet. He gazed at Lea, seven months pregnant now, her tiny frame all but consumed by her stomach, and he couldn't help but feel hopeful.

Lea carefully lowered herself onto a chair in the classroom, and then yelped in surprise when her brother and his husband burst through the doors behind her, carrying a dozen yellow balloons.

"What's going on?" Lea asked.

Chelsea breezed in with a large chocolate cake. "You didn't think we'd let you off without a baby shower, did you?" She placed the dish in front of Lea with a flourish.

"It's important to celebrate every beautiful moment that life gives us," said Sean. "And *this* is a beautiful moment."

The rest of the hour dissolved into merriment. Terrell had joined the new short-stringer dating app Share Your Time, and was asking for the group's approval of potential suitors before swiping. Maura and Nihal were relishing in Anthony Rollins's humiliation at the hands of his nephew. And Chelsea was trying to convince Lea to audition alongside her for the next season of *The Bachelor,* recently spun off into two separate franchises: *The Bachelor: Long Strings* and *The Bachelor: Short Strings.*

"Come on," Chelsea entreated. "You're under twenty-eight in both age and waist size. That's their favorite demographic."

"Maybe I *used* to be . . ." Lea looked down at her outstretched abdomen.

"You'll bounce back in no time," Chelsea declared. "And the surrogacy will make for the best backstory! I bet you'd be the fan favorite."

Though the evening bore an inherent note of sadness—the unspoken awareness that the twins would live most of their lives without Lea—there was something undeniably beautiful about the whole affair, just as Sean said. Lea was happy. Her family was happy. They were proof, Ben thought, that the world hadn't stopped spinning when the boxes arrived. People's lives still moved forward, new lives were created.

"And I want you guys there with me," Lea said.

"*With* you?" asked Chelsea, incredulous.

"Well, obviously not in the delivery room." Lea laughed. "But, afterwards, it might be nice." She rested her palm peacefully on her stomach. "I'm doing this for my family, of course, but I think there's a part of me that's also doing this for myself . . . and for all of us. Maybe it's just the hormones, or the fact that I can feel the babies kicking like crazy today, but I finally feel like a change is coming. Like, maybe we're going to be okay."

And the whole room understood.

They had all seen the viral video by now, a clip of a young woman in South Africa calling upon her fellow youths to fight this new surge of prejudice.

The hashtag #StrungTogether, inspired by her speech, was trending across the globe, being used by people to share stories of different acts of compassion: Companies pledging to hire more short-stringers. A college moving up its graduation ceremony so a short-stringer student could receive his diploma along with his class. There was even a town in Canada where short-stringers were encouraged to publicly identify themselves so their neighbors could provide support. Ben recalled one post: What if we knew that our waiter, our cabdriver, our teacher, had a short string? Would we show them greater kindness? Would we pause before we acted? #StrungTogether. A handful of journalists and politicians had already deemed it a "movement."

Later that evening, Ben stood next to Nihal.

"I think I might be coming around to what my parents said about rebirth," Nihal told him.

"What do you think changed?" Ben asked.

"Something about seeing Lea, maybe. And these twins she's about to give birth to, wondering where they came from," said Nihal. "I mean, obviously we know where they came from *physically*, but what about their *souls*? That just feels like something separate from the body, something more . . . eternal. And why couldn't they have lived before, and died before, and now they're returning to earth again?"

Ben thought for a moment about the woman from the park in October, breathing the air through Hank's lungs. Two people *truly* strung together, despite never having met.

"I think anything is possible," Ben agreed.

Nihal smiled. "At least, after all we've been through, I bet every one of us will get to come back as friggin' royalty."

By the end of the session, Ben found himself sitting with Maura, as usual, while the group finished off the last crumbs of cake.

"Do you ever think about kids?" Maura asked him, glancing down at Ben's sweater with a grin. "You kinda already dress like a dad."

Ben laughed and looked over at Lea, cradling her stomach, swapping smiles with her brother. Ever since that day in the storage unit, Ben had been thinking more about it. Of course, he'd thought about the proms and graduations and weddings. Everything he wouldn't get to see. He could still feel his chest constrict and a dark pit of bitterness swell up inside him whenever he thought of those things, and perhaps he always would. But he had discovered, recently, that he could calm himself down by thinking about all the other things—the ones he still might see, if he had children someday.

The first day of school. The dance recitals. The basketball games.

Sledding in the backyard. Trick-or-treating. Apple-picking in the fall.

The look on his parents' faces when they hold their grandchild for the first time.

"Maybe I'll be a dad . . ." Ben said. "But, hey, *I'm* not the one settling down, about to get married."

"Ugh, don't say it like that!" Maura cringed. "It makes me sound so *old*."

But Ben could see past her horrified pretense. He could see that she was happy.

And Ben thought about all the sessions before this one, all the Sunday nights spent in sorrowful solidarity, all the stories they had shared in fear and anger, all the violence they had seen. Something about *this* night reminded Ben of his college professor, explaining Newton's third law, pressing his hands against the blackboard to show how the wall pushed back on him. For every action, there is an equal and opposite reaction. Forces always come in pairs.

And now, at last, Ben could see the reacting force, pushing back against months of agony with a burst of brighter days. With this feeling, tonight, in Room 204.

MAURA

Nina had planned an entire day of wedding activities—the florist, the caterer, the bakery, the dress shop—every errand crammed into a single Saturday to accommodate the imminent nuptials, mere weeks away.

When Maura walked into the kitchen that morning, cell phone in hand, Nina was already cooking scrambled eggs on the stovetop, eager for an early start.

"That was Terrell calling," Maura said. "Apparently there's a huge rally planned for this afternoon in D.C. He and Nihal are going to rent a car and drive down."

"This is what, like, the third rally this month?" Nina asked. "Everyone at the magazine's been talking about them. That girl's video really did spark something."

"Apparently this one was planned as just a small demonstration by the MLK statue, at the same time as a Rollins fundraiser nearby," Maura explained. "But this Strung Together movement has really taken off online, and now it's supposed to draw thousands."

"That's incredible," said Nina, still stirring the eggs. "I'm sorry we can't go."

"Well . . . actually . . ." Maura bit her lip.

Nina placed the spatula down on a paper towel near the pan. "Are you trying to ask if we should cancel today?"

"I know the timing sucks, but I really want to be there," Maura said.

"Do you know how hard it was for me to get everything booked at the last minute?"

"I do, and I appreciate everything you've done. But it's not like I'm calling off the actual ceremony," said Maura. "It's basically just a day of shopping and tasting food."

Nina sighed and shook her head, before realizing that the eggs had started to burn on the stove. She quickly switched off the flame, grabbed the spatula, and began scraping at the crispy edges of the egg white that had stuck to the sides of the pan.

Maura stared at her back as she scrubbed silently. Nina's mood had been slightly erratic for the past few weeks, after getting into some sibling tiff with Amie—though Nina never looked to discuss it.

"Are we just dropping this?" Maura asked her.

"I don't know what you want me to say." Nina turned around to face Maura. "I thought today would be a milestone in our relationship. A day of celebration. But apparently it's just a bunch of superficial crap."

"That's not how I meant it," Maura said. "I just think this rally could be really important."

"And our *wedding* isn't important?"

"Of course it is!" Maura exclaimed. "But today is really just about a party. This rally is about . . . my *life*."

"And it pains me, knowing what you have to deal with," Nina said. "But you're already doing so much with your group. And you've gone to protests before. Maybe it's okay for you to take one day off and enjoy the *other* aspects of your life."

Maura paused for a moment and drew a breath. It frustrated her, sometimes, that Nina couldn't see things the way she did.

For Nina, their relationship felt like enough. Their engagement rings were platinum proof that Nina could look beyond the strings and love Maura for the woman she was, not the time she'd been given. The family they were building together was Nina's top priority. And, of course, that meant everything to Maura. But sometimes she just needed more. She needed to look beyond the small circumference of their lives, needed the rest of the world to see her as Nina did. As someone worth loving. As an equal.

"God, I *wish* I could take just one day off," Maura said, "but I *can't*. For my whole life, I've had to live *every* day making sure I don't seem too angry or threatening or undeserving, because that would make Black people look bad, and making sure I don't seem too sensitive or stupid or meek, because that would make women look bad, and *now* I can never seem too unstable or emotional or vengeful, because that would make short-stringers look bad. There *are* no breaks!" She let out a full, shaking breath. "And you know how much I've been searching for something, some way to feel like what I'm doing actually *matters*. Like I'm using my time for something good."

Nina nodded slowly, absorbing Maura's words. "You should go," she finally said, her voice sincere. "I can take care of everything on this end."

"Are you sure?" Maura asked.

"Yes. And I promise, next time I'll be there with you."

After they parked near the National Mall, Maura and her friends joined the crowd of nearly twenty thousand people spread across the base of the Martin Luther King, Jr., Memorial, spilling over to the nearby lawns, framed by branches now emptied of their rust-colored leaves. A large group at the center was cheering and chanting under a seven-foot banner reading "All Strings, Long and Short."

Half a dozen news teams covered the event, perhaps because of the rumors that Anthony Rollins's defector nephew might attend. But even with the added attention—and even with the groundswell of this new Strung Together movement online—Maura still wasn't sure that it would be enough to prevent Rollins from winning the nomination that summer. Anytime she saw the news of another shooting, or the wreckage of a major car crash, Maura found herself praying that a short-stringer wasn't at fault. The rest of her support group seemed convinced that the sands had already shifted. Every day that the hashtag trended, every public figure who expressed support, every news show that interviewed the student from South Africa, was proof, to her fellow group mates, that their lives could only improve. But Maura knew better than to blindly trust, or to risk growing complacent. She knew that things could *always* get worse, unless enough people kept on fighting.

When Maura returned to her apartment after a long day at the rally, she closed the door behind her as quietly as possible and stepped through to the dark living room, passing by the triptych of Ben's sketches on the wall, like postcards from her life. Nina had adored the images, she nearly cried at the sight, despite the fact that Maura's surprise had been upstaged by her proposal.

When Maura turned toward the kitchen, where Nina had left a single light shining, she spotted a piece of paper taped to the fridge, marked with Nina's writing:

> *Hope the rally went well. There's a cake sample inside. Trust me, you'll love it.*
>
> *I'm proud of you. Xo*

Maura didn't regret her choice. She was glad she went to D.C. But she was thankful that she could always return here, to her home, and to Nina, who at least accepted what Maura had to do, if she couldn't always understand.

Maura peered inside the fridge, where a slice of chocolate cake sat in a clear plastic carton, tempting her with the smooth curves of its frosting. When she lifted it up, she noticed another piece of paper under the box.

> *You were right, we don't need an elaborate party. We just need each other. And I don't want to wait any longer. If we're going to argue again, I'd much rather fight with my wife.*
>
> *Will you marry me on Monday at City Hall?*

Maura shut the door, shocked and silently elated. She crept into the bedroom, carefully unclasping a small gold pin with two intertwined strings from the top corner of her sweater, slipping off her clothes and dropping them into the hamper. Then she gingerly peeled back the sheets covering her side of the mattress and filled the empty space in bed, already warmed by the sleeping woman who, in just two days' time now, would become Maura's wife.

Maura knew that her parents might have preferred a church, or perhaps the lawn of a countryside estate, but a lot of what she had done in her life wasn't exactly what her parents would have wanted. After flitting from job to job, from girlfriend to girlfriend, at least she was finally staying put, getting herself properly hitched, and to a woman her parents genuinely liked. ("Nina seems like she has a good head on her shoulders," her father had said after they'd met.)

And Maura was actually quite pleased to have the ceremony at City Hall. The occasion didn't feel quite as overbearing without the long walk down the aisle or kneeling in front of the altar. And Maura never saw herself as the type to have a conventional wedding anyway.

The civil ceremonies were performed inside the Marriage Bureau, a large gray edifice surrounded by an array of municipal buildings in the middle of downtown Manhattan. Immigration services, the IRS, and the district attorney were all housed within a one-block radius of the New York Marriage Bureau, but its closest neighbor was the Health Department, where the city's birth and death certificates were filed. Maura found this oddly fitting. The Health Department recorded the beginnings and endings of life, while just next door, couples vowed to support each other through everything in between.

Inside, Maura thought the Marriage Bureau felt like a fancier DMV, with long couches lining one wall, a row of computers against the other, and large electronic screens mounted overhead, where couples looked to see their assigned number displayed, signaling that it was their turn to be wed in the private room in back. *The 24-hour waiting period between obtaining a marriage license and performing the marriage ceremony may be waived with proof of an expiring string,* read a poster near the entrance.

Maura could tell that Nina had been slightly distressed by the kitschy kiosk at the front, a small boutique hawking touristy "NYC" paraphernalia alongside last-minute wedding staples like flowers, veils, even rings. Perhaps, for a fleeting moment, Nina had even regretted her uncharacteristic impulsiveness that had brought them both here today.

But everywhere they turned, they saw love. Men in tuxedoes and women in gowns, young twenty-somethings in jeans and baseball caps, a handful of tulle-draped toddlers running amok. A few other couples had come alone, like Maura and Nina had, but most arrived with an entourage of guests, their cameras filling the hall with flashes.

Nina looked simple and elegant in cream-colored lace, while Maura had opted for a light gold dress with a bit more shimmer.

"I think you might be the most beautiful bride in here," Nina said to her, touching her cheek.

After their number appeared on-screen, Maura and Nina took their places before the officiant, a balding man with a mustache and glasses, practically swallowed whole by his baggy brown suit, who approached each and every ceremony with the benevolent energy of a man who performed only one of them per day, instead of dozens. The couple in line behind them—a woman in a red floral dress with a crown of flowers in her hair and a man in a matching red tie—had graciously agreed to bear witness, standing side by side, their hands linked together by two intertwined pinkies.

Maura had never expected this moment. Of course, before the strings, she had sometimes suspected that a proposal might be coming—in an incident of particular weakness, she had even peeked among the pristinely folded clothes in Nina's dresser—but everything had changed in March. Since then, even in their most intimate moments, even when swept up among the romance of Italy's cobbled alleys and quiet fountains, Maura never thought Nina would propose. Not after the strings.

And Maura never would have been the one to ask, to put Nina in that position. She didn't feel any shame at the thought of simply living with Nina, no titles. Maura didn't need to be one half of a marriage to feel whole. But once Nina had posed the question, once the possibility was suddenly real and standing before her in the shape of the woman who felt like home, Maura thought that maybe it would be nice to be married, to have something that felt solid and lasting in her otherwise upended life. Maybe, despite everything her string had stolen, this was one thing she could still have.

After the officiant pronounced Maura Hill and Nina Wilson newlyweds, the couple returned to the main gallery and exited onto a peaceful street. Nina clasped Maura's hand as they headed to meet their families and a few close friends at a restaurant just down the block—a near-miraculous feat that Nina had spent the weekend pulling together.

In a back room lit by candles, Nina's and Maura's parents sat together with Amie, while a few of Nina's favorite coworkers, some of Maura's friends from college, a couple of local relatives, and the members of Maura's support group gathered around three other tables.

Even before the strings, Maura had always believed there was something just a little bit crazy about marriage, committing the rest of your life to someone before you had even lived that much of it yourself. And surely, some might find her marriage to Nina even harder to understand. Yet all of the people in this restaurant, these family and friends, had canceled their plans at the last moment, rearranged their lives to be here tonight. To show their support for this crazy act. To fill the room with love.

After the meal was served, Nina walked over to a corner where Maura had been chatting with a cousin. "There's one more thing," she said.

Maura smiled, eyeing her with faux-suspicion, and as the violins began to play over the speakers, Maura suddenly realized the four tables had been arranged with a small opening in the center. This was Nina's plan all along.

Still surprised, Maura allowed herself to be pulled out of her chair and into Nina's arms, while the voice of Nat King Cole filled the air around them.

"I can't believe you did this," Maura whispered against Nina's cheek. "All of it."

"If anyone deserves it, it's you."

And the pair swayed back and forth together on the tiny makeshift dance floor, holding each other close.

That's why, darling, it's incredible
That someone so unforgettable
Thinks that I am unforgettable, too.

AMIE

Everyone around Amie stood up and headed for the patch of dance floor, leaving Amie alone at her table, admiring her sister and Maura as they weaved through the clusters of guests. She couldn't believe she had almost missed this. Thankfully, she had arrived at Nina's door just in time, overflowing with regret and apology. Only a few days later, Nina had called her to say that the formal wedding had been scrapped, replaced by an intimate dinner after a ceremony at City Hall.

Amie tried to focus her eyes on the dancers and stop staring at Ben, who was seated across the room, with the other members of his and Maura's support group. Amie had been too nervous to approach him earlier, and she assumed that Ben was understandably waiting on *her*. She was the one who had left his confession unanswered, after all.

She had already planned what she was going to say to him, some polite speech about wanting to stay friends, but as she watched Ben laughing alongside a pregnant brunette in a modest pink dress and a strawberry blonde with a spray tan, Amie felt inexplicably upset that he would be laughing with any woman who wasn't her. She felt her face growing flush and her heartbeat quicken. She was being completely ridiculous, she thought. She was a twenty-nine-year-old woman, for god's sake, not some jealous preteen.

Amie thought that she had made up her mind about Ben, that it would be safer to never act on her feelings.

But maybe she was wrong.

The song was still playing, she still had a chance. But would Ben even be willing to speak to her?

She drew a breath and walked over to his table.

"I'm sorry if I'm interrupting," Amie said shyly. "But I thought I'd see if you'd like to dance."

There was a brief pause before Ben smiled, and the relief warmed her body like sunlight.

"Of course," he said.

They moved together toward the center of the room, and Ben took the lead, his arm lightly encircling her waist.

It was Ben who ventured first.

"I was beginning to think you never wanted to talk to me again." He narrowed his eyes and raised his brow.

He was teasing her, Amie realized. A second relief.

"It wasn't you, it . . . I . . . Nina and I were going through a rough patch," Amie explained. "And it's honestly all I could think about these past few weeks."

"Oh," Ben said. He looked genuinely concerned. "Is everything okay?"

"It is now."

"So that just leaves you and me. And my letter."

"How did you figure it out?" Amie asked.

"Well, there were all these little hints, about you and where you lived and where you worked, and finally it all clicked when you mentioned that letter about Gertrude," he said. "Although I suppose I did take a bit of a risk that I had gotten it all wrong and the real 'A' would have been quite confused."

Amie laughed, and she could feel Ben's arm tightening around her. She stepped closer toward him in response.

"I'm sorry I'm not much of a dancer," he said.

"Oh please, all of my recent dance experiences have been chaperoning students who seem to forget that their teachers are watching."

"So you have to forcibly separate the poor hormonal kids?"

"Sometimes, yes," she admitted, "but not if they look like that . . ." Amie nodded toward Nina and Maura, twirling along the edge of the crowd.

"They look so happy," Ben said.

"And completely oblivious to anyone else."

Ben shrugged. "That's how it's supposed to be, right?"

He was looking at Amie with such kindness, such sincerity, that she needed to break away from his gaze for just a moment. She leaned her body in even closer, until her chin hovered above his shoulder, and her eyes landed safely on the back wall, while the music drifted around them.

And Amie thought of all the times that she had wondered about the person on the other side of her letters, and how remarkable it was that she was actually with him now, feeling his warmth and breathing in his cologne. Amie felt her body relax, at ease with Ben, as if they had danced together many times before.

Amie closed her eyes and tried to imagine the future, the way she always had, with the lawyer and the poet and the handful of other men who had held her in their arms over the years.

She pictured herself with Ben in Central Park, sitting on a bench near the lake, and painting the walls of a bare apartment with rollers. She saw herself in white, holding his hands before her, and then smiling in a hospital bed, both of them kissing the bundle in her arms.

She could see each scene quite clearly; they weren't blurred like some of her previous daydreams. She could see it, and she could almost *feel* it. And something about it felt right.

Unlike her visions of the men before, there were no caricatures of Ben's flaws. The problem holding Amie back wasn't a blemish in Ben's character, the fault not in himself but in his stars.

Amie blinked, and she saw herself standing in the grass, with two small children dressed in black, and then weeping inside a cramped kitchen, alone this time, while pots and pans and lunch boxes littered the counter before her.

Amie must have read his last letter ten times by now. She knew what Ben wanted, and that he wanted it soon. And he deserved to have it all.

Of course, he had never specifically said that he wanted any of it with *her*, but *she* was the one he had kissed only a few weeks before, the one dancing with him now, and suddenly it all felt like too much, too fast. She felt dizzy and overwhelmed.

"I'm sorry, I just have to get some air," she said, releasing Ben from her arms and escaping quickly toward the back door.

Outside, Amie sat down on the curb, rubbing her arms against the evening chill. Most of the buildings along the street housed government offices that were already closed, so everything around her was quiet.

She felt guilty and ashamed for running out on Ben, but she didn't know if she could go back inside, if the beautiful visions she had seen could ever erase the dark ones that followed.

An older couple walked past Amie, on the opposite side of the street, holding hands and whispering to each other, conspiring against the world. She thought for a second that they looked familiar, but in the dusky light it was hard to tell.

Of course, Amie wanted what this couple had, what her parents had, what Nina and Maura had.

"When you told me about the wedding, what I *should* have said is that you're strong," Amie had cried to her sister, just a few days prior, pleading for her forgiveness. "You are *so* strong, Nina. And so is Maura. You've chosen love over everything else, and I admire you for that. And I only hope that you can let me back into your life, so I can be there for you both. Because I know this will be hard. But I also know that it's right."

Amie wanted to be strong, too. She didn't want to be a coward, or selfish, or a hypocrite, all those jagged words that Nina had flung at her. She didn't want to be one of the people whom Ben had written about, forcing short-stringers into the margins, making them feel unlovable. The people who had driven thousands to the streets in protest.

If only it were as simple as her sister made it seem: Take a chance on someone. See where it goes. What do you have to lose?

Everything, Amie thought.

How did Nina do it?

And more than that, how did Ben and Maura and all the other short-stringers do it? How did they find the strength every day?

Amie remembered what Nina once told her: You don't know what you're capable of. And maybe Nina was right. But everyone around Amie just seemed so much *more* capable. She couldn't even open her box.

Amie pulled her knees into her chest, the blue fabric of her dress cascading down her legs, just barely missing the sidewalk, and hugged her arms around her bent knees, trying to decide what to do.

That's when she heard it.

Faint at first, but growing louder. Rising out of the silence around her.

When I was just a little girl
I asked my mother, "What will I be?"

"There's no way," Amie whispered to herself, not yet believing her ears.

She quickly stood up, trying to locate the source of the music.

"Will I be pretty, will I be rich?"
Here's what she said to me

The melody was coming from the end of the block, and Amie started running toward the sound, heels striking the pavement. She reached the corner just in time to spot the bicyclist from behind as he pedaled away from her, his purple blazer flapping gently in the breeze.

Que será, será
Whatever will be, will be
The future's not ours to see
Que será, será

Amie stood on the corner, dumbfounded and panting.

Then she started laughing. Louder and harder, until she almost felt embarrassed, despite the fact that she was alone.

As she regained her composure, a gust of cold wind blew past, lifting the edges of her dress, and she felt invigorated, awoken.

Amie knew that she had to go back inside.

She needed to find Ben.

What will be, will be.

ANTHONY

Anthony and Katherine were the last to leave the building. They had been meeting with the mayor in his office at City Hall as part of a brief campaign stop in New York, amid a larger attempt at damage control after Jack's stunt.

In the days following the incident, footage of Jack's outburst circulated online and replayed on air, while dozens of embarrassing memes were spawned from images of Anthony's seething expression. The Rollinses had been bracing for a disastrous month, to say the least. But nearly every politician or wealthy donor had a surprisingly similar tale of familial dysfunction, of children or grandchildren breaking ranks and siding with their opponents. ("You should hear what my niece and nephew would say about *me*," they all said with a laugh.) And while Jack's immature rebellion may have resonated with some undecided voters under age thirty, it ultimately had a negligible impact on much of Anthony's core base: older, anxious Americans who felt their tranquil, long-string lives were being threatened by the very anger and erraticism that Jack had displayed onstage.

Since they were hoping not to be accosted by too many people—either fans looking for a photo or protesters looking for a fight—Anthony and Katherine had scheduled their meeting at City Hall just before five P.M., so they could exit the office after most employees had already left for the night.

In this part of the city, the streets emptied after dusk, and as they walked out to meet their town car, they saw only one other person, a young woman in a blue dress and heels, sitting pensively on the curb. Katherine wondered aloud if the poor girl had just been stood up, or perhaps dumped during dinner nearby. Thankfully, she didn't seem to recognize them.

The car was late to pick them up, so they were waiting around the corner, slightly miffed, when Anthony's phone lit up with an advance copy of the next day's news. His numbers had dipped for the first time since June.

Katherine noticed the smallest of frowns tugging at her husband's lips. "What is it?" she asked, attempting to read over his shoulder.

"It's nothing," Anthony said. "A minor fluctuation in our stats."

"It's that Twitter crap, isn't it?" Katherine asked. "That stuff from the girl's speech? They're calling it some sort of movement."

"A hashtag doesn't make a movement," Anthony said. "There's no organization, just a bunch of sob stories online."

"Well, they've already pulled off multiple rallies," Katherine warned. "And now there are rumors they're trying to plan some sort of world-wide day of . . . short string *awareness* or something."

"A few scattered protests and some child's speech won't eliminate people's fundamental fears," he said. "The convention will be here before we know it. That's hardly enough time to mount a real offensive."

Anthony skimmed through the rest of the article. Senator Johnson's support had apparently risen for the first time since revealing his short string in September, though his numbers remained lower than his pre-autumn peak.

"See here," Anthony said, pointing to a quote from an interviewee.

Certainly, the incident onstage with Rollins's nephew was disturbing, but it doesn't take away from all the work that he's done. And, honestly, it just shows what we're up against.

Anthony smiled. "I'm sure there are plenty of others who *feel* this way, even if they won't *say* it. We both know that what people post online, and what they tell their friends, isn't always the way they vote when the curtains close."

Anthony and Katherine were feeling calmer now, when a familiar tune wafted toward them.

When I grew up and fell in love
I asked my sweetheart what lies ahead
"Will we have rainbows, day after day?"
Here's what my sweetheart said

They realized the music was coming from a cyclist, heading in their direction, with a stereo attached to his bike.

"New York is such an odd place," Katherine scoffed.

But Anthony was convinced that his triumph was nigh. Who cares what one article said? He was nearing the sun now, but he had no fear of falling, his wings built of something more powerful.

He stretched his arm out toward his wife. "May I have this dance?" he asked.

"Are you crazy? We're in the street."

"We have to practice for the inaugural ball."

Katherine relented with a grin and grasped the hand of her husband, just as the cyclist pedaled past, tipping an invisible chapeau in their direction.

Que será, será
Whatever will be, will be
The future's not ours to see
Que será, será

"We're going to look so much better than the last ones," Katherine said gleefully, spinning into her husband's arms. "Do you remember how horrendous the first lady's dress was?"

What will be, will be.

JACK

They were seven months out of college now, but nearly everyone at the New Year's Eve party was still getting drunk on cheap beer, just as they had done for the last four years. Only this time they sported glittery glasses and festive hats.

Standing in the living room of their friend's D.C. apartment, Jack and Javi were in the same space together for the first time since Javi had left for Alabama, and Jack could instantly sense the change in him.

Javi seemed confident and self-assured, regaling the group with tales from his first months of aviation training. He even looked taller than Jack remembered.

"And then, with zero warning, the pilot flips the plane upside down and does two spins in a row. The guy next to me vomits all over the side of the plane, and I couldn't eat a thing for the rest of the day." Javi laughed. "But apparently we'll get used to it."

Jack was struck by how different Javier's life had become. His friend was flying across the sky, learning how to conduct dangerous missions, while Jack was working a safe desk job in cyber operations (though his daily tasks felt more administrative than operative, his "short string" a barrier to any high-level clearance).

"Hey!" one of the guests interrupted the group, looking down at his phone. "Wes Johnson just released a new video."

"Is he dropping out of the race?" a girl asked.

"Why would he drop out now?"

"He's still lagging behind Rollins."

"Yeah, but a lot of people are pretty pissed with Rollins." The boy looked up at Jack, abruptly recalling his connection. "No offense, man."

Jack waved it off.

"I'm on his campaign site now," said another guest.

Jack and Javi joined the group that gathered to watch.

Wes Johnson sat in a leather armchair in what appeared to be his home office, decorated with family photos and framed diplomas and book-shelves packed with biographies.

"I'm going to keep this brief, so everyone can get back to enjoying the holiday," Johnson said. "I know there have been some calls for me to withdraw my candidacy, but I am here to assure you that I remain deeply committed to this campaign. I have discovered a new cause during my time on the trail, and I promise I will never stop fighting for all Americans with short strings and for anyone else who feels mistreated or marginalized by those in power."

He leaned forward in his seat, closer to the camera. "I know that, since the boxes arrived, it's often felt like we've been moving backwards, but the reason I wanted to say something tonight, of all nights, is because *this* moment, on the verge of a new year, is the only time when our entire world comes together in the hope for a fresh start and a better tomorrow. And I remain as hopeful as ever for the people of our great nation. I, too, have been following the many stories and voices of the Strung Together movement, and I invite you to place all of that energy and compassion and bravery—and, most importantly, all of that *hope*—into this campaign. I promise, this fight isn't over."

The crowd grew still in the wake of Johnson's statement, until one of the more inebriated partygoers slurred, "I fucking love that guy."

"But it sounds like he knows he's losing."

"No way! Haven't you heard about that huge Strung Together event next month? Apparently it's happening all over the world. I've heard Johnson is involved."

"That just sounds like a big PR stunt for short-stringers." Someone rolled their eyes. "A whole lot of hype for nothing."

"It's much bigger than that. You'll see."

"I don't know," a boy said, turning toward Jack. "Your uncle may be a son of a bitch, but at least he's tough. He could actually get shit done. Plus, he's brutally honest. You gotta respect that."

Jack shifted uncomfortably in his shoes, grateful when someone yelled, "Shots!" from across the room, and the group quickly dispersed.

It had been weeks since Jack last attended a campaign stop. His aunt had delivered the news in person, disinviting Jack from all future events, sealing his destiny to be cast aside. Jack still saw his father occasionally—as long as Anthony wasn't around—but he had come to realize that the family he was losing now wasn't really worth belonging to. At least, not anymore. Maybe when Grandpa Cal was alive the Hunters still stood for courage and country, but with Anthony and Katherine now at the helm, it was purely self-interest, winning at all costs. *Javier* was the one who was actually carrying on the original Hunter legacy, committing his whole life to service, in spite of its unjust brevity.

Before she left Jack's apartment for the final time, Katherine had even tried to excuse her husband.

"Look, Jack, I know this must be incredibly hard for you," she said. "But you have to trust me, your uncle knows that not all short-stringers are dangerous. He's just trying to protect us from the ones that are."

Anthony the defender. Guardian of the long-stringers. The man who would keep America safe, who would rule with an iron string.

Something had changed recently, that much was true. And perhaps Jack's interruption at his uncle's rally had played a small part in that. But Anthony was still unstoppable, Jack thought, no matter how many times #StrungTogether might be typed out on a keyboard, no matter how big this mysterious event might be, no matter how hopeful Johnson may feel.

How incredible that one dastardly clever performance—Anthony holding up his string back in June—had snowballed so fiercely, over the past six months, as the shootings and the bombing left people scared and vulnerable, as the failed attack in Manhattan turned Anthony into a hero, as Wes Johnson's short string made him look weak, and as many a downtrodden long-stringer listened to Anthony and finally felt powerful, at the expense of his short-string brothers.

How could this new movement, only just gaining ground, be enough to reverse all of that?

With the rest of the partygoers taking shots of tequila, Jack and Javi were left alone.

"I meant to call," Javi said. "But they've kept us so busy. This is literally my first break in months."

"It sounds like it's going really well," Jack said.

"It is." Javi smiled. "So, how angry was your uncle after what you did?"

"I think he's fully renounced me as his nephew," Jack said. "But at least he stopped talking about my string."

Javi nodded. "You know, you once told me that I was twice the man you are, but . . . that sure took a lot of balls," he said, laughing.

The debris from their fight still lingered in the air, tainting their words with an awkwardness that never existed before, and Jack wondered if things would ever return to normal, to the smooth and easy nature of their early days as friends.

"Hey, isn't that old vets' bar somewhere around here?" Jack asked. "You want to grab a beer?"

The two of them stealthily retrieved their coats and snuck out the front door.

Just a few blocks away stood an old-timey dive, with dark wood walls and dark green booths and all manner of military paraphernalia hanging from the ceiling. It was almost exclusively patronized by veterans, and whenever Jack and Javi entered the bar in their uniforms or old academy garb, they were welcomed heartily with tipped caps and raised mugs. Javi was wearing his army jacket, so tonight would be no exception.

The crowd at the bar was thinner than usual, mostly comprised of elderly men wearing caps embroidered with Vietnam or Korea, plus a few younger soldiers in camo.

On the television screens above, the celebrities hosting the night's entertainment were reflecting on the year that was ending.

"Well, to say this year has been a momentous one would be quite the understatement," one of the well-coiffed men joked. "Here's hoping that next year doesn't bring any *new* surprises."

Jack and Javi settled into a booth and spent the next hour reminiscing about their college years—the classes they had almost failed, the girls they should have asked out, the training days when they had their asses kicked so hard that it hurt to sit down *and* stand up. The memories somehow seemed further in the past than they actually were, and Jack wondered if this was adulthood, if life moved so much more quickly after you've grown up.

It was Jack who ultimately brought up the fight. "I'm sorry it took me so long to do something," he said. "To do *anything*."

"And there's plenty more to be done," Javi said. "But I lashed out at you for a lot of reasons, a lot of hurt, not *all* of which were your fault. And maybe I should have taken more responsibility for the switch, and the pressure it put on both of us. It's not like you forced me to do it. It was mutual."

"But you don't regret it?" Jack asked.

Javi took a sip of his beer, considering the question.

"I love the other guys I'm training with, and I have a lot of respect for the officers, so it's really tough to keep lying to them. But I wouldn't be there without it," Javi said. "I wouldn't be able to save people's lives, someday." He smiled and shook his head, like he almost couldn't believe it. "And no matter what went down after the switch, I guess I'll always have you to thank for that."

"Well, like you said, it wasn't just me. It was mutual."

Eventually the bartender started shouting across the room, "Ten! Nine! Eight! Seven!" The dozen or so strangers in the bar exchanged eager glances, joining in on the count. "Six! Five! Four!"

Jack reached into his pocket for the two small kazoos he had stolen from the party earlier, handing one to Javi.

"Three! Two! One!"

The two friends blew on their mini-instruments, while the rest of the crowd cheered, "Happy New Year!" in unison.

Then, at the farthest end of the bar, one of the oldest gentlemen began to sing, timidly and off-key, but with an earnestness that held everyone's attention.

Should old acquaintance be forgot, and never brought to mind?

Soon enough, every voice in the place was lifting his up.

Should old acquaintance be forgot, and days of auld lang syne?

As he sang, Jack thought about his aunt and uncle, who were no doubt clinking champagne flutes at a mansion just a few miles away, and about Wes Johnson, perhaps home with his family, resting after months on the road, wondering if he could still win.

We too have paddled in the stream, from morning sun to night.
But the seas between us broad have roared, from auld lang syne.

And Jack thought about his best friend Javier, admirably humming the tune in the places where he didn't know the words, and toasting the dawn of another year, even when the passage of time might not feel like something to celebrate.

Jack didn't know if Javi had forgiven him, or if his words on that stage had been spoken too late to ever merit his forgiveness. As long as Jack didn't ask, he didn't have to face the answer. All Jack could do now was hope that Javi knew he was sorry, and knew that he was trying.

We'll take a cup o' kindness yet.
For auld lang syne.

BEN

The whole world, it seemed, had gathered.

Everyone waiting to see what would unfold in this moment that had been spoken about and tweeted about and wondered about for weeks.

The locations had been revealed just three days prior, with hubs in two dozen countries, like a map mounted in a traveler's home, thumbtacks pinned on nearly every continent. It was the first time that the disparate voices of Strung Together had apparently managed to converge, to sing in one global chorus, and everyone wanted to know who was behind it, the organizers still anonymous. The names of Silicon Valley innovators and outspoken celebrities were whispered alongside prominent NGOs and local mayors and white hat hackers. Many wondered if Wes Johnson had lent his support. And what about that girl from the viral video? The mystery only deepened the marvel.

Ben's entire group had turned out that day, along with Nina, Amie, and a friend of Nihal's, all standing shoulder to shoulder in Times Square, where the city had celebrated the New Year en masse only a few weeks earlier. It was cold, but nobody seemed to mind, not with the presence of thousands of bodies, breathing into cupped hands, eagerly tapping their feet.

It started a minute past nine A.M. in New York—it was morning in the Americas, afternoon in Europe and Africa, and evening in the Asia-Pacific. All the screens in Times Square went black, before flashing the words "Strung Together" across their digital faces. The crowd erupted in cheers.

As Ben watched the display commence in Manhattan, he wondered, fleetingly, about the other countries, unaware that the very same video was being viewed by all. Playing across the LED billboards of London's Piccadilly Circus, and Tokyo's Shibuya Crossing, and Toronto's Yonge-Dundas Square. Projected onto screens and building facades in Mexico City's Zócalo, and Cape Town's Greenmarket Square, and Paris's Place de la Bastille. Streaming live, with no delays, on Facebook and YouTube and Twitter. Even the Google home page had been taken over in that instant, the letters of its rainbow logo linked by two twisting threads.

"Today, around the world, we honor the contributions of those with short strings," the video began, the stark white words like stars on a midnight screen. "These are just a few."

"Saved two hundred lives in surgery."

"Raised three children on her own."

"Directed an Oscar-winning film."

"Earned two Ph.D.s."

"Built an iPhone app."

With each tribute, each triumph, the applause grew louder.

"Married his high school sweetheart."

"Wrote a novel."

"Defended our country."

"Ran for president."

Ben looked around at the members of his group and wondered what the video might say for each of them. Nihal had been valedictorian, Maura was newly married, Carl was an uncle, Lea was carrying her brother's babies, Terrell was producing a Broadway show, and Chelsea made everyone laugh. Hank, of course, had been a healer. And there were a million other things, as well, that Ben still didn't know about these people, despite all the time they had spent together, sitting in Room 204. They had each fallen in and out of love, held jobs both dull and fulfilling. They were sons and daughters and brothers and sisters. They were friends.

"We love you!" someone shouted near Ben.

"Strung Together!" yelled another.

This wasn't what Ben had expected.

He assumed that he would hear platitudes from government leaders or actors. He assumed they would plead for tolerance. He assumed they might show photos of short-stringers already lost. He assumed the day would feel heavy and sad, a prolonged moment of silence. Like one massive memorial service.

But it wasn't like that at all.

It was boisterous and raucous and joyful. A celebration of life. An hour of untouched unity. In every location, every country, every public square, people leaned out of windows and stepped onto balconies and climbed up to rooftops, clapping and hollering and banging the rails.

For a nation—for a world—with no trouble starting wars, and stoking fears, and standing apart, they hadn't forgotten how to come together.

MAURA

Later, by the next morning, Maura would realize that it was perfectly, almost laughably, well timed. That something, fate perhaps, had allowed them to enjoy that moment in Times Square, blissfully and without disruption, before the panic set in.

The video had ended mere minutes before, and the people in the street and the windows above were still screaming and cheering, riding the currents of revelry, when Lea's face went ashen.

"Are you okay?" Maura asked her.

"I think my water just broke."

Within seconds Maura had rallied the group, forming a circular shield around Lea and pushing their way through the thicket of people. But the crowd was dense and the celebrants oblivious and the pace unbearably slow. Ben was hurriedly dialing Lea's brother and parents, and Maura glanced at her poor pregnant friend, who was trying to hold it together while contractions started pulsing through her body.

"Please get me out of here!" Lea begged. "I don't want to give birth in the Hard Rock Café!"

"Everybody move!" Maura shouted. "She's in labor!"

After an agonizing, indefinite number of minutes—the group would argue, that night, over how long they had *actually* been stuck in Times Square—they reached the edge of the mob and Carl hailed a cab.

When it stopped, Ben and Terrell gently loaded Lea into the back of the taxi.

"I can't go alone!" she shouted.

The members of the group exchanged rapid glances before Maura, seeing the squeamish faces and terrified eyes of her friends, quickly slid into the back of the cab, giving directions to the driver.

Lea spent most of the ride attempting to stifle her screams, strands of hair already sticking to the sweat on her forehead. Without any makeup, her cheeks pink and flushed, Lea looked so young, Maura thought. Only a girl. It seemed almost unfair to put her through such pain.

"Just keep breathing," Maura said calmly, not quite sure if that was right.

"Did someone call my . . . aghhh," Lea's words crumbled into groans.

"Your whole family's on their way," Maura answered, rubbing the top of Lea's white-knuckled hand, which seemed permanently fused to her seat belt.

"It'll all be worth it, once they're born," Lea moaned, placing her hands on her belly. "And we're all going to love them so much."

Maura was surprisingly moved by the girl's sense of assurance, the love that already flowed out of her. Nothing about Lea's current ordeal seemed appealing, but the thought still flickered within Maura. What she and Nina might be missing.

In a rare minute of reprieve from the pain, Lea whispered, "I'm so happy that I could do this for my brother. He's always been so good to me and . . . he's gonna make a great dad. They both are. And no matter what"—Lea tipped her head down toward her stomach—"I'll always be a part of their story."

But the beauty of the moment was broken by a passing contraction, as Lea clutched Maura's hand.

"We're almost at the hospital," Maura said. "You'll have pain meds in no time."

Lea shook her head vigorously. "No drugs."

"Are you crazy?"

"I want to feel it," Lea said breathlessly.

"But you're about to push *two* human beings out of your body!"

"I just want to know if it's true."

"If it's true that it hurts?" Maura asked. "I think you already got your answer."

Lea finally cracked a smile, her lips already chapped. "If it's true what I've heard," she said. "That it hurts like hell when you're going through it, but once it's over, you can't even remember the pain."

By the time Lea and Maura arrived at the hospital, Lea's family had thankfully appeared, relieving Maura's hand from any more squeezing. When she walked over to the waiting room, massaging her fingers back to life, Maura was stunned to see the entire support group gathered. Chelsea was sitting down next to Sean, her mascara slightly smudged. Terrell had somehow managed to smuggle in a bottle of champagne, bragging to Nihal about his exploits. Even grumpy Carl showed up.

And Maura joined her wife, standing now beside Ben and Amie, the three of them still in awe after the morning's event.

"This is turning into quite the day," Nina said.

"How's Lea doing?" Ben asked.

"She's got a way to go," said Maura, "but she's stronger than you think."

The following hours oscillated between caffeine- and adrenaline-fueled highs and a strange mixture of anxiety and tedium. When the wails were at last heard in the waiting room, Maura was returning from a coffee run, and she paused as she came upon the scene: Terrell pouring champagne into paper cups. Sean and Nihal high-fiving. Chelsea jumping up and down, her heeled boots clapping against the floor.

It was then that Maura realized this group of strangers had remarkably formed a family. One that mourned together, when Hank died, and celebrated together, now, as Lea brought two lives into the world.

Maura placed the coffee down on a nearby table and snuck up on Nina from behind, hugging her and kissing her neck, leaning into the warm feeling of the moment.

"There you are!" Nina smiled. "You almost missed it."

But she *hadn't* missed it, Maura realized. What she had witnessed in the cab, what Lea felt for her babies, that was *love*, in its most pure and intense form. And Maura hadn't missed out on that. Her arms, still bristling with energy, were, in fact, far from empty, wrapped as they were around Nina.

A few minutes later, the doors swung open, and Lea's brother walked out. "A boy *and* a girl!" he declared, looking awestruck by the fact.

How auspicious, Maura thought, to be born on this day, when the world came together for one briefly luminous moment.

And the group of people in the waiting room—giddy with delight and a little bit of booze—welcomed the newborn twins into their fold, the newest residents of earth, the latest members in a world of unimaginable pain and unfathomable joy, the two poles never so far from one another.

When Maura had a chance to visit Lea's recovery room, Lea looked up toward her, eyes brimming. "Thank you for being there," she said.

"It was my pleasure," said Maura, watching one of the twins rest in the nook of Lea's arm, both of them equally exhausted, and equally at ease with each other. Maura could practically read the answer in the curves of Lea's body, all inclining toward the baby, but still she was curious.

"Is it true?" Maura asked.

And Lea just smiled puckishly, as if privy to the greatest secret of all.

SPRING

AMIE

Amie had spent her whole life reading romance novels, fantasizing about love in her head. But seeing Ben at Nina and Maura's wedding reception reminded her that life was never as neatly packaged as the stories bound in books or the dreams she conjured up herself. And she simply couldn't turn away from Ben, without wondering forever what might have happened.

Even now, months later, she could remember every detail of their date. Ben had bravely asked her out again, just a few days after the wedding, and Amie had said yes. They met at the southeast corner of Central Park, still awaiting the season's first snowfall, then made their way north past the pond and the zoo, gradually turning westward toward the lake. It was one of those rare days, in the early winter, when the sun blazed bright and the wind held calm, and Amie and Ben hardly felt the cold as they sat on a bench near the water, looking out at the dual towers of the San Remo rising above the bare trees, which Amie pointed to as one of the most beautiful buildings in the city.

"The Corinthian temples on top of the towers were actually inspired by a monument in Athens," Ben said.

"You have a fun fact for every occasion." Amie smiled.

"Mostly architectural ones," Ben said. Then he leaned forward, raising a professorial finger and affecting a British accent. "*Did you know* there are nearly ten thousand benches in Central Park? And about half of them have been adopted."

"I assume that 'adopting' a bench requires a sizable donation to the park?" Amie asked.

"About ten thousand dollars." Ben laughed. "But you get to put a plaque on the bench that says anything you want, which is pretty cool."

Amie turned around to see if their bench was also adorned with a plaque.

"Oh, these benches by the lake were some of the most popular," Ben said. "They sold out years ago."

Indeed, Amie found the words of E. B. White engraved in a thin sheet of metal atop the wood panel behind her: *I arise in the morning torn between a desire to save the world and a desire to savor the world. That makes it hard to plan the day.*

In the weeks that followed their date in the park, Amie and Ben had done everything they could to savor their time together. Ben took her on a tour of his favorite buildings and landmarks, Amie brought him to all of her beloved bookshops. She joined him at the Strung Together event in Times Square, and he visited her class on Career Day, where Amie admired his ease with her students.

Through their letters, they had already grown close from afar, so once they were physically near, they felt almost instantly comfortable, freed from the typical tensions of early courtship. They both knew that the stakes of their budding relationship were higher than most, but Amie felt herself filled with the same urgent desire that had overcome her at Nina's wedding. Her future with Ben—be it only a brief affair, or something perhaps more lasting—was, at the time, still uncertain. All she *did* know was that she wanted to take this chance, to see where it might lead.

Of course, Amie hadn't forgotten her initial reluctance, or her lingering fears. She worried that she might not be strong enough for Ben, that she might not always be the woman from her letters, and that sometimes she would still be the flawed, anxious woman who couldn't help but dread the future, the eventual heartbreak.

And Ben wasn't blind to her conflict, either. When he asked Amie to dinner with his parents, he had couched the invitation in qualifiers.

"They'd love to meet you," he said, "and I'd love for you to meet them, but I don't want to move too quickly, if you're not comfortable. I never want you to feel trapped, in any way."

Trapped was such a loaded word for him to choose, Amie thought, clearly implying more than just one meal.

But she had agreed to join, she *wanted* to join. And she sat across from Ben's parents at the dining room table and swapped war stories from the classroom—the four inches of Amie's hair that were lost to an unrelenting wad of gum; the three pairs of his father's eyeglasses crushed by students' shoes; the two times that angry parents threatened to have his mother fired for failing their children.

While Ben's mother was slicing the coffee cake, Amie noticed her flash a look in her son's direction, one that Amie recognized as the same look she herself had given Nina upon first meeting Maura, nearly three years prior. A look that said, *I like this girl. She's good for you.*

It was a look that held excitement, and joy, and most of all hope, and Amie realized that this wasn't just about her and Ben anymore. She knew that Ben had wrestled with sharing the truth with his parents, before eventually telling them that fall. So Amie wondered if Ben's parents looked at her now and thought that all of their *own* dreams—their only son's future happiness, their chance to see grandchildren—possibly resided within her.

For one terrible moment, Amie wasn't sure if she could carry *their* desires, too, and her sense of ease began to falter. Until Ben's father surprised her by mentioning the strings for the first time that night.

"I'll tell you this, Amie, I'm glad Ben's mom and I retired when we did. I don't envy you having to teach right now, dealing with all the kids' questions and concerns."

"We've actually been instructed not to talk about the strings in class," Amie explained. "And honestly, it's been really hard for me. Sometimes I feel like I'm lying to my students, or letting them down by not engaging them in any deeper conversation. It's like I can't even dignify their questions with an attempted answer, however incomplete it may be."

"Well, it certainly sounds like your heart's in the right place," Ben's mother said. "All that your students really want to know is, if they're ever scared or hurt or struggling, they can come to you. And you can show them that without saying a word."

Listening to Ben's mother speak, Amie realized that was exactly how she felt with Ben. She trusted him with both the beautiful and the ugly parts of herself, and she *always* had, even in her very first letter. It didn't matter that Ben's parents had their own set of hopes, it was no additional burden. Amie was falling in love with Ben, clinging to the same fantasies they were.

And as dessert melted into a round of charades (Ben and Amie clinched a win with Ben's impression of the red pill/blue pill scene from *The Matrix*), Amie allowed herself to be wrapped, once again, in the same familiar contentment, the same relaxed intimacy that she had felt when dancing with Ben at the wedding.

She felt calm, even peaceful. The very opposite of trapped.

By the spring, Amie and Ben were already planning to move in together, and when Ben asked Amie to meet him one afternoon in Central Park, she knew what he was going to ask.

So she slipped into one of her favorite dresses and set out toward the park, hoping to walk off her nerves.

It was strange for Amie to think that the next time she walked down each of these streets, everything would be different. She would be engaged to the man she loved, the person she had trusted even before she knew his name.

Amie felt truly happy. So she was startled to suddenly find herself standing outside the wrought-iron gates of the Van Woolsey, wondering if perhaps she had been walking toward it, unconsciously, all this time.

She stopped in front of the building, as she had often done before, and tilted her head upward to take in its enormity: the Renaissance Revival facade, the rows of windows cracked open to attract a breeze, the imposing archway revealing the courtyard inside.

And as she stared at the Van Woolsey, the truth washed over Amie.

She would never live there now.

From the beginning, Amie knew that Ben wanted to raise a family in a small house in the suburbs, one like his childhood home, with a backyard where the ground sloped just enough to sled down when it snowed. It sounded perfect to Amie. But she also knew that, if she married Ben and had children, she would one day be a single mother, supporting her kids on a schoolteacher's wage, and who knows where they would live then?

Maybe after the kids left for college, Amie would move back to Manhattan. She would transport her empty nest—which, by then, would be emptier than most—into a building much cheaper than this one.

The security guard happened to be away from his post, so Amie crept closer to the gate and peered inside at the manicured garden. It was empty at the moment, and Amie was struck by the realization that the courtyard was *always* empty, whenever she walked past. In fact, she couldn't recall ever seeing a person sitting by the fountain or sipping coffee on one of the curved white benches, let alone a couple or family enjoying this private paradise.

Surely hundreds of tenants led happy lives beyond this gate, and yet the building seemed suddenly so devoid of life, especially compared to the ever-bustling sidewalks of Broadway behind her, where she and Ben had so often walked hand in hand.

"Excuse me, ma'am. Can I help you?"

The guard appeared from around the corner, eyeing Amie suspiciously.

"Oh, I'm sorry, I was just looking," she said.

"Are you a prospective tenant?" he asked her.

Amie paused, glancing back at the vacant courtyard, at the fantasy she had been nurturing for the past eight years of her life in New York.

"No," she said softly. "I'm not."

The guard gave her a slight nod, and she turned away from the building, from the dream that she wasn't meant to live, while her mind filled instead with new reveries. She must have played out ten different versions of the imminent proposal in her head: standing on Bow Bridge, drifting in a rowboat on the lake, sitting in the Shakespeare Garden. But, knowing Ben, it wouldn't be any of those public spots. It would be somewhere secret, someplace with a story that only he knew.

And as Amie walked down the street to meet him, she heard the melody play in her head, the song that had brought them together. *Whatever will be, will be.* Some things we just can't control, she thought.

But what about everything else?

What about all the choices that we make, each day? Who we choose to be, and how we choose to love? Every choice that was made to look, or never look, inside the box.

The choice that Amie made at her sister's wedding, to return inside to Ben.

The choice that she was about to make now, the answer she would give him.

And the life they would choose to build together. The dreams they would choose to chase.

BEN

One Sunday afternoon, Ben emerged from his apartment into the first blush of spring, the trees beginning to yawn awake, the scents of the grass and the nearby food carts carried along the breeze. His group was meeting earlier that day, instead of their typical evening time, in order to visit the new exhibit at the New York Public Library, commissioned by several prominent members of the Strung Together movement to mark the one-year anniversary of the strings' arrival last March. The center-piece of the temporary show was a sculpture crafted with five hundred of people's actual strings.

It was one of Strung Together's first organized ventures in the art world and the first big exhibition to tackle the strings, a retrospective on a phenomenon still ongoing. Perhaps, in the years to come, there would be more exhibits, Ben thought. Since the strings and their boxes couldn't be destroyed, museums across the world had assumed the hallowed mission of collecting and safeguarding these permanent artifacts, these relics of a life, from anyone who wished to donate. Those strings that weren't bequeathed to museums typically found their new homes among family heirlooms, on mantels, and in hope chests. Many boxes took the place of urns. Still others were ultimately buried alongside their owners, opened or forever unseen.

On the subway ride to the library, Ben thought about his support group, smaller now after Hank passed away, Chelsea joined the short-stringer home exchange network, currently living in a beach house in

Mexico, and Terrell moved to San Francisco. He had woken up one morning overcome with the desire for a clean start, and within a week he had moved across the country, spearheading the upcoming national tour of his entirely short-string musical.

Ben glanced at the scroll of advertisements running across the top of the subway: a diet company, a pill for erectile dysfunction, and a rose-covered promo for the dual premieres of *The Bachelor: Long Strings* and *The Bachelor: Short Strings*. (Chelsea's casting application had sadly gone unanswered.)

"I can't wait for the new seasons," gushed a teenage girl near Ben.

"I know. I'm definitely watching both," her friend agreed. "I'm worried the short-stringer version might be too sad for me, but it'll probably be more dramatic, if I'm being honest."

A conversation that nine months ago might have once filled Ben with a sense of dread, or loneliness, or anger, but now it merely blended into the background of his life, their words absorbed by the din of the car.

It wasn't that Ben had gone numb to it all. It still pained him deeply that most pundits were predicting Anthony Rollins would win the nomination in July, followed by the White House that November. It had certainly helped his campaign that, just prior to the first state primaries, the woman who shot Hank, Anthony's almost-assassin, had been sentenced to life in prison. She was the only assailant in the spate of short-stringer attacks to have survived and gone to trial, so perhaps her punishment served as symbolic justice for all those who had preceded her. (And the Rollins campaign had spared no dollar in depicting the defendant as a short-string terrorist, keeping the shooting top-of-mind and voters on edge.)

Anthony would claim victory—for now. Ben was disappointed, but he refused to despair. Real and lasting change would take time, Ben understood, demanding more than just flashy moments. But the path of Strung Together was evolving each day, learning from the movements that came before. After the event in January, people continued to share the contributions of short-stringers in their own lives under #StrungTogether. There were TED Talks and fundraisers and discussion panels. There were profiles of short-stringers and Strung Together activists in nearly every magazine. Short-string characters were even starting to appear on television and in films. The South African girl from the viral video turned twenty-two that spring and decided not to open her box. Many were expected to follow her lead.

And at least Ben's own future felt suddenly full. In a few months he would cut the ribbon at the sparkling science center upstate, the culmination of nearly two years' work. He had proposed to the woman who inspired him, and miraculously she felt the same. His parents were thrilled. Perhaps he had truly become better at living with his short string, like the support group's flyer had promised him once.

As Ben stood to exit the subway, he couldn't help but think how an entire *year* had passed since the boxes' arrival. Three hundred and sixty-five days. How so much of his world looked different now; so many of the people he cared about most he had met in that single orbit around the sun.

Inside the large marble library, Ben stood next to Maura. The two of them stared at the sculpture of a tree, nearly ten feet tall, whose branches sprouted strings in place of leaves. On the platform beneath the tree, five hundred names were inscribed.

"Nina's magazine did a profile on the artist," Maura said. "Apparently he made this whole project using people's strings, but he's still never looked at his own. He said that if he had a short string, he'd feel too rushed to produce good work, and if he had a long string, he might not feel rushed enough."

In another corner of the gallery, Lea and Nihal watched as a video played on loop, showing an interview with the artist, a man in his early forties wearing a shirt with a stenciled design and a heavy gold pendant swinging from his neck. Ben walked over to join them, just as the video started again.

"The idea for the project came when I was traveling in Japan," the sculptor recounted, "and I visited Teshima Island, where a fellow artist named Christian Boltanski created a piece in 2010 called *Les Archives du Coeur,* or *The Archives of the Heart,* a collection of the sound recordings of people's heartbeats from around the world. I wanted to do something similar with the strings. For many people, our strings, like our heart-beats, are something very private, that only ourselves and perhaps a small number of loved ones are ever going to see. So I wanted to create a very public record of these five hundred strings, these five hundred souls, born in different cities and different countries, with strings of all different lengths. But it was important to me that all the names, and all the strings, were treated equally. The viewers will never know which string belongs to which name.

"The tree, of course, felt like the perfect structure. The Tree of Life. The Tree of Knowledge. The reminder that we will all find our ultimate rest beneath the soil, nourishing the life that grows above us.

"We humans have an impulse to mark our existence in some way that feels permanent. We scribble 'I was here' onto our desks at school. We spray-paint it on walls. We carve it into bark. *I was here*. I wanted this sculpture to do the same, to let it be known that these people lived. A testament to the fact that these humans—with their long strings and medium strings and short strings—they were *here*."

SEVERAL YEARS LATER

JAVIER

Javi proved to be an exemplary soldier, not just respected by his comrades but genuinely liked. And he was always prepared for anything.

Even now, as he was facing alone what he knew was the end of his string, he was prepared.

He wrote a letter to his parents, explaining the lie that had launched his career, and hid it under his cot, where he knew someone would find it after he was gone, when his belongings were being packed. It had taken him months to decide what to say, but he couldn't leave his parents in a state of grief *and* confusion. They deserved to know the truth about the switch, to know that this was their son's choice. But Javi never named Jack in his letter, hoping that would be enough to protect him.

Every morning, like a ritual, Javi checked beneath his mattress to make sure the envelope was still there, touching it lightly with his fingertips before heading out for the day.

Javier was walking one afternoon with his buddy Captain Reynolds when the commanding officer called them over the radio. They were needed for the emergency recovery of a pilot and two medical personnel whose aircraft had just been shot down over unfriendly territory. All three passengers had successfully ejected and were currently presumed alive.

Javi and Reynolds quickly gathered their gear and headed toward the helicopter.

"Where are the PJs?" asked Reynolds.

"Here, sir!" The two pararescuemen appeared from behind the helicopter, ready to fly. Javi settled into the copilot's seat, to the right of Reynolds, with the flight engineer and two PJs in back.

As the chopper ascended, the voice over the radio prepped them. "You're looking for two males, one female. Our pilot and two civilian volunteers from Doctors Without Borders."

The sky was too overcast to spot the survivors and drop the rope ladder, so they were forced to land. Reynolds and the engineer stayed behind with the chopper, while Javi and the two PJs set out on foot, traipsing through the thinly forested terrain.

They got lucky, Javier thought. It was easier to camouflage among trees than desert plains.

About twenty minutes into their trek, the soldiers located the survivors, their faces and limbs smudged with dirt and blood, hiding behind the thickest tree trunk.

The two men were both injured—the pilot had been burned and one of the doctors had a bleeding leg—and the woman was attempting to tend to them both.

Javi radioed to Reynolds and their CO back at the base, "We've got all three survivors. Over."

The two PJs crouched down to examine the survivors' wounds, and Javi nodded at the woman.

"My name is Captain Javier García," he said. "You've done an excellent job here, miss."

"Anika," she said, "Dr. Anika Singh."

"Let's get you home, Dr. Singh."

The pilot could walk, albeit sluggishly, but the wounded doctor needed help just to stand. The six of them were about to depart, with the doctor leaning heavily on the junior PJ's shoulder, when the CO's voice came over the radio. "We have reports of hostile forces near your position. Do you copy?"

"Roger," said Javi.

Anika and her fellow doctor froze, looking to the soldiers for their orders.

"We'll be slow on foot." The senior PJ thought aloud. "And we're a big group. Easy to spot."

"With two people injured," Anika added.

As if on cue, the gravelly engine of a truck roared faintly in the distance.

Javi could see the fear on the two doctors' faces, still damp with sweat and possibly tears. *They're only civilians,* he thought, *here because they wanted to help, to make an impact.*

"I'll head off as a decoy," Javi offered. "I can run in the opposite direction, fire a few shots in the air to get their attention, then circle back around to meet up with the chopper."

"No, I don't like it," the senior PJ said.

"It's our best shot." The pilot winced.

"He'll be fine," said the junior PJ. "He's not gonna die, right?"

The senior PJ wanted to yell at his comrade, scold his casual attitude, but he knew that it wasn't the boy's fault. Most of the squad felt the same. Hell, he once felt that way himself. But then he had watched a friend walk straight into a field of IEDs, convinced he couldn't die, and he lost both of his legs instead. *It's the fucking strings,* the PJ thought. *Because of them, suddenly everyone is invincible.*

Until they're not.

"I won't go if you don't think it's the right call," said Javi. "But I'm ready."

The senior PJ hated to separate from one of his own, but he couldn't ignore the two civilians under their care now. And he didn't like their chances of walking more than a mile undetected, with two of his men barely hobbling.

"Okay," he finally agreed. "You're a good man, García."

Reynolds spotted the group through an opening in the trees. There were only five.

"Where's my copilot?" he shouted, as the PJs loaded the two injured men into the back of the chopper.

"He's coming," said the junior PJ.

The rest of the group climbed inside, and Reynolds was all set to fly. But Javi wasn't back yet.

A tense minute passed, followed by another.

And then they heard the engines.

"Shit." Reynolds felt a shiver of anxiety run through his body, but still he waited.

The rumbling grew louder. The injured doctor moaned. The rescued pilot was breathing rapidly, and the flight engineer tapped her fingers nervously on her knee. The senior PJ sitting directly behind him leaned forward. "Remember we have two civilians with us, Reynolds."

But still he waited. "I won't leave García."

The sound of the engine was approaching even closer now.

The junior PJ whispered, so as not to alarm the doctors, "We're fucking target practice on the ground, Reynolds."

"Just give him a chance to get here!" he shouted back.

Then Reynolds remembered something that his commander once told him: For all the damage they had wrought, the true gift of the strings—of every soldier knowing when he would die, and choosing his path accordingly—was that no soldier would ever have to die alone.

If he left now, Reynolds reasoned, abandoning Javi in enemy territory, at least Javi had a long string. At least he would survive.

The loud popping of nearby gunfire cracked through the silence.

"Goddammit Reynolds!" someone shouted.

He couldn't wait any longer.

"We'll come back for him," Reynolds said, for himself more than for anyone else.

From his spot on the ground, Javi heard the unmistakable sound of the helicopter passing overhead, his only shot at salvation flying away.

But it wasn't salvation. Not really. The chopper would have bought him a few extra hours, perhaps. A chance to send a final message to his parents back home. But he had already ended every phone call to his family, over the past five years, with the same three words that he would have said now. The only words that mattered.

So Javi pressed one last time onto the wound in his chest, the stray bullet burrowed somewhere inside, then lifted his hands to search his rucksack. It took him a minute, but he finally found it. A tattered old prayer card, its corners now smeared with the blood from his fingers.

He gripped it tightly in front of him, the same card that had been passed down from Gertrude to her lover, from Simon to his friend, from Grandpa Cal to his grandson, and from Jack on to him, even when he thought he didn't want it.

And Javi read aloud the words that all of the card's owners before him once read. So he wouldn't die alone.

JACK

The army had been shocked by Javier's death, believing him to be a long-stringer, and though they remained unaware of Javi's true actions and intentions, the top brass quickly assumed that some form of deception must have occurred in the days between Javier's graduation and his ultimate assignment. The strings never lied, but humans sure did.

A few army officials had contacted Mr. and Mrs. García, after delivering their son's belongings, and asked them not to speak with any members of the press until the military decided how best to proceed.

Javier was not the first short-stringer to die in combat after the STAR Initiative, since many soldiers were ultimately grandfathered in. But Javi's death *was* the first to spark suspicion of purposeful fraud. Javier's parents were given permission to arrange a veteran's funeral, but their son's precise function in the army—and, specifically, his clearance for active combat—was not to be discussed in public.

Not long after they received it, Javier's parents gave Jack a letter, which had been sent to them, unopened, by Captain Reynolds, a friend who had discovered the note in Javi's bunk.

The first time that Jack tried reading the letter, he couldn't get past the second line without crying. But he was determined.

Mami y Papi,
I know you're shocked and heartbroken right now, and I'm so sorry for the pain I've caused you. But I want you to know, I had to do this.

Five years ago, after the boxes arrived, a close friend and I decided to switch our strings, so I could present myself to the army as a long-stringer and be assigned a more challenging role, on the ground, wherever I was needed most.

I wanted to leave my mark on the world and really help people, the way that you both taught me to put others first. I couldn't let my short string hold me back.

And it didn't.

A year ago, I spotted a lost young boy who accidentally wandered into the line of fire, and I pulled him away before anything bad could happen to him. I think about that boy a lot now, with his dark, tangled hair and his skinny arms, like I'm sure mine used to be. Maybe you can think about him, too.

I pray that you will find comfort in knowing that we will see each other again. That I will be waiting for you, someday, alongside the rest of our family. It is that faith—the faith that you gave me—that has kept me strong, all this time.

I hate that I lied—to my country and to my family. But I don't think of what I did as hiding the truth about myself. I think of it as finding the truth about myself. I'm not just Javi anymore. I'm Captain Javier García of the U.S. Army, and I hope that I have made you proud.

Los amo mucho,
Javi

Javier's parents assumed that Jack was the close friend mentioned, and so Jack told them the truth, or at least part of it. He didn't mention his own motivations for the switch, or the fact that *he* was actually the one to suggest it. He didn't want to muddle the story of the switch as Javi had written it for them.

But Javi's parents didn't know what to do with the letter now. They hardly knew what to do with themselves, they were so gutted and depleted by grief. And they feared what might happen if anyone else were to read Javier's written confession. Yet, in concealing the truth about Javi's death, Jack knew that the army leaders were merely buying time

for President Rollins. His uncle was in the middle of his reelection campaign, and nobody wanted word to get out that a young Latino short-
stringer had intentionally conned the U.S. Army and evaded one of the
cornerstone policies of the administration. Jack was worried that his
friend's life, his greatest sacrifice, would be covered up, erased in order
to preserve his uncle's fragile reputation. And Jack couldn't let that
happen—no matter what consequences *he* might face if the truth were
to come out.

Jack shared his concerns with Javi's parents, telling them how their
son had encouraged him to fight on behalf of all short-stringers. Perhaps
he could do that now, Jack said, by sharing his and Javi's story.

All three of them knew that exposing the switch risked provoking back-
lash, but hiding it felt somehow shameful. And Javi's parents were not
ashamed. They were just as proud of their son as they had always been.

With their blessing, Jack drafted a plan.

Jack had requested a reassignment to New York four years earlier,
desperate to leave D.C. after his aunt and uncle moved into the White
House. He had made a few friends among the computer scientists at his
small cyber command outpost, and he dated a handful of pretty girls,
though most of them, believing Jack had a short string, only pursued
him in the hope of fulfilling some warped Jackie O fantasy, marrying the
doomed son of a dynasty. Jack had made a personal pledge to attend any
Strung Together events in his city, and he and Javi had mailed each other
letters several times a year, Javi's end of the exchange always infinitely
more exciting.

The thrill of defying his uncle had gradually faded, especially after
the election, and neither work nor pleasure gave Jack much fulfillment.
He had slipped back into his old aimless ways. Without the expectations
of his family propping him up, it was surprisingly easy to topple over, to
drift through the doldrums of the normal life he once craved.

But now, with a photocopy of Javier's letter in his hands, Jack finally
felt purpose again.

He arrived at the entrance to the brownstone where the Johnson
Foundation was headquartered. After losing his presidential bid, Senator

Wes Johnson had started the nonprofit to provide resources for short-stringers and promote equality of all string lengths. (Despite the great strides of the Strung Together movement, there was still much to overcome, as the bias against short-stringers proved easier to ingrain than to uproot.)

Jack had been following news of the Johnson Foundation for the past few years, the team working to establish legal protections for short-stringers facing discrimination across numerous fields: job hiring, school admissions, loan applications, health care, adoptions. The list seemed truly boundless. And they had recently launched a new initiative advocating for the right of short-stringers to die on their own terms, pushing for death-with-dignity laws to cover those at the very end of their strings, who would rather pass away peacefully, surrounded by loved ones, than leave their fate up to chance.

When Jack arrived at the Johnson Foundation, an assistant led him upstairs to the office of the newly appointed director of communications, Maura Hill.

"Please have a seat, Mr. Hunter." Maura leaned casually against the front of her desk, legs crossed at the ankles, while Jack sat down in a leather chair.

"I have to say, I was quite intrigued when I heard that the president's nephew wanted a meeting," she said.

Jack gave her a polite nod. "I'm here on behalf of my friend Captain García of the U.S. Army. He was recently killed in action." Jack took a gulp of water from the glass in front of him, suddenly parched.

"Oh god, I'm so sorry to hear that," Maura said.

Jack cleared his throat and steeled himself. It was the first time that Jack had spoken these next words to a stranger. "The truth is, five years ago we were both second lieutenants in the army, right when the STAR Initiative was announced. My friend Javi had a short string, and I had a long one, but we both knew that *he* was the one who was meant to be a soldier. To be a hero, really. So we switched our strings, and he was sent overseas in my place."

Maura's eyes widened, and she rubbed the back of her neck with her hand. "Holy shit."

Jack handed her the scanned letter that he had been carrying in a folder. "Javi wrote this, right before he died."

Jack watched Maura read the letter slowly, taking her time with each line. Her lips parted several times, as if she were about to speak, but she remained silent.

Jack hoped that he had brought the letter to the right place. For the past six months, the foundation had been powerfully backing Anthony's lead opponent for president, a Pennsylvania senator and vocal short-stringer advocate. Rollins was already bleeding support, especially after last year's revelation: the scrawled confession found in the cell of his attempted assassin, after she passed away in prison. The world had been wrong, five years ago. She was not driven mad by her string. She had never even opened her box, never seen what was inside. She was instead a grieving sister, still heartbroken after thirty years, angered by the ascendance of one of the men she blamed for the death of her brother. The woman had known, of course, that she couldn't murder Anthony— she had seen his long string on TV—but she still wanted to punish him somehow. To mete out the justice that had long been withheld. When an innocent man, Hank, got caught in the crossfire, she lost her will to come forward, forever silenced by her guilt.

After the true motive for the shooting was discovered, there were calls for impeachment, of course, but it was impossible to prove that Anthony knew anything more than the public knew. He denied any firsthand involvement in the death of her half brother, and as for his campaign's defamation of the woman, he had just assumed—like everyone else—that her string was to blame for her actions.

But now, in the most recent poll, the race for Anthony's reelection looked excruciatingly tight. It might only take one more weight to finally tip the scale.

"Why did you bring this letter here?" Maura asked.

"I want you to leak it to the press," Jack said. "Including my name, confirming that I was the one who switched strings with Javier. I'm hoping it might be the final piece of ammunition against the Rollins administration, to show people the damage done by his policies, and how stupid it was not to allow someone as brave and dedicated as Javier to openly serve his country. To fulfill his dream. It was Javi's courage, in his final mission, that allowed his team to rescue those three people. To save their lives." Jack paused for a moment. "But it's not just about the army. It's about every short-stringer whose path has been blocked off, because people are too afraid or prejudiced or ignorant. I'm hoping anyone who reads about Javi will see that short-stringers have just as much value as long-stringers. And they deserve the same opportunities to prove it."

Of course, Jack knew that reading Javier's letter wouldn't change the minds of people like Anthony and Katherine and those who had ushered them into power. It certainly wouldn't change everything. But maybe it was a start.

"You could get in a lot of trouble for confessing to this," Maura said. "Are you sure you want to do it?"

"I am," Jack said firmly. He was already estranged from his biological family; it was time for him to stand with the one he had chosen.

"Then I'd be proud to help," said Maura. "I think Javier's story deserves to be heard."

After Jack shook Maura's hand, leaving the letter in her care, he stepped out onto the sidewalk and looked up at the sky. Javi had been a pilot for the last four years. Who knows how many times he had flown up there, among the clouds?

Jack hoped that Javi, wherever he was now, would appreciate the irony in this moment. Anthony Rollins had callously used Javi's string to advance his career five years prior, and now that same string would hopefully play a part in his demise.

The memorial that week was small, attended only by Javier's family, Jack, and two soldiers on temporary leave.

Jack was standing near the casket, which was closed and draped with an American flag, when a woman came up beside him. "Your friend was a very brave soldier," she said.

The woman had arrived late, after the service already ended, slipping into the back of the room. Her face looked unfamiliar to Jack. "He saved all of us that day," she whispered.

Jack realized, then, that she must have been one of the two civilian doctors whom, according to Mr. and Mrs. García, Javi had rescued before he died. Anika Singh, he believed. All parties involved in the mission had allegedly signed NDAs, but Captain Reynolds had shared the story of Javi's courage with his parents.

"Javi didn't deserve this," Jack said. "He didn't deserve a short string."

Then Anika turned and looked at Jack with the kindness, the understanding, that he could only describe as the way a mother should look at her son.

"You know, your friend Javier reminds me of another man I used to know, whose string was also much shorter than it should have been. But he and Javier both made such a difference with their lives. Their impact will be felt for years, even generations," she said. "In a way, I think the two of them had the longest strings I've ever seen."

NINA

The anniversary of the arrival had come and gone, years had begun to pass, and soon enough the world was approaching nearly a decade of life with the strings.

Some ultimately felt grateful for the boxes, for the chance to say goodbye, to never regret the last words uttered. Others found comfort in the strings' uncanny power, enabling them to believe that the lives of their short-string loved ones were not, in fact, cut short. They were just as long as they were meant to be, since the moment they were born and the length of their string was seemingly determined. It made losing them somehow easier to accept, trusting that nothing could have changed the ending, that their deaths did not hinge upon any particular decisions they made, what they did or didn't do. Because of the strings, there was no need to wonder what might have happened if they had lived in a different city, or eaten different foods, or driven a different route home. The loss still hurt, of course, still didn't make sense, but it was almost a relief not to be hounded by what-ifs. Their lives were simply the length that they were always going to be.

But this wasn't a comfort to the short-stringers themselves, the ones who confronted the injustice most intimately. It was a comfort to the long-stringers who survived, the ones who continued on in their absence.

• • •

Maura's parents asked Nina to speak at the funeral.

It was the first eulogy she had ever delivered, and it took nearly all the strength she could muster to let go of her mother's hand, leave her seat in the first pew, and stand before the crowd of mourners.

Nina quickly scanned the room, looking for a face to settle on while reading her remarks. Nobody in the first few rows would do: Maura's family members were all crying softly, and she didn't want to look at Ben and Amie, who were probably thinking about their own version of this funeral, which would be held, inevitably, a few years from now. So Nina spoke instead to a handful of strangers in the back, perhaps colleagues or old acquaintances of Maura's whom she never had the chance to meet.

Nina spoke about her wife's passion and fearlessness and wit and the impressive speed with which she made friends. She relayed how Maura had learned about the Johnson Foundation and promptly left her job in publishing to work for the senator's team—her sixth job overall, but the first to feel like an instant fit. She had finally thrived at work, found a place to channel her energy, working with the foundation to protect her fellow short-stringers.

Nina didn't want to talk about the final days, about the rare abnormality in Maura's heart that had gone undetected. She didn't want to talk about the ending. So she talked about the story itself.

"It's easy to look at our time together and think that we were so unlucky. But isn't it better to spend ten years really *loving* someone, rather than forty years growing bored or weary or bitter? When we think about the greatest love stories ever written, we aren't judging them by their length. Many of them were even briefer than my marriage with Maura. But our story—mine and Maura's—it felt *deep*, and it felt *whole*, despite its length. It was an entire, wonderful tale in and of itself, and even though I've been given more chapters than Maura, *her* pages were the ones you couldn't put down. The ones that I'll keep rereading, over and over, for the rest of my life. Our decade together, our story, was a gift."

The faces in the back were growing blurry now, so Nina wiped her eyes with a crumpled tissue and looked down at the speech before her. She owed it to Maura to finish.

"And, in true Maura fashion, she even gave me a final message to ensure that hers was the last voice we would hear at her service: 'Tell them that I always wanted to be an explorer. That I always tried to take the first step, to be the first one to dive into the freezing water, the first to taste the strange-looking food, the first to get onstage and sing. And now I'll be the first to know what happens next, the first to find out what's waiting for us all. I promise to do enough recon that I can tell you all about it when you get here.'"

A few weeks after the service, Nina finally left her parents' house and returned home, alone, to finish her book. A compilation of stories inspired by the strings, and the people who used them for good, that she had been working on for nearly three years. The dedication page was already typed—*For Maura*, simple and honest—but Nina was reluctant to part with the manuscript, to pass it off to her editor.

So that night Nina read through the stories again.

The woman born with the BRCA mutation, who never expected her long string, now spearheading advancements in breast cancer research. The twenty-three-year-old raised in a gang-ridden neighborhood, whose long string offered him the hope of escape, now running an after-school program for at-risk youth. The short-stringer who carried his box on his back while he summited Mount Everest.

Maura lived within the manuscript, too, in her role at the Johnson Foundation. The woman whose public awareness campaign, whose tribute to the sacrifice of a young short-string soldier, helped lead to the STAR Initiative's ultimate defeat in the Supreme Court. A greater legacy than she ever could have imagined.

Maura would tell her to hand in the book, Nina thought. *Try to let go*. It was time.

Nina remembered one of the last conversations she'd had with Maura. "You were always the stable one, the rock, the one with all the plans," Maura had said. "So I need you to be that person now, okay? You can't fall apart. Amie and Ben need you, and their children need you, and your *life* needs you. Promise me that you'll still be the rock. That you'll keep on making plans."

But Nina had only two plans right now, publishing this book and getting through the next year. Tomorrow, she would start on the first. Tonight, she needed one more moment alone with these stories, with Maura's story, before sharing them with the world.

AMIE

Like all married couples, Ben and Amie argued.

She would grumble at him for failing to empty the trash, for not loading the dishwasher properly. He would sometimes question her cautiousness, insisting that their children, Willie and Midge, were indeed ready to take off the training wheels.

They rolled their eyes and raised their voices, but they each found a surprising comfort in their quarrels, in this natural part of marriage and parenthood, realizing that their own lives—despite their unusual challenges—could still be so conventional, so deliciously *normal*.

Ben wanted everything to happen fast. He put a down payment on a house in the suburbs before Willie was even born, and he and Amie were gifted with two children who progressed rather rapidly. Their first steps, first words, first hobbies, all came in quick succession, and soon enough they were learning how to play piano and shoot basketballs. Ben and Amie did all that they possibly could to give them memories for the rest of their lives, recollections of their time as a foursome. Ben coached both of his kids' Little League teams and took painting classes with each. Amie read to her children in bed at night, whisking them off to faraway lands. Both Amie's and Ben's parents moved nearby and doted on their grandchildren, filling the house with toys and treats, while Nina became the "cool aunt," as she and Maura had joked about once, inviting the children into the city for monthly sleepovers at her apartment.

And whenever Ben and Amie paused, amid their hectic days, to look around their house, they saw the very things that Ben once doubted would ever exist—the records of their family, of their very full life together. The shelves that were once stacked neatly with Amie's favorite novels, now crowded with children's books. The postcards from summer in the French Riviera and winter in St. Petersburg, two journeys before Willie arrived. The blue serving platter that Ben had chipped on the first Thanksgiving they hosted. Scooters, puzzles, an electric keyboard, from birthdays and holidays past. Framed blueprints of the buildings that Ben helped design, and framed letters from three of Amie's former students, grown up and now teachers themselves. And, in a scrapbook tucked away in a desk, every letter they once wrote to each other.

Ben and Amie were not surprised when they received Ben's diagnosis. They were prepared. And Ben knew immediately that he wouldn't move into the hospital. He would stay home, with his wife and kids, just as they had planned.

Nina asked her sister if she would return to the city after Ben was gone, and Amie pictured her life in the house without Ben: the fridge stuffed with frozen casseroles, the neighbors shaking their heads solemnly every time they walked past her lawn. But it was still the house where Ben had insisted on carrying her across the threshold when they moved in, despite the fact that she was five months pregnant. It was still the house where he spent an entire week building a swing set in the backyard. She couldn't leave their home.

One night, Nina sat at the kitchen table with Amie and Ben, as Ben finalized his will. To Nina's surprise, Ben leaned back in his chair, looked at them both, and told them that he was satisfied. Satisfied that his open box had been forced upon him when he was younger, satisfied that he had shared the happiest years of his life with Amie, Willie, and Midge, and satisfied that he would not be leaving his family in a state of disarray.

After Ben went upstairs to sleep and the sisters were left alone, Nina asked Amie if she, too, felt satisfied with her choice.

"I suppose I *may* still change my mind," Amie said. "But I don't think

I will. I used to spend so much time inside my head, fantasizing about all these potential futures and different what-ifs. But ever since Willie and Midge were born, I haven't really had any more visions like that. I think becoming a mom has made it so much easier to stay in the present."

"Because you lose focus for one minute and they've stuck their hand on the stovetop?" Nina asked.

"Well, yes, there's that." Amie laughed. "But it's not *just* that. I always used to wonder about these other versions of myself potentially leading different lives, but now I know that *this* life is the one I was meant for. I can feel it every time I kiss their pudgy little cheeks, or watch Ben lift them up on his back."

Amie was quiet for a moment. "Of course, seeing a long string, like you did, is the greatest blessing," she added. Then she lifted her phone to look at the home screen, a photo of Ben and the kids trick-or-treating last Halloween. "But I still feel pretty blessed myself."

Willie and Midge's college savings accounts; the mortgage on the house; the updated version of Ben's will—everything was all in order. And everybody—from Ben's and Amie's parents, to Nina, to Willie and Midge—was as ready as they could be.

But nobody was ready for the call from the police department, reporting that Ben and Amie's car had been struck on the highway, while driving home from one of Ben's doctor's appointments.

"I'm very sorry for your loss," the officer said.

But it was more loss than anyone expected.

The morning after the accident, Nina, grief-stricken and sleep-deprived, stumbled into her sister's closet and pulled out the box that Amie had kept there, unopened, for the past fourteen years. Nina already knew what was inside, what her sister had never seen, but she wanted to see it for herself.

Amie's string.

With the same ending as Ben's, all along.

Nina tenderly lifted the string from the box and held her sister's life in her hands, then pressed it gently against her chest as she wept and wept.

NINA

Children were never part of her plan, but Nina adopted Willie and Midge without a moment of doubt. Though only eleven and nine years old, they reminded her so much of Amie. They had her imagination, and they had her eyes, and having the two of them was like having a piece of her sister that would remain with Nina, always.

She knew that Amie wanted her children to continue living in their home, so Nina sold her place in Manhattan and moved into the house in the suburbs, with both Ben's parents and her own parents in apartments nearby, so Willie and Midge would never be alone.

Nina knew that she would never stop missing them, Amie and Maura and Ben. But she would honor her promise. She would not fall apart. She would be the rock, now, for Willie and Midge. She would keep making plans, for all three of them.

And after about a year had passed, Nina and the children had managed to rebuild their lives together, as a newfound trio. As a family.

Every few weeks, Nina took Willie and Midge on a trip into New York City, where the threesome would visit a museum or the zoo, or Nina would let the kids wander, awestruck, through the aisles of FAO Schwarz.

On the rare occasions when they spent the night, after a late Broadway show perhaps, they always stayed in the uptown hotel with the Beaux-

Arts facade, one of Ben's last projects in the city. The yearlong restoration had transformed the century-old hotel, a blemished jewel in disrepair, into a palace worthy of its history. Ben had purposefully chosen the hotel for his final undertaking. Something about giving the building a "second life," if Nina recalled. A life that his children were now a part of.

One such evening in the city, after a long day studying dinosaur bones in the Museum of Natural History, Nina led the two children across the street and into Central Park. Under the shadow of the trees, the last light of the day piercing through the branches, the family of three stopped to see Amie's bench.

Nina reached out her hand, where the loose folds of skin had only recently begun to betray her as a woman in her mid-forties, and ran her fingers along the smooth silver plaque, which Amie had gifted to Ben on their tenth anniversary, after spending the previous nine years secretly saving up for it.

Dear B,
No matter what happens, I still feel the same.

—A

Nina lowered herself down onto the bench, while Willie and Midge sprinted to the playground nearby.

Watching the children run, smiling, from the swings to the monkey bars and back, Nina marveled at their resilience. Amie and Ben would be so proud of them—the sweet, inquisitive, playful little humans they created.

In moments like this, Nina was glad that Amie had never opened her box, never felt the anger and anguish that plagued Maura, and never had to look at the soft, round faces of her babies with the searing knowledge that she wouldn't see them grow old.

Nina even wondered, sometimes, whether Willie and Midge would have ever been born, if Amie had looked at her string. It was difficult enough for Amie to plan on raising a family without Ben. What if she had known that *she*, too, wouldn't be there? Perhaps Amie's decision to never look, to never *know,* had given both sisters the gift of these two precious souls.

Of course, Nina strove to be the mother that Amie had always been, so attentive and affectionate, but she also wondered about the kind of mom that Maura might have become, and it was Maura's sense of fun and fearlessness and spontaneity that Nina wished to instill in these kids. An eagerness for life that both her sister and her wife had shared. Nina thought about how often she saw the phrase "Live Like Your String Is Short" emblazoned on T-shirts and tote bags and posters. The popular refrain was heard a lot nowadays, much more often than back at the beginning, when short-stringers were overwhelmingly cast as dangerous and depressed, rather than purposeful, open to life.

Nina watched as Willie and Midge quickly made friends with two other children on the playground, the four of them taking turns on the plastic yellow slide, shrieking with delight as they slid down. It always amazed Nina how children could forge such instant, honest connections, only to thrive on division as adults.

Nina's fingers crept toward her neck and touched Maura's pin, the two gold strings, that she had slipped onto one of her mother's chains after Maura died. She had a habit of rubbing her thumb against the pendant like a talisman whenever she was deep in thought. Few people wore that pin every day, as Nina did. It was mostly reserved for special occasions or political events, like the pink ribbons that appeared each October, now that the overwhelming shock of the early years had largely petered out, aided by the fact that there were never any mass waves of violence perpetrated by short-stringers, as some had cautioned. Former president Rollins, once the loudest voice of warning, only rarely reappeared in the news, to promote his memoir or give a speech.

Despite the ongoing efforts of the Johnson Foundation and Strung Together, allegations of illegal string discrimination still persisted, of course, and the more intimate, personal prejudices against short-stringers were perhaps too slippery, too invisible, to ever truly stamp out. Protests still erupted sporadically, in response to particularly egregious cases, and Maura would be pleased, Nina thought, to know that they hadn't been silenced.

But when Nina watched the four children play together, friendships formed in a matter of minutes, she wondered if, this time, they might hold on to their childhood gift of easy, unbridled empathy, even after they grew up. It's certainly what Amie and Ben and Maura would have wanted for them, and how Nina would do her best to raise them.

An older woman took a seat next to Nina on the bench, pulled a magazine from her purse, and started to read. Nina recognized the past issue for having featured a profile of Jack Hunter, the famous nephew of an infamous president, whom Nina would always remember as having turned to Maura in his time of need. After confessing, with Maura's help, to swapping strings with a friend in the army, Jack had enjoyed a few years as a minor celebrity. The article recounted his rapid fall, stripped of his military title, followed by his eventual rise, finally unencumbered, as it seemed. At the time of the interview, he was working at a nonprofit supporting veterans with PTSD, his wife expecting their second child.

The picture of Jack Hunter's pregnant wife, in a corner of the magazine cover, vaguely reminded Nina of Maura's old friend Lea, who had nearly given birth in Times Square, after the first of many Strung Together events. Willie and Midge still had playdates in the backyard with Lea's twins, who were just a few years older than they were, while Nina and Lea's brother kept watch from the terrace, both tending their sisters' legacies.

Someday, Nina thought, these children would all have children of their own, born into a world with little memory of the time before the boxes, when Nina and the other long-stringers of her generation would retreat to the stillness of old age, reminiscing about the arrival of the chests like her own grandparents once spoke of the Second World War, a seismic shift that everyone else merely learned about in textbooks and novels. Something so unfathomable for the two young sisters reading in a bookshop, for the shy boy drawing buildings on a sketchpad, for the carefree woman singing karaoke at a bar, would someday be just another part of growing up.

But would people still look inside?

Nina's colleagues had all been talking about the recent Gallup poll, the latest national survey about the strings. For the first time, the number of people deciding not to view their strings had risen significantly. More and more boxes were remaining closed, especially among the newest recipients. It might just be a trend, people theorized, they might all change their minds. But Nina wondered if it might be a sign. If, after fifteen years of chaos and fear, the world had seen enough strings— short and long and every measure in between—to know that *any* length was possible, and so, perhaps, the length didn't matter. That the beginning and the end may have been chosen for us, the string already spun, but the middle had always been left undetermined, to be woven and shaped by us.

Of course, people still wondered, would *always* wonder, where the boxes came from, and why they were sent. Were they meant only for the individual, to use the knowledge of your own life span however you saw fit? Or were they offered to the world in communion, to prompt some greater global change? Some predicted their true power would only be unlocked once every single person had looked. Others had begun to believe that they were never even meant to be opened, that the gift was simply receiving any string at all.

And though her own string still stretched out long before her, Nina wondered if perhaps she herself could try living as if it were short, unafraid of the unexpected, embracing the chance to say yes.

She never imagined herself as a mother of two, yet these children were the light that had broken the darkness. Who knows what else awaited her? Perhaps she would finally agree to being set up on one of those dates her friends were always offering. Perhaps she would update her book with new stories. Perhaps she would take Willie and Midge on an adventure somewhere. Perhaps she would show them the world.

But for now, on a bench in Central Park, Nina simply willed her mind to rest, to focus on the present. She lifted herself up and joined her children on the playground, clasping their hands within hers, as she twirled them around and around.

And somewhere, a few blocks north of them, on the edge of the park and just out of earshot, a man on a bicycle pedaled on, with a stereo strapped to his back. His legs labored more than they used to, the wheels turned a little more slowly. But the melody played as clearly as ever, and all the people walking around him, busy and distracted as always, paused for a second and turned their heads, trying to see where the music was coming from.

ACKNOWLEDGMENTS

I want to thank everyone who played a part in the journey of this book, bringing a dream to fruition. The depth of my gratitude cannot be fully conveyed here.

Thank you to my incredible agents at CAA, Cindy Uh and Berni Barta, the fairy godmothers of this book. I cannot imagine bringing this story into the world without their wisdom, dedication, and guidance.

Thank you to my remarkable editor, Liz Stein, who touched every page of this novel with her brilliance and compassion. I could not have asked for a better partner and a greater champion of this story.

Thank you to Carla Josephson, for her endless passion and creative leadership in bringing this book to UK readers.

Thank you to the powerhouse teams at William Morrow, Borough Press, and HarperCollins, especially Liate Stehlik, Jennifer Hart, Kelly Rudolph, Ariana Sinclair, Kaitlin Harri, Brittani Hiles, Elsie Lyons, Dale Rohrbaugh, and Dave Cole. I pinch myself each day.

Thank you to the unparalleled team at CAA, especially Michelle Weiner, Dorothy Vincent, Emily Westcott, Jamie Stockton, Khalil Roberts, Jason Chukwuma, Adi Mehr, Sydney Thun, and Bianca Petcu.

Thank you to my aunt, Aimée Fine, for her initial feedback; to Sumya Ojakli, for her early faith in this book; and to Mady Despins, for her invaluable kindness.

Thank you to all of my professors at Harvard and Columbia, and to my teachers at School of the Holy Child, who nurtured my desire to write and pushed me to be better.

Thank you to the circle of incredible people whom I met in Cambridge and New York, for your love and support during the years that I worked on this book. You have all made my life so much richer, and I will always be grateful.

Thank you, at last, to my family. To my grandparents, Mary and Walter, for laying the foundation of my life spent loving books and inspiring me each day, and to Nancy and Everett, for helping me reach for the stars. To my parents, Laura and Jim, for shepherding me through every step of my life and for the unwavering encouragement that raises me up. (A special thank-you to my mother, my original editor, for reading this book more times than anyone else.) To Landy, my sister and my very best friend, for sharing her enviable talent and creativity with me. Being loved by all of you has made me who I am.

And to any reader who picks up this book, thank you.

READING GROUP GUIDE

1. If the box from *The Measure* arrived on your doorstep, would you open it? Is there perhaps a particular age or moment in your life when you would be most inclined to view your string?

2. Knowing the length of their string causes many characters to rethink their careers, their dreams, even their views on marriage and children. Some people quit their jobs and shutter their businesses; others travel to distant lands. How would knowing about your string—or *not* knowing about it—affect the way you lived your life?

3. Ben initially feels conflicted over telling his parents about his string, while Javier chooses to hide the truth from his. Do you think family members have a right to know about each other's strings?

4. In today's world, do you think the arrival of the strings would bring out the worst in people, or the best? Would you view the boxes as a gift or a curse?

5. The world of *The Measure* feels familiar to our own, except for one powerful twist. What is the benefit of setting a novel in a slightly altered version of our world? In what ways did this fictional society's reaction to the strings mirror the behavior of our own society? In what ways did it differ?

6. Do you think any members in the public arena—such as doctors, employers, or government officials—should be able to know the length of someone's string? Should short-stringers be able to publicly identify themselves in order to receive legal protections or government aid? Do you think political candidates should be able to use their strings during a campaign, like Anthony did?

7. In the support group, Maura argues that "We never should have allowed them to start labeling people as 'long-stringers' and 'short-stringers.'" Do you agree with her? Do you think it would create more division or strengthen community in society?

8. Nina worries that if Maura were to enter the hospital, she might face multiple biases as a Black woman *and* a short-stringer. How does the experience of short-stringers in the novel reflect any of the past or present injustices facing historically marginalized groups? How do they differ?

9. Religion takes on varying degrees of importance in the characters' lives. Javier is Catholic, Nihal is Hindu, and other characters aren't observant. How do you think the arrival of the strings might impact a person's religious devotion, or lack thereof?

10. In the world of *The Measure*, people receive their boxes upon turning twenty-two. Do you think that's too young to be facing such a choice? Or should the choice be offered to people even younger?

ABOUT THE AUTHOR

Nikki Erlick is a writer and editor whose work has appeared on the websites of *New York, Harper's Bazaar, Newsweek, Cosmopolitan,* the Huffington Post, Indagare Travel, BookTrib, and the Verge. As a travel writer, she explored nearly a dozen countries on assignment—from rural villages in France to the arctic fjords of Norway. As a ghostwriter, she has lent her voice to CEOs, academics, and entrepreneurs. She graduated Harvard University summa cum laude and is a former editor of the *Harvard Crimson*. She earned a master's degree in global thought from Columbia University. *The Measure* is her first novel.